fall to grace

KERRY CASEY

This is a work of fiction. In other words, I made it up and no one should get bent out of shape over content.

ISBN-13: 978-0-9769765-0-9
ISBN-10: 0-9769765-0-1

Library of Congress Catalog Number: 2005929586

Printed in the United States of America

First Printing: July 2005

09 08 07 06 05 5 4 3 2 1

Published by:

five friends books™

fivefriendsbooks.com

The best books come from friends. That's why Five Friends Books™ puts the destiny of a book in the hands of readers, not in the hands of a large, impersonal publishing company. Please pass along your bookmarks to five book-loving friends. How far this novel spreads depends on you. And 5% of profits go to public literacy programs. Find out more by visiting us at **fivefriendsbooks.com**.

five friends books™

For Kelly, Sully, and Teddy: my grace.

BOOK One

FALLING

In falling, you're thrown into a new mystery.
Certainty belongs to yesterday's steps.

— *Father Pat*

PART ONE

October 15, 1973

JOSEPH.

"Mistake."

That was the last earthly word spoken by Joseph Blackholm's father before the logging truck piled into his pickup at 65 miles per hour, killing him instantly. He was a man of few words, right to the end.

A full-blooded Ojibwe, Joseph's father refused to live on the nearby reservation. Dependency meant you'd sold your single irreplaceable possession: your spirit. Instead, he and his 13-year-old son and his wife, HomeSky, lived near the Minnesota-Canada border, north of the reservation, on a hardscrabble quarter section of land his family had worked for four generations. It was lonely flat country where the wind blew so unchecked, when you stopped to retie a bootlace, you'd hear your name sung high in the treetops. For most, this country was painfully quiet. Unless you learned to listen. Listen truly. This was the secret Joseph was learning from his father.

It's safe to say people weren't lining up to scratch a life out of the rocky soil of Northern Minnesota. It turned out bushels of character, Joseph's dad said, but hard little more. He occasionally joked about this with his wife in the early dark before daybreak as he threw back the blankets and put his bare feet to the cold plank floorboards. But when he sensed her concern, he rubbed her back a few strong strokes and kissed her cheek, taking her aroma with him as he went out to scratch some more. That was their life. That and their wondrous boy. He felt rich beyond measure, stepping out under the morning stars, dirt under his boots, humming an ancient chant on the way to the old barn.

On the morning of his accident, Joseph's father was going to town for a drum of grease. The axle and springs on the plow were in need of service. Joseph asked could he race the pickup on his bike the mile stretch of gravel to the highway. His dad allowed it. He told Joseph, *To the highway. No farther, you hear?*

Inside the duct-taped cab of his 20-year-old Chevy, Joseph's father squinted into the hard-slanted morning sunshine. He listened to the radio station broadcasting from the reservation as the chatty DJ reminded everyone that the coming Saturday they were to bring their best moccasins for the traditional dance, along with a dish to pass. In his truck mirror, he watched Joseph racing behind him, dark hair wild in the dusted brilliance of the autumn air, his butt never touching the seat. *Such a little bike*, Joseph's dad thought. *The boy's bigger by the morning.*

Downshifting as he approached the highway, glancing again in the rearview mirror to watch his son wave and circle back toward home, Joseph's dad pulled out into the highway, blinded momentarily by the low, early morning sun.

He heard the air horn before he ever saw the 40-ton logging truck burst out of the yellow-white brightness.

The impact of his father's pickup nearly cut in two echoed for miles. Joseph skid-stopped his bike. Life flicked by in slow-motion frames. A crow wheeled from the ancient stand of Norways, losing a feather. A deer looked up from watering in the creek, muzzle dripping. Joseph's mouth opened. Truth had found him like a finger of lightning.

Then the rage of adrenaline released. In the middle of the unpaved road, Joseph threw aside his bike. He sprinted toward the highway, feeling no contact with the ground. His arms and legs pumped in perfect synchrony. The wind howled, trying to hold him back. The clouds pushed lower, begging him to stop. Leaves wrapped his ankles, unable to deter him.

Joseph ran. His breathing grew heavier with every stride. Soon the word he was repeating with each step became audible above the slap of his shoes on the gravel.

"Please. Please. Please …"

CORY.

The chestnut-sized aneurysm in his father's brain burst.

One moment, Cory's dad sat erect at the tiller of the 25-horse Mercury. Then he grit his teeth, released the throttle, grabbed his ears like they'd been set on fire, and hit the aluminum hull of the fishing boat face-first.

Cory heard nothing of this over the din of the wide-open motor and the large waves thumping beneath the boat. He faced forward in the bow as they sprayed east, straight into the bright, early morning sun, cutting across the Canadian side of Lake of the Woods.

Cory was studying his leather boots, vibrating on the thin aluminum hull. Shivers jolted through the rubber soles, branched through his entire body. His teeth chattered, primed by the cold, then set machine-gun rapid by the paint-shaker ride. This time of year, the water temperature dropped to near freezing, making the water dense enough to rattle fillings from your molars.

The throttle remained wide open. The boat sped ahead, hooking right slightly as the last involuntary twitch fired through Cory's dad's gloved hand. They were headed for the rocky shoreline of an island.

Cory's hood was drawn up tight, exposing the least possible area of his face to the biting wind. His view through the opening was about the size of a grapefruit. It couldn't have been more than a degree or two above freezing. Cold. That was the only thought stirring in the boy's mind. He blinked through the wind-tears, not yet grasping that they were speeding toward the rocky shoreline. His hands were shoved deep in his pants pockets to conserve every trace degree of body heat. It was a picturesque fall morning as the fog lifted from the warm-water bays. Frost and ice capped the rocks on the north-facing shore. There wasn't another human being to be found for miles.

The boat closed fast on the island. Now the certainty of their fate electrified Cory. He craned back to see what his dad was doing; it was unlike him to horseplay. Cory saw nothing but an empty boat cushion perched on the rear seat. The outboard engine roared ahead. Cory yanked one hand out of his pocket and began to tear at his tightly drawn hood, widening the view. Face down in the hull, his dad was tangled in the landing net. As Cory stood to go to him, the boat tore into the rocky shoreline. He shot out of the bow like a missile and landed some 40 feet inland on a thick patch of knee-high pine seedlings. The boy never lost consciousness. Quite the contrary: Cory, to his death, would vividly recall—with no small amount of guilt—the surreal pleasure of the moment. The flight through the air. The slow revolution of his body, landing face up as he came down in that mattress-soft spot of immature underbrush. All of this, quite unbelievably, with one hand still buried in his pants pocket, warm as a muffin under a napkin.

Cory hit with a soft thud. Air wheezed out of his lungs. Then a singular, sharp thought crystallized. He tried not to think it. He squeezed his eyes shut in an attempt to banish it. But the thought was overwhelming. He opened his eyes to the electric blue sky and said it aloud.

"Free."

FATHER PAT.

It was one of those squeaky-clean mid-October mornings in Baudette, Minnesota, where the yellows and tangerines cascading from the tree crowns left a person staring up in idle adoration for such a stretch of time he was likely to develop a stiff neck.

Father Pat had on his brown gardening gloves, but that was as far as he'd gotten with the yard work. After being dumbstruck by the maples, oaks, and birch on the grounds of the St. Francis Mission Church, he moved to the pole barn just down the hill from his residence, where he'd been looking high and low for a rake. Not only had he come up empty on the rake, but he had lost his mug of coffee somewhere along the way, too. Having arrived at the Reservation Mission Church just three weeks ago, Father Pat was still feeling his way around.

If you asked him, he'd say his reception on the Ojibwe Rez was warmer than he could have hoped for. Being a fairly young, blue-eyed Caucasian, he'd quite expected to run into more resistance from the native tribe. But almost without exception, this 35-year-old was readily accepted.

Father Pat was inspired by the open, non-judgmental nature of the Ojibwe. He theorized that because for so many years they'd been pre-judged, they chose not to make that mistake with him. In just three short weeks, the Indian friendships he was forming opened his eyes and heart to the generous, joyful qualities of his unique congregation. They accepted that he was sent by God; who were they to question that endorsement?

Frustrated by his unproductive search for the rake, Father Pat needed some air. Walking out of the pole barn, he caught the faint odor of the skunk living under the crawl space. He kicked through the leaves, enamored by the youthful sound. Maple, birch, oak, sumac; he shuddered in his new glorious surroundings. God felt closer here. This reassignment was a blessing.

His church, the rectory, and the grade school lay on 25 acres of land beneath towering, one-hundred-year-old white pines. *Maybe I can get it together here.* Failure wore on Father Pat in none-too-subtle ways. He looked older than his mid-thirties. His thinning hair. His face with deep lines of sadness, which he tried a little too hard to animate in the company of others.

As he strolled toward the rectory, hands clasped behind his back, he heard the phone ringing. Father Pat snapped into an easy jog, jumped the porch steps two at a time, and reached the phone slightly out of breath.

"Mission Church, Father Pat."

"Oh, so you are there. I was just about to hang up. Counted 13 rings."

"Yes. Sorry. I was out back. How can I help you?"

"This is Sheriff Harris in Baudette. We have a problem here in town that requires some, well, spiritual assistance."

"What is it?" Father Pat pulled up a chair and reached for a pen. Pat hadn't felt much needed since his rather uneventful arrival at his new parish. He was eager to get on with the business of service.

The Sheriff continued, "An Indian boy lost his dad to an auto accident a few hours ago. He's gone missing and his mom is needing a priest. Seeing as she's an Indian and you're the new Rez priest, well, that's why I called you instead of Monsignor Kief from town here. Can you come?"

"Certainly. Where are you, Sheriff?"

"County Courthouse. Red brick building behind the Dairy Queen, which is closed up for the season. Guy'd have to be blind to miss it. What do you say, Padre?"

"I say I'll be there." Father Pat scribbled down *Boy* and *Dairy Queen*, a little rattled. "I'm glad you called me, Sheriff. What did you say the boy's name is?"

There was a pause as Father Pat heard what sounded like a piece of paper unfolding on the other end of the line. "Blackholm. Joseph Blackholm. Missing since the accident."

Father Pat wrote the name on a spare offering envelope. Unfortunately he had far too many unused boxes of those around. "How's the boy? Was he in the accident?"

"We found the boy's bike near the site, but that's the only sign. Likely, he witnessed it."

Father Pat winced. "My Lord."

"The driver of the other vehicle saw the boy squatting next to his dead father, right up real close, near what was left of the cab of the truck," Sheriff Harris explained. "Says he saw the Indian boy talking right along and nodding his head saying 'okay, okay, uh-huh,' and the like. Says he's having a regular porch-side chat with the deceased. Then the boy took out his pocket knife, cut a lock of his father's hair, and made off to the woods faster than a deer's been shot at. Not a trace since. What do you make of that, Reverend? Seems something strange to me."

"Did you say he cut his father's hair?"

"I did."

"Why on earth would he do that?" Father Pat asked.

"You're the Indian priest. You tell me why their kind do what they do."

With that, Father Pat knew where the Sheriff stood.

"Father, you there?" the Sheriff asked after a long pause.

"Yes, yes … So the only trace of the boy is the bike?"

"Up and vanished. The boy's mother is awful upset. Lost her husband and misplaced the kid." The Sheriff chuckled. "I tried to get her up to the hospital for a couple of pills, but she's asking to pray with a priest."

"How old's the boy, Sheriff?" Father Pat asked, crisply.

"Thirteen."

"Good Lord have mercy," Father Pat whispered to himself. He stood up quickly. "Tell her I'll be there in 15 minutes. Tell her not to worry. Tell her I'm praying for her family."

With that, Father Pat hung up and ran out the door through the blowing leaves. He got in his car, but got out just as quickly. He ran back to the rectory and grabbed his car keys off the desk. The wheels spun on the damp leaves as he took off. He got no more than 10 feet when he stomped on the brakes and jumped out again. The car sat idling, driver's door open, as Father Pat sprinted back up the rectory stairs.

When he slid back behind the wheel, he was wearing his clerical collar.

THE STONE.

When Joseph got to what remained of the truck, his father was most certainly dead. Joseph's whole body trembled. A leaf blew across his father's upturned wrist. Joseph's mind grasped little. He stroked his father's hand. This calmed him. His breathing slowed. He closed his eyes and opened the gate of good thoughts, as his father had taught him.

He saw his yellow dog, Lick, down by the creek shaking water off his sunlit back. There was his mother's face below him, through the summer leaves of the climbing tree. He saw the glen in the back pasture white with June daisies. He opened a second gate and a story was waiting for him, the one his father had told so many times Joseph could recite it to the word. The story was passed down while they sat together on the tractor planting corn, or after splitting wood, or on blue-bird days when the duck hunting was slow. It was the story of Joseph's great-grandfather's grandfather, Red

Hawk, born in 1835, an honored warrior and trusted friend to the Ojibwe chief Hole-in-the-Day.

While in their teens, Red Hawk, Hole-in-the-Day, and a dozen other young braves ventured out to steal ponies from the rival Sioux tribe. They rode most of the day, slept in the warmth of the afternoon, and planned to slip in during the dark before moonrise for their mischief. The braves gathered around Hole-in-the-Day as the first stars awoke in the evening sky, passed a ceremonial calumet pipe, and bragged about how many ponies they would ride away with. Hole-in-the-Day was the best horseman, the surest archer, and his calm, beguiling personality drew the others in.

Joseph's great-grandfather's grandfather, Red Hawk, was the quietest member of the group, as well as the strongest. Most times, as Hole-in-the-Day paired off the braves before an attack, he chose to ride with Red Hawk.

The band of young Ojibwe belly-crawled down a ravine, two by two, into the lower field where the ponies were hobbled next to a wide, shallow creek. Each pair of braves picked out two horses, untied the ropes strung between the front and rear legs, and quietly led them back up the hill, feeding them slices of apples. In all, there were seven pairs of braves. Hole-in-the-Day and Red Hawk had chosen to go last.

As they crawled down the ravine, Hole-in-the-Day stopped Red Hawk and whispered a new plan. Red Hawk was amazed, but not surprised. Hole-in-the-Day planned to sneak past the remaining horses at the creek, slip into camp, and steal the wedding ponies of the chief and his new bride. What a sight they would make, returning home, sitting tall on the backs of their ponies!

The two made it to the chief's ponies, but a dog scented them and howled out an alarm just before Red Hawk could slit its throat. Sioux and chaos descended. Rifle fire and arrows whistled overhead. The whooping and clamor brought the other Ojibwe braves thundering down the ravine into camp. Hole-in-the-Day signaled retreat. He told Red Hawk to lead them, using the creek as an escape route. Meanwhile, he would circle back through the woods and surprise the Sioux at their flank. No sooner had Hole-in-the-Day peeled off into the trees than Red Hawk and his fellow braves found themselves backed into a steep bluff, cut off. They were outnumbered five to one. The fighting was hand-to-hand. They fought valiantly, but by the time Hole-in-the-Day had circled around to the Sioux flank, most of his friends were dead. Hole-in-the-Day attacked with such a lack of self-regard, the Sioux rode off, laughing that they needn't kill the crazy one.

Hole-in-the-Day and Red Hawk were the only survivors. They rode all night and arrived at daybreak back at their village on horses wet and ready to collapse. Hole-in-the-Day, ashamed by his failure, asked the chief to gather the warriors and attack the Sioux. The chief said it was nearing winter. It wasn't wise to ride until spring. Hole-in-the-Day asked for a fresh horse and enough warriors to go back and bury their dead, but the chief, knowing Hole-in-the-Day's true motive was revenge, forbade it. Proud Hole-in-the-Day fell to his knees and begged. The chief walked away. Hole-in-the-Day ran to the nearest horse, mounted it, and rode off. Red Hawk tried to follow, but his father stopped him.

Hole-in-the-Day rode back to bury his friends. According to legend, the Sioux kept back because Hole-in-the-Day was conversing with the dead. The Sioux claimed to hear voices of such variety, they had to be the spirits of the many fallen warriors. They rode off quietly, leaving Hole-in-the-Day.

It took a full day for Hole-in-the-Day to bury his friends, each in a sitting posture, facing west, with the traditional journey articles of moccasins, blanket, flint, and axe. He then went down to the creek to wash. As he finished, he took a small, smooth stone from the water and braided it into his hair behind his left ear. This is how he would honor his friends who died at Massacre Creek, how he would carry their strength with him and keep their voices close to his ear to advise him. He took another small stone from the creek to give to Red Hawk to wear behind his ear, so he too would always walk with the counsel of fallen friends.

Not long after the massacre, Hole-in-the-Day and Red Hawk went their separate ways. Hole-in-the-Day pushed south, trying to drive the Sioux from the state. Red Hawk's band stayed behind to fight and raise families in northern Minnesota. In 1877, as one of the last Ojibwe still refusing to submit to the white man's reservation, Red Hawk was tracked down by men of his own tribe and killed by the soldiers they guided. But not before passing the stone on to his oldest boy.

The eldest son of every Blackholm thereafter received this same creek stone from his father on his 16th birthday. Each boy would braid the stone behind his left ear while reciting the oral tradition of Massacre Creek—how the dead braves sat up as they were being prepared for the spirit road, how they embraced Hole-in-the-Day and calmly told him not to question the massacre. It was part of the Great Spirit's plan to make Hole-in-the-Day and Red Hawk stronger and more daring—the two marking feathers of a warrior. Hole-in-the-Day and Red Hawk each rode with a stone behind his ear, knowing that their friends' deaths should weigh on them no more than this memorial.

Now, 96 years later on a highway where his great-grandfather's grandfather once galloped horses into battle, Joseph held that very same stone.

"This stone is your link to me and those of our blood who have come before us. With it, you walk with the strength of many behind you. You will never be alone. You will hear us speaking in your ear. You know this to be true, don't you, Son?"

"Yes."

In the quiet highway ditch, Joseph sat cross-legged near the shredded cab of his dad's pickup. The woods were mute. Tears wet his face as he listened to his father's spirit speak.

"There is a plan for you, Good Thunder. You will be an honored leader. The hand of the creator has reached into a valley of wildflowers and picked you. From millions, you. My great son, you must understand, no ordinary life awaits you."

"I'll try, with all my heart I'll try," Joseph said to his father's spirit, which was sitting upright.

"Joseph, I have no single regret, so you have no burden to carry forward. Be faithful to yourself; you are old enough to see all around you now. Know I have loved you like eight sons. Go now, Good Thunder."

"Dad ...?"

"Run past this darkness. Run to the daylight."

"Please, Dad ..."

"Go now."

Joseph pulled out his pocketknife and in a single upward stroke cut the lock of hair that held the stone behind his father's left ear.

Meanwhile, the driver of the logging truck radioed for emergency assistance. He ran up the highway, trying to find the pickup he hit. Two hundred feet from the point of impact, the driver slid down the ditch on the seat of his pants toward the wreckage. He was surprised to see a young Indian boy next to the mangled vehicle.

"Hey kid, you okay?" The boy didn't acknowledge the driver.

"Hey," the driver approached, "are—" he stopped, stock-still, shocked to see the boy talking to the obviously dead man. And then the boy, with tears running down his face, cut a lock of the dead man's hair.

"For the love of Jesus ..." the driver uttered.

The boy, oblivious, said, "Yes, Dad," and sprang into a fast jog, crossing the road to the adjacent field, gaining speed as he headed for the woods. Off in the distance, the sound of the first emergency vehicle came in on the wind.

Joseph left the stubble-cut field, ducking into the edge of the forest. The woods thickened and darkened as he weaved like a deer through the trees. Effortlessly, he cut around obstacles, but the tears obscured his vision. He leapt high over a deadfall and went face-first into a low-hanging branch.

Lying there, unconscious, the first of two visions that would forever change Joseph's future visited.

HOME BASE.

Cory stood. He brushed the soft pine needles off his wool pants and looked himself over, slowly, quite surprised to find himself in one piece. He tested limbs and joints. *How could it be? Not even a lousy scratch.* His fingers searched his face, feeling for a stinging spot. Nothing. Yet there, only 40 feet away, was his dead father, face up and spread-eagled next to the bent, overturned boat.

Cory approached the body, the cold island rocks grinding beneath his boot soles. He knew his father was dead, but he needed to break the eerie spell of quiet.

"Dad?" Cory said, voice cracking. Then louder. "Dad, it's me. Cory." He knelt, unable to look away from his father's face. His father stared up at him with lifeless, wide-open eyes. Cory had never seen his dad's eyes so wide open. They were doll-like.

Cory knew that TV policemen would wipe a hand across the eyes of the deceased to close them. He tried. One remained wide open, accusing. Cory rolled his dad over.

From his father's back pocket, a folded map of Lake of the Woods stuck out toward Cory. Taking it to the water's edge, Cory sat. He had a vague idea of where he might be, remembering they were headed straight into the morning sun as they motored across the main channel of the lake. The resort they were staying at was marked with a red circle, so he wasn't entirely lost. But there were thousands of islands on this lake, so getting back wasn't going to be easy. Especially this time of year, when fishermen were scarce.

Cory's spirits weren't heavy. He was terrified, but invigorated. His skin prickled with an awareness of life and death, how closely they resided. Boy alive, father dead. Cory looked out at the endless empty of the blue horizon. The realization shook him by the shoulders: he'd have his chance right now. He wouldn't wait until he was eighteen or twenty-one to be his own person. It was just him now. Cory Bradford. Thirteen years old. Now was his chance to find out if his recurring suspicion was true: that he was best alone.

Things came easily for Cory. He had a nearly photographic memory and an instant grasp of the most obscure details: cousins' zip codes, old grocery lists, capital cities of foreign countries, math equations, sports stats, middle names, conversion tables, neighbors' favorite colors. He'd take apart a lawn mower, leave it for two weeks, and put it back together. Answers were always there. But finally, a real challenge. To find out who he is now that he's no longer his dad's son. It was a sin, Cory thought, but it made his skin tingle.

When allowed to, Cory trusted his instincts implicitly. He attacked problems knowing he'd find the answer in due time. His father was the opposite. He'd follow the map, follow the operating instructions, heed the popular opinion. The proven way was the only way. Cory's greatest punishments came when he struck out on his own, oblivious to worry. His father boiled into a fury over Cory's disregard for those more experienced. *You're too cocky,* he told him. *You don't have the judgment to weigh the consequences.*

Cory didn't concern himself with the existence of failure. Failure was a temporary setback. This was how he was made. His father was the other: a slave to the possibility of mistakes. And now, after all the careful planning and preparation, there he was.

Dad is dead.

How strange those words. Cory ached for the loss, but he couldn't keep his mind from racing forward. *I can move without hesitation.* The spark that was placed in Cory upon creation was about to be fully expressed.

Cory licked his lips and flipped the aluminum boat right-side up to examine it. It was beat up, but sound. The motor had been ripped off the stern, and lay in the shallows just below the waterline. His boots and socks removed, Cory waded into the ice-cold water for a closer look. The lower unit of the motor was mangled beyond operation. His feet ached in the frigid water, but calling on all the strength he had, he lifted the 25-horse Mercury up off the lake bottom and got it standing. He leaned his weight down on it, drilling the shaft back and forth into the sand-and-rock bottom.

The motor stood on its own. He set large rocks around the base to keep waves from tipping it. Numb and aching, his fingers worked as if separate from the rest of his body. As always, he had a plan. Unlatching the cowling, he lifted the top off the motor, exposing the engine. Then Cory waded back to the shore, tore off a square of lunch bag, and printed a note:

> *To anyone finding this,*
> *My name is Cory Bradford. It's October 15, 9:30 a.m. We had a boat accident. I'm okay. I'm heading straight west back to Monument Bay Resort. I have my dad with me. He is dead. Please come looking.*
> *Cory Bradford*

Cory waded back out to the motor, teeth chattering, put the note on top of the flywheel and slid the cowling back on top to keep the note dry. Rather than latching the top, he left his pen sticking out so anyone finding the motor would have a clue a note was inside. He hummed as he worked.

Next Cory pulled the boat into the shallows and watched for leaks. There was one: a thin, two-inch fountain springing up near the bow. A seam rivet had popped, leaving a small hole. Cory knew if he had a screw with a tip about that diameter, tightening it in would stop the leak. In the bottom of his dad's tackle box was an emergency kit. He found two screwdrivers—Phillips and flat-head—a small ball-peen hammer, cotter pins, an assortment of screws, Band-Aids, a needle, heavy thread, and antiseptic. Classic Dad, he thought. By the third turn of a small screw, the boat was again watertight.

Cory looked at his dad. He wasn't going to leave him on the island for the birds and scavengers to find. *Can I do it?*

He began to roll his dad like a log the 30 feet back to the water-line. An arm would flop over on each turn, striking the ground. On the third rotation, his dad's watch crystal broke on a rock. Finally at the boat, Cory discovered his dad was too heavy to lift inside. He was stuck.

Taking a few steps back, he looked over his situation. Ominous, heavy clouds were multiplying to the west. *Storm's coming.* He paced the length of the boat, stopping often to challenge and rework the plan he was developing. Finally Cory grimaced and got to work.

He pulled the boat up the rocky shore, beside his dad, and flipped it over so it covered the body. Cory lay on his stomach next to the boat. He closed his eyes and took a deep breath. He got a shoulder under the boat and wiggled himself the rest of the way beneath it. Pulling in his foot, he allowed the boat to drop down over them. Sealed underneath, in the nearly pitch black, he could hear his breathing reverberating within the small space. The smell of his father, bowels and bladder released upon death, was trapped underneath. Cory could only take short breaths. With every one, the urge to roll out into the fresh air scratched at him. Cory grit his teeth.

He tied his dad's hands and ankles to the boat seats using the anchor rope. For the plan to work, his dad had to be secured. Cory tried not to think about what he was doing. The lack of light under the boat saved him.

Finished with the last knot, Cory slid out and gulped fresh air. He felt about to vomit. After a few minutes, he began to stretch his legs and lower back.

Cory wedged the wooden oars under the lip of the boat, knowing if the weight of the load snapped them, he was stuck on the island. Crouching, he positioned the oar handles on his shoulders, and lifted with everything in his legs and back, inching slowly toward standing. The boat raised on its edge and, just as planned, his dad's weight shifted lakeside.

The boat struck the water with a mighty splash, sending out an icy spray. Cory simply nodded. Floating in nine inches of water was his way off the island. Quickly, he busied himself collecting only the gear he needed. Rod, tackle box, net, lunches. Sweating, Cory unzipped his coat. He kept an eye on the blackening sky.

Map in his back pocket, Cory rechecked his compass and his watch. It was eleven o'clock, over three hours since they'd run aground. As he pushed off from the island, he drifted by the motor standing sentry in the shallows, the waves lapping around its shaft. "Do your thing," he said aloud. The boat slipped into deeper water. The island behind him appeared so peaceful … beautiful. He turned away, pulled on his dad's gloves, and gripped the oars. "Gloves," he reminded himself. "You don't need blisters." Locking his toes under his dad's body for leverage, Cory pulled hard, feeling the strain in his back. Heading due west, it was all big water speckled with small islands. Black wall clouds shouldered out the last traces of blue sky. Ducks wheeled overhead in large 30-bird flocks. Cory checked the boat leak. It remained tight. Pulling up his hood, Cory leaned into the oars, settling into a rhythm, helped along by a strong southeast wind. With each stroke, he felt himself gaining strength.

All of this made for quite a picture: dark forlorn water as far as the eye could see. Smothering charcoal skies, pressing lower and lower. Bobbing silver rowboat with a body curled on the floor, lashed to the seats with yellow anchor rope. And a 13-year-old boy—13-year-old man—with a look best described as intrepid, putting his back into the oars. West. Do or die, they were headed west, back to Monument Bay.

By the smudged light of evening, the storm crouched on the doorstep ready to pounce. The temperature had pushed below freezing. Fat, wet snowflakes began to unpin from the clouds. Cory had rowed nonstop for six hours.

The wind suddenly swung around. Cory edged along the umpteenth small island, fighting to keep the bow straight, snow spitting in his eyes. Through this veil, he saw what looked to be a sign of human life.

"Dock," Cory whispered hoarsely.

Jutting out from the shoreline was an old kattywompas boat dock with a thin skin of snow. Cory knew he hadn't made it back to the resort, but maybe where there was a dock, there was a cabin. Maybe someone was home. Maybe there was a telephone.

Rowing hard, Cory released the oars and grabbed the surprisingly sturdy old dock piling. He pulled the boat to it, overwhelmed by the feeling of arrival. He had no idea what was ahead, nor did he care. Just to hold fast to something man-made, as bent as it was, unwound him. His back, neck, and shoulders ached from rowing, but he felt none of it, his arms around the dock post. The storm blew harder, trying to peel him away. Cory held with one hand and tried to loop a line over the post with the other. The last of his strength was dissipating. *So sleepy.* He stared glassy-eyed into the white haze; the notion of drifting away under a blanket of snow seemed so simple. He shook it away, rallied his will, and pulled with everything he had left. The boat banged the dock, and he lashed the bow. He was home. Visibility was hardly farther than 30 feet. All was an unreal, swirling, white, black.

Cory splashed a handful of water on his face. Revived, he thought to make note of the time of sunset, but it was impossible to distinguish in the storm. It would be good to know when to expect darkness as he searched for the resort in the coming days. If there was shelter on the island, this would be his home base.

Cory reached for the two lunches his dad had packed that morning. He tried not to notice the snow accumulating on his father. The flakes didn't melt on his face. Cory looked away as he took off his jacket and laid it over his father's head.

On the dock, shivering, Cory scanned his new island, recording the details. Just enough light remained to trace silhouettes of four weathered martin houses on 20-foot lodge poles ringing the rocky shoreline. A dovetailed plank boathouse slouched unlocked. Twisting away from the shoreline, a scrubby path disappeared into the oaks and pines, presumably leading … where? Snow dropped into the lake's mesmerizing blackness. The temptation was to sit and watch, but Cory knew better. He stiffly made his way up the three lengths of dock, away from the tireless wind.

Under the outstretched boughs of the mighty pines, all became quiet. A sharp jolt of the same freedom Cory had experienced earlier charged through him. Why, he wondered, stepping across the roots on the worn path, why hadn't he wailed and beat the ground with his fists? Why hadn't he cried for his loss? Why hadn't he cursed the unfairness? Cory was quickly reassured. He was acting entirely as his father had hoped. No futile emotional discharge.

Snow flecked the path. Cory ascended the gradual rise. Then in a single, powerful heartbeat, two words slipped from his lips: "home base." Crouched under the protective pine trees, a humble log cabin. It was quiet-dark. The cabin appeared to be closed for the season, windows shuttered. Off to the side, a yard light glowed. *Power.* Earlier on the trip, Cory's dad had pointed out how electrical service came to a select few islands by underwater cable. Phone service came in that way, too. Some islands were given permanent lights, landmarks for the pilots who flew in fishermen. *Looks like I got lucky.*

True dark was fast coming. Cory walked around the cabin, checking both doors. Everything was bolted up tight for winter. Cory knew this meant the water would be shut off and drained, too.

An old long-handled pump sat under the yard light. A toothbrush and a small mirror hung from nails on an adjacent tree for morning toiletries. A bucket of priming water was skimmed with ice. Cory put his boot through it, primed the pump, and after ten hardy cranks, water surged out onto the ground, melting through the accumulating snow. Cory refilled the bucket. At least there was water. One less thing to think about.

On the cracked concrete doorway slab, Cory sat, his back leaning against the weathered pine door. He pulled his legs to his chest, balling up against the cold. Here he was out of the wind and dry overhead. He watched the fat flakes materialize out of the black nothingness, cut through the yellow glow of the yard light, and disappear again. It was coming down hard. Time to eat, his stomach growled.

As he opened one of the two brown-bagged lunches, a small, adult-like smile crept onto his face. He thought of his dad, how he always packed lunches the same way: a ziploc with one diagonally cut sandwich on top. Bag of chips in the middle. One cookie on the bottom. Dessert came last. Everything in order. Cory's dad was big on order. Cory pulled out the cookie and turned it over in his hand.

Cory's dad began packing Cory's school lunch because he didn't care for the way Cory's mom did it. A bag lunch, the way Cory's dad saw it, was an instrument of learning. In the fourth grade, Cory forgot his windbreaker at school and it was stolen. For the next six weeks, Cory's lunch cookie was put in the pocket of his new jacket as a lesson. His father's instructions were clear: walk to school without eating the cookie. Have your lunch at noontime. After school, walk home without eating the cookie. When your new jacket is hung on its peg in the hall closet, *then* you can take the cookie out of the pocket and eat it. This went on for weeks until one day, after coming home and hanging his jacket, he reached in the pocket and there was no cookie. Cory asked his father about it while wiping the supper dishes. His dad told him, "You'll never forget your jacket again. Look for your cookie back in your lunch bag from now on." That was the end of it.

The trees above creaked in the wind. Cory put the cookie aside and ate his sandwich and chips. He couldn't bring himself to eat his cookie, though. It made him think of his jacket, which was in the boat lying over his father's face. He snapped the cookie into small pieces and left it for the chipmunks.

Finished, Cory folded the empty lunch bag neatly and slid it into his back pocket. *Good kindling.* With all the doors locked, before he went to break a window, Cory played a hunch. He looked under the welcome mat, felt above the door, checked under the two dead potted geraniums, but came up with no key. He picked up a rock and walked over to the warped storm shutter. But as he lifted the shutter he found the window open a crack. Why? Providence? Dumb luck? Rather than dwell on his good fortune, Cory pushed up on the sill and the stubborn old double-hung released, rattling up. The smell of cedar wafted out. He climbed through.

The complete darkness of the cabin was more exciting than frightening. Inching toward where the door must be, Cory visualized what the place might look like. Rustic. Chinking receding from time-varnished logs. A fieldstone fireplace, maybe a wood-burning stove. Old stuffed fish and deer heads and cool outdoor relics. His hands felt their way slowly along the logs until they slid up on the switch plate. His urge was to flip the switch right away, but a different notion won out. Would the cabin lights go on? Or had the fuse been unscrewed from the box when the cabin was closed for the season?

"If the lights go on, I'll play pro hockey," Cory announced to the dark room, his fingers steady on the switch. "If they don't, I'll die out here with Dad." Cory squinted as if a bomb were about to detonate. He threw the switch.

THE CALLING DREAM.

As Father Pat drove the two-laner into town to meet with the Baudette county sheriff, he reminded himself not to take the curves too fast. He was in a '66 Toronado that he and some kids rebuilt in shop class the winter before his "reassignment" to the Rez parish. The car flat-out flew. And he couldn't help himself. Ever since he'd hotwired cars as a teenager, Pat was no stranger to speed.

But speed was hardly the root of the excitement arcing through his body. Father Pat had been waiting for this very day since he first heard the calling to the ministry 17 years ago. He was sure of it! He was destined to meet this Indian boy who'd lost his father. This was why he'd become a priest.

Up to this point, Father Pat considered himself a 35-year-old flop, as did most who knew him. As a priest, he'd washed out of parish after parish, finally to be, essentially, banished to a tiny northern Minnesota reservation.

Pat had an unseemly temper, surely his greatest vice. His taste for liquor was a close second. Usually, Father Pat was able to keep the two at arm's length, but on the occasions they came together, the result was regrettable. Certainly two substantive vices were enough for one priest, but Father Pat, a handsome man, was also vain. It didn't help any that he was quite popular with the female contingent of his congregations, or that he couldn't seem to divert his eyes from the raised hemlines of the Sunday skirts in spring. Last but not least, he drove too fast. No doubt, Father Pat was no angel—as he was known to say. Others were known to say it as well. He'd hear of his shortcomings often, through the grapevine, or directly in the form of written complaints addressed to the bishop.

Despite this, deep below his frayed exterior, holding Father Pat together inside was his Calling Dream. There was no questioning its divinity; it shone beyond a doubt. It was the single aspect of his entire life Pat didn't question.

When he was 17 and living in a halfway house—which by Pat's reckoning meant he could spend half his nights wherever he damned well pleased—he was out looking for a place to flop. He found an open car door on a tree-lined side street. Pat slid in the back seat. A quick survey of the car made Pat snicker: a small statue of the Virgin Mary on the dash. A rosary hanging from the rear-view mirror. A bible on the floor of the back seat. Pat dismissed them as trinkets, stretched out in the back seat, and quickly fell into a deep dream sleep.

A young boy walked toward Pat through an uncut meadow. Tall prairie grass swayed above the head of the four-year-old as he parted it. He was weather-weary, clothes torn, soiled, but he shone a radiant, electric white. The child sobbed, his cheeks hand-slapped red, his arms outstretched toward Pat.

Suddenly, then, the boy and Pat were both teenagers. They stood in front of a department store with heavy bricks. It was late night and they were about to break in. Pat looked at the boy and knew he'd do whatever Pat did. Pat threw his brick through the window. The boy next to him collapsed like a tent with the poles pulled. *We've got to run*, he told the boy, whose skin grew paler with every eye blink. The store alarm wailed. Pat tried desperately to resuscitate the boy, whose breathing became fainter. Pat found his voice and yelled for help. No one answered his calls. The boy's eyes fluttered and closed. He had trusted Pat, this boy. He was dying.

Then Jesus was at Pat's side. It was the same storybook Jesus that Pat had doodled on since grade school: incandescent robe, gentle countenance, long slender hands and feet. "Wake him," Pat was calmly instructed. Pat went to shake the boy, but instead Pat in the car was shook from his sleep. Someone was bent over him. Pat looked up at the figure who simply said, "He needs you." Pat bolted upright in the back seat, heart pounding, but no one was there. His head snapped right to left. He was alone. More inexplicably, when he unclenched his fist, the rosary from the rear-view mirror was in his hand. Pat jumped out of the car ready to confront whoever it was who was messing with him. There was no one, up or down the street.

It was in that spot, under the quiet elms of the sleeping neighborhood, that Pat's breathing slowed. His heart calmed. He slipped the rosary into his pocket. And from that night forward, he began looking for the "he" who needed him.

Eighteen rocky years later, as Father Pat accelerated his coupe down the empty two-lane highway toward an anonymous speck on the map called Baudette, Minnesota, he had his answer. There was a mother waiting, a mother of a suddenly fatherless boy; a boy missing, a boy swallowed by the forest. Pat was certain that his Calling Dream had come to fruition. He looked up at the old rosary hanging from his rear-view mirror, filling with purpose. Finally. His ministry, his failings, his luckless life, they all pointed him here to this overlooked place, to this particular boy. "He needs you." At last, those words had an object. Joseph Blackholm needed his help.

But in typical fashion, Father Pat was quite mistaken. As it turned out, it was the boy who was sent to help Father Pat.

TWO VISIONS.

Unconscious, under an ancient pine, Joseph was shown this by the Dream Spirit.

He was walked far back in time, before the vista was scarred by the white man's paved roads and endless power lines. Joseph sat cross-legged on a hill atop a grassy valley pasture, braiding the stone behind his ear. Finished, he ran down the slope, the stone tapping him with every stride. Running alongside him was another boy Joseph knew to be Hole-in-the-Day. They were in their early twenties. Joseph was fascinated to see himself so powerfully grown. They played lacrosse, slipping past their opponents as naturally as the wind. They scored goal after goal and hugged and laughed. When the opposition came toward them with the ball, they easily intercepted it and raced toward the goal, passing with unmatched skill.

The game ended and everyone clapped one another on the back and talked about the prowess of Joseph and Hole-in-the-Day. There was no resentment, only laughter. Joseph filled with the feeling of great camaraderie and a purity brought on by athleticism and sweat and sun. He so loved to play, that while the others talked endlessly of the goals, all he could think about was playing more. But the others were exhausted. Except Hole-in-the-Day. So the two of them slipped off to practice and to play keep-away. Their skills grew and Joseph was utterly light, almost bird-like, hopping among heavy river rock. He felt a genuine love for himself. Few people achieve this, except those doing precisely what they were created to do. The vision ended as it had begun: Joseph and Hole-in-the-Day, running, laughing.

Joseph awoke. His nose was swollen, congested with crusted blood from the branch he'd struck. He sat up expecting to feel deep grief. Rather, he remained light like the bird on the river rock. He felt strong and athletic. He accepted this positive feeling without reflection. The spirits of his father and forefathers were with him.

As he stood, he reached into his front pocket for the stone from his father's hair. It was gone! He checked every pocket, flush with a rising panic. He searched the ground where he'd fallen. There he found the strands of his father's hair, but the stone was missing. Joseph instinctively felt behind his left ear. There, in a small braid, he felt the pea-sized roundness of the stone tightly cocooned inside. *How could it be?* Did his hands do this unconsciously during the vision? Touching the braid erased his anxiety. *It happened, is all.* The mystery connected him to something significant and ancient. As Joseph walked, the braid swayed, gently touching him, reminding him that he did not walk alone.

Farther into the woods, a trickle of a creek branched through the forest floor. Joseph washed the blood from his face. It was late afternoon. He'd been unconscious for hours. A storm closed over the sky like a gray glove. Snow was coming. Joseph went about collecting wood for a fire and branches to build a lean-to. He would fast for the rest of the day, more if necessary, to grieve his father. A sign would come instructing him what to do next. As he went deeper into the trees, collecting wood, Joseph's mind drifted.

When his father was alive, he'd pull Joseph up on the old green John Deere tractor in the spring to turn the fields and lay the seed. When the planting heat finally arrived in northern Minnesota, it was well into May. But when it did come, it came in earnest, the sun so close it felt right in your pocket.

Joseph sat on an extra seat his dad had welded to the tractor, facing toward him so they could hear each other above the rumble of the old machine. Joseph looked closely at his father, listening intently as he told stories of the ancients. The oral history was passed on this way for generations. Joseph's dad talked reverently of his grandfather's grandfather and Hole-in-the-Day, how they refused to come into the reservation, long after all the others relented. He talked of how their arms were held back by their own people as the soldiers' bayonets cut into them.

"Before the reservation," Joseph's dad had said, "this treachery didn't exist in our blood. The reservation was the deadliest of the white man's epidemics. Before this, an Indian wouldn't eat before he was hungry or sleep before he was tired. Now we're fat and indolent. The white man's cage broke us."

Joseph had heard the stories many times, and understood the importance of collecting them and living their lessons. Actions showed he'd listened. Listening was their secret. A person who listens is hard to surprise. That was the Blackholm way.

"Some day," his father had said, "you will be alone, like Hole-in-the-Day and Red Hawk were. You must not be distracted by the lazy way or the greedy way. Take the true Indian path."

Joseph's father would smile and stroke the boy's hair, warm in the sun, as a signal it was time to be less serious. "What bird do you hear?"

"Jay."

"What else?"

"Red squirrel."

"What else?"

"Deer. John Deere."

They would laugh from the tractor as the discs tore into the black, cold earth, laying it open to steam under the spring sun.

Even death couldn't separate them. As Joseph built his lean-to in the woods, his father's words whispered in his ear: "Lay the thickest boughs down exposed to the northeastern wind. That wind carries in a storm." And "Layer them angled away from you so the weather will run down to your trenched perimeter, unless you want to wash into the creek and swim with the brook trout."

Joseph watched the sky as he wove the pine bough roof. He had no rope lashings, but it was very secure. The storm was ready to unload, and Joseph wasn't alone in the forest preparing. A covey of ruffed grouse was busy up on the ridge filling their crops with poplar buds before burrowing under a thick deadfall. Joseph was downwind from them. He could actually smell the birds in the thick, moist air as they hopped from ground to tree, feeding.

Joseph gathered cattails from the nearby swamp to make a sleep mat. A buck and doe, already bedded down for the storm, leapt off, startled, crashing through the thicket in search of another swamp for the night.

"Sorry, friends." Joseph waved as they bounded out of sight.

Beneath the sloping pine canopy of the lean-to, Joseph started a fire. The sparks and small flames curled around the kindling. There's something in the hypnotic dance of flames that causes reflection. Joseph thought of his father and the long, winding bloodline that connected his family. *My strength comes from the others.* The fire crackled with growing intensity. There are answers in a fire, always answers. Joseph, like his ancestors before him, squatted close to the flames, looking for more than warmth.

The sky neared dark. Large, wet snowflakes began to fall from the heavens, quietly spiraling down. Many caught on branches, but a select few made it to the forest floor. Joseph took a charred stick from the fire and let it air-cool. With his knife, he scraped soot onto his hand and made his mourning face. He would fast and listen. He knew there was meaning to the earlier vision of himself and Hole-in-the-Day playing lacrosse in the ancient pasture, but he wasn't sure what to do next. The fire illuminated his blackened face. He watched the few flakes among the many weave their way through the tree's canopies, parachuting down onto the forest floor. *For every one flake that makes it to the ground, so many are caught in the trees.* That thought occurred to him, and Joseph knew it was sent by his father. Joseph pushed away the creeping sadness. He strengthened as the storm began to blow.

Stroking his lock of braided hair, he rolled the small creek stone between his fingers and said, "The wind blew, but he was warm. The snow fell, but he was dry. His stomach was empty, but he wasn't hungry." Joseph lay down on the matted cattails, brought his knees to his chest, wrapped his arms around his knees and slept. A second vision visited.

Rather than playing lacrosse with Hole-in-the-Day, he saw it was winter; large, soft snowflakes were wafting down from the sky. Joseph sped across a pond on a pair of ice skates. He was with a friend who was like a brother, but he couldn't see who it was. *Was it Hole-in-the-Day?* No, he thought not.

Joseph's speed and skill on skates were astounding. He flew. Then in a flash of blades, he cut to a stop, sending shavings high into the air. He could explode with speed, like a grouse bursting from cover. He'd crossover and make turns without losing speed. The wind pulled through his long black hair as his legs pumped. He had the same feeling of camaraderie and athleticism that he'd experienced in his first vision.

Next to him, the other boy skated. They passed a puck back and forth, lost in the natural simplicity of their skills. They would curl and curve, dropping passes to each other, almost reading each other's mind for where the other would be. Like friends since birth, they moved in unison, receiving the puck with a sharp snap as it zipped from stick blade to stick blade.

They didn't get tired or cold. It was effortless. As the vision continued, Joseph's view pulled back, and back, and back, until finally he watched the two skaters as an eagle might from a treetop, high above the pond.

The snow swirled. The skaters weaved and accelerated and swung into smooth, powerful turns. The air was full of sounds: blades shaving ice; the puck crisply received; laughter; playful boasts and taunts. From this higher vantage point, Joseph recognized the pond; it was on their land. He could see his white house with smoke curling out the crooked chimney. The boys skated and skated. Each knew what the other was thinking.

Who was it he skated with? Was it his dad as a boy? He wasn't sure. He felt a closeness, a kindred spirit, but this other boy was more like a brother. Someone like himself, but not a carbon copy. Their skills on the ice were different enough that they made the other better. Complementary, not identical. Who, though?

There, in the forest, Joseph's blackened mourning face dream-twitched in the flicker of the dwindling campfire. Night, silent night, closed around the lean-to. Snow fell from the heavens. Clouds, heavy, watched over young Joseph. Behind them, stars stacked up, yearning to sparkle down on the boy. Stars of such bewildering magnitude and radiance, to see them in a night sky is to doubt your eyes. But shine not yet, stars. Now was darkness. Soon, in what seemed like only a breath, the stars would come out for this boy. Soon, but not yet.

SHERIFF HARRIS AND MONSIGNOR KIEF.

"I'm looking for Sheriff Harris," Father Pat announced as he strode into the dingy Baudette county courthouse, crossing its alternating pattern of tan and chocolate floor tiles. All was quiet in the reception area except the dull hum of excessive fluorescent lighting.

"Good thing he ain't looking for you, luv," the receptionist shot back, nose stuck in a paperback so well worn it was an obvious constant companion. When she finished reading her sentence, glancing up, her eyes quickly found Pat's clerical collar. She fell over herself apologizing. "Gracious me! Father, I'm so sorry. I didn't realize who you were and all. A priest, by gar! I mean, what I said … I didn't mean no disrespect."

Father Pat smiled graciously at the dyed-blue hairdo peeking over the top of the romance novel. On the paperback's cover was a half-dressed woman busting out of her bodice splayed out in hayloft straw. The receptionist set her book aside self-consciously.

"No offense taken," Father Pat said. "I assure you." The two looked at one another in an uncomfortable silence.

"Sheriff Harris ...?" Father Pat repeated, lifting his eyebrows.

"Oh, mercy yes. Last door on the right, end of the hallway. Forgive me, or, I mean, of course you could forgive me but I didn't mean it like that. Ah, hell. I should be wearing my Bad Day t-shirt."

Father Pat nodded and started down the hallway before the receptionist did any further damage to her blood pressure.

Light fingered out of the Sheriff's office. Father Pat stepped over a smelly old black retriever sprawled across the threshold. If that dog wasn't already dead, he wasn't far off. In the office sat an immense uniformed man with closely cropped brown hair and a boulder-size head. He made the desk in front of him look miniature as he focused intently on the act of spinning a coin on the ink blotter. Something appeared wrong with the Sheriff's left hand. Across the office, at the window with her back to the Sheriff was, in all likelihood, Mrs. Blackholm.

Father Pat cleared his throat. "Sheriff?" This startled the old retriever, who let out a single low bay, trying to make his feet. The Sheriff lurched upright, accidentally flinging the coin he was fiddling with over his shoulder. The woman at the window didn't so much as move a muscle. "Excuse me ... I'm Father Pat. We spoke on the phone."

"Shitfire, man!" the Sheriff coughed, startled, swinging around to squint at Father Pat. "Them Rez Indians got you sneaking up on people already." The Sheriff wiped a few potato chip crumbs off his uniform shirt.

"Sorry for the start. Thought you saw me come in."

Sheriff Harris gave him the once-over. "You sure don't look none like an Indian priest, Padre." A rubber smirk formed on his face. "Not hardly." All the Sheriff needed was a cheekful of chewing tobacco to be the consummate cliché small-town lawman. "Good of you to drop by, Reverend."

"Sheriff, please, call me Father Pat." Pat could feel the initial traces of his temper beginning to prickle.

"Sure 'nough, Padre. Whatever you say," he winked. The Sheriff hooked his hands behind his meaty neck and leaned back in his office chair, which gave out such a protracted groan, it seemed certain to implode. Pat half winced, half smiled. "This here is the Indian boy's mother." The Sheriff gestured in the direction of his office window. That's when Pat noticed the artificial fingers on the Sheriff's left hand. He wore a prosthesis.

The woman remained looking out the window. Outside, through the dirty glass, the early afternoon sky had gone mean and threatening. When she turned to face the room, Father Pat was nothing less than stupefied. She was undoubtedly one of the most striking women Father Pat had ever encountered. A fact not lost on Sheriff Harris.

"Sit. Sit," the Sheriff commanded. The dog in the doorway tried to sit, but his front paws slid away from him, dumping him back on his belly. "Not you, Deputy," the Sheriff said. "Poor old boy. He's been with me, what, 13 years. Huh, boy?" The Sheriff's voice carried the first touch of softness Father Pat had heard thus far.

Father Pat and Mrs. Blackholm sat opposite the Sheriff at his large walnut desk. The Sheriff pulled a folded piece of paper out of his shirt pocket and went over his scribbled notes in wheezing silence.

Concluding that the Sheriff wasn't going to properly introduce them, Father Pat leaned across and whispered to Mrs. Blackholm, "I'm Father Pat. So sorry for your loss." He patted her hand.

Mrs. Blackholm looked back at Father Pat now for the first time. Her eyes were deep black and shone with a mystery. She was tan-skinned with high cheekbones, a long slender nose and a squared jaw line that gave her a regal aspect. Her straight black hair was pulled back in a braid tied with a thin strip of black leather. She spoke to him as if they were alone.

"I'd like to pray with you for Joseph's safe return."

"Joseph's the boy," the Sheriff interjected, reasserting his presence in the room. "Been missing since early morning, like I said over the phone." The Sheriff turned his attention to Mrs. Blackholm. "We'll have to run a blood-alcohol on that husband of yours. See if he was drunk."

Father Pat was appalled. "Sheriff! For heaven's sake. You yourself said the accident happened at eight in the morning!"

"Reverend," the Sheriff said with a thin smile, "you're a new pea in the pasture there on the Rez, aren't you? They get started on the lightning syrup mighty early."

Mrs. Blackholm interrupted before Father Pat entirely lost his temper. Her cool hand came down gently on his arm. "I'm afraid the Sheriff's right, Father. Drinking at that hour is nothing new to the reservation. But I'll remind you, Sheriff," Mrs. Blackholm turned her intensity on him, "we don't live on the Rez."

"Standing procedure is all," the Sheriff said, jotting a note on his folded paper, retreating from her stare. He pulled open a desk drawer and produced an ashtray in the likeness of an Indian's head wearing a feathered war bonnet. "Cigarette?" he asked his guests. Father Pat's neck was getting very hot.

"Sheriff, have you put a missing persons out on Joseph? We should organize a search party and go looking for the boy. C'mon, it'll be dark in less than four hours. Let's get on with it!" He stood up from his chair, anxious to be doing something.

"Way ahead of you, Padre. But Mrs. Blackholm here, she doesn't want no search. She wants to pray, like I said."

Father Pat looked across at her. His voice softened as he asked her, "But we could go looking too, right?"

"I've got both Camels and Vantage," the Sheriff said. "Any takers?"

"Please, can we talk in private, Father?" Mrs. Blackholm asked.

"I keep the Camel straights in the right pocket, Vantage filtered in the left." The Sheriff tapped the front pockets of his uniformed shirt. "The best way to restrict my tar and nicotine intake is to rotate—"

"SHERIFF! If you please. Can we have a moment? Alone."

The Sheriff let out an exasperated grunt. He shrugged his shoulders and unstuffed his 280-pound frame from his office chair. "I needed to go check a few things anyway," he said, looking down at them. "Pastor, I want to talk to you before you head back to the Rez tonight. I'll be taking supper at Lu Ann's. It's the only diner there on Main Street. Can't miss the neon, even blindfolded. And Mrs. Blackholm, you've got my number should you change your mind on how to handle this situation with your boy. I'd listen to the Reverend there and reconsider putting out a search." With that the Sheriff decided on the Vantage filtered in the left breast pocket, shook one out, and lit it.

No one said anything.

"C'mon Deputy. It's chops tonight at Lu Ann's. There'll be bones." He exhaled, and the dog and his master trudged out of the office.

"Can you *believe* that man?" Father Pat said, his voice starting to wind up. "I can't believe that man!" But already Mrs. Blackholm had stood and begun to walk back to the window. The sky outside was bruised and gray. A storm was certain; the only question was when. She worried about Joseph, although she knew he was fully capable of spending the night in the woods. Silent, she pressed her fingertips to the cold panes of glass.

"Mrs. Blackholm, if I may, what's your objection to the Sheriff's search party? I don't understand."

She turned to face Father Pat. "Please. Call me HomeSky."

He asked again, "Why no search party, HomeSky?"

"Father, to us, our land is sacred ground. I could no sooner permit strangers with packs of dogs on our land than you could let them loose in your church."

"But your son is lost."

"Father, my boy knows every stump on that land in the dark. Joseph's not lost. He's missing."

"So how can I help you? Why call me?"

"To pray. And ..." she paused, "I asked to speak to you privately because what I'm about to say would have made no sense to Sheriff Harris. I can't even pretend to understand it."

Father Pat frowned, waiting for her to continue.

HomeSky walked toward him and looked intently at his face, studying the detail. "I dreamt about you. A few months ago. You were with a child. Your presence brought great peace to his suffering. When I saw your picture in the paper announcing your arrival to the area, I recognized your face as the face in the dream."

Father Pat stepped closer to HomeSky. He took her hands in his, looking earnestly into her eyes. He was afraid, he was excited; he wanted to sing out!

"You dreamt that—about me and the boy?"

"Yes."

"Praise be. That's my Calling Dream. It's why I chose this vocation, or it chose me. My destiny is to help your boy."

HomeSky shook her head. "Father, the boy in my dream wasn't Joseph. I'm not even sure Joseph is connected to this dream, or to you. I just know I was sent your face in the night."

"I'm sure you're mistaken, HomeSky. Who could it be but Joseph? Will you kneel with me to say a prayer for guidance?"

The two knelt on the olive carpet, below a framed picture of the Sheriff in blaze orange grasping the antlers of a 14-point buck. "What's your husband's name?"

"RiverHeart. William RiverHeart Blackholm."

Father Pat closed his eyes. "Heavenly Father, please welcome William RiverHeart to your side. We ask You to guide Joseph home safely, and also give us the wisdom to accept the mysteries of Your ways and find our place in them." Then Father Pat added in silence: *I've been called by You to be of service to this family. Help me now. My life has been directed to this moment from inception. Show me what to do, Lord. Don't let me fail them like I have the others.*

Father Pat and HomeSky stood and looked at each other in silence. The Sheriff's phone rang; they both jumped.

Father Pat spoke up. "I'm not sure how to interpret your dream, but I have faith the reasons will show themselves. Are you okay, HomeSky? I feel I've done so little."

"Father, you're here to help me. What more could one person ask from another?" She smiled weakly. Obviously the tremendous strain of the day had depleted her. The spark in her eyes lacquered with tears.

Father Pat squeezed her hands. He quickly scribbled his rectory phone number on a scrap of paper. "Call me—on the hour if you like. Even if nothing changes and you just need to talk. Also, if you need help with the funeral arrangements, just let me know."

"I was hoping you could say the mass. There will be a small gathering. We kept mostly to ourselves. My husband was clear about his opinion of the Rez."

HomeSky's eyes brimmed once again with tears.

Father Pat took HomeSky's hands.

"There is one thing, Father. I hate to ask …"

"Don't be silly."

"Our truck was lost to the accident. I came into town with the Sheriff. Could you possibly drive me home? I'm just north of the reservation."

Father Pat thought for a moment. "I need to see Monsignor Kief, the head of our diocese here in town, about the arrangements. Plus, as you heard, Sheriff Harris wants to see me for dinner for some reason or another. Take my car. Keep it for a few days. I'll see about getting a loaner from Monsignor Kief. I'm sure he'll be happy to help out."

"I couldn't possibly—"

Father Pat put the keys in her hand. "It's the least I can do. It'll make me feel useful. It's the green one out front."

"Are you sure?" she asked.

"I've never been more sure of anything in my life."

After seeing HomeSky off and making preliminary phone calls about the funeral from the Sheriff's office, Father Pat, hands clasped behind his back, walked up the empty sidewalk to Lu Ann's diner. Snow had begun to spin out of the low black sky, swirling fat flakes through beams of streetlights. The effect was magical.

Up ahead, sure enough, a person couldn't miss Lu Ann's with its bright green neon coffee cup being filled and refilled, hung over the entryway of the old brick restaurant. As the cup topped off, a red slogan illuminated: Lu Ann's Bottomless Cup. No wonder the streets were empty, Father Pat smiled to himself. Every soul in town had to be in the diner.

Pat stepped over Deputy gumming a bone just inside the noisy entrance. He scanned the tables for Sheriff Harris. The place was hot and packed. After an uncomfortable 20 seconds he heard "Padre!" shouted from a back booth. A hand shot up with a half-gnawed pork chop in its grasp. It was the Sheriff with his back to the door.

"Pretty good trick, Sheriff," Father Pat said, slipping off his coat. "How'd you see me faced this way?"

"Born with eyes in the back of my head," the Sheriff snickered, wiping the grease off his mouth. He added the crumpled napkin to the hill he'd created on the table. "That's how I knew I'd found *my* true calling, Pastor."

"Sheriff," Father Pat crossed his arms, exasperated, "do you mind calling me 'Father Pat' or 'Father' or just plain old simple 'Pat?'"

Delaying the request, Sheriff Harris slid a pack of Camel straights from his right shirt pocket. Then he reconsidered, pulling a pack of Vantage filtered from his left. "I switch off," the Sheriff said. "Sometimes I lose track which pack I'm on. One thing's sure, those Camel straights are gravediggers. Smoke?" He offered Father Pat a cigarette.

"Not me," Father Pat said, trying not to stare at the prosthesis on the Sheriff's left hand. Two of his fingers were certainly artificial.

A malicious twinkle came to Sheriff Harris's eyes. "You don't look the type that doesn't smoke, Reverend. It's my job to be observant, and I'da bet my last nickel you were a smoker."

"Never touch 'em," Father Pat said, looking out the big plate-glass window as the snow came down with greater authority.

The Sheriff exhaled toward the ceiling. "So, the reason I asked you over here is I'd like you to get Mrs. Blackholm to reconsider her decision not to search for that kid of hers."

"Joseph," Father Pat inserted.

The waitress came over, refilled the Sheriff's cup, and asked if Father Pat wanted anything.

"I'll take a cup of that, thank you," Father Pat said, offering the waitress a distracted smile. "Sheriff, I believe her mind is made up. She says Joseph knows those woods like the back of his hand and will come home in due time."

"The hell," the Sheriff rebuked. "That boy is in shock, you hear? He's 13 years old and he seen his dad die this morning when he shoulda been eating cornflakes. Do you think that sets him as capable of deciding when or when not to come in? The driver of the logging truck—hell, he said the boy was talking to his deceased dad, nice as can be. Like the two of them were sitting on the porch glider. I saw the corpse. I tell you, that boy was conversing with a man near decapitated."

Father Pat swallowed some of his acidic coffee, and exhaled deeply. "Okay, Sheriff. You've made your point. I'll call HomeSky and see if she'll reconsider. But she seemed to have her mind made up."

A gleam came to Sheriff's eyes. "Sooo, you're already on a first-name basis with the widow Blackholm *and* you've got her phone number. Not bad for an afternoon's work, Pat." The Sheriff licked the tip of his index finger and used it to pick a few crumbs off the table.

"Excuse me, Sheriff?" A surge of heat bloomed up Father Pat's back.

"I saw the look on your face when you first laid eyes on her, Padre. She sure is something, huh?"

"Sheriff, do you have anything the least bit worthwhile to discuss? Otherwise I'll be on my way."

"I just call 'em how I see 'em. I'm a born observer of human nature."

"Shame on you, Sheriff." Father Pat's voice was rising.

"Look," the Sheriff said quietly, trying to bring the volume down. "I'm not going to sit here and ask you to lie to me and say it ain't true how you looked at her, so let's just drop it. Just see if you can get her to reconsider about the kid. It's heading below freezing tonight and it'll snow straight through. Out there is no place for a 13-year-old, even if he is a damn Indian."

Father Pat could sit for it no more. He pushed away from the table and stood, light-headed with temper. His fists balled. He tried to count his breaths, to level himself. It was too late. He ground his teeth, sputtered something entirely incomprehensible, and turned to make a fast exit. He strode straight into the waitress coming for coffee refills. The pot crashed to the floor, the waitress landing butt-first behind it. The whole diner swiveled around to see what the hubbub was about. The place went library-silent at the sight of a priest standing over a waitress as coffee pooled onto the floor and tip money skittered in every direction.

"Hey, everybody," Sheriff Harris boomed, turning his hulking body around in his booth to address the stunned diner, "this here's the new Rez priest. He prefers to go by Father Pat, or Father, or just plain old simple Pat."

After what seemed to be an hour of silence, in a voice barely audible, the priest said, "Sorry … good evening," tucked his jacket under his arm, lowered his head and was out the door.

"Not much for small talk, is he?" someone cracked from the front counter. A swell of laughter went up and the previous din returned. The floored waitress asked if anyone was going to help her up, which brought the eligible bachelors quickly to their feet.

The Sheriff swung back around in his booth, slid a few bones into a napkin for Deputy, and wondered if he'd been a little rough on the greenhorn priest. Hell no, he concluded. He unfolded a square of paper and looked at his small, neat, handwritten notes on the Blackholm case. Aloud, he said to himself, "There's a boy in those woods and the snow's coming hard. Whatever it takes to shake him out." He lit a Vantage filtered and double-checked the pertinent details of the accident inked on the paper. Now and then, when the bell over the diner entrance would tinkle, he'd see who just came in by checking the reflection in the window in front of him. "Eyes in the back of my head," he chuckled, as the cigarette smoke roped toward the yellowed ceiling. "That city priest will last about as long as a mud turtle crossing the highway."

Pat snapped his jacket collar up against the wet snow. It was coming down heavy and silent. A few big flakes found the nape of his neck, exactly the cooling required. After five blocks, he was sufficiently collected.

He made his way up a long, gradual rise of residential sidewalk, watching attentively as the street numbers closed in on the one he held in his hand. Heavier coat and gloves: Pat made a mental note as he crunched through the sticky snow.

Monsignor Kief was the head of the Catholic parish in Baudette and had been good enough to phone Pat upon his arrival weeks back and extend an invitation to coffee. The invitation was intended for a more reasonable hour—Pat knew this, but considering he needed advice about handling a funeral and was without a car, the time seemed right. He was sure the elder priest could be of help. Something about his voice weeks ago lingered, positive and gracious.

Saint Olivet, a turn-of-the-century sandstone Catholic church, stood at the crest of the hill, just next to the water tower. Pat subdued a smile, thinking of all the holy water jokes that must have inspired. Four inches of snow had accumulated on the walkway up to the three-story brick rectory. Pat rang the illuminated doorbell, and despite a very substantial oak door, he easily heard the bell play inside the house. The elder priest must be hard of hearing, Father Pat surmised, shifting from leg to leg in the dampness.

The porch light snapped on and the door creaked open, revealing a distinguished-looking, vigorous older man.

"Monsignor Kief?" Pat asked.

"The one and only."

"Hello. I'm Father Pat. The new priest out on the reservation. We've spoken by phone."

"Why sure enough; I recognize your voice! What a pleasant surprise! Please, come in where it's warm. Put your jacket on a peg there." Father Pat followed him into the entryway, thinking of freshly laundered clothes. He realized Monsignor Kief smelled faintly of bleach. They stood just off the entryway. The interior rooms were a wonder in wood.

"Is it snowing?" the Monsignor asked, excited.

"Indeed. Flakes big as hubcaps. It appears winter will get an early start this year." Father Pat shivered abruptly as the warm air curled around his legs like a stray cat.

"Ahh. My bet, it'll be gone come Monday. So, Pat, what brings you out on a night like tonight?"

"Well, Monsignor, sorry about the hour, but it's a rather long story ..."

"Ex-ceptional," the Monsignor clapped his hands together, smiling. "My favorite kind!"

Father Pat watched as the elderly man with his exuberant youngish face stared past him, obviously preoccupied with what he was doing before the interruption. Embarrassed, Pat continued.

"You see, well, Monsignor, there was the invitation for coffee—I know I didn't call ahead—but, truly, I happened to be in the neighborhood."

"Of course, and here we stand. Where are my manners! Do come in and sit. The pot is always on here, Pat, my boy. Always on.

But what we *really* need at this hour is ice cream and vanilla wafers. Sinful, but only mildly so. What do you say? Can I make you a bowl to go with your coffee? It's no trouble."

"Thank you, no, Monsignor. Just the coffee."

Monsignor Kief's face slackened, but he rallied quickly. "Would the fact that it's mint chocolate chip help you to reconsider such a hasty decision?"

"No. I've had my fill of cold for today."

"Oh yes," he said. "You've had a long-storied day. What would you say to a dram of brandy with your coffee?"

"That would do nicely. Thank you."

"Done," the Monsignor said, walking toward the kitchen. "Make yourself comfortable in the great room there. I'll be but a wee minute. Then I need to hear all about that tale of yours."

Father Pat walked into the stately room. The woodwork was ornate and exceptionally maintained. Cherry, mostly, and mahogany. Three of the four walls were spectacular floor-to-ceiling bookshelves. Other than the seminary library, Pat had never seen so many hardcover books. Along the great room's fourth wall was a massive fieldstone fireplace. Books were stacked neatly on the mantel for lack of alternative space.

"It appears you're a reader, Monsignor," Pat called out. The shelves were immaculate—not a book spine out of line with its neighbor, the rows flush, tight. Pat walked along them, his finger dragging along the leather bindings.

"It's true, books are my great weakness—along with ice cream." The Monsignor approached, smiling, holding the tray of treats. Lamplight danced through the small crystal of neat brandy, steam lifted off the cups of coffee, green mint ice cream rose high above an ornate china bowl with a row of vanilla wafers placed on edge running the length the mound. Monsignor Kief stood in front of his guest and positively beamed. "I do enjoy company." He stage whispered, "Truth be known, it's my second bowl tonight. Inevitably, when company comes to call, there I stand with my head in the freezer." He shrugged innocently.

"It looks delicious."

"Not too late to change your mind," the Monsignor gave it one last valiant try.

"No, no," Pat stood and took his coffee and brandy from the silver serving platter. "This is more than enough, thank you, Monsignor."

"Please, Pat, Monsignor seems so formal. Frank fits better with vanilla wafers and ice cream, wouldn't you agree?"

"Yes. Certainly. Frank."

"Please sit." Monsignor Kief chose the smaller wooden rocking chair, leaving the stuffed high-back nearest the fire for Pat. The warmth of the hearth was another in a string of kindnesses he'd felt since ringing the rectory doorbell. Unaccustomed to such treatment, Pat felt a twinge of melancholy. He took a swallow of brandy that went through him like he'd touched an electric fence.

"Frank," Pat began slowly, holding his coffee with both palms, "as I alluded to, the motive for my visit isn't entirely social. There's been a terrible accident on the reservation today. A young boy named Joseph Blackholm lost his father."

"Oh, dear Lord, no. I know that good family. But they don't live on the reservation, if I'm thinking of the right Blackholms."

"No, no, you're right. They're just north. I understand they own a small farm."

The Monsignor nodded his head. "That would be them, yes. Strong family. I knew the father back when he was in high school. Great person. A standout athlete." Monsignor Kief's brow creased. "How ever did this happen?"

"His pickup was hit by a logging truck."

"Curse those things. Every year we're burying another family on account of those monsters. They just can't clear the land fast enough."

"They found his son, Joseph's, bike near the accident. I'm afraid he may have witnessed the whole terrible thing. He's run off to the woods and no one has seen or heard from him. That was early this morning."

"The poor boy."

"His mother, HomeSky, says he's gone to mourn. She—well, actually Sheriff Harris—called me in to town. She asked me to pray with her. Her family car was lost to the accident, so I've loaned her mine to get back home. Frank, I know I'm rambling, but there's a 13-year-old boy in tennis shoes in the woods, he's lost his father, snow's beginning to pile up, I've got no car, a funeral to arrange, and the Sheriff's hounding me to go back out to her farm to convince her to let a search party find her son. I'm in over my head here."

"Well, all I can say is thank God you *are* here, over your head or not." Monsignor Frank Kief reclined in the firelight. "Let's take them one at a time. You say HomeSky is confident her son will be okay? He's 13? You'd be humbled by how much the Ojibwe have been taught by 13. If the mother isn't worried, I'd follow her lead on that."

Father Pat began to relax in his chair. He put his head back, looked up at the ceiling, feeling suddenly quite tired. "Sheriff Harris is strongly advocating I try to change her mind."

"I'd just ignore Sheriff Harris for the moment, Pat. He means well for the boy's sake, but he tends to bully. Fortunately, I've been around here long enough to have known him when he was just a playground malcontent. If you'd like, I'll get him on the phone and we can discuss it. I know he can be difficult, but life has dealt him some pretty crummy cards. That's a different story for another time and another bowl of ice cream."

"Thanks. The Sheriff is a strong flavor. I don't quite know how to handle him."

The Monsignor swept his hand through the air putting an end to that discussion. "Now, as for the funeral, I can surely help there. Is HomeSky planning on a mass and Christian burial here in town?"

"We haven't discussed the details. I need to go see her tonight—which brings me to my third pickle. I was hoping you could drive me out to the Blackholm place." Father Pat sipped his cup of coffee, relieved to have such an ally to help sort through all this.

A great smile spread across Monsignor Kief's face. A smile untouched by artifice. A child's smile.

"Oh, Pat, I know you're a man of great faith, but I don't think you'll want me driving you out to the Blackholm farm." Frank's smile broke into a chuckle. He tried to stifle it with his hand.

"Sorry. I don't catch your meaning," Father Pat's brow wrinkled.

"Son, I'm blind. You wouldn't care much for my driving." Monsignor Kief broke into a hearty laugh.

Pat looked across at the elderly priest. In that moment of recognition, he lost the grip on his coffee mug. It crashed on the hardwood floor, sending ceramic splinters in all directions. The crash caused both men to jump.

"Ah, shit!" Pat quickly tried to regain his composure. "Excuse me for the language—and the cup. It's just, I had no idea. You hardly seem blind, what with the low light and your skill getting around and all the books. Let me clean this mess." Father Pat hopped to his feet, completely flustered.

"Please, please. Be calm a moment. Leave that just now. Sit down, and listen to me." Monsignor Kief leaned in closer to Father Pat, firelight cupping his face. He spoke in a melodious voice that instantly put Pat at ease; a voice equal parts paternal, saintly, friend, practical joker. "Don't be embarrassed you didn't know I was blind. It's a high compliment. I sensed that might be the case and I was stringing you along a bit. Forgive me, but there's a twinkle of my grandfather in me that can't let an opportunity like that pass. Please, feel free to take the rectory vehicle and keep it as long as you and HomeSky may need. It was left to the church by a parishioner and only gets used by my housekeeper for grocery runs. I may ring you when the pantry runs bare." The Monsignor smiled to further break the tension. "And when you leave tonight, I'll phone our good Sheriff Harris and tell him we've got the right man helping with this tragedy. It'd be wise for you to call him first thing in the morning with an update. The Sheriff is a good man—more God-fearing than he lets on. In time, you'll figure out his bark-to-bite ratio."

Father Pat closed his eyes, rested his head back in his chair and listened to the sound of Frank's voice in darkness. He heard the fire, the refrigerator, the wind pressing on the windows. Eyes shut, he wondered about blindness: were the nuances always this pronounced, or did they dull and fade away? He bathed in the friendly authority of his newfound colleague.

"I can't believe you pulled me along like that."

"I'll be sure to say one extra rosary as penance. Now," the Monsignor continued, "about that broken mug ..."

Father Pat snapped open his eyes and hopped to his feet. "Yes. By all means."

"You'll find a broom and dust pan in the closet past the coffee pot near the back door. Paper towels are hung on the roll just to the left of the toaster."

Father Pat hustled into the kitchen and found everything precisely in its place, just like the books in the great room. As he finished cleaning the spill, he asked the Monsignor about the floor-to-ceiling bookshelves.

"Are all these books braille?"

"All except the shelves left of the fireplace. Those are books from my youth or titles left to the church. I like to loan them out to friends. You're welcome to any of them."

"On my next visit, I would love to. But right now, with all this going on, I'm afraid I don't have time to read."

The Monsignor stood to stretch his back. He warmed his hands and legs by rubbing the front of his corduroy trousers. The damp cold of the evening was settling in the as the fire burned down. "Pat, if there's anything you recall about your first visit with Monsignor Frank Kief, I sincerely hope it's this: there is no such thing as being too busy to read. The fine irony is, the answers to the questions we're so busy wrestling with, they're pressed between the pages. Waiting. One need only pause. You'll find books reinforce what you already know, and confirm what you've always suspected. What I mean is our instincts are right, mostly. Sometimes we just need a gentle reminder from an outside source. That's the power of reading others' words. It's reassurance that even from great distances, we human beings do come to the same conclusions. To know we're not all so different after all, that is the shared humanity found in the counsel of good books."

Father Pat looked at the enlightened priest. "I don't know what to say, other than I've never heard it put that way before. I better get busy cracking some books."

"That's the spirit! Now …" The Monsignor walked over to the bookshelf by the fireplace. He ran his long index finger across the hard-covered spines, stopped midway along the third shelf and tipped out a single thick volume. He smoothed his hands over the front cover, assessing it. He judged the heft of it in his right hand. Satisfied that he had found the book he wanted, he held it out to Father Pat.

"I believe this is T.R Pearson. He writes of small town idiosyncrasies with as much humor and insight as any author of any time. A few pages each night. I assure you, it's time well spent."

"Thank you. Do you mind one more question?"

"By all means."

"How long have you lived here? In this small town."

"I was born in St. Paul, about 360 miles south. Started coming up here 50 years ago as a boy with my dad and uncles to hunt and fish. I fell face-first in love. Never had I seen anything so green and blue and wide open and untouched. The pageant of colors every fall. I even love the winters. I call it God's playground. I've always felt a few feet closer to heaven here."

The two sat and let the tranquility of the thought sink in. Ashed wood shifted in the hearth and let out a waning string of smoke. The elder priest yawned and rubbed his hands together.

"Now, about that car. You'll find the key in the ashtray. The garage is unlocked just around the back. Suddenly I'm pooped, so I think I'll get started for bed. Thank you so much for your company tonight. What a pleasure to meet you finally."

"No, thank you. For your help and your friendship and your warm spirit. And for the book."

The Monsignor led the way to the front door. His hand swept beneath the coat pegs in the entryway until it bumped into Father Pat's coat. He held it out.

"Tell me, Pat, is it still snowing those large flakes out there?"

Father Pat stole a long look into the face of this wise old priest. He saw a face of almost exclusive peace and misleading youth. The man was indeed beautiful, if such a word could be used. Pat quickly glanced out the little window cut in the front door.

"Still coming down."

"Oh, how I can remember the muffled spectacle of the year's first big snow. The white-flocked pines. The yellow evening light in the warm houses. The kids throwing snowballs long after their mitts soaked through."

Father Pat stood at the door, knob in hand, as the Monsignor reminisced in his velour voice. He wondered how long Frank had been blind. He said he had come here as a boy to hunt and fish, so obviously he had been sighted. What fire had his soul endured to produce such exquisite certainty? Pat pulled open the door, recharged, optimistic.

"What a difference the thickness of one door can make," he said, as much to himself as to Frank.

"How's that?"

"Oh, I was just thinking how I felt lost standing on the opposite side of this door, and how much better I feel now."

"Well, Pat, it seems it's you who has taught me something. I'd never heard it said that way; the thickness of one door. How true. I hope you don't mind, but I'm going to toss my Sunday homily on the fire, and pilfer your words."

"I'd be honored. Well, I'll be off."

"I feel the moisture in the air," the Monsignor smiled. "The smell of chimney smoke … the wet snow seems to pull it to the earth for us to enjoy. Do drive safely. Call me bright and early and we'll talk about the funeral and what's next to do."

Father Pat, much to his own surprise, stepped forward and gave the elderly priest a hug. He received a hardy embrace in return.

"Thank you so much, Frank," Father Pat said, a shiver of cold making its way up his pant leg.

"The Lord loves you more than you could ever know," Frank said, seemingly able to divine Father Pat's deepest doubts. He gave the young priest a hardy slap on the back. "Now, straight to the Blackholm farm. No stopping at the pub," the Monsignor joked. "If the locals see my car parked in front, I'll never be able to deliver my temperance sermon again."

"Straight to the farm, then," Pat repeated as he walked down the steps, laughing.

As the like-new 1968 Cadillac DeVille crunched through the six inches of fresh snow, Father Pat's head swirled with the day's details. It was almost overwhelming, yet his sense of purpose was renewed. On the dark Main Street, his was the only car moving. Snow humped up on a few parked along either curb, making them indistinguishable from one another.

Ahead on the left, Lu Ann's diner glowed warmly. The large neon coffee cup over the doorway was muted beneath a new buildup of snow. As Father Pat got closer, he slowed, seeing the hulking silhouette of the Sheriff in the doorway. Inside the brightly lit diner, the locals looked up from their pie, gesturing good-bye with forks. The old labrador, Deputy, waited curbside.

Pat considered rolling down the car window to blurt something about how easy grand theft auto was in these parts, but wasn't up to another encounter with the Sheriff. He pulled to the curb and snapped off his headlights. Snowflakes the size of 50-cent pieces descended onto the windshield, instantly melting. The wipers traced the wet glass, removing the plump water droplets. As the car idled, Father Pat slunk in his seat, and said a quick prayer that the Sheriff wouldn't notice him.

A half block up the street, the massive Sheriff stepped across the snowy sidewalk to join Deputy. He looked both ways, up and down Main Street. Satisfied, he moved to cross. But before doing so, he did something that Father Pat wouldn't have believed had he not seen it with his own eyes. Sheriff Harris made the sign of the cross, touching his forehead, chest, and then crisscrossing his jacket. Then the Sheriff pulled on his gloves, stepped into the street, shuffled across, heading in the direction of the courthouse. Behind him, Deputy's belly pushed a wake of snow. It was a lonely sight, the two of them. It caused Father Pat to wonder. Had he misjudged this man? As his new friend Monsignor Frank Kief had said, the Sheriff was more God-fearing than one might imagine. Father Pat was reminded again of the complexity of the human experience and the foolishness of judging a person. "Maybe he's not so bad after all," he said to the Cadillac, patting the leather upholstered seat. Once the Sheriff and his dog had disappeared into the night's shadows, Pat put the car in gear and crunched away from the curb through the snow.

Slowly, in near white-out conditions, Father Pat navigated his way north from Baudette on the thin white ribbon of highway. Only the yellow road signs illuminated in the headlights gave perceptible warning of the highway's twisting course. Despite his intense focus, Pat thought about his new friend. What had he said? He talked about hunting and fishing as a boy, about being transfixed by the spectacular colors of summer and fall, about the books of his youth. What trauma must he have endured in losing his eyesight? What did the crucible of that experience do to his faith? He had so many questions. The Monsignor seemed resolutely calm and affable. What demons had he faced down? And Sheriff Harris with his chain smoking and his disfigured hand. What secrets were tamped down in the bowels of his soul? And HomeSky? Father Pat was ashamed of the moment of distraction her physical beauty caused him. He admired her strength and faith in the face of this agonizing day. He was anxious to see her tonight, to be of service. But selfishly, he was also brimming with questions about her dream. She, too, had dreamt of him with the child. How was she so sure it wasn't her son in that dream? Father Pat was convinced it was, and this tragic glittering moment was what all his life had been in preparation for.

A strange, exhausting day. Father Pat bore down on the leather steering wheel as the beam of headlights framed a swatch of snowflakes out of the darkness. It was impossible to see where the road ended and the ditch began. But he had a recharged faith. He'd get to where he was going. He was doing God's work.

The right front wheel drifted onto the shoulder of the road, causing the car to lurch powerfully toward the ditch. In the span of time it took the wipers to swipe the windshield, the car's red taillights left the highway. Down the bank it hurtled. Just before the car flipped a second time, in the near silence of this snow-muffled empty stretch of night, three words were borne into the blackness:

"Shit damn piss!"

CORY'S NIGHT.

The lights went on! Cory stood by the worn switch plate notched into the log and breathed out in relief. It was cold enough to see his breath, but the presence of light made the cabin feel infinitely warmer.

His eyes swept the inside perimeter, stopping on a quaint, yellowed needlepoint in a wooden frame on the wall beside him. Welcome Home, it read. Each hand-stitched word radiated a feeling of safety, triggering a stab of sadness, an inner tug of something indescribable—something forever—pulling in his stomach. *Mom's back home.* At least she had his two sisters, Cory reassured himself. Mom had her daughters and her husband had his son. That was the unspoken arrangement.

"Welcome home," he was surprised to hear himself whisper. His eyes continued their way around the cabin. He forced a laugh, for courage, but the more he saw, the more he did feel at home here.

Breaking the spell, Cory clapped his hands, rubbed them briskly, and got busy looking for a heat source. Lips pursed, brow furrowed, his was his dad's countenance.

The fieldstone fireplace had a knee-high hearth ledge extending into the room. On it was split oak in a spot-rusted tin tub. The fireplace box was loaded with kindling, dry pine needles, and a few logs pyramided for the next fire. Cory was impressed; the owner thinks ahead. Hanging on the flue pin jutting out of the fireplace's rock face was a small, hand-made sign showing which way was open and which was shut: *Don't forget to shut the flue or you'll be living with a bat or two* was patiently hand-cut into the wooden sign.

Near the opposite wall in the main room was a space heater. Cory found a panel that opened to the pilot light. Taped inside the panel door, in the neatest hand printing Cory had ever seen, were full instructions on lighting the heater. The directions ended with a paragraph on how high to set the heat.

Lighting Wisdom:
On a one-blanket night
set it for two.
If it's two-blanket cold
go for four.
When it's just too cold
to get out of bed
stay where you are
and sleep instead.

Cory followed the lighting instructions. He stood back as the space heater whoomphed to life. The old steel frame popped and pinged, expanding as it warmed.

He looked the heater over carefully. A cord ran out the back, but sat unplugged beneath an outlet. A blower to push heat into the room, he assumed. When Cory plugged it in, sure enough, the blower kicked on.

On every fishing and hunting trip he and his dad went on, they always spent a painful amount of time going over the workings of things. How to take a reel apart. How the toilet ballcock worked. How to gap the plugs on an outboard motor. How to read a map. How to fillet a fish. How to rewire a lamp. How to put a thermocouple on a water heater pilot light. How to take apart a jammed shotgun. How to this. How to that. It's almost as if his dad knew to cram a lifetime of these lessons into the short time they had together. His dad wasn't going to raise a fool, he often reminded Cory.

Which was quite the understatement. Cory needed to see things done once and he had it. Curious, intuitive, he was a quick study. Regardless, his dad was judgmental. Rather than tell him how well he did or how much he loved him, he restated how much he expected of Cory. Cory hardened. He, too, grew judgmental, often disappointed in people—he himself topping the list.

As the cabin warmed, Cory checked for food, formulating a plan for getting back to the resort. One lunch remained of the two that were in the boat, so he wasn't bothered that the refrigerator and pantry were bare. The cabin had been closed up for the winter. Any liquid left behind would freeze and burst. And food just attracted mice. He found a lonely can of lard, some salt, some pepper, and a can of tuna fish. Cory put his lunch in the fridge, but didn't bother plugging it in. The cold of the cabin was sealed inside. He'd have one sandwich for breakfast and then head out on a day trip looking for the resort. He knew it got dark somewhere around six, so he'd go out for about five hours and if he came up empty, head back for the cabin, careful to return before dark. Maybe he'd get back with time enough to put a few walleyes in the boat for supper. Each day, he'd take a slightly different track around the islands until he found the resort. As long as there was shelter to return to, he'd be fine. He'd be mindful of the space heater, though. In tomorrow's daylight, he'd check how many gallons of fuel were left in the tank. And look for more wood, too.

The cabin was mostly one room with the fireplace and heater. Off to one side were a narrow kitchen and tiny bathroom. Cory tried the kitchen faucet. It just let out a whisper of pressure.

The owner had an assortment of handmade signs hung and tacked in every room. *Bacon grease down the sink gets you dishes for the week!* was warned over the drying rack. Over the toilet, *Fussy Flushing Saves a Septic: If it's yellow let it mellow. If it's brown flush it down.*

Off the opposite side of the main room were two bedrooms hardly bigger than their sagging double beds. Further down there was a heavy pine door that opened onto a screened porch. Cory unbolted the door and took a peek. Wind-whipped snow had filtered through the screens like flour through a sifter, settling on the plank flooring. The cold blew into the cabin. Cory closed and re-locked the door quick as a shiver.

The main room was a cacophony of fascinating outdoor stuff. Hanging from the ceiling with heavy monofilament was a group of stuffed bluebills, wings set like they were about to decoy. A mounted walleye was over the door leading to the kitchen. Above the mantel a huge muskie was chasing a fat smallmouth. Deer heads and a bearskin rug took up another wall. There was a beaver playing cards and antique fishing lures hooked to petrified driftwood as if they'd snagged there decades ago. Old snowshoes crisscrossed above the entryway and antique outboard motors stood sentry on either side of the fireplace. There was hardly a space that didn't have something stuck to it, dangling from it, or propped up in front of it. It was the coolest place Cory had ever seen. He spent over an hour examining things, picking them up, fingering them, and then carefully putting them exactly back where he had found them. It was like being in an outdoors museum.

During this get-acquainted time, Cory realized there was no phone. He double-checked every room. Maybe it was a hard-and-fast rule that went back for years—to remain unconnected, to escape all that. But it seemed dangerous. The owner would have something in case of an emergency.

Back at the resort, they had phones and marine-band radios. A lot of folks on the lake communicated over the radio. Cory looked through all the drawers and closets, but had no luck with the radio, either. He did find a lined canvas coat, which he hung over a kitchen chair to warm. His coat was still down in the boat, over his father.

He got on his stomach and looked under the beds. There was a cased 12-gauge shotgun and a box of shells three-quarters full. Cory put them back. No radio. No phone. It just didn't add up. Maybe the owner had a ship-to-shore radio in his boat, which this time of year would be stored mainland.

Cory pulled on the coat and took two large stockpots out to the hand pump. The wind had laid down, snowflakes zigzagging out of the blackness, large, delicate, landing on Cory's upturned face and eyelashes. The season's first snow is an awakening. The sight, the smell, the quiet of it. Deep emotions are conjured, even if you're only 13. Cory set the dented pots in the snow, and allowed thoughts of a particular first snowfall to rush in.

It was a few years back. He had just run back inside the house to find his dad behind a wiring manual for the blender.

"Dad, it's scented! It's perfumy! No kidding!"

His dad squinted at him. "What are you talking about?"

"The new snow outside. You can smell it. Come out and see—I mean smell!"

His dad gave him that *look.*

"I swear, Dad!"

They walked out the back door and stood on the patio as the big flakes tumbled and descended and accumulated. Sure enough, somewhere in the fresh inches of that first snowfall was the hint of a sweet scent.

"Do you smell it, Dad? I smell it, do you?"

For a moment, his dad was bewildered. He, too, smelled it, but it made no logical sense. Then, in a rare display of spontaneous emotion, a smile spread across his face.

Cory noticed this and smiled too. "You do smell it. I told you, but you didn't believe me." He was so excited that he had shown his dad something, rather than it always being the other way around.

"What direction is the wind blowing, Cory?"

"South. Southern wind brings the moisture in," he recited the old outdoorsman's rhyme.

"Okay. So let's go see what's upwind." They walked around to the side of the house where the dryer was vented to the outside air. Cory's mom had a load of laundry going. Steam was rising where the warm and cold air met. The distinct smell of scented dryer sheets filled the air.

"So, what do you smell, Cory?"

"Mom's got the dryer going." He was disappointed.

"How come you could smell it all the way in the back yard tonight, but not other nights?" Cory's dad quizzed.

"Because the wind is blowing it that way."

"Any other reason?"

Cory thought hard. He couldn't offer one.

"Why, Dad?"

This was the question his father enjoyed most. 'Why, Dad?' was music to his ears.

They returned to the spot where they first stood. "This snowfall has a lot of moisture in it," he explained. "Moisture holds scent much better than when it's dry. That's why when we're pheasant hunting, the dogs do better flushing birds when the ground's wet. If it's dry and windy, the dogs aren't much good. So moisture content and wind direction is why you smelled what you did."

"Cool. Let's get Mom out here and trick her into thinking the snow has perfume in it. I know we could."

"She's busy with your sisters." With that, he went back inside to his blender manual.

As Cory stood on that little island somewhere in the middle of giant Lake of the Woods and looked into that black sky with soft flakes suddenly materializing, melting on his face, he inhaled deeply in all directions hoping for a trace of that safe, sweet smell. What he got instead was a quiet so profound it hurt. Warm tears at the corners of his eyes melted with snowflakes, tracing cold down his face.

If ever there was a moment of childhood lost, of the raw tragedy of this transition, here under the starless sky, feeling the sting of new snow, wrapped in unknown silence, alone, except for memories barely aromatic, it was this plaintive moment. Cory took the oversized coat sleeve and wiped it hard across his eyes.

"Knock it off," he said aloud. And after a few cranks of the pump handle, the water flowed into the large stockpots. He brought them inside and got a glass from the cupboard. He dipped it into the pot and drank so fast he coughed most of the first glass down the wrong pipe. "Slow down," he reprimanded himself. "Don't be an idiot."

Next Cory found a flashlight and went out to the unlocked boathouse he'd seen when he arrived. There might be an outboard motor he could use tomorrow to go looking for the resort. His hands had blistered from rowing all day despite wearing gloves and being mindful to alternate his grip. There wasn't much in the boathouse, but there was a tarp he could use to cover his father. He cringed at the thought, but his dad out in the boat being covered by snow was worse yet. He made his way to the dock.

The flashlight beam found his dad, Cory's small coat over his head. Cory shook out the folded tarp and let it fall over the body. He lifted the legs and tucked the edges beneath, away from the wind. The legs were like logs. He did what he did, but at times couldn't help but pull his hands back to his chest and stare. This was his dad just 12 hours ago. Cory clicked off the flashlight and continued to tuck the tarp around the body.

In the utter blackness, rocking in the wind, Cory fluctuated from the surreal confusion of *where am I?* to absolute clarity about his task. In a moment of confusion, he almost got out of the boat on the waterside rather than dockside. Cory took off his gloves and rubbed his face. "I don't know," he said. Cory snapped on the flashlight, found the dock, and got out of there.

"Enough for now," he said, the sound of his voice reassuring. He quick-stepped up the path toward the cabin, pulled by the amber glow in the windows. The certainty, the companionship of this light, started him crying again. "Idiot. What good is that going to do?" He remained outside, not permitting himself back in until he stopped.

Inside, it was warming nicely. Cory sat with a glass of water at the kitchen table. The chair seat was still cold, but the room was feeling good, welcoming. In the middle of the table was an oversized leather-bound book. He spun it around to read the cover: *Cabin Log* was embossed in yellowed scripted type. Inside, page after page journaled the stays of the owners and their many guests. Each entry would tell a little of the weather, the meals of fresh fish, the berry picking results, the bird sightings, the spectacular sunsets, and of the simple times had by all. It was full of memorable incidents of poison ivy, of snapping turtles picking a stringer of walleyes clean to the gill plates, of running out of gas in the middle of the lake, of a rod taken overboard while a fisherman dozed. Most of the entries were signed off Bud & Lois in the same neat printing Cory had seen in the lighting instructions on the space heater. There were jottings about different schemes to keep deer out of the vegetable garden, tulip bulbs that didn't blossom, bears swimming across to the island, parts of docks that blew away in the storm, spring hatches of goslings waddling to the water, friends they had seen on the lake, and many, many, fishing reports. Most talked of big muskies caught, in the 45- to 55-inch range. Cory had seen pictures of fish that large in his fishing magazines. He'd always wanted to fish for muskies, but his dad was a self-described "walleye man" and that was the end of it.

As Cory flipped through the entries, he looked mostly for the fishing reports because they were more interesting than the number of hummingbirds at the feeders that day. Halfway into one entry, he stopped, frozen by adrenaline.

The entry read:

July/1969. Perfect, overcast morning. Air thicker than the Sunday paper. Decided to run up north to Monument Bay for muskies ...

Cory's eyes held on the words Monument Bay. That's where he needed to get back to. *Decided to run up north to Monument Bay ...* Right there was the information he needed.

Quickly, Cory unfolded his lake map and spread it across the kitchen table. He was looking for two things: islands south of Monument Bay. And of those, the ones marked with dotted lines coming into them signifying underwater power service. He circled a group of islands south of the resort.

Next, he penciled a line going out of Monument Bay heading east. That was the general direction he and his father had taken; he remembered squinting into the sun. After the accident, Cory was sure he rowed west all day because he watched his compass. The obvious conclusion was his dad and he were actually heading more south east when they left the resort. Everything fit. He'd come back far enough west. Now to the north he'd find the resort.

Only three of the forty islands in that area indicated power service. He circled them. One of them had to be his present location. Trial and error would tell him which. If he just took it slow and smart, he'd be fine. He'd do it.

He rolled out a sleeping bag in front of the space heater and read through the log by the light of a table lamp he brought to the floor. More than a few times it was noted that a big muskie was caught and released in Monument Bay. With each reading of those words, he came closer. But something was missing. Something pulled at him. A clue? His dad taught him to always go slowly and double-check things, because usually in the awkwardness of haste, you'd overlook the obvious. It's right under your nose, he'd say with a frown.

Cory snapped off the lamp and the red glow of the space heater lit a small radius of pine plank floor. He rolled to his side, and recited the same prayer he'd said every night since he was taught it:

"Please, Lord, help me not to be selfish. Amen." He always allowed himself one extra prayer, what he called a special prayer: "my special prayer is for ..." he paused, thinking. He knew it'd be wrong to pray for himself. "My special prayer is for Mom. When the news comes."

Cory punched the musty feather pillow and settled into its coolness. His body began to unwind. Overstimulated, his mind swirled with the day. He listened for his breathing.

What am I missing? The exhausted 13-year-old boy drifted toward sleep. *Something's missing.*

The cabin creaked and popped as the temperatures outside and inside moved in opposite directions. The wind began to blow, the snow petered out. One by one, the clouds peeled back, exposing the night sky. Hundreds of stars sat in front of thousands.

Cory slept. He dreamt his failure dreams. Hockey pucks rolling just wide of goal posts, punts bobbled and dropped, destinations unreachable despite the running. But then, for a moment, something was there, bright and glorious and good. He tried to hold fast to this dream-feeling. He wasn't alone now. In that dream moment, the next mistake wasn't breathing down his neck.

Hard days end quietly, it's good to know. Even this October fifteenth parted in silence, with a quiet turn, before moving away.

Cory lay curled in the red glow of a heater in a cabin built of logs that were ancestors to the trees towering high above.

Joseph, in the woods, slept on a mat of cattails, three-quarters of a mile from the farmhouse where he was delivered, and his father before him, and his father's father.

HomeSky, cold, barefoot, stunned, in the farmhouse kitchen, looking out the window into blackness, held a half-peeled orange, unable to bear the sight of her husband's empty chair at the kitchen table, so she put it out on the porch where snow was blowing up around its legs.

Sheriff Harris, home, alone, in pajamas his wife had years ago sewn for him because his size was rarely stocked, was looking over the blood-alcohol report of Joseph's father as Deputy pawed at the air, dreaming of fast-running rabbits.

Father Pat, pressing a snowball to the blood-crusted gash over his eye, was trying to get comfortable beneath a mildewed army blanket from the back seat of the DeVille he'd rolled twice before coming upright in the ditch.

Monsignor Kief, showered, teeth brushed, rinsed, and spat, in the humid dark of the bathroom, paused to kneel, to say a petition for Joseph before rising and walking to bed.

These people were now and forever altered. October fifteenth would never again pass through a calendar year without each of them, for the rest of their lives—long or short as they may be—giving pause, to press that day with a fingertip and hold on it. Their life paths converged at this single point, came to a hard stop, and then branched out, entangled.

None of them would ever be as lonely, as independent, as pained, as frightened, or as perplexed by life's ways as they were on this day. None of them would ever be as trusting or as innocent or as easily surprised. They tasted the unapologetic shove of life. For some, it was their first taste. For others, it was familiar.

If there is true good to come of a hard day, it is the quiet bond that forms among the newly tempered few. If there is true sadness, it is the false hope that this bond encourages.

No less. The day, finally, agreed to go. Bodies rested. Breathing found rhythm. Fists unclenched. Shoulders went slack. It was as if something incomprehensibly powerful said, "Enough, already."

PART TWO

October 16, 1973

MORNING. JOSEPH.

Joseph opened his eyes to a blue sky so diamond-clear it hurt. Yesterday's heavy snow was already melting under the bright sun. As sagging pine boughs shed their snow, they snapped back toward the heavens. Joseph knew the feeling. Lithe and at peace, he walked to the stream to rinse the mourning ash from his face. The gentle tap-tapping of the stone braided in his hair steadied him. He was ready to go back to his mother and help her see that they would be fine.

Rising from the stream, he looked all around, pivoting slowly. The pristine blanket of snow lay unblemished, reflecting millions of sequined pinpoints. The season's first snow always possessed this capacity to amaze, but there was more to it. Joseph was strengthened by the *now* of things. He resolved not to bank his admiration of today on tomorrow. A smile tickled through him.

He began to run. He loved to run, muscles stretching, springing. Through the woods he went, surefooted as a buck. How little energy it required, how effortlessly movement came to him. The stone tapped. The rhythm was as musical as ancient drums.

He came out of the silva and sprinted across the open field to the highway, black hair flying out behind him. Ahead was the intersection where his father had been killed. The highway had a brilliant sparkling white blanket of snow pulled over it. Joseph knew this was a sign from the Great Spirit. Renewal.

Before he crossed the road, he looked in both directions. About a half mile to the south, Joseph caught a reflection, sunlight glancing off something down in the ditch. The man in him said investigate, but the child said hurry back to Mom. He started down the road.

His were the only tracks on the highway. Ahead of him, it became clearer and clearer there was a car in the ditch. Joseph quickened his stride.

The bank showed signs where the car had left the highway and rolled. He could see the windows were frosted, a good sign. Whoever was in that car must be alive, or the windows wouldn't be fogged.

Joseph tried the driver-side door. It was locked. Same for the back door. He rapped on the glass. It was quiet enough to hear drops of melting snow falling from the wheel well, plopping onto the rubber tire. Crows cried out from treetops a half mile away. The temperature was climbing fast behind the warm sun.

Joseph rapped on the window harder this time. Through the frosted glass, something stirred. He could hear a hand fumbling with the back door handle. Joseph took a step back.

The door opened a crack, but no farther. Snow was packed up tight against it, high as the handle. Not a word was spoken. Inside, weight shifted on the car seat. Joseph took hold of the door handle, set his feet, and gave a mighty pull. At the same moment, Father Pat put his shoulder to the inside of the door. The door flung open, sending Joseph airborne, backward. He landed in the snow with a great "uuff!"

Father Pat crawled out of the car and got his very first look at the boy who he was immediately certain was Joseph. Full of snow, flat on his back, arms splayed, unable to contain himself, the 13-year-old laughed with such contagious joy, Father Pat began laughing himself.

Pat always treasured their first meeting. For his entire life, he could only wish for such strength of spirit. *Imagine what Joseph had just been through,* he'd say, *yet there he was, in a snowbank, laughing. So irrepressible. So clear about himself. Such a good heart.*

And although those words were true, they were inadequate. Father Pat felt something uniquely powerful come from this boy before a word was exchanged. "You, I'd wager, must be Joseph Blackholm." Father Pat stretched the night's kinks from his back.

"Did you see how far I flew?" Joseph said, eyes ablaze. "Had to be 20 feet!" He paced off the distance from where he landed. "That could be some sort of record." He shook his head in amazement and looked up at Father Pat, who at six feet, was only an inch taller. "You sure picked a funny place to park." Joseph was amused by his own wit.

"Ah, yes." Pat's legs were asleep and not quite responding. "I was on my way to see your mom last night when I encountered this little detour." Father Pat tapped the roof of the car. "I'm Father Pat, the new priest on the Rez." He put out his hand to shake Joseph's.

"Nice to meet you, Father. I've got to be telling you, we steer wide of the Rez. No disrespect." He shook Father Pat's hand. Pat couldn't help but notice the size and strength of the boy's hand.

"Actually, I met your mom yesterday in town at the sheriff's office. She filled me in on your family's feelings in that regard. My visit is about … your mom asked if I could help with your father's service." Father Pat looked at the boy. The sparkle left Joseph's eyes. "I'm so sorry about your loss. I'm sure your father is resting in the love of God now."

Joseph studied the priest, backlit in the sun. He was a well-framed, blue-eyed man with a face that was both rough and kind.

His eyes, though, were sad. Maybe it was the fact that one was gashed from the accident, but Joseph didn't think that was all there was to it.

"I'm thankful for your helping Mom. She's religious—I mean in a Catholic way. My dad, he was religious, but in a less Catholic way. Does that make sense?"

"I think I follow you. How about you? Are you religious? Will your faith help you get through this difficult time?"

Joseph looked off at the trees and suddenly smiled his infectious smile. "Already has, Father. It's just my way is more like Dad's. He said start by being faithful to yourself."

"I think my Boss would agree with that." Pat smiled and patted Joseph on the shoulder, letting the idea sink in.

Joseph's thoughts came back from the trees. "We should get up to the farm. Our tractor'll yank you out of here easy as pulling carrots on a rainy day. I've helped my dad do it lots of times."

Father Pat kicked the snow in the highway ditch. "So I'm not your first uninvited visitor to these parts?"

"Hardly. See that creek back there?" Joseph pointed down the road. "It cuts under the highway. There's a bridge not two cars wide under that snow. That's always the first patch to ice up. The wind blows under the bridge, turns it into a skating rink. Plus there's just enough of a curve to shoot plenty of cars our way. We still get Christmas cards from some of the families we've pulled out. Mom always said that creek had a way of sending people our way. Do you believe that, Father?"

Pat blew into his cold hands. "I'd have to mull that one over."

"Looks like that roof of yours will need repair." Father Pat didn't hear him. He was focused up the road, wondering about that creek bridge shrouded in snow. *That creek has a way of sending people our way …*

Father Pat and Joseph sidestepped up from the ditch bottom. Joseph made it up first and reached out a hand.

As they headed back for the farm, the two walked in silence down the county road. Pockets of gravel were beginning to show through where the sun had melted away the snow. The day was edging toward beautiful.

"What would you guess the temperature at, Joseph?"

Joseph cocked his head. "Low 50s. Snow'll be gone after lunch."

"You must be hungry. When did you last eat?"

"Yesterday, breakfast," Joseph said. "Around this time. Before the wreck."

Father Pat lowered his voice. His eyes narrowed with concern. "Did you see the accident, son?"

Joseph thought for a moment, then stopped walking and looked up into the crowns of the trees lining the road. Tears shone in his dark eyes. His voice dropped to a deep whisper. "I heard it. On my bike. Dad told me I could follow down to the highway. We were racing. I turned back for home." Joseph paused. "How could he pull in front of that truck, Father? He's so smart." Each tear grew until its weight moved it slowly down his face. He looked at Father Pat, waiting.

Pat was at a loss. The boy obviously needed something more substantial than *the Lord works in mysterious ways.*

"I wish I could say, but I don't know. I do know the Sheriff was out here yesterday talking to the trucker. When we get to your house, we'll call him and see if he's found anything. I promise you, I'll try to get an answer."

"But there is no answer, is there?" Joseph said.

"What do you mean?"

"I think things happen. A lot of it is just luck—good and bad. That's what I was thinking in the forest last night. Some people are just lucky. My dad wasn't. There's no why to it."

"What about you?"

"I'm lucky. Always have been. Maybe it goes in waves. Maybe I got my dad's luck." Joseph wiped his tears and they resumed walking. "I don't know. It's confusing if you let it be."

Father Pat looked at the boy, wishing he could inject some insight. All these years of service and he had no more to offer than a mute tongue.

"I'm glad you're here, Father."

"Well so am I. You're a pretty amazing guy, do you know that?"

"I don't know. I feel something good today. It's a ways off, but it's coming."

"I feel it, too." Pat looked up. "Good things on the horizon."

"How far off, Father?" Joseph looked harder now at the priest.

"Close at hand, I think. Around the bend."

Joseph nodded. He picked up a rock and winged it effortlessly a good 40 yards. They made their way up the gravel utility road toward home.

"See that field to the south?" Joseph pointed in front of them. "That's ours. Those standing strips are food plots. Sorghum. Corn. We leave them out all year for the deer. There's even a lost pheasant or two up here. We run around on the tractor in the summer planting for winter—food plots to help them get through. When Dad was my age, he and his dad planted these fields by pushing a plow behind a cow. Can you believe that? That's all they had. He said everyone called them rock farmers 'cause that's mostly what they raised. But they made it. We will, too, Mom and me." In silence they went, letting the lonely beauty of the landscape speak.

"That's our wheat field on the other side of the road here. Once lightning hit the hill and killed five deer where they stood. We found them laying there stone dead. Had venison steaks for a month." The thought of eating like that made Joseph smile. He was a boy with an appetite. "The wheat and straw gets us just enough in town to buy seed to plant again next year. Dad taught me a lot about the land. He says the land can only make you so strong, so it makes you smart, too. Dad was a great man." Joseph tugged the stone behind his ear.

"I would have loved to know him," Father Pat said.

Joseph smiled.

Father Pat let those words settle in around them. *Great man.* What two words could any man more hope for? What mark would he rather leave? Like a pattern etched into a rock that few see because they alone were fortunate to know of it. Time may diminish it, but cannot remove it. Pat thought that the mark most truly great men leave is private.

"There's my house!" Joseph startled Father Pat from his ruminations. He broke into a sprint that Pat couldn't have kept stride with even had he a notion to. The boy flew toward the white one-story farmhouse just up the rise, tucked behind a shelterbelt of oaks. The snow had sloughed off the black-shingled roof with its lightning rods standing guard on either gable. Smoke curved from the crooked chimney. Father Pat recognized his Toronado parked in the back of the driveway loop.

The old farmstead looked straight out of a picture book of midwest farms. Modest. Weathered red barn and outbuildings tilting this way and that, trimmed white, built on fieldstone foundations. The white clapboard farmhouse had a wrap-around summer porch and hanging swing. A yellow dog barked out a greeting as he circled Joseph. Just then, the front door banged open and HomeSky rushed out. Father Pat was far enough away that she didn't notice him. Everything had a surreal touch from this distance; a miniature scene in a wind-up music box. HomeSky's arms went out, but her legs were glued to the porch floorboards. Joseph ran to her, dropped to his knees and buried his head in her stomach. She curled over him and they rocked back and forth. Father Pat's eyes filled. Even from this distance, he could feel their strength going into each other, resuscitating each other. They swayed on the porch, mother and son. To witness such a thing did wonders for his faith. Father Pat knew he was watching Joseph's last childhood moments. A boy knelt, a man would stand.

After a time, Joseph turned toward the road, cupped his mouth with his hands, and in his inimitable way hollered, "Hey, Father. You get lost or something?" Pat waved an arm, and headed toward the house. The sun was warm on his back. He felt needed.

Inside the kitchen, HomeSky put out three unmatched cups, a pot of hot coffee, and fresh-baked oat cakes on the table. The room's walls were horsehair plaster, painted clean white. The space was neat. The refrigerator looked to be from the early fifties. The oven appeared older yet. It must have been so empty here for HomeSky last night, Father Pat thought. Again, for an instant he wasn't proud of, he was struck by her, watching her move through this raw, plain space, offsetting it.

Father Pat got back to finishing the story of his last 24 hours. HomeSky leaned on the sink, listening. Joseph sat directly across the table, peppering in questions when he wanted more detail.

"Next thing I know, the car settles upright. I knew I was stuck for the night. I made two snowballs to cut the swelling around my eye, got comfortable in the back seat, and this morning, Joseph comes to call."

"I'm sorry for all this," HomeSky said.

Joseph chimed in, "He went off by the creek, Mom. You know the spot."

"That godforsaken road." HomeSky grit her teeth, stopping herself before she said anything more. "Joseph," she restarted, "Father Pat is going to help us with the funeral. I'd like for it to be tomorrow. Morning, if that's possible, Father. I know that's short notice, but like I said yesterday, it'll be small. The way your father would want it."

Father Pat and Joseph waited for her to continue. "Father," she said, "there's a small place on our property here … for the burial. Is there anything in your doctrines keeping you from giving the final blessing here?"

Father Pat looked at her, considering the question. "This is a special situation. If on your land is what's right, then that's what should be done. What's tougher to avoid are the legal issues. How do we get the Sheriff to release your husband's body to us?"

"They can't do that, can they, Mom?" Joseph interrupted. "It's our business, not theirs."

"I don't know. White laws are powerful. They're made to protect and serve white customs, not ours. No offense to you, Father." HomeSky looked at him.

"I'm on your side on this. But laws like this aren't easy to sidestep." Father Pat sighed, thinking. He looked like a brooding prizefighter with his cut eye half shut.

"HomeSky, do you know of a blind priest in town, Monsignor Kief?"

"Sure. I've gone in for his masses many times. He gives homilies worth driving for."

"That's his car out in the ditch. I met him last night and he was good enough to loan me the rectory vehicle. Anyway, he seems to know the ins and outs of this town. I've got a hunch a crafty old fox like him could dodge us around the Sheriff's red tape. Do you mind me speaking to him about our predicament here? I trust him—although we've just met."

"I know what you mean," she said with such certainty, and a trace of a smile, that he was momentarily confused. Then it dawned on him that they, too, were essentially strangers. Yet here they sat talking as if they'd grown up together. Father Pat returned her smile. Joseph smiled too. An unspoken link had begun to pull them together.

"God is at work here, that much I know." Father Pat beamed with a sense of purpose he hadn't felt in far too long. "We'll find a way."

Joseph pushed his chair back from the table. "Well, if the Monsignor from town is going to help us, we better get in his good graces by putting his car back on the road." He went to the closet. "Too warm for overalls, too sloppy for shoes," Joseph said with his back to them, pulling on his boots. HomeSky jumped like she'd leaned up against a pin. It was as if she'd heard the voice of her husband coming from that open closet. It was exactly what he'd have said. Father Pat couldn't help but notice her reaction.

"Father, you should care to that cut of yours," HomeSky said, distracted, coming around the table, but watching her boy, how he moved there, bent over, pulling on one boot, then the other. She nearly walked right into Pat's chair. "There are some things in the bathroom."

"It'll be fine," he said to her.

She looked down at him, focusing now. She pushed his hair to the side and furrowed her brow. "Sure could take a stitch or two, but it looks to be too late for that now. It'll leave a scar."

"A scar on a priest, cool!" Joseph said. And just like that, he was her boy again.

Pat walked to the bathroom, also somewhat enamored with the idea of a scar marking this turning point. It would bring some purpose back to his reflection. He wasn't particularly fond of what he'd encountered in the mirror lately.

The bathroom was beyond the only two bedrooms in the farmhouse. The master bedroom came first. Then Joseph's room. Father Pat peeked around the doorframe into a sparse, neat room. Against one wall, under the room's only window, was a single bed that looked too small for Joseph. There was a desk with a few schoolbooks stacked on one side. And one single poster hung in the room, centered over the desk. It was a famous photograph of Boston Bruin Bobby Orr stretched out airborne two feet above the ice after scoring a spectacular goal. Father Pat recognized the shot. It was the game-winner in the Stanley Cup when Orr and the Bruins beat the St. Louis Blues on their home ice.

In another corner of the room, Joseph's skates and hockey stick were propped up neatly. Father Pat didn't play much organized sports growing up. No one was there to expose him to that pure thrill of being a kid, pulling on a uniform, belonging to a team. Pat went into the bathroom to clean up. He heard the phone ring as he turned on the faucets.

HomeSky was still on the phone when Father Pat reentered the kitchen. She nodded at the kitchen table where he saw she'd refilled his coffee and put out another warm oat cake with homemade blackberry jam. Joseph was cramming his fourth into his mouth while translating the phone conversation.

"It's the Sheriff," he said to Father Pat. "Sounds like the whole town pretty much thinks I've run off for good, or may be dead. They think maybe you're a goner, too."

HomeSky clasped her palm over the phone. "Joseph!" she shot him a look that could melt glass, and then went back to the conversation. Joseph lowered his voice. "They've been trying to reach you all morning. The Sheriff went out to your place and saw no tire tracks. He called around to see if you stayed in town on account of the weather and found out you had the Monsignor's car last night. Most likely, you've gone off the road someplace, he guessed. As for me, he just figured I was laying frozen under a foot of snow with crows fighting for my eyeballs."

"JOSEPH BLACKHOLM!" HomeSky warned, this time not bothering to cover up the phone. Obviously Joseph hadn't lowered his voice enough. He gave the priest a little shrug. It was his nature to bedevil, even at a time like this. "I'm going to run the tractor up to the road and pull the car out."

"We could call the service station," Father Pat offered.

"And pay 25 bucks!? It'll take me 10 minutes to get things set up. Why don't you drive up with Mom."

"You want me to come now? It's no trouble."

"Nah. Nothing to it. I'll just get things ready."

"See you up there, then," Father Pat said, finishing his coffee as Joseph opened the door to leave. "We'll be along in a few minutes."

HomeSky hung up, looking very concerned.

"What is it?"

She shook her head and sat down to her cold coffee. "That boy of mine, talking lighthearted about his death like that. He's always had a lot of nonsense in him."

"I think he realizes today could use ... something not so heavy. He really is a miracle."

"His dad always said it was foolish to dwell on a thing. Move on. Life changes its mind daily, he'd say."

"I was talking with Joseph about him as we walked to the house. Sounds like your husband was quite a person."

"I've never met another like him. I don't know how to take the next step, not now. I consider myself an independent woman, but … I don't know."

"That's to be expected. Thankfully, you've got a lot of your husband in Joseph, so you're not completely without him. That and your strong faith will guide you."

"Thank you for saying so. You're right. I'm not completely alone here. With Joseph, and now with your help."

Father Pat smiled. "What else did the Sheriff have to say?"

"He was calling to see if Joseph was still missing. I told him the two of you showed up on my porch an hour ago. He wants you to call him."

"I'd like to call Monsignor Kief first. I'm hoping he can help us with the funeral. Maybe he can find a loophole or something. Plus, I don't feel like talking to the Sheriff just now."

HomeSky nodded. "The phone book is in the drawer under the phone. Then we should get to the highway to help Joseph. I don't like him up there alone."

"Maybe we should go now?"

"Oh, no, he'll be fine. He's done it with his father before. I guess I'll just have to get used to it. Trust he'll be safe. I can't keep him locked in the house. He's bigger than I am." HomeSky managed what was her first hint at a carefree smile since Father Pat had met her. It was beautiful, that smile, incomplete as it was.

"HomeSky, I've known your son all of …" Father Pat looked at his watch, "an hour and forty-five minutes, but I know he'll be okay. He's unusually capable. It's hard to believe he's only 13."

HomeSky nodded. "Father, if I lost him I wouldn't know what to believe. I'd come unpinned from this earth. I don't—"

"There's no need to think about that. You've got a special boy there and the Lord has a purpose for him. I can feel it."

"Thank you. I guess I always sensed it myself, but I attributed it to a mother's bias."

They smiled tentatively at each other as the sunshine spilled in through the kitchen window, making the room a little less drafty, a little less empty. Father Pat tucked the phone between his shoulder and ear. He dialed with one finger, pointing to the number in the phone book with the other. Father Pat listened as the phone was picked up.

"Monsignor Kief?"

"No, sorry. Monsignor Kief is out giving driver's education lessons, can I take a message?"

"... He's what?"

A giggle came from the other end of the line.

"Monsignor, it's not nice to pick on the rookie. It will surely be recorded on the heavenly tally."

"I recognized your voice. I'm terrible, I know."

"Monsignor—"

"I'll only remind you one more time, it's Frank."

"Frank. I have good news and bad news. The good news is I'm out at the Blackholm place and Joseph is safe and sound."

"Wonderful! That will certainly diminish any bad news you could have."

"Glad to hear you say that. But I'd like to deliver the bad news in person. Do you have lunch plans?"

"Are you buying?"

"I am."

"My, that must indeed be bad news. Yes. I'd love some lunch."

"What do you say I pick you up around one and we have a bite at Lu Ann's?"

"Excellent," Frank chimed. "Lu Ann's will be grand. But I'll meet you there. The walk will do me good. It's such a beautiful day. If I leave at noon, by the time I've kindly declined all the lifts people will insist on giving me, I should be arriving about the same time as you."

"Fine. I'll see you at one."

"You will indeed, Patrick. Bring your checkbook. I'm particularly hungry."

Father Pat shook his head and smiled as he hung up the phone. "That Monsignor Kief sure is something."

"Do you think he can help us with the arrangements?" HomeSky asked, concerned.

"If anyone can, he's the one. Now, as to tomorrow, would you like me to say a word or two about RiverHeart, or would you prefer to?"

"Could you, Father? I'm not much for speeches. I'll write some things down for you, and ask Joseph to do so as well. You could speak from that, couldn't you?"

"Yes, sure. When I come back out this evening with details on the service, if you and Joseph might take some quiet time today to think about what you'd like said, that'll be of great assistance."

"That's just what we'll do. I'll take a walk with Joseph." HomeSky pushed away from the old kitchen table, gathering her resolve. "We should be getting up to the road."

"Indeed," Father Pat said, getting up stiffly from the table. The rollover and night in the car had left him sore.

The two of them, together, stepped out of the farmhouse into the brilliant reality of sunlight. On the porch, he felt the sun on his face, yet despite a strong sense of purpose, he paused there momentarily.

"You coming?" HomeSky asked quietly, looking back at him, seeing the sun on his unshaven face. "Is everything okay?"

"Yeah—yes, sure. Just got a little disoriented for a second. It's been one heck of a day—night—well, you know."

She came toward him. "You've taken a good knock. Maybe you should see a doctor."

"Nah. Silly cut, is all. I was blessed with an exceptionally hard head."

She touched over his eye very gently. Father Pat watched her. "You're going to have something to remember us by, no doubt," she said. They looked at each other. She was meant to be in the sun, Father Pat thought.

"Let's go get a car out of a ditch," he said.

"I bet that boy of mine has it out already."

They held each other's glances, and then dropped them, like something distant, something small and far off and impossible. They stepped off the porch into the mud of the melting snow. All around them there was sunshine, there was future.

MORNING. CORY.

Cory awoke, disoriented, confused—but certain of this much: he'd wet himself in his sleep.

Morning sunlight pushed through the windows and put down bright yellow mats on the pine-plank floor. He looked around, lost, light-headed, sweaty, helpless. These were feelings Cory had little time for. He jumped to his feet, kicking out of his sleeping bag.

"You turd! You baby shit!" He accosted himself. "You pissed your pants. What a fuck-over!" Ashamed, he knew his dad knew.

Near the kitchen sink was a pot of water he'd taken in for the night. Cory snatched it roughly off the counter, spilling. "Dipshit." He ground his teeth, marched into the bathroom and dropped his pants. "Fuck-over," he said, yellow stain in his briefs. He flung them against the wall and scrubbed himself raw with the cold water.

In the bedroom bureau he found some underwear. Quickly pulling on his jeans, he sat down on the bed, rubbing his eyes. "You're not going to cry now, too?" He stared at his feet. "Dammit!" Cory listened to his breathing, trying to settle down. Slow down. Slow down.

Cory reminded himself of the things he'd done correctly after the accident. "Dammit. Dammit, dammit, dammit, dammit," each time said less emphatically. He shrugged. "I don't know what happened. Sorry."

He went to the kitchen table and opened the journal. He liked to read from it. There was a sense of belonging as he got to know the people. The final entry of the fall included the cribbage standings for the season: Bud 113, Lois 121. Bud promised to get her next year. She added, *p.s. Don't count on it.*

All the entries in all the different handwriting, Cory found fascinating. Notes from the guests, family, friends. He felt a part of it somehow. He unclipped the pen from the inside cover and started on his own entry. He went slowly, choosing the words carefully. Cory didn't like to write in ink. He didn't like mistakes to show. He inched along. When he finished, he checked on the sleeping bag he'd cleaned and left to dry over a chair back. The little cabin warmed, the space heater kicked out a dry heat. Cory was parched. It was five minutes to eight and the morning sun was shining full. Water dripped fast off the roof above the kitchen window. It looked to be a warm day, which made the thought of getting back into the boat and searching for Monument Bay Resort less daunting. In fact, Cory filled with a nervous anticipation.

Outside, he watched the towering pines swaying in the wind. They shook off the snow like a wet dog does water. Cory primed the hand pump and filled his stockpot. He ladled out and drained three consecutive glasses of pure cold water. Refreshed, he no longer felt any of the earlier disorientation. "Must have been one tired puppy." He went to the dock to check on things. Burnished by the sun and wind on the open dock, the last trace of fatigue disappeared as Cory tested the knots securing his boat. They were sound.

The snow on the wooden planks was snowball-sticky. Cory hurled one as far as he could. It bobbed once on the surface and was swallowed by the giant lake. The wind had shifted, now out of the west. "It'll have a head of steam today." The distant whitecaps pushed endlessly on.

From his pocket, Cory pulled out his compass and oriented it north. Then he made his way around the riprap perimeter of the island, through the tangled brush, until he was on the side facing due north. He remembered the journal entry in the cabin log: *ran north to fish Monument Bay.* Looking that way, Cory knew what had to be done. There were islands for as far as the eye could see. Some large enough to be mistaken for mainland Canada. It was too easy to get turned around out there. Bewildering, murderous, beautiful, the water waited.

Cory scanned the horizon but saw none of the channel markers that dot the main navigation routes on the lake. They were out there, somewhere. The heavy waves crested white, pushing west to east. It was strangely quiet and serene where Cory stood, on the northern tip of the little island, out of the wind, warmed by the sun. He was careful not to be deceived by the spot's tranquility.

"I'll go slow, that's all," he said aloud, for the comfort of his own voice. "I'll be careful. Head north for four hours, if I don't find anything, head back. That'll be eight hours of daylight, which leaves two in case I get lost. Simple. I'll have time to catch dinner. Next day, I'll go again, a slightly different heading. How hard could that be?" *Home base.* He liked the sound of that, but nervousness gnawed at the emptiness of his stomach. "You'll be fine," he said to the wind.

Turning to walk back, he heard the distant drone of an engine. A float plane? He listened without moving a muscle. A boat? A boat! Yes! Out there, a speck in the distance, coming around an island and heading south in Cory's direction. The boat was a good ways out, but if he ran out to the end of the dock and started waving his arms, chances are he'd be seen. Rescued, was the word that popped to mind.

Cory crouched in the underbrush. He wanted to scream. He wanted to jump. He wanted to run and flail his hands. But instead he crouched, holding very still. With every fiber in him, he denied the urge to run toward that sound. The boat kept coming. Getting louder. Closer now. Close enough to see it was a lone man in with a red hat at the center console. Cory remained still. The boat roared by, heading away, getting smaller, smaller, quieter. Only when the wake from the boat washed up on the shoreline did Cory stand.

He walked to the dock and looked out as the pinpoint-sized boat disappeared into the blue. *I have to do this. Just me. Otherwise how will I ever know?*

Through the melting snow, he slowly walked back up to the cabin, feeling the oncoming weight of sadness. Like he'd parted company with a friend. "Buck up, now." He sounded something like his dad.

Cory ate his last sandwich and studied the map, comfortable in the silence of this familiar little cabin. Leaning back in the creaky wooden kitchen chair, he knew now he'd made the right decision to not flag down the boat. He didn't know why, exactly, but he knew. Maybe, it occurred to him, I was even *told* to do it this way. He didn't dwell or pick at it. Just as yesterday he hadn't lingered over the decision to take his dad's body and set off in the boat—which led to him finding this cabin. That decision he'd made alone. He'd continue alone; not by waving his hands like a lost fool. Cory hadn't realized it, but he had chosen a path, there, crouched, and that decision would define him throughout a very difficult life.

"Me, myself, and I." He swept the breadcrumbs off the table into his cupped hand and tossed them out the door for the chipmunks. He came inside, leaned his back against the log wall, and closed his eyes. One last time, he went through the process of trying to visualize where he was on the giant body of water. Monument Bay Resort was clearly marked on the map, as are all resorts on the lake. He knew his home base island was south of there, from what was written in the logbook. There were three islands in the large area south of the resort that the map showed had power coming in. He opened his eyes, held his map up to the door, and double circled one of those in pencil. "It's got to be you," he whispered.

Cory slid the map into his back pocket. Coat on, he filled a Thermos with water, and turned off the heater. He wondered, would he be back? "Will this be the last time I see you?" Cory said, feeling the smoothness of the log walls. He went into the bedroom and stripped off a bed sheet. Before leaving, he had one last look around. From the moment the lights snapped on and his eyes were filled with turn-of-the-century logs, mottled white chinking, and rustic knickknacks tucked in every nook and cranny, this cabin had taken hold of him. He didn't see the mouse droppings, the doorjambs akimbo, the warped plank floor, the sagging ceiling. It was his home base. Full of spider-webbed, generations-old outdoors stuff that you don't see in the city. Huge fish on the wall that had been pursued for so long they took on names. He walked over to the yellowed needlepoint that had Welcome Home stitched across a quaint log cabin. Removing it from the wall, he traced his fingertip over the bumps and contours of the careful old threadwork. He turned it over in his hands and looked at the waxed back where the knots were hand-tied. Suddenly he put the keepsake in his coat pocket. The old tongue-and-groove cedar had a lighter square where it had hung all these years. The bare brad nail stood out, accusingly. It was unlike Cory to steal, but even more unlike him to be moved to this kind of sentimentality over a craft.

The cabin had been so good to him. Was it betrayal to take it? Or betrayal to take nothing? From the cabin's first moment of light, that Welcome Home needlepoint had been exactly in his sightline, like it had been waiting all these yellowing years.

At the kitchen table, he opened the cabin log, and amended the journal entry written earlier in the morning. He added a P.S.

October 16, 1973

Hello,

My name is Cory Bradford. I found your cabin by boat after my dad and I had an accident. I'm okay. My dad is dead. I spent yesterday trying to get back to Monument Bay Resort. I've got a compass and a map and I'm sure it's north from here so I'm not worried I'll find it. I'm using this place as my home base. I took your thermos, and a warm coat. When you read this, write me at 1206 Bayard, St. Paul, MN 55105 and tell me where to send them. I'd say call me but there's no phone here. Thank you.

Cory Bradford.

P.S. I took the Welcome Home sign from the wall. It's a good luck charm. I hope you're not mad.

With a quiet snap, Cory closed the journal and got on with leaving. Now he was ready. He locked the front door from the inside, planning to leave by the same window he'd entered. He took his last look. "Good bye, home base. Maybe I'll see you again, maybe not." He walked to the window, slid it up, tossed out the bed sheet and followed it out. He left the window cracked open, as he'd found it. His boot tracks in the snow from last night had sunk into themselves and the sun would soon take them entirely. It would be a nice day, surely. The snow would be gone come lunchtime, Cory guessed, as he slopped down the path with his bed sheet and Thermos.

Something still nagged at him. Some detail unseen in the shadows. What was it? He couldn't put a finger on it, but he was overlooking something that could help him—that he knew.

There was no phone; he'd triple-checked. There was no outboard for his boat; he'd looked in the boathouse and shed and found nothing but a push lawnmower and two badminton rackets with broken strings. *What?* He shook his head.

Cory put the Thermos on the dock and stuffed the bed sheet inside his jacket. Up and up he climbed into a giant pine at the waterline. He wondered how long it had been since a boy had climbed this tree. He felt welcome in the limbs of the big Norway. Like climbing into the arms of a grandfather who'd not held a child for years.

Swaying in the highest branches, where they grew thin and began to bow under his weight, Cory tied off the four corners of the bed sheet. He had stretched it fully. The wind blowing in off the lake pressed it against the needles, dimpling the texture in the angled sunlight. This would be his marker should he need to return to the island in the evening. All the islands looked so alike from the water, but this would bring him home.

On the dock, Cory oriented his map, wind blowing up the bill of his cap and almost taking it into the lake. He pulled it down firmly on his head. "I'll find my way. It can't be that tough."

Cory planned to head north, then swing around the west side of the largest island, which was just in sight from the dock. That would put him in the main channel of the lake, where there should be buoys marking the route. Careful of his fishing poles and tackle box, Cory climbed in the boat and stepped to the bow to tuck the tarp flaps more securely under his dad's body. Cory's stomach turned. He wasn't prepared for how stiff his father's body had become.

The sun was bright and warming. Cory was rested. He had a plan. He checked his watch: "8:30. I'll row until 12:30. If I don't find anything, I'll turn around and be back here no later than 5:00. It doesn't get dark 'til past 6:00, so I'll have time to catch a few walleyes."

As Cory pushed away from the dock, dipping the oars, he looked back. "So long, home base." The white sheet luffed in the breeze against the green backdrop of layered pines. What was it like, he wondered, to be a tree, so permanent? The oars cut into the cold, dense water. The sting of yesterday's blisters snapped him into focus. He pulled hard and his back and shoulders ached, but stiffly obeyed. "Okay," he told himself with as much certainty as he could rally.

Cory's mind settled in for the long pull. The squeal of the oarlocks was abducted by the wind. The waves slapped the boat in a trancing rhythm. The sweat beneath his many layers trickled. Cory would occasionally check his compass, verifying his course. He tried to keep track of time, but he thought less and less about it the farther into the blue he went. As he looked back toward his island, seeing the white bed sheet hardly bigger than a postage stamp, Cory bit his lip and looked away, entertaining no further thoughts of comfort or log book friends.

"Me," he said, pulling on the oars. "Myself," he said on the next pull. "I," he said on the next. Over and over and over. From all sides the water diminished him. A few feet at a time, the small boat nosed forward.

Cory cranked hard on the oars, swinging the boat behind the big island, cutting off visual contact with his home base. Ahead of him lay what he guessed to be the main channel of Lake of the Woods. As the 13-year-old rowed toward the unknown, a warm flood of adrenaline filled him. He was learning that moving away from the familiar was greatly rewarded; a lesson he'd find hard to unlearn.

Finally, one look over Cory's shoulder, out into the big water with its sharp whitecaps, showed him what appeared to be a marker buoy tilting in the distance. If it were true, he'd found the main channel that would take him to Monument Bay Resort. He checked his watch. He'd been rowing two hours. It was getting warm. He unzipped his coat. He didn't want to overheat, or get overconfident. It's one thing to think you know where you're going on Lake of the Woods. It's another to get there.

At almost straight-up noon, Cory came around an island and saw the white-trimmed log cabins of Monument Bay Resort. He'd made it! But rather than rowing faster to get around the rock jetty and glide into the docking lagoon, Cory released the oars. Removing his gloves, he put each blistered hand in the water for as long as he could bear the cold. It was a beautiful day, the sun was shining hot on his back, the birds were soaring, and the resort he and his dad had departed from 29 hours earlier was only shouting distance away. He'd accomplished his single-minded mission of getting back, but Cory was as lost as ever. He just drifted, staring at the boathouse with the big painted sign reading Monument Bay. In the bow, his father's body was heaped under the tarp. Cory hadn't thought beyond this point. His every atom of energy had been brought to bear on getting here, and with that accomplished, he didn't know how to proceed. He was scared. For his mom and sisters, for all the kids at school who'll look at him funny, for the emptiness of the car, the quiet of the house, of the yard, of the garage, he was scared. The thought of home seemed further away than ever.

The wind began pushing his boat back around the point toward the main channel of the lake. Cory sat with his blistered hands on his lap, listening to the oars bump loosely against the side of the boat. From the corner of his eye, he saw someone come quickly down the dock, waving her arms. He could hear nothing—the strong wind blowing her words back to her. It was like the mute button had been pressed over the picture he saw.

"Is that you, Cory?" Darlene shouted at the small boat silhouetted by the hard sun. She held her hand over her eyes. "Get in here, son, out of the wind! Can you? Can you hear me? Cory, that's you, isn't it?"

Cory snapped out of his trance and focused on the white-haired lady on the dock. He recognized her as one of the owners. She and her husband ran the resort. Her name was Darlene and she had a handshake that could squeeze four fingers into one.

Cory raised a hand to her before taking hold of the oars. He started to pull again. "Yes, ma'am," he whispered. "It's me."

AFTERNOON. FATHER PAT.

Pat pulled up and parked alongside Lu Ann's diner. He stepped out of the car into the little remaining slush washing down the gutter. The car roof and door showed signs of the accident, as did the purpled swelling around his eye reflected back at him in the car's window. His shoulder was stiff and he had a headache, but mostly he felt lousy about denting the mint-condition Cadillac. Pat's years of assisting in shop class told him that those dents could be punched out, but the paint would never be the same. "That'll be the first to go to rust. Right up there for God to look down upon." He wasn't quite sure how to break the news to his new friend, Monsignor—he corrected himself—Frank.

Approaching Lu Ann's from the street, there's a large plate-glass window that gives you an advance look at who has taken up residence at the diner. Pat saw no sign of Frank. The smell of overcooked bacon pulled him toward the front door.

Inside, Father Pat was surprised to hear himself called by name. He swung around into a pair of deadpan looks—one belonging to the waitress he ran over in his hasty exit the night before, and the other belonging to a cook getting a refill from the coffee station. "Well, say here, if it isn't Father Pat, the Rez priest," the cook said. "And two days in a row. You must really like the coffee." The cook raised his eyebrows and shot him a plastic smile. It was all a part of the small-town hazing, Father Pat told himself as his skin began to prickle. Don't let them rattle you. He decided to fight fire with fire.

"Well good afternoon to the two of you!" Father Pat said loudly with mock enthusiasm. He walked directly to the cook. "I recognize the woman there, and I apologize again for my quick exit," Pat said to her, "but I can't say I've had the pleasure of bumping into you, good sir." Father Pat shook the cook's hand, going extra on the squeeze to send a clear message. The cook's face wilted. "No sir, I have not had the pleasure," Father Pat repeated, pumping the man's arm like he was jacking up a car. "Nice to see all of you again," he addressed the quiet diner. He looked them all in the eye, one by one. "I'm Father Pat. The Rez priest." And one by one they mumbled hello and went back to picking at their pie. Just like that, the attitude was drained from the room. He'd made his point. He could be as brash as a local.

"Name's Tim," said the cook, meekly, after the handshake ended. "And she's Lu Ann. She signs the front of the paychecks." He crossed his arms for safekeeping.

Lu Ann chimed in. "Didn't mean to give you a rough time, Father. Just, the way you left here in such a huff last night, thought it might be the chow. I get a lot of ribbing. This town has a weird sense of humor, if you ask me."

"No, it wasn't anything with the food," Father Pat said. "I just needed to get up the road to see Monsignor Kief." Both Lu Ann and the cook stood a little straighter after Father Pat dropped that name. Pat figured the Monsignor was a good ally to have in a town this size. Then for added oomph, he asked very conversationally, "By the way, you haven't seen Frank? We're to have lunch." Not only name-dropping, but now the blatant use of the first name. Check and checkmate. They'd probably known the Monsignor 30 years, and never had the nerve to call him Frank.

The obvious intimacy between the two priests put Lu Ann and Tim on their best behavior. Tim disappeared to the kitchen while Lu Ann wiped down ketchup bottles and personally saw to it that Pat's coffee cup never got below three-quarters full.

"Sorry again about last night," Father Pat said after one of the refills. "It's just the Sheriff and I don't quite see everything eye-to-eye."

Lu Ann bent down and whispered conspiratorially. "That Sheriff can be a real horse's ass sometimes. Forgive my French. Lousy tipper, too. Say, you know, up close in the daylight, you're almost too good-looking to be a priest. Hope there's no sin in saying. That's a heck of a shiner you got there. Oops, got a table to clear." Lu Ann flashed him her new dental work and was off with the energy of a hummingbird.

There's one like Lu Ann Cunningham in almost every small town. In high school, Lu Ann was a bright-burning star. She was the head cheerleader and voted MLTMD—most likely to marry a doctor. Among her many admirers at school was the new biology teacher, Mr. Klinedorsk.

Klinedorsk was from the "new school" of teachers who, green out of college, raring to make a difference, asked his students to call him "Mike." Word of *this* quickly got around town.

Teachers were needed in the more depressed areas up north, so Mike decided to shove everything he owned in a duffel bag and hitchhike nearly to the Minnesota-Canada border to teach biology in Baudette. Not even through his first year of dissecting worms and microscoping plankton, he'd gotten Lu Ann pregnant. There were fewer than five years between them and they were in love. They talked about getting married after her graduation and making a life right there in town. And they might have, too, if it weren't for Lu Ann's father.

He had some big dreams for his daughter. Certainly bigger than a hitchhiking biology teacher who the kids called "Mike" at basketball games. She was destined to marry a doctor, or at the very least a banker. So one night after more than a few tappers at the Mutineer's Jug, he and the rest of his bowling team paid Mike a little visit. They wrapped his head in a pillowcase and took turns beating his body with golf balls in a sock, addressing him as "Mike" before each blow. "How are you tonight, Mike?" WHACK! "How 'bout that basketball game last week, Mike?" WHACK! "How would you like to be arrested for statutory rape, Mike?" WHACK!

They told him he'd be looking at jail time unless he left that night after signing a letter saying he didn't really love Lu Ann and he'd joined the Peace Corps to teach the less fortunate in Africa. The Peace Corps angle was especially convincing because everyone in town knew of Mike's almost religious zeal for teaching.

Lu Ann's father made it clear that if Mike ever set foot in Baudette again he'd unload his deer rifle into him, then tie him to his truck bumper and drag him until the gas tank ran dry. But before that, he'd see to it that Mike's teaching license was revoked. This, of all of the threats, hit home. Mike could live with bruises, but he couldn't live without teaching.

Lu Ann's dad drove him six hours to Minneapolis in silence and told him to get out at the bus depot. He gave Mike 100 bucks and instructed him to buy a one-way ticket and some condoms. And that was that, or so he thought.

What Lu Ann's father didn't foresee was that Mike's letter calling out his insatiable love for undereducated Africans would spiral his daughter into a deep, prolonged, chocolate-coated depression.

Lu Ann never stopped eating candy bars after she read that goodbye note. Sure, she was pregnant, so a few pounds were par for the course. But Lu Ann ate steadily—right through delivery, everyone in town said. Most agreed it was her way of getting back at those reed-thin kids in Africa shown on the commercial breaks during the afternoon movie doubleheader. Lu Ann had a particular fondness for Kit Kats, Baby Ruths, Heath Bars, and cream soda.

Her weight ballooned from a sprightly prenatal 102 to 186 at delivery. After a modest postpartum decrease—Lu Ann delivered fraternal twins, a boy and girl appropriately named Lou and Anne—her weight pretty much plateaued at 170.

Her father finally came clean with her about Mike's goodbye note. He said he forced it because he loved her more than the stars and the moon and only wanted the best for his princess. She responded by rifling a can of cream soda his way, opening a five-stitch cut on his forehead. She packed up her new family and moved downtown to a small apartment across the street from a greasy spoon called Gracie's. Lu Ann hasn't had a cream soda or candy bar since.

As a waitress, Lu Ann essentially raised her twins at the diner. Customers finished their plates, and were handed either Lou or Anne for bottle feeding and burping. Lu Ann went from waitress to owner in under five years. She went from 170 to 118 pounds in the same time span. Her secret to weight loss—beside the breathless schedule of being a single mother of two—was working out. Lu Ann loved to lift weights. Loved to run. Loved to do anything to purge the anger rather than consume it. When she wasn't clocked in at the diner, she was in her apartment pumping iron. The super allowed her to set up some garage-sale fitness equipment in the laundry room where she worked out while the kids teethed on the corners of an old wrestling mat donated by the high school. She won regional and state bodybuilding contests. Her physical transformation was so stunning, a before-and-after picture of her was displayed at the Science Museum in downtown St. Paul. She had the picture signed by the mayor, hanging proudly in the diner.

Her high school confidence returned and Lu Ann was back turning heads again. But she had little time for men, except for a few moderately misleading dates with Allan Watson, a bookish associate vice president at the bank, who was so smitten by her, he personally co-signed for the small business loan she needed to purchase the diner. He took up jogging so they'd have something in common but quickly realized this was a woman he literally and figuratively could never catch.

With its new owner, Lu Ann's diner remained the meeting place for all townies. But now the mistreated, the lonely, the discarded, and the cheated were warmest welcomed and the first served. Lu Ann would feed them, pep them up, and tell them spilt milk deserved no tears so get happy and get going 'cause the world needed them and she needed the table. And off they'd go, bolstered, though soon to return hungry for the sustenance only Lu Ann's heaping portions of mashed potatoes and TLC could provide.

There was little remaining evidence of her old, love-struck wounds—nothing more than a sign hung in the front of the diner next to the register reading We Reserve The Right Not To Serve Anyone, followed by a handwritten list of the eight men, beginning with her father, Reg Cunningham, who ran her one and only love out of town. Everyone else was welcome and no one left hungry. Her servings were immense, buttered, creamed, fried, and gravied—the daily specials never under 3,000 calories. Maybe it was a fault of hers—the bigger her customers got, the more it offset her small muscular body. Or perhaps she was still mourning the fictional version of Mike who left to work with the starving Africans. Or maybe her customers were starved in an altogether different way and food was the closest form of comfort Lu Ann could offer. One thing was sure, her place was always jammed.

"So what'll it be today, Father Pat?" Lu Ann asked. "I'm still serving breakfast. I've got biscuits and gravy simmering in the back. That'll help you fill out the vestments. What do you weigh, don't mind my asking?" She squinted as she looked him over, calculating a rough estimate. "One-sixty?"

"Closer to 170."

"Oh, that's far too light for a man your size. Biscuits and gravy coming up. With a glass of whole milk and a side of bacon. Say, how'd you come by that shiner, anyway?"

Father Pat smiled at the woman's energy and curiosity. "Well, after my little run-in with you last night, I went up to see Frank to borrow his car. I had an accident going back out to the Rez. With all the snow, I couldn't make out where the road ended and the ditch began."

Lu Ann smiled as she was turning back toward the kitchen. "Had a few nights like that of my own. But it weren't on account of no snow." She winked, and then got busy pushing dessert options on folks not yet half through the main course.

Just then, Monsignor Kief was making his way up the slushy sidewalk in front of Lu Ann's big picture window. The sun shined on his thin, gray hair. He had a mischievous grin filling his face. He used his cane to tap the glass a few times—his calling card. The place buzzed with a warmer energy.

"Hello, Lu Ann," he said as his hand found the empty coat peg with his name written on a strip of white tape below it. He hung his jacket. "I see no one claim-jumped my spot today. Hello everyone," Monsignor Kief said, turning to the diner, "Lu Ann *has* to be here. What's your excuse?" A hearty laugh went up from the regulars.

"If that's the case, Monsignor," one of the regulars quipped with his mouth half full, "what are *you* doing here?"

The Monsignor allowed just enough time to escape so everyone was listening. "Son, if that's lunch you're finishing, I'm here to perform your last rights."

The place exploded in laughter.

"Has Father Pat O'Rourke made his way in yet?" Monsignor Kief asked as the laughter subsided.

"Back here, Frank." Pat got out of his chair to assist the blind priest. "Right this way." He took his elbow.

"Well, I gather you haven't started without me, Pat," he announced loud enough for the diner to overhear. "You're still walking." And the laughter rang out once more.

They sat down to fresh coffee. Father Pat didn't quite know how to jump into the subject of last night's rollover and the damages. He fiddled with the corner of his menu. He tapped his silverware.

Finally Frank interrupted. "Pat, you seem … tense," he offered. "Is it about the funeral arrangements?"

"Before we go into that, I've got something I need to tell you."

"I'm all ears. In a manner of speaking."

"Remember on the phone I told you I had good news and bad news and the good news was Joseph was home, and the bad news … well, I'm not sure how to broach it."

Monsignor Kief's voice got quieter. "What is it, Pat?"

"I've … I've had an unfortunate accident with your car. Last night, the whiteout conditions, I'm afraid I rolled your vehicle. Nothing serious, mind you," Pat quickly explained, "just cosmetic. Of course I'll handle the repairs."

There was a long pause. "Pat, that car was quite special to me. I can't believe what you're saying."

"I'm very sorry."

"I rarely let that car out of the garage. It's my baby."

Father Pat felt the perspiration beading on his back. Quite honestly, this was a side of the Monsignor he hadn't expected. Surely, he'd be upset, but it's just a car. He didn't even think to ask if Pat had been hurt. "You have every right to be upset, but the snow—"

"I trusted you, son," the Monsignor said sternly.

Father Pat looked down at his coffee.

"I can't do it anymore!" Monsignor Kief burst out laughing. He slapped his hand down on the table in delight. "Boy, did I get you. I'm so sorry, Pat. I couldn't resist. How could a blind man care about a few dents on the roof of a Cadillac?" He was laughing so hard, heads turned to see what the ruckus was all about.

Pat shook his head and looked at Frank. He had certainly made the Monsignor's day. Then it dawned on him. "Just a minute. How did you know it was just a few dents *and* on the roof?"

"I have my connections," Frank said, pointing a thumb upward.

"You nearly gave me a heart attack."

Frank stopped laughing. "Forgive my childishness. But it was just such an opportunity. I couldn't stop myself."

"Seriously, Frank, how did you know? Out with it."

"HomeSky called. She told me about the mishap and said you were feeling low when you left the farm. I figured you could use some cheering up. And what better way, I ask you, than a good practical joke? What better way? I was planning it the entire walk over. Laughing to myself."

"At least now I'll know to keep my guard up."

"At all times, Pat." The Monsignor put up his dukes and threw a mock jab. "At all times."

"HomeSky says you were cut above the eye. Is it serious?"

Father Pat considered returning the practical joke, but decided to save it for a better time. "Except for looking like I just got out of the ring with Joe Louis, no."

"Our vocation could stand a little toughening around the edges," Frank proclaimed. "Get people to sit up straighter on Sunday."

The food came and the Monsignor made an obligatory wise-crack to Lu Ann about how everyone had a cross to bear and his happened to be the hot beef and gravy on white. Once her back was turned, he shoveled it in like a farm kid.

After a few minutes of loud eating, Frank grew serious and dropped his voice to a whisper. "Pat, HomeSky mentioned on the phone the two of you were wondering about arranging for the burial out at the farm?"

Pat pushed away his biscuits and sausage gravy. "I am. HomeSky and Joseph will do it, with us or without us. There's no compromising for them, and rightfully so, I think. What do you say? Can we do it?"

"I've done some soul searching. As long as the service doesn't include the Eucharist, according to ecumenical law, we're in pretty good shape. As for the legal implications, that's another kettle of fish."

"In other words," Pat interjected, "Sheriff Harris."

"Yes. But I think we have a loophole if we're smart about it. If I can talk the Sheriff into signing the burial record over to the Rez, because it's a sovereign nation, then he's free of any infraction of the law."

Pat thought for a moment. "Even though the Blackholms don't live on the reservation? In fact, they're adamantly opposed to everything about it."

"That's where you come in. You need to convince HomeSky to sign reservation intention papers, and then, a day or so after the internment, she can cancel them. You just need to keep the papers yourself, rather than submitting them to the Indian Council, because as you know, there's no love lost between the Rez and the Blackholms. They could use this document to publicly mock the family name."

"Could it be that easy, Frank?"

"I think it could be that simple. Easy, that's another thing. You and I haven't persuaded the principal members of this plan to cooperate, so let's not count our chickens yet."

Father Pat was nonetheless very excited. "It's brilliant. It'll work. I'm sure of it. Frank, it's such a blessing having you. I wouldn't know where to turn."

Frank blushed. "You're counting chickens again."

"Sorry. What's the next step?"

Frank pushed away from the table and rubbed his stomach. "To try to digest this brick."

Father Pat smiled in admiration for his new friend. What a positive force a sense of humor can be. He'd forgotten that. He'd gotten glum, pensive. He made a mental note to take Frank's cue in this regard.

"My next step," Frank inserted, "is to go to work on the good Sheriff Thurgood Harris. Remember, I've know him since he was just 'Turdy,' an overweight playground bully who pushed kids down in puddles so he could reject them before they could reject him. Shoot, all he wanted was to be liked. He used to get sent to me when he had exasperated all of the teachers, including the principal."

"What about his parents?"

"Sheriff Harris lost his mother at a young age. A family car wreck."

Father Pat said, "We have more in common than I thought."

"How's that?"

"It'll have to keep for another time, Frank. That's at least a two-bowls-of-ice-cream epic."

"Excellent. I'll hold you to that." The Monsignor smiled before continuing on about the Sheriff. "For all intents and purposes, he lost his dad in the wreck, too. The accident broke his back and he was confined to a wheelchair. His dad said he couldn't properly care for the boy and made him a ward of the state. The poor kid bumped around a few foster homes in town, but spent almost as much time living at the rectory with me and my widowed housekeeper. What a pair he inherited. Me, blind. Her, a closet drinker and gun enthusiast. She'd hide her empties down in the basement. Then on Sundays after church, she'd sneak them out to the dump on the edge of town and plink away at them with Thurgood. He became quite a marksman."

"He wasn't in the car wreck with his parents?"

"He was, but wasn't hurt. He believes the hand of God protected him. To this day he carries an irrational fear of driving. He walks everywhere. Only gets in his cruiser when he has to. Imagine that? A sheriff who's afraid to drive. What a town of misfits we are."

"That explains it!" Father Pat exhaled. "Last night, driving from your house, I passed the Sheriff leaving here. Before he crossed the street, he made the sign of the cross."

"Yes. I've heard he does that," Frank said. "Like I told you, he's more God-fearing than he comes off."

Father Pat heard the door open, tickling the little bell on the doorframe. "G'afternoon Lu Ann," the Sheriff bellowed. "I'm here to see a priest. From the looks of it, you've got 'em coming out of your ears." The gruff voice got Father Pat's back tingling. As his stomach roiled, he reminded himself, *just think of him as Turdy.* But looking at the hulking figure zagging through the tables, slapping shoulders and making snide comments, he felt like he was 10 years old and the playground bully had him in his sights.

"Easy, Pat." Monsignor Kief used the same whispering tone a veterinarian might use around a high-strung colt. Somehow this blind priest could feel the tension drawstringing inside Pat.

"Thurgood. Sit down, young man," Frank commanded in an altogether different tone. Father Pat noticed how the Sheriff winced at the use of his first name, but did precisely as instructed. He obviously wasn't comfortable being addressed informally in public, and in uniform, especially in front of a relative stranger like Father Pat.

"Monsignor. Padre," the Sheriff said. "L'Ann, bring another cup," he bellowed. Then thinking a little better for it, added, "if you'd be so kind." It was as close as he could bring himself to saying please.

"Good," Monsignor Kief said. "I see you haven't lost your manners entirely."

"No. That was beaten into me pretty good as a kid with a long-handled ruler," the Sheriff shot back. Then switching subjects, "So, Monsignor," he said, "did some vandals get after that car of yours, or were you out driving again?"

"Vandals … that's one way of putting it." The two priests snorted and chuckled. The Sheriff looked on, uncomfortable being an outsider to the joke.

"And what's so funny about vandals? You'll need to come in and make a report."

"A report!" they giggled. Father Pat jumped in. "Oh, he's already caught the perpetrator. In fact, turns out Frank was an accessory in the bludgeoning." The both of them laughed even harder. The Sheriff squinted down his nose at the two of them, unwilling to go any further. He knew Monsignor Kief liked nothing better than a joke, and now he had a co-conspirator.

"L'Ann!" he hollered. "Coffee!" Reaching in his right shirt pocket for the Camels, the Sheriff studied the cigarette. "Well, I imagine all this has something to do with that eye the new pastor here is sporting."

Monsignor Kief abruptly stopped laughing. "Thurgood, his name is Father Pat. Show some respect." When Monsignor Kief decided to get serious, there was no mistaking it. The Sheriff felt the sting. He pulled over an amber glass ashtray and changed subjects.

"Got a phone call just before I came over. Something I think you two might find quite interesting." He tapped the cigarette on the rim of the ashtray. "The call came in from a police detective down in the cities. Seems a boy and his dad were out fishing yesterday on Lake of the Woods, no more than 60 miles from where we sit." The Sheriff lit up, stretching the story like homemade taffy.

"Last night, they never made it back to the resort they were lodging at. Remember how hard it was snowing here? You can be sure it hit up there even harder. So the city detective says to me that resort owners from around the lake went out looking for them. Anyone who's been on that water knows trying to find one fishing boat on that lake is harder than finding a sober Irishman at closing time. But out they went to shake it."

"That lake's a monster," Frank agreed. "All but abandoned this time of year."

The Sheriff stubbed out his Camel, and reached in the opposite pocket for a filtered Vantage. "Just over an hour ago, I get a call back. The city detective again. The kid shows up at the dock of the resort. The kid rowed all the way back."

"Rowed? Did they have engine trouble?" Pat asked.

"What about his dad?" Frank added.

"Here's where it gets interesting." The Sheriff looked out the window at the sun melting the last of the snow off the roofs across the street. He rubbed his eyes and lowered his voice. "The boy's dad passed while fishing. They had some sort of accident that knocked out the motor. Turns out the kid's now something of a lake legend 'cause he *rowed* the two all the way back to the resort. What's more, the kid's 13. Damnedest thing, ain't it? I got a police detective telling me about a 13-year-old kid who's lost on the lake, his dad is dead, and all the while I'm thinking we've got the Blackholm kid, 13, also missing, and his dad is dead, too. Same age, same day. Never heard of such a thing."

"My good Lord in heaven," the Monsignor whistled through his teeth. "So young, the both of them, fatherless."

Pat was almost speechless. "What does it mean, Frank?" He looked at him earnestly. "Have you ever heard of two boys like this?"

"And them being pretty much only 60 miles apart when it happened," the Sheriff added. "Only time stuff like this happens is war."

The Monsignor shook his head and put his hand on his chest. Surely, he'd never heard of anything like it. The table was silent.

"So," the Sheriff continued, "the city detective tells me the mother and her daughters want to come to my office tomorrow since we're the nearest town of any size to the lake. He asks me if I could go up to the resort first thing and retrieve the boy and arrange for the father's body."

"I'd like to go with you, Sheriff," Father Pat interrupted, speaking directly into the eyes of the Sheriff. "I'd like to have the funeral tomorrow morning at the Blackholm place, and we could drive up after that."

"Ho, now. Slow down, Padr—Father. What's this about a funeral at the Blackholm farm?"

"Sheriff, Frank will explain everything." Pat got up, putting his hand on the Monsignor's shoulder. "He'll explain it all, right down to the dents in his car and this prize of an eye of mine. I've been in these clothes for over 24 hours. I'm heading home, going to take a run, a hot shower, and sit down to write a eulogy. Frank, I'll go see HomeSky about what we talked about. You see if you can get our friend here agreeing with the best way of handling things. Sheriff, I'll see you at the farm tomorrow. Bright and early. We'll drive to

Lake of the Woods afterward to bring this poor boy back to what's left of his family. My good Lord, what's the boy's name?"

The Sheriff, taken aback by Father Pat's burst of authority, pulled a small square of paper from out behind his cigarettes. "Bradford, Cory. From St. Paul. But I don't know—"

"Got to go. Much to do." Father Pat gave the Monsignor one last pat on the shoulder. "You'll take it from here, right?"

The Sheriff glared up at Pat. "You've been a busy man, Father. The last time we met you were stumbling over Lu Ann."

"These are busy times, Sheriff. I trust you'll facilitate things out to the Blackholms. My guess is around eight. Let me talk to HomeSky, see what she has in mind. I'll be in touch. We're counting on you."

"Don't be so sure, Father. You're not the only man in town with a busy schedule."

"He'll be there, Pat," Monsignor Kief assured him. "Let's you and I talk later by phone …" But Father Pat was out of earshot by the time Frank finished his sentence. He nearly ran over Lu Ann again, who deftly veered out of the way with a tub of dirty dishes.

"Slow down, Father!" she hollered after him, shaking her head. "City folk."

"Monsignor?" The Sheriff swung his attention to him. "What's all this about a funeral out on that Indian farm? You know I can't be doing that."

"I know nothing of the kind. All you need to do is certify on the burial document that the reservation is the place of interment. Father Pat will see it gets misfiled on the Rez. The sovereign nation status keeps anyone from ever looking any further."

"It's against the law. In case you've forgotten, Monsignor, my duty is to *uphold* the law."

"Thurgood, I've known you a long time. I've known you to get creative with the rules when the situation calls for it. I tell you, this situation calls for it. This is a chance to do what's right rather than what some statute deems correct. I wouldn't ask you otherwise."

"Monsignor, let me ask you something, off the record."

"What is it?"

"What's your take on Father Pat?"

"What do you mean? Obviously I thought enough of him to approve his relocation here."

"Yeah? I'm not so sure. I've been doing a little digging."

The Monsignor took a drink of his cool coffee. "Thurgood, I get a good feeling around Father Pat. It's unusual. Not like what I've felt in the presence of other priests, and I've met my share. It's not an overly devout feeling. Or the stale, bored-out feeling many priests unfortunately emanate. Losing my sight, I *feel* how people are. It's like hearing body language. Father Pat transmits a presence of … I don't know, anticipation. Something's coming. Something powerful has begun and it's on its way. This little town of ours is a stopping point in the journey. I'm able to read it, I don't know, like you read barometric pressure. It's anticipation of … grace, I guess. I couldn't put my finger on it until just now. Yes, it's grace, and it's coming and we're all part of it."

The Sheriff straightened and reached for a Camel in his right pocket. "No disrespect, but I'm no feeling-reader. I'll tell you this, though: I've got a knack for people, too. This Father Pat, let me tell you, he's no saint. You should see how he looked at the widow Blackholm."

"THURGOOD! What kind of thing is that to say!"

"Monsignor, I saw what I saw. She's an attractive enough woman, to be sure, but he sparked to her more like a man than a priest."

"Thurgood, first of all, he's just a man, as am I."

"Monsignor, you're a whole different league—"

"Don't interrupt me, son." The Monsignor rarely lost his temper, but at the moment, he was holding on by his fingernails. "Secondly, you have not been put here by God to judge this man—or any for that matter."

The Sheriff felt his cheeks burning. "All I'm saying, Monsignor, is he's no saint. I've got a nose for people."

"Father Pat's sainthood is not for any of us to canonize. I do feel—no, actually I *know*—we're all somehow part of this and it will take us somewhere. This place, this time, these events, these boys, it's significant. It needs due time. And it begins with the funeral at the Blackholm farm. We need your help there."

"Okay. I'll stand aside and trust you on this one. It's just not my nature to break the law."

"Nor is it mine, Thurgood. But this is no ordinary day. You can see that as well as I. I know your occupation involves solving things, but this is somehow bigger. Agreed?"

The Sheriff managed a nod and stamped out his cigarette with his good hand. Everything about this man was oversized. His knuckles were like dresser knobs. "I'll have the body out to the Blackholm farm for the service." Then the Sheriff added, more to himself than to the Monsignor, "Won't be easy, though. Trying to do anything quiet in this town is like balancing a pea on the back of a spoon."

"I truly believe you're doing the right thing. We'll all look back and recognize that."

"I'll just have to take your word on that one."

"Good. Now get on with whatever you've got to do. Daylight's burning and it'll be tomorrow before we know it." The old priest shook his head. "Two boys' fathers. Just 13. Sometimes the hand of God drops awfully hard."

The Sheriff went to push away from the table, but his chair remained and instead the table slid. He groaned, hopped his chair back and stood, towering. The Monsignor thought about the day and all that was left to do as he unconsciously worked a sliver of bacon free from between two molars.

"Be sure to take your own medicine on this one," the Sheriff said, leaving the Monsignor. "Don't think on it too hard." With that the huge Sheriff lumbered up to the cash register, belching into his fist. Deputy lay on the floor, ignoring the half of sprinkled donut someone left just off his nose. Up on the Formica counter, next to the cash register, Lu Ann had strategically placed a replica hand grenade. Attached to the pin was a tag with the number 1 on it. COMPLAINT DEPARTMENT: TAKE A NUMBER, she'd written.

"This should cover our table."

"Picking up a tab?" Lu Ann chortled. "My, my, all this time with priests lately, you're brimming with the virtue of charity."

The Sheriff hardly heard her. He was looking over her head at his reflection in a mirror on the back wall. "Don't count on it. Let's move out, Deputy. Least you're smart enough to stay away from the grub here."

The two slowly made their way out into the sunlight, into the warming afternoon. The snowmelt ran down the slope of the street. Above, in the crystalline blue, the last colorful leaves of fall clung to their branches, refusing to release this moment, this day—tenacious. "Don't feel nothing like funeral weather, Deputy." The Sheriff squinted as he looked both ways down the street, sun sparkling everywhere. He crossed himself, stepped off the curb, and headed toward City Hall.

"Lu Ann. I need one of your famous desserts," Monsignor Kief called out.

"What'd you have in mind?" she barked from across the room.

"Ice cream and vanilla wafers?"

"Sorry. All I got is gingersnaps."

"Store-bought or real molasses?"

"Monsignor, you insult me!"

"Sold, then." And with that, the blind Monsignor, in his 73rd year of life, sat in the tangle of the mystery, trying to make his peace. Grace has a way of revealing itself, he concluded. And there's nothing like ice cream and gingersnaps to keep one company during the wait.

But his mind refused to rest. Why Father Pat? Why had God sent this man? Certainly, the Sheriff's intuition hadn't failed him when he said Pat was no saint. He had bounced around over seven dioceses in his thirteen years since ordination, being asked to leave more than once. But there was a radiance about him, a vibration, gaining tune and clarity. Monsignor Kief knew it like he knew stepping from the shadow into the sunlight. But the Sheriff was right to have suspicions. And knowing the Sheriff's tenacity for detail, soon enough he'd come across Father Patrick O'Rourke's full record. He would find evidence that their new priest was no saint, indeed. In fact, just a few years ago, he was known as the Suicide Priest. Not only in private, but to his face.

CORY AT MONUMENT BAY.

"The boy's come in!" Darlene, the resort owner, hollered to her kitchen helper from the front deck of the main lodge. She was out shaking rugs when she noticed a boat drifting in front of the docks. "Get on the radio and tell everyone. The boy's come in." She ducked back into the main lodge and threw the old hooked rug on the floor. Strange, it occurred to her, she couldn't recall seeing anyone else in the boat.

Out on the docks, Darlene hollered out but the boy didn't reply. He just stared off at the long horizon. He'd let go of the oars, which bumped free along the sides of the boat. The boy's in shock, she thought.

"Is that you, Cory?" Darlene shouted at the small boat. She held her hand over her eyes. "Get in here, son, out of the wind now!" She thought about climbing in a resort boat and going to get him, but every spare boat was on the water, looking for the pair. "Cory! Can you hear me?"

Suddenly, he could. He blinked, considering her for a moment, standing there, her white, wiry hair pushed by the wind. He reached down and gripped the oars.

Inside the great room of the lodge, sitting in a large rocker, facing a blazing fire with a Hudson Bay blanket up around him and another at his feet, Cory thought of nothing. He was exhausted and hollow. Darlene came out of the adjacent kitchen. "How are you feeling? Warming up?"

"A little too warm, now." He began to unwrap the blanket. The fieldstone fireplace was big enough for him to walk into without hardly stooping. There were eight logs burning in there. Cory had counted.

"You just keep that there a little longer," Darlene said, patting his shoulders with her strong hands. "Your system's had a shock out in those temperatures. One minute hot, the next, cold. You'll come back to balance here shortly."

"Yes, ma'am." Cory could see there was little sense in arguing. He'd never looked at Darlene up close, but judging from the depth of the lines in her face, she knew about things where this was concerned. Things about the water and cold and how a person would be affected by them. She was someone who knew things for sure, or didn't speak of them.

Indeed, Darlene was an extremely capable woman. She could bake apple crisp to die for in the dark of the morning and put new bushings in the generator before lunch. Self-sufficiency was the way of life if you owned a resort on an island in one of the largest freshwater lakes in the country. Self-sufficient, or out of business. Or even worse.

"Here, Cory. Drink this." She handed him a small jelly jar glass with three fingers of bourbon. "Ever taken a drink of whiskey before?"

Cory looked at the amber-colored liquid. "No, ma'am. Had a few sips of beer when my dad's back was turned. Didn't care for it."

"Me neither, truth be told," Darlene pulled a chair up next to him.

Cory took a sip. It shot electricity through him and raised goose bumps on his arms. He felt warm inside. He smacked his lips and pondered the taste and the effect. Darlene waited for a report, but Cory just smacked his lips and had another little sip.

Strange, quiet boy, Darlene thought. She'd known him from three seasons of coming to the resort. She'd serve him and his dad their meals in the main lodge. Breakfast before fishing, dinner after. They packed their own lunches for the day. Neither of them was hardly good for a peep. Not only to her, but to each other. She'd crowbar a few words out of them about the fishing or the way the boat was running, but they weren't talkers. In that regard, she liked them. So many of her guests were such prolific gabbers it wore her plum out for listening. Serving a nice quiet meal to this pair was a pleasure. It reminded her of why she'd moved to this forgotten island in the first place.

"Whiskey stings going down. I always thought it'd be smooth. It looks smooth as syrup." Cory looked over at Darlene, his eyes sparkled some. He was coming back from wherever it was the last two terrible days had taken him.

"Up here, they call that stuff lightning syrup. You're best staying away from it except on those occasions when the cold has gone clear to the bone."

"I'm tired now."

Darlene looked at the boy. His face was flushed from wind and cold and more recently from heat and whiskey. He was a handsome boy, a bit undersized, with blond wavy hair and hard gray-green eyes and dimples he used only rarely.

"Cory, do you want to talk to me, or my husband, Stu, or anyone—I don't know, a doctor or a priest—about what happened? Out there … you know, only if you want to." For one of the few times in her life, Darlene was flustered.

Cory took in the question and dealt with it with his usual full introspection. Did he wish to talk to anyone? He'd already been on the phone with his mother. He took care of that the moment he got in. He told her Dad was dead, but kept her from the details. He didn't tell her about his night alone on the lake, or how Dad had died. She kept saying, "What do you mean he's dead? Cory? How can he be dead? Let me talk to your father. Please." Cory would start talking again and his mom interrupted with those same questions. She must have asked five times. After that, she just broke down. Cory gave the phone to Darlene, who instructed her to get in touch with the local authorities.

The fire crackled and spit. A log shifted. Although it was only early afternoon, it felt like midnight.

"I don't know if I want to talk about it. Not that I mind. I do have a few questions. I'd like to hear from a doctor about what killed Dad. I'd also like to see on a map where the accident happened exactly. I have an idea. I want to know if I'm right."

Darlene thought it a strange request, asking about the exact location. "What did you tell your mother on the phone?"

Cory sat up straight, and his eyes shone serious. He looked Darlene square. She knew men three times Cory's age who couldn't look at a person that straight in the eyes. "My mother is not very strong. I don't want her upset any more than she already is. She doesn't need to know all of what happened. Okay?"

"Your choice. I told your mom I didn't know much because you hadn't said much. I said you looked fine. But if you feel like talking about it … If not, that's okay, too."

Darlene watched Cory stare into the fire. She knew he was back out on the lake somewhere, alone with the waves, only 13 years old, having done what most are never asked to do even in their adult years. He had arrived here in her chair in front of her fire with these memories to take home with him.

Cory spoke to the fire. "I didn't know where I was." His voice was hoarse and distant. Cory leaned in and reached inside his blanket. "About the time the snow came, I was ready to quit. I was so tired. I came around a small island and there was this rickety old dock. Like an arm reaching out. That's what I thought."

Cory blinked a few times, pulled his hand out of the blanket and unfolded the map he had in his back pocket. He seemed more alert now. "My dad had this. He never went out on any lake without a map." Cory unfolded it and put it on the log coffee table in front of them.

"It was snowing pretty good, getting dark, and I figured dock means cabin so I tied up. On the island, sure enough, there it was. A log cabin, like out of a dream. It was all shut up for the winter. Except for one window opened a crack, like someone knew I was coming."

Cory pointed to the map. "I think I was on this island here. The one with the power line coming in underwater." Cory pointed to a small, jellybean-shaped island. Darlene got up and found her reading glasses.

"I need my cheaters to see the small islands," she said. "This one here?"

"Yeah. There's power to it, see the dotted line coming in?"

"That's the Goetz's place. Bud and Lois."

Cory's eyes sparkled. "You know them?"

Darlene nodded. "Bud always leaves the front window open a crack. Sometimes squirrels get in through the chimney and get trapped in the cabin. They see daylight through the windows and try to chew their way out. Makes for a real mess. But if they smell fresh air they'll squeeze out the crack. Those damn squirrels can make themselves paper thin."

"That's where I slept. Bud and Lois's place. I saw their names in a log they keep. They wrote about running north to Monument Bay to fish big muskies. That's how I found my way back."

"Pretty smart for a city kid," Darlene kidded, taking off her glasses. Her only hint of vanity was that she hated being seen in glasses.

"My dad taught me to pay attention. I see something and it sticks. The rest was luck. Like me seeing their dock when it was getting dark and starting to snow hard. And the window being open and there being power and heat to the cabin. Dumb luck."

"We all need luck. And can't be too proud to recognize it," she told Cory. "This time of year, with most of the boats off the lake and resorts closed for the season, we're lucky to have you back here."

Cory nodded. "Before I go home tomorrow, could we go back out? I'd like to find the island we crashed into."

"You crashed? Is that how he ...?" Darlene was prying. She had no patience for priers. She didn't finish her question.

A quiet filled the space between them. Cory drifted back. "Dad was driving. It was so cold, so windy ..." He stared into the fire. "We were going into the sun; I remember squinting. That's how I knew to come back west. We're goin' straight for an island. I waited for Dad to veer off. I thought he might be kidding, but Dad didn't do that. I looked back. He was on the bottom of the boat. We hit the shallows in front of the island. Snapped the motor, sent me into the trees. Didn't get a scratch. Musta been a heart attack Dad had. Like to know from a doctor for sure. It's better if Mom doesn't know about the island stuff. I'll just say we were fishing and he tipped over, peacefully. That's easier."

"You tell your mom what you must," Darlene whispered over the hard silence, "but she deserves to hear the truth. I know I'd want to know. Wouldn't you if you were her?" Darlene looked at him.

"She's not us," Cory returned her gaze. "She loses it. Her knowing all that would do more harm than good."

"She may surprise you. And it might be good for you to tell her. So you don't have to keep it all to yourself."

"Could be," Cory said in a way that Darlene correctly interpreted to mean there wasn't a chance he was going to reveal much. "Is she coming up here to get me?"

"No," Darlene said. "After we talked to her, she called the St. Paul police. They got in touch with the sheriff from Baudette. He'll be coming up around lunchtime tomorrow. Baudette is a couple hours out by the time you boat here to the island. Your mom and sisters will be driving up from the cities. They'll wait for you in Baudette."

"Will my dad go back with me and the Sheriff?"

"I don't know how that's arranged exactly. But don't you worry on that."

"Where do you have my dad now?"

"He's in one of the spare cabins."

"Will he be okay in there?"

"The cabin's shut down for the season, so it's plenty cold."

Cory nodded. "If the Sheriff's coming around lunchtime and I have my stuff all together tonight, do you think we could take the boat out in the morning and look for the island? I marked it. Stuck the broken motor in the water just off the shore. I put plenty of rocks around it to keep it standing."

"Why go to the trouble?" Darlene asked.

"I left a note under the cowling. Put in the time, compass heading, and the resort name. I knew sooner or later someone would come looking. Find the motor, see the note. Might help you find me. Plus everything but the lower unit is in perfect working order. Be a shame you not getting that motor back."

"You're a smart one, no doubt. We'll talk to Stu when he gets in. Somebody reached him on the radio and told him you were back. He should be here any time."

"Do you think I could have some more of this?" Cory held up the empty jelly jar.

Darlene thought it over. "Just a sip, for medicinal purposes. When you decide what you'll tell your mother about what happened, this whiskey could be one of those parts you leave out."

Cory smiled. His dimples curved to life and it nearly broke the old resort owner's heart. Darlene was as tough as they came, but when she went back in the kitchen, she wiped a tear from her eye. A 13-year-old boy, fatherless. He had an obvious love for the outdoors. Would all that end now? Would this be the last time she saw him? Was going out in search of the accident site his way of saying goodbye to the lake and its haunting memories? What remembrance will he have of her and this resort? Could there possibly be any good in it? She poured him a tiny splash, and herself a healthy one. Then, after consideration, she gave him a skosh more. This is no boy, she thought. He saw his father die. Brought him in from the lake, alone, through a snowstorm. No, this is no longer a boy. And that, she thought, was a damn shame.

"Here then," she said, giving Cory a little more whiskey. She took a healthy pull off her glass and winced. They watched the fire burn down. Out the window, squirrels chased each other, corkscrewing down the tree in the afternoon sun.

"Are you hungry for a late lunch, Cory?"

"No, thank you. I think I'll go pack up our gear. I've got some sandwich fixings back there." Cory started to lace up his boots.

"Suit yourself, but it's no trouble."

"Nah," Cory said as he finished off the whiskey.

"You will have dinner with Stu and me," Darlene said, trying to be stern. "I won't hear it any other way. I'm making roast chicken, mashed potatoes, and blueberry pie. Stu will have a story or two about this week's duck hunting. I'm sure he'll want someone to tell, and I've heard 'em twice already."

Cory stood up from the rocker and folded the two Hudson Bay blankets into neat squares. "What time would you like me?"

"Six sharp. If you get all your packing done, you'll have time for a nap."

"See you at six then. Thanks for the medicine." Cory smiled, a half-moon of one dimple made a brief appearance. He walked out the door and stood just outside the doorsill, spat on the grass, and pulled the heavy oak door shut tight behind him. The air was full of wood smoke, a smell Cory loved.

"Strange, quiet boy," Darlene repeated to herself, feeling lonely. She wasn't prone to spells of melancholy, but this boy, how he sat so still, how he looked off somewhere past the cabin, past the trees, to somewhere locked inside. Just now, how he rose from the chair, slow, wary, it awoke feelings long ago put away. She wanted to hold him. Run with him down a hill. Swim with him. Mother him. Smell his hair. Hear him laugh. "I don't think I'll ever get to hear this boy laugh," she whispered to the empty room. A tear rolled down her weather-cragged face. "Silly old coot," she said of herself. She abruptly wiped her nose on her sleeve, wristed back her whiskey, and went into the kitchen to see about dinner. "I'm getting moody as April," she chided herself. She pulled the kitchen curtains and looked out the side window to watch Cory, hands in his pockets, walk through the slush and autumn leaves into his cabin. "Moody as April."

At six o'clock on the dot, Cory walked in, Sunday-school clean. His hair combed, he wore a turtleneck under a flannel shirt. He carried a white envelope.

Darlene's husband, Stu, was fiddling with the fire. The room smelled of roast chicken and something sugary. Pie, maybe.

"Right on time, boy," Stu called out, still looking into the hearth, puzzled by the amount of smoke the fireplace was producing.

"He's got a name, Stu," Darlene said from the other room.

"I'm aware of that. Is this firewood wet? Darlene, what do you know about this smoky firewood?"

"I know if you'd sit down and stop poking at it it'd burn just fine."

"Cory," Stu said, still staring into the hearth, "have a look here and give me your diagnosis."

"Stu," Darlene barked from the kitchen over the rattle of pans, "if you're not in your chair ready to say grace in one minute I'm going to take that fire iron to you."

Cory stuck the envelope into his back pocket and walked over for a look. Stu watched as the boy quietly scanned every inch of the fireplace. Picking up a quartered log from the wood bin, Cory studied it top to bottom. "That's poplar you're burning. Poplar always burns dirty."

"That's not poplar. It's birch."

"No sir. See the green tint?" Cory showed Stu the log, holding it out into the room where the light was better. "That's poplar. See how soft it is? Put your nail to it." Cory pressed his fingernail into the log's end.

"I'll be dipped in bacon fat and grilled over coal! It is poplar. Darlene! Why we burning this scrub?"

Darlene was carrying a hot pan of roast chicken. A trail of steam followed behind. "All right you two, get yourselves seated or I'll set this out for the dogs."

"Just can't figure where that poplar came from," Stu mumbled to himself, walking toward the dinner table. "Would have sworn it was birch. Good catch there, Cory."

Chicken. Gravy. A basket of rolls wrapped in a red gingham cloth. Side-by-side sticks of butter. A pitcher of milk. Corn. Jell-O with little marshmallows. Darlene just kept bringing it.

Stu whispered to Cory. "She goes back for one more dish and the table will give out." He winked. Cory winked back.

"I heard that." Darlene came in wiping her hands on her apron. She untied it, gave it one quick fold, set it down on the wooden chair seat and sat on it. "Stu, lead us in grace." They took one another's hands. Cory felt his getting clammy. He was unfamiliar with this type of closeness.

"Lord, straight off the top, thank you for bringing Cory home. I know his father is with you now and is surely proud of the way this boy's handled himself. Thank you for our good fortunes, each other, and this wonderful food on the table. Thank you for clothes on our backs, and fire in the hearth, even though it's scrub poplar and I don't know how it got there. Amen."

"Amen," Cory and Darlene repeated as they released hands. "It got there," Darlene informed, passing the chicken to Cory, "'cause I went and cut it, split it, and carried it in is how it got there. It's from the one that went down in the storm over by cabin three. Take another piece, Cory."

Cory absorbed the large room. The butterscotch-colored log walls had clean white chinking. The fire in front of them spat an occasional ember on the oak floor. The steam from the chicken broth and mashed potatoes intertwining as it rose above the long harvest table. And the three of them, squeezed down on one end of the table like family. It felt pretty good, Cory thought. Suddenly, he was famished. He didn't look up for some time.

"I don't recollect *ever* seeing someone your size put it away like that," Stu said, lighting a pipe and leaning back in his chair 20 minutes later. "A sight to see."

Darlene hissed at him. "Never mind that. Cory, can I get you another slice of pie?"

"That'd make four!" Stu said, coughing out pipe smoke in disbelief.

"Hush you," Darlene snapped. "Cory?"

"No thank you. Stu's right, mostly. I'm stuffed."

"What do you mean right *mostly*?"

"You said four when actually one more piece would make five."

Stu whistled and chewed on his pipe thoughtfully. "You know, that reminds me. I ate a pie and a half one day. Darlene, you remember that?"

"Like Hades, you did."

"When I get to telling, you'll remember it like yesterday. It went like this, Cory." Stu leaned back, loosened his belt a notch, and prepared to launch one of his patented whoppers.

"I was out bear hunting on Blueberry Island just east of here. Actually, I was guiding this yahoo from … where was it? Down south somewhere, Oklahoma. No, Tennessee. Hell, it ain't no matter except to say this guy was a few sandwiches short of a picnic. So we boat over and I pull us up on the sand and right out, we see 'em." Stu repacked his pipe for dramatic effect.

"Big around as a car steering wheel, no lie. Paw prints. Black bear. A female. In the wet sand by the waterline. Never seen prints that size before. Sunk deep, too. I says to the yahoo, 'She'll go eight hundred pounds if she goes an ounce.'"

Cory got comfortable in his chair. Darlene folded her arms, thinking that bear put on weight every time Stu told the story. The firelight flickered in the room. A cat leapt onto Stu's lap and licked chicken grease off his fingers.

"The yahoo gets one look at those fresh bear prints and he nearly wets his drawers. Next thing, he's uncasing a brand-spanking-new Weatherby, hands shaking so bad he's dropping cartridges on his boots.

"'That rifle looks awfully new,' I says to him.

"'Ought to,' he goes. 'Never been fired.' Damned if I shouldn't have grabbed him by the collar and throwed him back in the boat right there and then. You don't break in a rifle on a bear, right Cory? You learn her inside and out in the gravel pit. You sight her in, get familiar with the safety, touch off some rounds, see how she kicks—all that. You know? Am I right, boy?"

Cory nodded.

"Anyway I says, 'By this light, looks like a Weatherby you got there, fella. That's a safari rifle if I'm not mistaken.'

"'Elephant gun,' the guy tells me with a big smile. 'This load ought to give that bear a migraine.' He holds up one of his cartridges. The thing's the size of a salt shaker. 'I bet that gun kicks like a hornet-stung mule,' I say. 'We'll soon see,' he replies, finally getting it loaded. I just shook my head.

"So I tell him to follow the bear tracks into the woods. 'She must have a berry patch in there. She's got a trail knocked down. Just follow it in a ways, get set up by a stump and sooner or later she'll come out the way she came in. You'll have your trophy.'

"So the yahoo reaches into his backpack, I'm assuming for his lunch. He pulls out a big thick reading book. 'What in hell's that for?' I say. He says, 'Don't want to get bored.' He goes whistling off into the brush with that elephant gun slung over his shoulder and his reading book. Disaster on rails."

"I thought this was a story about you eating a pie and a half," Darlene interrupted.

"I'm getting there. I'm getting there." Stu chewed on his pipe stem.

"So with the yahoo in the woods, I push my boat off the island to try and catch a bass or two. I sneak out a ways and drift over a sunken gravel point. The smallmouth are in there like ants on a cupcake. I keep four for dinner and throw the rest back, working up an appetite in the process. I got two pies in the boat for baiting bears and I thought one slice won't hurt none—catching smallmouth is hungry business. Before I knew it I had half a pie completely ate."

"What about the yahoo on the island?" Cory asked.

"He's been in the trees over an hour and all's quieter than Sunday morning. So I roped out an anchor and got comfortable. Darned if the warm sun and that pie didn't put me to napping.

"I woke to a gunshot. BOOOM! Like a cannon it echoes. Just one single report. I sat up and hollered, 'D'ya get 'er?' I hear nothing back. I holler like that a few more times. Not a peep. I yanked up the anchor and got in there. Now I always keep a pistol in the boat, but this was no pistol-sized animal we were bothering.

"I followed the tracks in. The bear had knocked a path through the underbrush from all the coming and going; it was like walking blacktop. I get in about 100 yards and hear this moaning. 'Ohhhhhhhhhhhh. Mmmmmmmmm. Eeeeeeeeeeeeee.' I look over by a stump and I see the yahoo on his back. He's trying to sit up but he keeps rolling over. His face is all blood. I'm thinking he took a paw.

"I get the guy sitting upright and I see it ain't too bad. He's got a deep gash over his eye and all the blood made things look worse.

"'What'n hell happened?' I ask the yahoo.

"'Ohhhhh, ahhhhh,' the guy's still pretty out of it. 'Was reading … heard a buzzing sound … buzzing, buzzing, buzzing. I look up and there's a monstrous bear, 30 yards away, staring at me, sniffing. Must have been a thousand flies around her. The gun's at my side so I start to bring it slowly to my shoulder and just as I go to sight the bear, it goes off. Guess the safety wasn't on. The gun kicks and the scope clobbers me above the eye. That's the last thing I remember. I don't know if I hit her 'cause the gun went off before I could settle the cross hairs.'

"I tell him, 'That bear's hit because I woulda heard her come crashing off the island otherwise.' I used his belt and a piece of his shirttail to hold the bleeding over his eye, put the rifle safety on and gave him his gun back. The yahoo looks like a deranged pirate. We checked to see if there was any sign of the animal being hit. Sure enough, there's drops of blood the size of silver dollars and some hair on the ground."

Cory was watching Stu closely now. Stu's voice dropped to a whisper.

"'Get ready,' I says, 'because we're going in for her and she's not going to be happy to see us.' We walk another 100 yards and next thing, she roars up from behind a deadfall. She can't stand; I figure she's spine-hit. Even from her knees she's over six foot. She lets out a roar that could curl a guy's hair.

"'Finish her!' I scream. But the yahoo was shaking so bad he can't get the safety off. When he finally does squeeze off a round, it hits her in the meat of the shoulder. That accomplishes making her madder yet. Her legs aren't working. She starts pulling herself toward us across the ground, moving fast as a grown man jogs. 'Finish her!' I yell again, and the yahoo empties his clip without touching another hair. I wouldn't be here in this chair if I hadn't brought along my pistol. I put six shots into her mouth before she collapsed in front of me. Went nine hundred pounds.

"As it turned out, the yahoo wrote me a check for three thousand dollars to have that pistol to mount alongside *his* bear. Told me to tell everyone that what he started with his rifle, he had to finish with his pistol. Told me to go along with the story or he'd cancel the check. The resort got new plumbing and a septic tank with that money. Seeing as all the crap he was slinging, seemed the proper way to spend it."

Cory wrinkled his brow. "But that's just half a pie you had in the boat. You said you ate a pie and a half."

"Glad you're staying with me," Stu winked at Darlene. "You see, we boated back to the resort, rounded up the eight strongest men

I could find and dragged that bear out. By the time we were done it was past dark. Having had no lunch or dinner, I finished off the first pie and had half of the second. The yahoo dug into the last half when my back was turned." Stu patted his stomach, "One and one-half pies in a day. And a trophy bear to boot. That's how I done it, as I sit here, not a word stretched in fabrication."

"Well it's sure getting deep where I sit," Darlene said, smiling at Cory. She sat up straight. "Guess I better get after those dishes. I sure don't remember you taking two of my pies out to bait bears. Lucky I didn't catch you or you'd have been worse off than that animal."

"Let me help you," Cory pushed his chair out and started gathering plates and silverware. He was full as a June tick. "You don't happen to have a picture of that bear anywhere? I'd sure like to see her." Cory and Stu cleared the table.

"When we're done, I'll have a look. I keep a shoebox full of photos in the closet. I bet I can put my finger on one. Sure do miss that pistol, though."

When all was quiet and the warm dishes were stacked back in their rightful places and the pots dried in the rack and every last crumb had been swept into cupped hands to be tossed in the fire, they sat down with the box of pictures in front of the hearth. There were photos of muskies the size of golf bags and bears as big as sheds. There were endless limits of green-head mallards and Canadian geese laid out in front of hunters with their hats tipped up. Deer with antlers spread wide as coffee tables. Unshaven men in flannel shirts and canvas oil-cloth coats grinned like boys. Cory loved it. Mesmerized, he sat fighting the day's exhaustion, looking at each picture, asking questions, smelling the paternal aroma of Stu's pipe smoke. Then he grew silent for a time. His brow creased.

"Stu, do you think in the morning we can take a look for that island my dad and I ran up on? I marked it with the broken outboard engine. I'd like to get your motor back."

"You're not worried nothing over that, are you, son?"

"I know it can be repaired. But mostly I'd like to know where that island is."

"I guess we could," Stu said. "Darlene, we've got 'til noon before the Sheriff's expected, is that what you said?"

"The man said noon."

"Cory," Stu asked, looking at him, concerned, "is there any reason you can talk about on why you want to get back to that island?"

Cory watched the fire. "I'm not sure, really. I just don't remember it that well. It's hard to explain. I'd like to know where it is, exactly. Mark it on the map. See it one more time."

"Can you get us back there, you think?"

"If we backtrack the way I came, I think I can. Those islands look a lot alike, don't they?"

Stu nodded and thought about when he first navigated those islands as a boy himself. "I've been looking at them all my life and I still get turned around. The fact of you getting back here to us, cripes, most city people couldn't make it. You're built for the outdoors. You just take to it."

Cory blushed and Darlene patted his hand.

"Before I go to bed I'd like to settle up." Cory reached around to his back pocket and pulled out the envelope. "Here's what we owe for the five nights, plus meals and boat rental. About the motor, I'm going to need a little time for the money on that." Cory tried to hand the envelope over.

"Slow down, now," Stu said. "There's no hurry on any of this."

"Really, you just put that away and we'll talk about it later," Darlene insisted.

"My dad always squared with people. It would take it off my mind knowing it's done. Please. Take it." Cory looked earnestly at Stu, who was about to object again. "Please."

Stu took the crumpled envelope, feeling lousy about it. But the boy had made up his mind.

Cory stood, stretched, smiled slightly, and walked toward the door. "If you would, just give me a knock when you're ready in the morning. I wake up at six out of habit, so I'll be up. Thanks for the pictures and the dinner and all. Tomorrow, we'll go find that island. Good night."

"Good night," the two resort owners replied in duet.

Cory pushed his way out the door, spat, and leaned on the heavy oak until it clicked shut. Billions of stars seeded the night sky. He shuddered in the sudden crisp cold, chilled now, outside the company of Darlene and Stu. Sadness found him, but Cory did his best to shake it. He had tomorrow to look forward to. The island. And, he said to himself, the bill's squared.

THE FARMHOUSE.

The light was dynamic. Dying fast. Showing the final deep purples of evening. Father Pat wheeled into the Blackholm sideyard and shut off the engine. He looked at the farmhouse with its warm amber hue cast from rectangular windows. There was something about the fast-closing darkness and the yellowed window light—those paired opposites—that caused him to feel the plangent pull of family and wonder what might have been. These familial feelings were long dead and buried, or so he had thought.

He was never close with his father, whose appetite for tavern cheeseburgers and 8-ball continued to grow, even now. Pat's dad was a loser; that was the simple handle many used, and it fit. He was always one day away from the big job, the big break, the big payday, the big win. So close, but someone, somewhere, always screwed him. So the family would yank up stakes and go looking for the next big thing.

Pat's dad was injured in high school as a standout football player, so God screwed him. He got fired for skimming money from construction bids at work, so his boss screwed him. He spent weekends in detox and lost his driver's license, so the cops screwed him. He had a no-good son who got in trouble and then, worse yet, became a high-and-mighty priest, so Pat screwed him.

As for his wife, she screwed him, too. Well, actually, she screwed a few other men around town first, and finally packed a suitcase. Pat lived in a motherless house. Then a duplex. Then an apartment. Then a trailer. It got worse from there.

The deal was, Pat and his dad were always one address ahead of bounced checks or overdue payment notices. As they moved, Pat stopped building new friendships. He and friends had been pulled apart too many times. He was getting smart. Hard smart.

One of his favorite school activities was hooky. When he was 15, the school of the moment was near a church that had a small, quiet cemetery around back. While Pat's classmates were learning composition, Pat was in the cemetery stubbing out cigarette butts on headstones that he fantasized belonged to his parents. The resident priest would walk out, hands loosely folded, and talk quietly to him. He'd pick up the butts. He'd sit next to Pat, often asking or saying nothing. This priest didn't have a judgmental bone in his body. He wore Pat down with kindness. Pat had never witnessed such determination. No matter what Pat said or didn't say, there that priest would be. Smiling. Picking up those cigarette butts.

Pat never gave the priesthood a second thought until he had his Calling Dream. And that's when the hardest kid in the district showed up at the door of the seminary, pleading to come in.

Father Pat stepped out of the car, leaving the door open. His hands traced over the roof dents in the DeVille. It was the braille of his life. He watched, transfixed by the image inside the farmhouse: HomeSky, through the window, hands in the sink, soaping the supper dishes as Joseph dried. Mother, son. Togetherness in the closing night. It was like he was watching a movie; it had a surreal quality he understood but couldn't fathom.

Quietly, he spoke to the farmhouse window. "How can such pain be mixed with this tender beauty? Is anything as it truly appears?"

Pat stepped out from behind the car door and shut it hard to announce his arrival. HomeSky bent to the window and cupped her hands to cut the glare. She smiled a small smile. Father Pat waved. HomeSky turned and said something. Joseph's large frame ran past the window toward the door.

"Hi, Joseph," Father Pat said as the boy yanked open the sticky front door. "Careful you don't pull that thing off its pins." He rubbed his hands together as he stepped in. "Hello, HomeSky." Joseph leaned on the creaky old door, his weight shutting it tight. "It'll freeze tonight," Father Pat said. "Not a cloud in the heavens."

"I was going to start some coffee, would you like some, Father?"

"I would!" Joseph edged in quickly.

"Joseph, your manners!" HomeSky furrowed her brow.

"If it's no trouble," Pat said, letting the cold tingle out of his legs, "coffee would be perfect."

Father Pat took a chair at the sparse kitchen table, unsure whether to dive into the details of the funeral in front of Joseph. The three sat in careful silence.

Pat waded in slowly. "Joseph, I saw the hockey poster in your room this morning. Are you a fan?"

"I'm a player, Father. Field hockey and lacrosse are Indian games, did you know that? There'd be no hockey without us."

"I guess I didn't. Wasn't that Bobby Orr on the poster? He was a Boston Bruin. I lived in Boston for a while. Spent many a night listening to the Bruins on the radio."

Joseph eyes twinkled. "St. Louis Blues. 1970. Stanley Cup. Bobby Orr gets the puck and comes out from behind his net. Skates around a few Blues as he picks up speed crossing the red line. Weaves through the defense, cuts to the side of the net, and just as he's tripped, flips the puck in to win! It's the most incredible goal in hockey. I love that picture."

"What position do you play?" Father Pat asked.

HomeSky turned to watch her son answer his favorite question.

"All of them. There's not one I don't love. Goalie. Defense. Forward. Sometimes, if we're winning, I'll play goalie to hold the lead. It depends on what the coach wants. I love to handle the puck and play offense, but Bobby Orr played defense so I guess I like that best. Do you play?"

"I picked it up late, but I really like to. I skated in church league. It was good and rough with all the checking. You can't keep hockey players from checking—not even in a church league."

"I love the hitting, too. But it has to be clean. There's nothing like putting a good shoulder to somebody." Joseph's eyes gleamed. He was big and very solid for his age. At 13, he already weighed 170 pounds. And thanks to the farm work, it was nothing but muscle.

"I saw Orr play once, in the Boston Gardens when I was with a church on the south side. He was something. A natural."

"Mom, did you hear that? He actually saw Bobby Orr skate. What was he like?"

"So smooth. He made skating effortless. He flew down the ice."

"I'm going to play in the pros some day," Joseph said flatly, like he was stating something that hardly needed mentioning.

HomeSky interrupted. "Joseph, what has this family agreed to about hockey?"

Joseph looked out the kitchen window. The yard light rocked in the blackness as the wind blew. The house groaned in resistance. He thought about his dad. Gone now. He got so much from his father. He hadn't lost all that, but everything was different. Life now moved faster.

"I know, I know. Play for fun. To be athletic and strong. Professional sports are not dream-worthy."

HomeSky could feel the "but" coming.

"But Mom. Look at Bobby Orr. Even Father Pat saw the …" Joseph struggled for the word. "The good in it. When done right. Right, Father?"

Pat knew better than to get tangled up in this issue. He was rescued by HomeSky.

She brought over the coffee. "By the way, when did you start being such a coffee regular, young man?" She poured three cups.

"When Dad and I got up for morning chores while you were still warm in bed dreaming of another lazy day." Joseph laughed and smiled. Father Pat and HomeSky shook their heads; they couldn't help but join in.

"What news do you have of the funeral?" HomeSky looked at Father Pat. This was the lead he'd been waiting for. Obviously, the funeral could be discussed openly, as he had hoped. Joseph, like it or not, was now man of the house.

"As we discussed this morning, it's against the law to bury your husband out here on your land, but—"

"Against *whose* law?" Joseph asked, seriously. More serious than Pat thought him capable of.

"Joseph, let him finish," HomeSky said, gently but firmly.

Pat continued, "But Sheriff Harris has agreed to look the other way if you sign a document that says you intend to take up residence on the Rez and your husband will be buried there. Since the Rez is exempt from the Sheriff's jurisdiction, that absolves him of any legal consequences."

"Out of the question." HomeSky folded her arms. Her eyes ignited with conviction. "This family will have no association with that filth. I thought you understood that." She looked at Father Pat like she'd never seen him before. It stung him, but he knew he had to be persistent.

"You can cancel the paperwork one day after the burial and I'll misfile the document and that will be the end of it. It's the only way." He looked her in the eyes. "Like it or not, you, me, Joseph, all of us are under the jurisdiction of the white man's law. No matter how wrong it may be, we can't fight these idiocies with obstinacy. Not if we want to win. *Outsmart* them, HomeSky. No one will know of the misfiled record, I'll see to that. It's the only way. Do you think I would suggest it otherwise?"

HomeSky unfolded her arms. She looked at her son. They studied each other. "What do you think?"

Joseph had grown quiet, listening. "The idea of outsmarting white laws, I like. If Father Pat says it's the only way, then I believe him. Whatever it takes to keep Dad on our land."

Pat was impressed by Joseph's maturity. "I sincerely believe it's the only way, HomeSky."

"I don't like it, Mom, but I'm for it." Joseph watched his mother.

HomeSky went across the cold, small room to the kitchen window. She looked through her reflection and saw nothing but blackness covering their land. She was part of this dirt. Every contour, each dip and rise, each rock pile, each shelter belt, each cattail slough. In the darkness, she couldn't see the front pasture leading away from the house, stretching out flat toward the ridge, but she knew every step of it. This was their hard-earned land to do right by! Why should she sneak around like a thief? Falsify documents. She made a fist and stood firm at the sink. Tall and lean. Despite the cold, she stood in her bare feet. The night wind leaned on the spare wooden farmhouse, and it popped and rattled and complained. All was quiet in the kitchen. With her back to the table, HomeSky slowly wiped her tears. And in the next breath, a peace came over her like warm hands on her shoulders. She relaxed. Her fist unfurled. She asked finally, "Father, did you bring the documents to sign?" She turned and faced them.

Father Pat talked about the service he had in mind. They worked out the details and drank coffee and talked quietly as the wind blew under the stars. "Do we have enough men to get the casket up to the top of the ridge?" Pat asked.

Joseph answered. "We have a cousin with a pickup I can call. With the frost in the ground he'll be able to drive up through the field."

"HomeSky," Father Pat asked. "How many people will attend?"

"I think no more than 12 or 15. Mostly neighbors my husband has helped out over the years. A few cousins may come up from the Rez. We kept to ourselves, mostly. I haven't told many people because I didn't want to bring attention to the farm and the burial."

"Unfortunately, that's probably for the best. Is there anyone you'd like me to notify on the Rez? Anyone at all?"

"No. The Rez is best left out of this. My husband's life offended them; it exposed the truth of their decision. He didn't have friends there."

"Maybe not, but he did have admirers. I heard some talk at the gas station before I came. They were speaking very respectfully. They asked me what I knew about the arrangements and I told them to call you. I hope that's okay."

"I have gotten a few calls that I didn't expect. But it will be a small gathering. And Father, with you being assigned to the Rez, I hope you take no offense by our family's stance on this matter."

"No. I don't. I agree it's in bad shape. But my job is to make it better. My work is in the middle of the Rez, not on the edges. I've met a few people who share in this desire. All we can do is our best."

"They're lucky, you coming," Joseph said. "But for every good one that finds you, there will be ten tearing down what you build."

HomeSky looked at her boy. It was like she was hearing the voice of her husband. Father Pat was impressed by the thoughtfulness of this young man who, not ten minutes ago, was talking like any kid might about playing a pro sport. If Pat had met Joseph out of the blue, on a road, if he knew nothing about him, if he saw him hulking over his undersized bike, Pat would have surely misjudged this boy—underestimated him. What arrogance! To assume you know someone by only seeing him. To do this is to take his mystery away. And that's among the gravest of sins. He made a mental note to write on this subject for Sunday's homily.

He asked, "Did you two collect your thoughts on what you'd like said at the service?"

"I wrote something," Joseph said, reaching into his pocket, pulling out a folded piece of paper, passing it to Father Pat. It read:

My dad, William RiverHeart Blackholm, taught me to laugh when no one was looking because first you must please yourself. Not many knew it, but Dad laughed a lot. Because he loved me he let me catch him at it.

My dad pushed a canoe over thin ice, jumping in the boat when he finally broke through, to free a large buck that had gone through. I asked him why do such a thing when just a week before we shot a deer to eat. He said this deer told him it was not time to die. My dad knew how to listen for such things.

Dad grew corn in dirt where others couldn't grow weeds.

Dad said all that died returned new again. In spring, we'd race to the top of the ridge and lean over and let the sweat roll off our faces onto the new shoots. We called it sweating on Grandpa.

I love my dad and wear his stone behind my ear as did his father and his father's father back to Massacre Creek. We are all shaped by the ones who came before. My clay is firm. I will honor our name as much as I will miss him. I will thank him for my life by the way I live it.

My name is Joseph Good Thunder Blackholm and I love my father and mother.

Father Pat tingled. He didn't know what to say. "Wonderful," he managed, looking at the boy. Joseph beamed from ear to ear. "If it's okay with you, I think I'll read it just as it is tomorrow. I could stay up all night and not improve on it." Father Pat handed the writing to HomeSky.

"Yes," she said. "I've read it. It is wonderful. Just like the author." Joseph beamed all the more and looked down at his hands, embarrassed.

"HomeSky, how about from you?"

"I've written a poem. If you could read it tomorrow as well, I'd be grateful.

My husband was named RiverHeart
Because a strength flowed in him
No droughts could long dry
Nor winter freeze solid
Winding past objects man-made
Unstoppable peacefulness
Sourced by a depth
Few of us toe
The day's outcome
My RiverHeart would say
Has been trusted to the rock
For time
Not man
To chisel away
The Great Sky
May have called his body
But his Spirit
Replenishes
Those who love him
Advances
Those who walk alone
There is a river

A strength
Called serenity
I have swum in it.

Father Pat folded his hands and let his nose drop to touch them. The wind against the four walls refused to relent. A tear came to his eye. He usually swallowed such emotions publicly. Priests are to be level-strong. But maybe crying in front of this family was the ultimate show of strength. For the first time he could remember, he didn't feel the need to hide vulnerability.

"It's a beautiful tribute." He thumbed the tears away and smiled. "Tomorrow will be a day of honoring. There will be tears and laughter. But before I leave, I need to speak to you both about one final thing." Father Pat's face tightened. He shifted in his chair, struggling for an entry place. "I realize it's been an exhausting day, but I learned something in town this afternoon that you should know." Pat rubbed his forehead. "Some important mystery has chosen us. I'm sure of it. But I'm equally sure I don't know why. Joseph, the morning your dad died, another boy's father also passed away. Up on Lake of the Woods. The boy's name is Cory. He's 13, too. He and his dad were fishing, There was an accident. The boy's fine. Tomorrow, after the funeral here, I'm to drive with Sheriff Harris to pick him up." Father Pat shifted his attention across the kitchen table to HomeSky. "I don't mean to alarm you, but my heart tells me these boys are to meet. This has been preordained. I'd like to get them together, with your permission."

HomeSky and Joseph sat stunned. Father Pat saw his news was a lot to absorb, given everything they were dealing with already. He repeated himself, "I really believe Joseph and Cory should meet. I hope you agree."

HomeSky looked from Father Pat to Joseph. The kitchen was quiet except for the hum of the old refrigerator. "Joseph?" she whispered.

Joseph went around the table to his mother. He looked down at her and, of all things, smiled. "Mom, when I was in the woods, I had a dream about another boy. We were skating on the pond behind the house like brothers. The vision must have been about this Cory. I want to meet him."

She hesitated, but only for a moment. "I think so, too," she said.

Father Pat exhaled, relieved. Everyone was smiling, but shaking their heads. Father Pat spoke up. " I hope you don't take this wrong, but this is strange stuff."

"*Weird* is the word I was thinking," Joseph interjected.

"Me too," HomeSky said.

"Okay. Same here," Pat confessed. And they all continued to shake their heads, lost in the meaning of it.

"Does this stuff happen often, Father?" Joseph asked. "With two kids like us?"

"I've never heard of anything like it. I'd say we're all on new ground here."

They sat in the silence of the moment, knowing they were in the presence of something profound. Whether by coincidence or providence, these lives now stood bundled. The what and why of it, there was no telling. But what was conclusive for these three, sitting in the night-cold farmhouse kitchen, was that somehow it was good. They didn't, any of them, feel fear. They felt, unexpectedly, impatient. Like they needed to take a next breath, quickly, to prompt the mystery's telling.

"When will Cory be here?" Joseph asked. "Mom, could he come to supper tomorrow?"

"Tomorrow? I guess. It depends on their plans, though." She looked at Father Pat. "Is Cory's mother going with you to Lake of the Woods?"

"No. The Sheriff said the mother and her two daughters would drive only as far as Baudette. They have funeral arrangements to make at home in the morning, then they'll get on the road. They're expected around two. The family will need some alone time in the afternoon when we get Cory back. I could ask if they'd like to come here to supper, but that's a lot of work for you. When I talked to

Monsignor Kief about all of this, he suggested we try and get everyone to eat at the rectory. He's got a housekeeper who lives to cook. I said I'd have to ask you and the Bradford family. How does dinner at the rectory sound?"

HomeSky shrugged her shoulders. "Well, it's been a time since I've seen Monsignor Kief. But if it's his suggestion, I'm fine with it. Okay with you?" She looked at Joseph.

"What are we having?" he asked with a sly grin. Joseph never missed an opening.

"Great. Everything on this half is settled then." Father Pat clapped his hands together. "I'll talk to Cory's family. To be completely honest with them, I should tell them about your family's loss, so they know the whole story, too. I hope that's all right."

"I was thinking the same thing," HomeSky said.

"Good. Well, it's getting late. I'll be back out here bright and early. The service will begin around nine." Father Pat stood up stiffly from the table. The aches from last night's detour weren't going away anytime too soon.

HomeSky stood as well. "I can't tell you what a blessing you've been to us these last two days. It's like you fell from heaven." She stepped forward and embraced him. Father Pat stood tightly, hands momentarily at his sides, not quite certain how to reciprocate. His feelings for HomeSky weren't entirely clear, and the occurrences of the past 48 hours fuzzed his thinking further. He gave her a quick squeeze and stepped away. They looked at each other for an odd moment.

"Good night," Father Pat said.

"Good night to you," she replied.

"I'll go out with you," Joseph said, pulling work boots over his bare feet.

"Take a jacket," HomeSky said, shooting a wary eye at her boy. "That wind has teeth."

Father Pat and Joseph stepped off the porch. It was like they were covered in stars. Out in the great wide open, the night sky is so radiant, it makes a person question if it's real. "So many stars," Pat said aloud to himself.

"My dad told me every time you did something good, another star got pinned. He'd say, 'When you get out of the bright light of the city, you can see there's a lot of good in the world.'"

Pat looked around at the sky, wincing now and then, his neck in stiff disagreement. They stood in the sideyard, mouths slightly open.

"Hear those chimes, Father?" The wind chimes hung on the porch, swaying and bumping out a sweet opera.

"Yeah. Nice."

"Father, remember when we were talking about hockey earlier?"

Pat looked over at Joseph, who was still staring upward. "Sure."

"I want to skate like those wind chimes sound." Father Pat watched as a smile stretched across the boy's face. "Do you know what I mean?"

"I'm not quite sure I do," Pat said.

"I want to skate easy. Like I was moved by something that can't be seen. I know that sounds goofy, but that's how hockey feels to me. I get lost in it. I just go. Does that make any sense? Or am I just losing it?"

"Do you believe in God, Joseph?"

"I believe in the Creator, the Great Spirit."

"That is the unseen source that moves you. In whatever you choose—skating or whatever—stay close to that force." Pat contemplated the notion for a moment. "Like wind through the chimes. Yeah, I like that." Father Pat threw an arm over Joseph's shoulder and they continued to admire the stars.

HomeSky glanced out the kitchen window and saw the two. She allowed herself the momentary delusion that the nightmare had ended and her husband was back. She watched their shapes. She felt something inside her move, ever so slightly. Something came to life, almost imperceptibly. Like a tiny fold of grass, nudging toward daylight. She rested her hand on her stomach, where the feeling originated, but it was gone.

Father Pat said good night to Joseph and climbed stiffly into Monsignor Kief's Cadillac. Joseph went to the barn, hung the trouble light, and used the hoist to put the shovel blade on the tractor. Tomorrow, he would need it to cut through the frostline for the burial. Wrenching on the iron blade was cold work. Joseph stopped to blow in his hands. He walked to the open doors of the barn to listen. The wind had lain down. The chimes hung silent.

Finished, Joseph latched the barn doors. The reality of night's cold crept in and took hold of the farmhouse. But as Joseph climbed the porch steps, he reached over and ran his fingers along the chimes. They sang an a cappella into the stillness of the night. Beautiful and random, the notes scattered.

Inside, he leaned on the door to close it tightly. As he shut off the kitchen light, in the stillness, he waited as the final muffled note of the chime rang out against the night.

NIGHT. SHERIFF HARRIS.

It was a typical October Saturday night for Sheriff Harris in Baudette. Outhouses at the city park were overturned. Firecrackers were lit and dropped in the book return at the library. Two women traded blows in the bowling lanes over alleged score-doctoring in league playoffs. An emergency vehicle was dispatched to the VFW senior potluck dinner where a rabbit bone was temporarily lodged in a member's throat. Underage drinking and a bonfire without a permit were reported on the old logging road by the garbage dump. The front door of the Chamber of Commerce was egged.

Mostly, Saturday night did what Saturday nights do in these parts: came and went. The small ration of driving Sheriff Harris endured consisted primarily of a nightly patrol within the city limits. It revealed little more than rectangles of TV-blue flashing in living rooms as couples nodded off with empty ice cream bowls on their laps. The aluminum-sided ramblers were shut up tight for the night.

Sheriff Harris backed the cruiser up his driveway so it sat nose toward the road. He turned off the police radio and sat for a moment. The engine ticked as it cooled. He hated driving. He was tense, constricted, and overheated inside a vehicle. That, and he was afraid. Cars had terrified him since the automobile wreck as a boy. Took his mother and brother and left his dad an angry cripple. Cars were dangerous. They went too damn fast. They carried too goddamned much gasoline.

Sheriff Harris remained buckled in his seat. He glanced at his watch. Four more minutes to go. His mind caromed, seeking a distraction. He thought of Deputy, curled up on the back seat. He had to boost the dog up by the hindquarters to get him in the cruiser now. They'd been together a long time. Eleven years, maybe more. Deputy was a great duck dog in his prime, but the Sheriff couldn't remember the last time they were on the water. No damn ducks left. Indians shot 'em all up. Speared most the walleye, too. Asshole Indians. Blight on our country. Sheriff Harris didn't care for technicalities like who was here first. We won the land—fair and square. All these goddamned treaties and special hunting and fishing privileges, no wonder there was no game left. It was all in the freezers of those lazy-asses.

Still buckled, he checked his watch again. Three more minutes now. Perspiration rolled down the inseam of his undershirt. Try to think of something pleasant. He thought of his wife, his Amanda.

They were good, Amanda and Thurgood, although everyone concurred they were a strange pair, she being 19 years his senior. It was love at first sight for Thurgood. She was his piano teacher. He was 10 and she was 29. On their third lesson, Thurgood promised to marry her. Miss Amanda smiled and told him to concentrate on his scales. Twice a week they played, all the way through high school. He proposed weekly. He never loved anyone else.

Thurgood thought Miss Amanda was the most beautiful woman in the world. Most of the town saw her as a bony spinster. Introverted, she rarely spoke unless spoken to. And to say she was exacting in her ways was to put it kindly. But to an overweight kid with few friends, she was non-judgmental and, best of all, attentive. Thurgood had been thoroughly shorted in that department. Piano lessons, Tuesdays and Sundays—those were his week's highlights.

On the outside, Thurgood was built for football, but on the inside, it was piano. When he was on the playing field in high school, he always worried about his hands. He caught endless grief from the coach for playing "LIKE A GIANT PUSSY!" but when he did sprain a finger, it meant two weeks away from his duets. That was unbearable.

The only reason he played football was because they needed a body on the front line, and it lessened the ridicule at school. Miss Amanda showed him how to tape his fingers to protect them. He learned the art of tackling by never using them. He'd just lay that overgrown body on whomever he could and knock them silly. When he missed, he missed badly, and would go down face-first in the mud. Everyone laughed. He was a big joke. But as long as his hands stayed out of harm's way, Thurgood didn't care. His hands were precious. The rest of himself he had deserted long before.

Miss Amanda would guide his large hands. She would marvel at their tremendous span to reach keys. He'd blush with pride; he'd thank his hands under his breath. Piano was his only consolation. He forgot his size, his ugliness. The piano made him forget his dad in a wheelchair. The piano made him forget that the only foster home to keep him was the church. When he played, people smiled at him. It was the only time.

But in the very beginning, he chose the piano for one reason and one reason only: it made him look small. At 10 years old and already 170 pounds, he chose this instrument from all those the music teacher presented because of its size. Thurgood hid behind its bulk. He only came to love piano because of Miss Amanda.

Sheriff Harris looked at his watch. The seatbelt felt like it was slowly tightened by some relentless force. Two more minutes would make five that he'd been sitting in his car. It was all part of an experiment (he didn't cotton to the word therapy) to overcome his fear of automobiles (nor did he care for the term motorphobia).

He was seeing a doctor once a month in Minneapolis. For the first year, he had to take the bus seven hours each way to see her. As the therapy progressed, Monsignor Kief, who recommended the psychologist in the first place, rode along as the Sheriff drove. He was making progress. The Sheriff could now drive the entire 720-mile round trip alone. And when the state slashed his budget, eliminating his deputy, he could manage driving himself daily pretty well. But whenever possible, he walked, especially downtown. Rattling doorknobs, making sure everything was buttoned up tight. He used to meet Amanda at Lu Ann's after foot patrol for a malt and a wedge of cheesecake. But she passed unexpectedly two years ago. Cancer came and stole her in the blink of an eye. Gone at 65 years of age; far too young.

Thurgood played the piano at his wife's funeral, to the astonishment of the town. Few had ever heard him play, but the story of a boy smitten with his piano teacher and eventually marrying her and going off to Korea and coming back with part of his left hand blown off was a story regularly circulated at church socials or holiday picnics or wherever three or more chatterboxes gathered. They'd gossip about the same half-dozen subjects, and Sheriff Harris and his wife, "nineteen years his senior, of all things!" were second or third on the list—coming in just after the most current pregnancy and alleged infidelity. But for the town to actually hear Thurgood at the piano, they were dumbstruck. How could something so delicate come out of this mountain of a man with his mangled hand? There wasn't a dry eye in the church.

When Thurgood returned from Korea, it was public knowledge that he refused to go near the piano. He had artificial fingers replacing the two he lost in combat, and his disfigured thumb was a transplanted section of his big toe. He demanded the piano be removed from the house. Amanda, in quiet persistence, struck a deal. The piano would go the basement. A custom ramp was built. It took eight men and Amanda to get that piano on its side and down the basement steps. Thurgood would have no part in it.

Then there was talk he was playing again, with his good hand, and the index finger of his left. It was slow going. Many nights, rumor had it, he stormed out of the house, slamming the door so loudly "it shook apples off the Clancy's tree three blocks away."

"The piano is back upstairs," was the next report, according to a second cousin of Hal Johnson of Johnson and Sons moving. To hear it, old man Johnson nearly lost one of his seven boys trying to get the damn thing back up the basement steps to the living room. Thurgood, who was supervising operations this time, was said to have been sent away to clean the garage by Amanda just as the Johnsons threatened to walk off the job with the piano stuck halfway up the incline. "Don't think you'll be getting no 50 percent leaving it there!" Thurgood screamed from the service door of the garage.

"They're playing duets," was the gossip at the Cut 'N Curl barbershop with the ladies' beauty parlor in back. Summer evenings, Amanda and Thurgood could be seen through the front picture window squeezed onto the piano bench. Thurgood loved duets because he would play one hand, his wife the other. Not long after, Amanda was back in her regular place, to the right of the piano in a straight-backed chair, setting the metronome in swing, instructing her husband.

"He's trying to play with two hands again and it ain't going so hot," this according to Mrs. Schmitz, wife of Mike Schmitz of Schmitz Plate Glass and Window. Rumor was that during a difficult stanza of a Souza march, Thurgood threw his prosthesis through the bay window. Mrs. Shields put the record straight: it was the metronome that went through the plate glass, not the artificial hand. She knew. She waited on the Sheriff when he came into her card shop the next day for a scented candle and a lovely apology card for his wife. "While I was wrapping the apricot candle, the Sheriff was inscribing the card," she said. "He inquired as to the spelling of metronome. Luckily I've always been a whiz with words," Mrs. Shields told her Ladies of Commerce luncheon group.

On the day of Amanda's funeral, the entire town of Baudette packed into St. Olivet, watching as the Sheriff seated himself on the piano bench to play. It was so quiet you could hear the bench groan before he touched out the first notes of Amazing Grace. But it was unanimous. Everyone repeated the same thing for weeks. "When he finished, there wasn't a dry eye in the church. Not a dry eye."

Sheriff Harris looked at his watch. One more minute. The doors of the patrol car were pressing in. He did as he was taught in his meetings. (He didn't like to call them sessions.) He tried to conjure pleasant thoughts. He remembered how soft Amanda's hands were. How gently she would help his fingers stretch to strike an F minor or a D flat. Her hands on his, this was the touch that introduced him to the notion of love. No one touched Thurgood. He was clumsy. He was in the way. But the touch of Amanda Kipshaw, to this day, that tenderness lingered. It kept him above water when most else whispered *let go*.

"Time's up!" Sheriff Harris flung off his seatbelt and slid out of the car as quickly as his 280-pound frame could maneuver. For the longest time, even after becoming relatively comfortable driving, he couldn't buckle himself. It took him back to the accident. His sister out of the vehicle, banging on his car door. It was locked from the inside. He couldn't see his dad. Mother was bleeding. Thurgood couldn't unlock the door. He was tangled in his shoulder harness. He was too fat to get his hand around to the buckle release. The flipped car had him. He smelled gasoline. A fire ignited. His younger brother was screaming. THURGOOD! He smelled smoldering rubber. Smoke filled the car. Trapped! Too fat! Someone broke the window with a branch. Unlocked the door. Got Thurgood out. The car filled with flames. His younger brother calling his name. THURGOOOOD!

The Sheriff pushed himself away from the cruiser. Breathing hard and beaded with sweat despite the below-freezing temperature, he ran his good hand through his hair. He opened the back door of the cruiser and whistled softly to Deputy. The old dog stood shakily and looked at the Sheriff.

"Come on, old boy," the Sheriff said gently as he hoisted the dog out. He set him down on the driveway and held the back door open. Inside, in the front of the cruiser, a 12-gauge shotgun was racked in the center console. He looked at the gun. He looked at it for longer than a man, alone, should. Then he slammed the door and locked it.

This was Sheriff Thurgood Harris's life: at the end of the day he was greeted by a green stucco three-bedroom bungalow just eight blocks off Main Street. The carpet smelled of cigarettes and dog despite the vigilant vacuuming and shampooing (Amanda's training). What qualified as a homecoming surprise for the Sheriff was flipping the light switch and having a filament blow. He tossed his keys on the kitchen table and snapped on the light over the sink. There was one bowl in the dish rack. One fork. One knife. One cup.

He sat down heavily at the kitchen table, reaching into his right pocket for a Camel. Thinking better of it, he went to the left for a Vantage. A clean Welcome To Las Vegas ashtray sat in the middle of the table. He pulled it toward himself, thinking, even though Amanda had passed almost two years ago, how he still kept the house spotless. Amanda was the type that not only straightened before company, she'd walk around touching up the paint. The Sheriff finished his cigarette, emptied the ashtray, and went to the refrigerator. Three cans of Pabst Blue Ribbon came out.

He lined the beers side by side on the kitchen table. He took a fresh glass from the cupboard and blew in it. Not that the glass had any occasion to collect dust. He kept only four glasses in his working rotation: Beer glass. Juice glass. Milk glass. Company glass. The rest he boxed up and stored in the garage. Actually, he needed no more than three. The fourth, for company, that one gathered dust.

For Thurgood, it was always three cans of beer to a sitting, just as Amanda's father had done his entire adult life. Amanda had told him about this shortly after they were married. She mentioned she thought Thurgood had too much of a taste for beer. She suggested he do as her father did when he came home from a long day with the Public Works Department cutting roads through the northern forests. Three beers. No more, no less. The first for thirst. The second for flavor. The third for relaxation. That's what her father said. Three to a sitting. Always out of a glass. Like a gentleman.

Sheriff Harris cracked open and poured the first can. "For thirst," he said, raising the glass in a toast. He drank the beer in his home's silence. The resolute, clear winds of the approaching winter contracted his house, which popped and settled in the seasonal shift. Thurgood looked out the window. The empty road led south to town and north to the nothingness of the Canadian Shield. He contemplated tomorrow. He'd have the coroner drive to the Blackholm farm and leave the body. He'd then send him ahead to Lake of the Woods. He and Father Pat would go up after the funeral. Thurgood was sure the coroner would keep his trap shut about the unusual funeral arrangements. The Sheriff knew for a fact the coroner was playing pat-a-cake with a young cashier who rung at Bonaducci's Grocery. He also knew for a fact that the coroner's wife wouldn't be too thrilled about her husband's new grocery item. So when the coroner pressed with one too many questions about why the Blackholm body wasn't going directly to the Rez, the Sheriff winked at the coroner and asked him if he didn't have some melons to squeeze at Bonaducci's instead of asking so many questions. That pretty much moved the coroner off the subject.

Up at Lake of the Woods, they'd get the Bradford kid. The coroner would take the boy's dad back to Baudette. Damnedest thing, these two kids. Same age, same day, losing their dads like that. In all his years, he'd never heard anything like it. But that's the thing about small-town sheriffing. Just when you think you've seen everything, something new drops on your doorstep.

The Sheriff poured his second beer. "For flavor," he toasted. He wondered how much of what he'd uncovered about Father Patrick O'Rourke he'd delve into on their ride north to Lake of the Woods. He'd done the usual background stuff, typical work whenever he had a new person in the area. Then, after they met, something gnawed at him, so he followed a hunch to dig deeper. Father Pat had registered vehicles in six different states in the past 10 years. Obviously this guy didn't sit still long. A few phone calls to various city police departments turned up that the good Father Pat had been arrested in two of the cities. Once for disturbing the peace. Once for public intoxication and brawling. This, from a *priest.* But it wasn't until a few calls later that the Sheriff hit pay dirt.

Sheriff Harris went into the living room with his third beer and sat in his recliner by his puzzle table. He and Amanda had always worked puzzles in the evening. It helped with his dexterity and was a habit he still found therapeutic in many ways. He unwound after a full day of sheriffing by working the puzzles. The sense of accomplishment, the tangible results of the work, the gratifying formation, the control, the measurable progress—he slept better, just a half-hour on the puzzles. He liked European Landscapes best. They were challenging, but not impossible, like The Impressionists, which Amanda preferred. He poured his third beer. "For relaxation," he quietly toasted.

In the endless quiet of that Saturday night, Sheriff Thurgood Harris sat, staring past the half-finished puzzle, looking out his front bay window at the blackness covering the road. It was a cold, pathetic road, empty as a villain's soul. It was nothingness. Not a thing moving in or out of town. No single sign of life, except for the rise and fall of Deputy's raspy breathing. He pulled a Camel out of his right pocket and lit it. Amanda never allowed smoking in the front room. Even today, Thurgood felt a shot of guilt when he lit up in the recliner. Across the room, window-side, matching his-and-hers armchairs were covered in plastic to keep the daylight from fading the olive upholstery. Thurgood didn't care for using those chairs. Sitting so close to the window announced his aloneness to anyone passing by. He spent his time in the dim half-light of the background, in the recliner.

Thurgood snapped on the floor lamp and let his thick fingers push through the scattering of delicate puzzle pieces. He found a sloping edge of the church spire and snapped it in, giving it a tap for good measure. He reached for his cigarette and inhaled deeply.

With the smoke swirling in his lungs, he pondered. Would he broach what he uncovered with Father Pat—or, as the Boston cop referred to him—The Suicide Priest?

That ought to get the Padre sitting up straight in the car seat, the Sheriff thought, a smug little smile coming to the corners of his mouth. And with that, his fingers went back to work, scavenging for the next puzzle piece.

PART THREE

October 17, 1973

BOOM ISLAND.

The morning was nothing shy of magnificent. The sun was on a mission with a clear-blue sky escort. It would be warm, no doubt.

The frost on the grass sparkled like miniature crystal figurines. Those who weren't up early, like Cory was, missed it because it was burning off fast. Steam rose from the east-facing slope of the cabin roofs. The asphalt shingles curled slightly as they warmed.

Cory was awake before six, straightening up both his and his dad's gear for the trip home. The Sheriff was due at noon. With all their stuff packed, he'd get that chance to take a last look for the island.

The island wouldn't leave him.

He dreamt about it again last night. He was walking barefoot, searching every inch of undergrowth. A very serious expression on his face. Don't worry, he said to his dream self. Slow down. But there's no line of communication to yourself in a dream. You just watch helplessly. You're never so alone as in a dream. Cory woke up, breathing hard, before he found what he'd been searching for.

The light of morning comforted him. In the cold shower stall, he stood aside as the temperature became more bearable. His dad had taught him to conserve water. "Get in while it's warming up. You'll end up feeling warmer 'cause you started cold," he told him. "It's invigorating." Cory stepped into the stream of water and grit his teeth as the cold water drummed off his taut skin. He knew that from heaven his father could see all. Quickly the shock of the cold wore off. He scrubbed, and cranked the handles off. Often, he would time his shower, like his dad did. He'd count the seconds. Just over a minute and he was out.

In the chill of the cabin bathroom, Cory stood naked and looked at his face in the mirror. He looked hard, without coming to any conclusions. Teeth brushed, he got dressed, pulled on his canvas coat, stepped out the front door of his cabin, and spat. He thought about the day. Not specifically about what was to be done, but about the day in general. It would be warm. The high sky meant high barometric pressure. Little wind early, but it would be humping pretty good out of the west once things warmed. It was shaping up to be tremendous. He got lost momentarily in that thought. When he snapped out of it, he went back to his reflection in the mirror; he wondered if he was okay, or was he a bad person, walking around absorbing such a beautiful day, considering everything that had happened.

Cory stepped back into his cabin, took a deep breath, and began emptying the cabin of their things. He picked up his dad's army-green duffel and fishing rods and started for the dock. "The first trip down is the worst," he said to himself, seeing the outline of the boathouse through the pines.

Stu caught up with Cory. "With all this early morning commotion, I thought we had a bear in the bird feeders. Can I give you a hand with that stuff?"

"No thanks. I've about got it licked. Good day for a boat ride, though, wouldn't you say?" Cory looked up. Stu couldn't help but agree.

"Tell you what we'll do. We'll get in a good breakfast, then we'll go out and see about that island. Sound okay?"

"Boom Island," Cory said. "That's what I'm calling it. I want to mark it on my map."

Stu winced at the name. "If you've got this gear under control, I'll get on the radio before breakfast and talk to a few guides around the lake. Maybe they can help us find the island once you get us close. There are over fourteen thousand islands out there, did you know that? That's how Lake of the Woods got its name. It's a forest on water."

"Couple more trips and I'll have it all sewn up on this end," Cory said.

Stu laughed.

"What?" Cory asked.

Stu shook his head. "Ah, you just have some funny ways of putting things. See you up at breakfast." Stu clapped him on the back.

"I didn't think I could eat after last night's dinner. But a few times down and back to the cabin changed that right around."

Stu laughed and waved and headed toward the lodge. He felt something deep for the boy. Smart as a whip, he is. Up before dawn, handling chores. After all he's been through, he wants to go back out and find that godforsaken island. Gutsy kid, for sure. Probably wants to put some closure on the whole thing. Take one question mark out of the damnedest mystery someone that age ever had to face. The kid was old enough to entirely grasp what happened but too young to have any experience coping with it. It couldn't have happened at a worse age. Stu found it difficult to fathom why a God who made a day as spectacular as the one they were breathing would stick it to a kid like that. "Don't make no sense at all," he said to the sky. What more could be said? Maybe you're never old enough to untangle a knot like this. Maybe the young are better off because they don't care to try. It made Stu's head itch thinking about it. He picked up the pace toward the main lodge.

When Cory stepped inside to join them, Stu was just finishing up on the marine band radio and Darlene had the room smelling so strongly of bacon, it had sunk into the log chinking.

"Good morning," Cory said, poking at last night's ashes in the hearth.

"Jeez Louise!" Darlene jumped. "Don't sneak up on me like that!" She gathered herself. "How'd you sleep?"

"Very well, thanks. And believe it or not, I'm hungry again."

"You're still making up for all that rowing you did. Plus, I heard you out there this morning. You're up before the birds. My mom had to dynamite me out of bed in the morning when I was your age."

"I hope I wasn't too loud," Cory offered.

Stu chimed in. "Don't let her fool ya. Darlene is up before the sun every morning. She sleeps a lot less than most of my other girlfriends." Stu shot Cory a wink. Cory returned the gesture. Darlene winged a buttermilk biscuit across the room, catching Stu flush on the forehead. "A damn crack shot, too," he added, picking the biscuit off the floor. "Mmmmm. Not bad. Little heavy on the salt, though." Darlene sent him a look that quieted him right down.

"All right. Everyone better be sitting in one minute or I'll set this out for the dogs," Darlene made her usual pronouncement as she came out of the kitchen. They all took the same places they had last night. "Stu, lead us in grace." They took one another's hands. This was less uncomfortable to Cory than it had been 11 hours ago.

"Thank you, Lord, for another fine morning to be witness to. We appreciate this food, this company, and especially this boy you've seen clear to send us. Bring a peaceful resolution to all this and help us to understand your way in it. And get them ducks flying into my decoys. I can't make the long shots like I used to. Amen."

The breakfast didn't feature much talking. There was warm maple syrup for the pancakes. Enough bacon to feed a lumberjack camp, fresh cornbread biscuits with sausage gravy, honey, sliced apples, orange juice, milk, and coffee. After five minutes of uninterrupted eating, Stu took a short break. "I've got the boat gassed up, Cory. When we're through with the dishes here, we'll go see about finding Boom Island."

"Stewart!" Darlene shot her husband a horrified look.

"Well that's what the boy calls it," Stu defended himself.

Cory interrupted, "Honest. I call it Boom Island."

Darlene just shook her head, folding her napkin. "Seems you could find another name," she said, looking out the window.

"I talked to a few of the guys on the lake," Stu said to Cory. "Resort owners, guides, whoever I could scrape up. Some might be coming by to help. I hope that's okay with you—them coming too."

"Sure. If I can get us close, somebody will see that motor stuck up out of the water. I believe with a little work that motor'll be good as new."

"Son, there's plenty of motors around here where that came from."

Cory looked up from his pancakes directly into Stu's eyes. "It's more than that. Getting the motor back will make me feel better. The engine's fine. It didn't hardly get wet."

Stu nodded. He couldn't help but be impressed by this boy with the curly hair and the distant gray-green eyes that revealed little. "We'll all get on one radio channel out there, that way we can talk back and forth."

Darlene jumped in. "I want you both back here by 11:30, no later, you hear? That Sheriff's coming up from Baudette. I've met him once before. He's an owly SOB. Don't leave me here feeding him lunch when he's anxious to get back to home."

The table was silent.

"Are your ears working?"

They both kept their heads down chewing. "Loud and clear, dear," Stu replied.

"Yes, ma'am," Cory answered.

"I'll see to the dishes. You two get."

"Are you sure?" Cory asked. "Things could wait until we got these dishes done."

"Just rinse your plate in the sink and leave the rest to me. I've cleaned up after a lot more than the likes of you two." She patted Cory's hand. "Nice of you to ask, though. Stewart, you could take a page from this boy's book."

He's a real good one, she thought, watching Cory. But she worried. She talked with Stu late into the night about going out to that island. It just didn't seem right to her, the boy being obsessed with it. But Stu convinced her it was just Cory's way of putting it behind him. He'd be fine. Stu would see to it the boy'd be fine. Get some sleep, he said. But she couldn't.

"You two beat it. Eleven-thirty sharp!" Darlene boomed as they went out the door.

She sat for a minute with her warm coffee cup against her cheek. What would come of the boy? How would his insides be years after a fall like that? She wanted to meet his mother, but it was none of her business. Nonetheless, the boy had stirred feelings in her that had long been cold. She sat at the table until she noticed the coffee cup on her cheek had lost its warmth.

"Silly old bat," she said to herself as she pushed stiffly from the table. Walking to the kitchen, she said a quick prayer that the Lord's will be done on the lake today.

When Cory descended the slope that opened up to the lake, he couldn't believe his eyes. He stopped dead in his tracks and looked up at Stu to see if he wasn't imagining things. Stu had a big smile on his face.

Boats! Twenty, maybe thirty of them. All makes and models and colors. Tied up to the docks and then lashed to one another once dock space ran out. Men and women and a few dogs had come to Monument Bay from all over the lake to meet the boy who rowed in from the big lake—two days, alone—through the snow, to bring his dad back to the land to be rightfully laid to rest.

The word had gone out to a few of them, and the news had carried. They'd come to see and help the boy, this Cory. Standing on the docks were guides and resort owners who had feuded over fishing spots for years, who hadn't spoken since they couldn't remember, but now they were together, talking, waiting to help. It was a sight to behold.

Stu put his hand on the boy's shoulder and said in a low voice, "Looks like we got us some help. What do you say you go meet a few of the best fishermen to ever set foot in a boat?"

Cory smiled up at him and nodded.

Cory shook a mess of big hands and got plenty of claps on the back. He had no trouble remembering their names; that was something that had always come easily. He met Scratch, a young Indian guide with a fur hat that looked recently skinned. Ron, a big blond man, who once won a cabin and a boat in a 25-minute fist fight; three summers later he lost the boat and his wife in the rematch. Dancer, a small, hard tangle of a man who'd been on the lake since before electrical service. Legend had it that when he finally wired his place, not having the ground wire hooked up, he grabbed two overhead lines and danced on the end of a ladder until his sister kicked it out from under him. She saved his life, but the fall busted up his legs and back and left him curled. Peter, a businessman who'd owned half of a world-renowned tackle company, but said the hell with it, sold out, bought a houseboat and lived a recluse, fishing and selling oil paintings in the winter. A lot of the guys hadn't seen Peter up close for years, but there he was, smoking a cigarette on the dock, looking to meet the boy legend. Apple, an Indian who made hard cider that he traded with barge captains for gas and provisions. There was Chip, a half-breed woman who was as tough as any man on that dock, but looked ready to cry when she shook Cory's hand. Poose, the youngest of 14 children, was big and strong enough to wrestle bears, which he did at the county fair until the animal-rights people filmed a clip that made it onto national news. Poose and that muzzled bear were soon out of the carny business. There were others. Cory met each of them. And filed their names away so later he could get their addresses from Darlene to send thank yous.

"Give me your attention here," Stu barked through his cupped hands. "We got 'til noon to find the island where Cory left the motor. He's got a pretty good grip of the lake, so I'll let him explain the plan, if that's okay with you, Cory."

Cory nodded up at Stu. It got quiet on the docks. The boats squeaked against the bumpers. "My dad and I were running southeast out of Monument here," Cory pointed the direction. "I can't say how long we went, but it was no more than 30 minutes. We were in a resort boat like the one tied up there with a 25 on the back, so you can guess better than me how far we got. I'm thinking the best chance of finding the island is to backtrack the way I came home. That was by way of Bud and Lois Goetz's place where I slept the night." Cory paused to see if everyone was with him.

Stu interrupted, "Everyone knows the Goetz place, right?" Heads were nodding so Cory kept going.

"The Goetz's cabin was eight hours of hard rowing from the island. I was heading due west. If we drop down to Goetz's and head east, we should find it. The motor we sheared off is standing straight up off the west-facing shore. That'll be the sign we got the right island."

Cory stopped and looked up at Stu, who took over. "Let's everyone get on channel 19 so we can talk. My boat will lead to the Goetz cabin, then we'll go east, get in the general neighborhood, and spread out. Once you've checked an island, if there ain't no motor, mark it off on your map. If we haven't found it by 11, we'll meet at Ron's resort and compare maps so we're not all covering the same water. Any questions before we head out?"

There were none. Of course, these weren't talking men. They all stuck their hands in their pockets. Then it dawned on Cory he'd forgotten something. "One last thing," Cory hollered. Everyone stopped untying their boats and turned to listen. "The island isn't huge like Cochrane here. It's smallish, like the one the Goetz's place is on."

The group nodded as they climbed in their boats. Most had to do a fair amount of digging in their storage space to find lake maps. The maps they carried were in their heads. Plus, the smaller islands weren't officially named. As a result, everyone had put their own names to them, like Crooked Tree, or Three Sisters, or Dead Pelican.

The wind was beginning to kick up out of the west. The sun had warmed the October morning into the 50s, and it was only 9:00. As the boats motored out of Monument Bay, if you didn't know better, you'd have thought it was a fishing tournament. In unison, the bows reared up, sun careening off the windshields and top-decks, then planing out, heading south at full throttle. It was a sight to see. Stu's Boston Whaler out front with Cory standing next to him at the center console, hat pulled low, squinting ahead, regularly checking his compass, his map folded in front of him, tucked behind the windshield as he traced his finger along the boat's path. Cory knew where he was on the map by cross-referencing the islands on either side as they went.

"Is that the Goetz's island two up on the right?" Cory pointed, yelling over the engine. Stu looked at the boy and smiled. "Hell, boy. You should be driving." That was all the answer Cory needed.

The boats roared past the Goetz pier and turned due east. A few men pointed at the bed sheet tied in the pines. Cory told Stu it was his marker to get back in case he couldn't find the main channel. Stu winked at the boy. Cory winked back.

Stu calculated an average adult could maybe make five miles rowing all day, winding through these islands. Seeing this was Cory, he went seven and pulled back on the throttle. He looked out behind him at the 20 boats throttling down. Stu got on the radio. To his left was a well-known island called Ike. "Let's do it this way. A third of us will check the dozen islands to the north. A third of you split up the islands south of Windigo. The rest start picking your way back around the islands we just came through; the boy may have never got this far. Cross off islands as you go. And stay on the radio. Out."

Cory had thought about it last night in bed. Would he be scared when it got to this part of the trip? To be so close to where his dad died. He'd given it more thought again in the early morning as he stayed warm, pinned under layers of blankets. Now the moment was here. Squinting, he raised his hand to shield the sun. There were islands in every direction. He swallowed hard.

The group that was staying with Stu idled up and shut down their engines to talk. They agreed on how to split up the islands. "If anyone sees anything, give a shout on 19," Stu instructed. Then the Whaler roared off for the islands ahead of them.

Cory and Stu were checking the second island on their list when the radio crackled to life. "Dancer to Stu. Dancer to Stu. You there?"

Cory and Stu froze. They held each other's glances as the boat idled down. Stu took up the hand-held.

"Go ahead, Dancer."

"I think I've got your island. There's a Merc 25 stuck outta the water. That's got to be Cory's marker. I'm between Monkey Rocks reef and Pine Island. You know the spot?"

"I know it," Stu said. "Everyone else keep looking, 'til we're sure."

Cory and Stu raced over. Cory wondered if he'd recognize Boom Island. As they got closer, to his surprise, he did. He remembered the two tall dead pines off the face.

Stu could tell by the tears welling up in Cory's eyes that they'd found it. He clicked off the radio and idled down to give Cory time to compose himself. But instantly, it all came cascading. A few large tears rolled down his cheeks, then they came faster, then sobs that shook and convulsed him. Cory was fighting hard, but it was runaway. Finally it plain took the feet out from under him. Cory went to his knees and Stu turned the boat out to deeper water. He knelt next to the boy, taking him up in his arms. Cory was wound tight as wire. He sobbed fiercely for five minutes against Stu's chest. Dancer sat in his boat by Boom Island and tried not to listen to the boy over Stu's idling engine, but soon he too had tears sliding down his face.

Cory gathered himself. He took a deep shaky breath. "Didn't see that coming. Sorry. I'm ready to go in now."

Stu looked him in the eyes. Cory worked up a smile and said, "I know you weren't convinced it was a good idea coming out here, but it is. It's the right thing."

Stu gave him his best attempt at a smile, dragged his nose along his coat sleeve, trimmed up his motor, and they crept in to Boom Island, past the outboard standing sentry in the shallows.

"I'm okay now," Cory said, reading Stu's thoughts. "Go ahead. Call the other boats in. No sense in them looking any longer than they need to."

"Cory, if you want five minutes, I don't think that would hurt," Stu said.

"Call 'em in. That's the best way."

The keel of their boat drifted up on the riprap at the shoreline. Cory hopped out with the rope and tied up while Stu got busy on the radio. The boy walked along the shoreline looking down for a trace of the accident. His shadow eased over the rocks next to him. The sun warmed the back of his coat. His legs were no longer shaky. There was no trace that any human had ever been here before.

Inland about 40 feet, he found the patch of white pine seedlings that he'd been thrown into. They were each about 20 inches high, so similar in size and spacing it was as if they'd been planted by hand. But on an island so remote, that wasn't possible.

The stems of a few young seedlings were broken. The tips of the needles were beginning to brown. The rest of the green, resilient seedlings had sprung back up, leaving no trace of ever being disturbed. Cory touched the long needles, ran his palm over the top of them. "A soft place to land," he whispered.

Cory walked to the waterline where Stu had taken off his boots and socks, rolled up his jeans, and waded out to retrieve the broken motor. Stu's feet ached from the water's cold. The motor's cowling was jimmied up with a pen. Stu lifted off the hood and on top of the flywheel was the note Cory had left. He scanned it. *Had an accident ... straight west ... Monument Bay Resort ... He is dead ... please come looking.* Stu folded the note carefully and put it in his pocket. *What the boy faced alone here*, he thought. *What mark will it leave?* He ripped the motor out of the lake bottom. Damn it all, he thought, lugging it in.

Cory asked, "Did you find the note?"

"I did." Stu took it from his pocket.

"I'm not sure what I'd do with it," Cory said.

"Would you like me to keep it?" Stu and Cory watched each other.

"I think so," Cory said.

Stu pulled on his boots as Cory walked back to the patch of white pine.

"Stu?" Cory called. "Can you come have a look at this?"

"Be right there," he shouted back. The other boats were starting to roar into the area. They circled out in the deeper water off Boom Island and cut their motors. They rafted up and drifted as a loose bunch.

"What do ya got?" Stu bent down next to Cory.

Cory brushed his hand over the little pines. "What kind of seedlings are these?"

"Them's white pines, pretty sure," Stu said, putting his large hand on one. "Yep. You can tell because the needles are long and flat and come five to a bundle. See there?"

Cory examined the needles. "What would cause them to clump so tightly in a small spot like this? They look like somebody came in and planted them."

Stu looked over the small patch. It was a ten-by-ten-foot area. "My guess is they're all the same age. Seeing as there's no old growth around, probably a lightning-strike fire cleared the island. When the big white pines go up, the cones burst in the heat, sending the seeds away from the fire. That's nature's way. Fire soil is prime growing soil. I'd say these here all must have come from one tree."

"How old would these little ones be?" Cory asked.

"Hard to say for sure. The first years are the slowest growing. Maybe five years, maybe more. What's got you all interested in seedlings, Cory?"

"They broke my fall. The boat ran aground there at full speed," Cory pointed to the waterline. "I landed here. I was standing up to get to the motor's kill switch when we hit. Feel how soft these seedlings are. The needles aren't even sharp yet. Like yarn. I didn't get a scratch. If we had come up 15 feet to either side of where we did, I'd have come down on those rocks. Hard to figure."

Stu felt the softness of the young needles. He imagined the awful screech of the aluminum hull coming up on the rock and sand. How this beautiful young boy was shot out. The viciousness of that moment. But then to be caught, gently, in this patch of new growth.

"I don't claim to be on the best terms with the Lord, or claim to understand all about His ways," Stu said, "but I'd say He put down a soft place for you to fall. Looks like He saw to it that His plan got a chance to show itself. Something important is down the road for you, sure as I'm standing here."

Cory looked up. He saw in Stu's brown eyes the absolute conviction of a man too smart to ever be so sure of much. But he was sure. They looked long into each other's eyes and were so suddenly connected, a stream of silent communication traveled back and forth. The more time Stu spent with this boy, the more he knew he was in the presence of something ... he didn't have the word for it, maybe miraculous or divinely directed or something. Stu had seen plenty in his day, but when he looked at Cory, he sensed potential beyond his understanding.

Cory looked up at Stu and hugged him. Cory felt changed inside. He wasn't embracing Stu to be consoled, but the opposite. Cory knew this hug was the reassurance Stu needed. Stu nearly took the wind out of Cory with the completeness of his end of the hug.

"Stu," Cory wheezed. "A little too tight."

"Oh, damn. Sorry, boy. I lost track of things. You're not hurt, are you?"

"No, no," Cory said, trying not to gasp. "Think it'd be okay if I dig up two of these seedlings? Take them back with us?"

"Let me see what I've got for that," Stu said. He came back with a large plastic bailing bucket and a Buck knife. Cory dug carefully around the perimeter of two seedlings and got them out, roots, sandy dirt, and all. They packed them in the bucket, gave the pair a few handfuls of water, and set them in the boat.

"I'll just have a walk around the island before we go," Cory said.

"Sure," Stu replied, a little hesitantly, as the boy walked away. It was already 11:30. They were supposed to be back on the dock about now. He got Darlene on the radio and told her they'd found the island and would be home shortly. "Any sign of the Sheriff?" he asked.

"Nothing yet. I imagine that crew you're with will be hungry. I pulled some fish out of the freezer. Tell them there'll be lunch."

"I'm the luckiest man on the lake."

"And don't you forget it," Darlene shot back.

"No, I mean it, Darlene." Stu lowered his voice, "I love you."

"Stu, everything all right out there?" Darlene asked, concerned.

"We're great. We'll see you soon. Out."

"I'll be here. Out."

Darlene walked to the sink to run water on the frozen fillets. She remained there with her hand on the handle, thinking about the last time Stu had actually *said* he loved her. It wasn't in his constitution to be vocal about such matters. She knew he loved her, he showed her so dozens of times a day, just in little things he'd do. But to come out and say it. To literally broadcast it over the airwaves. It made her feel good, but worried. What happened out there to trigger something like that? Then she stopped worrying, and just felt good about it. "If I need to concern myself with anything presently," she said aloud, "it's whether we've got enough fish to fry for *that* pack. And I imagine the Sheriff will need filling, too, after his drive up."

Back on the island, Cory walked through the brush as the sun came slanting down from above. He walked to the shoreline opposite where the boats were gathered and looked out at the lake. "All these islands," he said to himself. "Fourteen thousand, Stu says … why here, Dad? How many did we go past? How long were you down, me just bouncing along?"

Cory sat on a large boulder. He took off his right boot, slid off his sock, and then laced his bare foot back in the boot. He put the sock in his pocket. Down on his haunches, he found a baseball-sized rock. He placed his left hand on the boulder; it was baked warm from the sun. Curling his fingers under his hand, leaving just his index finger exposed, he looked out at the forever blue of the water. He heard the waves lapping the shore. Rock in his right hand, lifted high above his head, he brought it down with a ugly thud, shattering the bone. A fine spray of blood speckled across the boulder. Cory closed his eyes and grit his teeth. He relished the pain. The only noise he made was to exhale 15 seconds later. He looked at the throbbing finger. The tip was gruesomely flattened, the nail was half peeled off. It pumped out a surprising spray of blood with every pulse. He went to the waterline and laid his hand in the lake, watching the blood flow out to mix with the clear water. The pain thumped in his head. The bleeding slowed in the ice-cold water. He took the sock from his pocket and wrapped it tightly around the finger. Then he headed back through the brush to the other side of the island where Stu was smoking his pipe.

Cory was sweating. He was pale. He smiled. "We better be getting back before Darlene has our hide."

Stu banged the pipe bowl clean on the tread of his boot. Then he took notice. "Cory, boy! What the hell happened there! You're bleeding."

Cory saw that the bleeding had soaked through the sock. "Ah, it's nothing. Klutzy mistake. I fell on the other side of the island and my finger got pinched between two rocks."

"Let's have a look at that thing. I've got a kit in the boat. We'll get a proper dressing on it."

"It's nothing," Cory said, looking away. "We'll get it all fixed up when we're back. We're late. Darlene—"

Stu took Cory's hand. "Cory, let's have a look at that now. It won't take but a minute."

Cory unwrapped the sock. "It looks worse than it is. It just got pinched."

Stu winced. "Good mother Mary! What a mess. That finger's broken, sure. How in the hell did . . . ?" Stu stopped at that moment. Realization flashed through his eyes. "Ah, Jesus, Cory."

Cory looked down. They stood in silence. "I'll get the kit," Stu said, walking fast to the boat.

Stu cleaned the finger with antiseptic, wrapped it with gauze, and splinted it straight. "It looks like the bleeding's mostly done, but you're going to need a doctor. Infection can get into the bone with a break like that."

"Really, it's not so bad." Cory glanced up, but he couldn't hold Stu's eyes. "Ready then?"

"Sure. Let's get on back. I radioed Darlene. She's making fish fry for all of us. The other guys are already on their way."

"Sounds good." Cory hesitated, "You're not mad, are you?"

Stu looked at the boy. "Accidents happen to all of us. Just be more careful next time, okay?"

Cory smiled. "I will."

"Promise me now. No more accidents, right?"

"I promise."

They pushed off from Boom Island with the mangled outboard, two pine seedlings, and one broken finger.

"You want to take her home?" Stu asked, after firing up the motor.

Cory's face lit up. He pulled out his map, checked his compass, and got behind the wheel. He pushed the pain out of his mind. He rejected it, and at the same time, welcomed it.

"Monument Bay, here we come." Cory cranked down the throttle, the bow rose, then quickly planed out. They thumped across the big blue chop under a brilliant sun, taking their caps off and tucking them in their jackets as the wind mussed their hair. Stu looked over at the boy captaining the Whaler, standing in the crisp, yellow sunshine of fall, and a thought shimmered through him clearly and certainly: despite everything, the day was a gift.

"Sit. Sit. Help yourself now before that fish goes cold!" Darlene shooed the fishermen closer to the tables. "C'mon now, before I put it out for the dogs." She tried without much progress. The men milled about tables in the lodge, scratching, each waiting for the other to pull out the first chair. "Cory," Darlene said, "show these men how to eat, would you, please?"

Cory took a place at the table and the other fishermen followed like ducks dropping into decoys. Each man removed his hat and set it on the floor next to his chair. Soon there was only the sound of chewing and slurping coffee.

Fishing guides eat like no other creature on earth. They lower their heads, square their shoulders, and shovel in food with one hand while keeping a firm hold on the coffee mug with the other. It's like that mug is going to walk off if they let go. Darlene circled the long harvest tables, refilling plates with steaming beer-battered fish on the first go-around, refilling coffee mugs on the second. She counted eight laps before hearing the first sounds of chairs pushing back from the table, followed by the low, pleasured groans of stuffed fishermen.

Cory stood up from his chair and addressed the group. "I'd like to say my thanks to you all for the help this morning. I appreciate you're busy with fall chores, and putting aside the time to help is no small thing. I'm thankful. I felt very safe and sure out there with all of you. I want you to know, especially Stu and Darlene, thanks to you I carry no fear of this lake. I'm even hoping to come back next summer. Stu has asked if I'd work as a dockhand and if he thinks I'm ready, maybe even do a little guiding. I hope if there's any favor that needs doing at your resorts next summer, I'll be the first you'll call. I'd come over on my off weekends. And I could use some hot fishing tips if you have any to spare." All the guides smiled and nodded. "So until next summer, then." Cory sat back down.

Very unexpectedly, Dancer started to clap. And then another. And another, and another until the whole room was applauding. Cory looked up shyly, a smudge of blush in each cheek, and couldn't help but smile. His half-moon dimples made an appearance. Stu, still clapping, caught something out of the corner of his eye. Standing, watching through the screened doorway of the lodge, was an eclipse of a man in a crisp sheriff's uniform. Next to him was a thinner man who wore a clerical collar under his unzipped buffalo plaid coat. And the priest, if Stu wasn't fooled by the light, had one hell of a black eye.

FUNERAL ON THE RIDGE.

Father Pat rose at six and stretched on the floor for his regular morning run. He always said his morning prayers while stretching. Get two birds with one stone, to his way of thinking. No sin in that. He had a friend in the seminary who said his morning thanks on the toilet. Kept the bible in there. He was one of the most spiritual men Father Pat had ever known. Claimed to be one of the most regular, too.

Father Pat told HomeSky he'd be at their farm by eight. The service would begin at nine on the ridge above the pasture. Father Pat also talked to Monsignor Kief who confirmed that the Sheriff would cooperate. They'd be out for the service in the morning, he and the coroner. After the funeral, they'd all drive up to Lake of the Woods to pick up Cory and his father's body. Then they'd return to Baudette to meet Cory's mother and sisters. If the Bradfords were willing, they'd all gather for supper at Monsignor Kief's so the two boys could meet. It was going to be a whirlwind day.

Father Pat pulled on a light windbreaker and an old Red Sox hat and walked out into pink-sky embrace. It was crisp as an orchard apple. Last night's frost curled what was left of the flower gardens along the rectory foundation. The fall weather reminded Pat so much of home in Boston. Except the quiet here. He loved the quiet here.

Pat touched his shoelaces, the muscles in his back loosening, but under protest. He was still feeling the effects of the rollover. He hopped into a stiff-legged jog down his gravel driveway that led to the two-lane highway. Take a right, go north to Canada. Take a left, go south to town. There's something comforting about having so few options.

Sometimes his running companion would include a deer, grouse, a loud pileated woodpecker, osprey, bald eagle, or a porcupine—the only animal slower than himself, he'd tell the porcupine that waddled across the blacktop, disappearing into the high ditch grass. Pat would run along the road's shoulder, on the soft pine straw, rarely seeing a vehicle at that early hour. Occasionally an over-the-road trucker would come blasting by to spoil the moment, but he'd be gone quickly and quiet would retake possession.

On either side of the highway, the rundown Rez houses and trailers tilted, discarded appliances rusting in the sideyard. The contrast to the pristine wooded backdrop was disheartening.

Father Pat thought about the day ahead. He mentally reviewed his words for the funeral, not so much a eulogy, because he didn't feel he knew enough about RiverHeart to properly eulogize him, but a few thoughts around the theme of moving forward: a subject he felt all too qualified to speak to.

What was responsible for the anxiety gnawing in his gut was the upcoming ride to Lake of the Woods with Sheriff Harris. The man was about as pleasant as soap in the eyes. He had a deep prejudice against the Rez, and he didn't take to outsiders. "People who came from off," as he called them. Pat, an outsider *on* the Rez, had two strikes against him. The thought of getting into the patrol car and driving up to the big lake with him made Pat's stomach clench. Pat even went so far as to call Monsignor Kief last night and invite him to come along. The Monsignor simply replied, "What would a blind priest do, navigate?" Then, in his trademark fashion, he gently got to the heart of the issue: "He won't bite, Pat. It will be good for you—both of you. You're good people who just need a little time to recognize that in the other. Nothing like tight quarters to bring out the best in folks, I've always said." Pat acknowledged he was probably right and thanked him for the advice before adding that the quarters weren't too confined for one more. They both chuckled at that.

Pat had been running for three miles. He turned around at the cranberry bogs, which were just harvested and skimmed with ice, and began his way back. He spun his Sox cap backward, Pat's way of announcing he was on the backstretch.

In Baudette, Sheriff Harris rose at five. He was an early riser; Amanda had always seen to that. "Early to bed, early to rise, eat your vegetables, tell no lies," she'd singsong. She had been such a positive force in his life.

He missed her. Especially on those cold mornings when he liked to put on the coffee and then creak back into bed and lay next to her and listen to her snore just ever so quietly. It was warm in that bed, and the aroma of coffee and the faint traces of Amanda's perfume would mix there, above the quilt. He'd gently wake her and tell her she'd been snoring and she'd say, "Thurgood, the good Lord has a place for husbands who lie to wives, and you don't need an overcoat there."

On this clear October 17th morning, the Sheriff felt especially cold. And old. Deputy's collar tinkled as they went to the front door, both shuffling out and over the threshold in a mighty effort. The Sheriff cinched up his bathrobe and stepped out onto the driveway to get the newspaper. No one could say why exactly, but in Baudette, newspapers were delivered to the driveway, spring through late fall. Once a snow stayed on the ground, the paper came to the doorstep and was delivered that way through the winter. Then, constituting one of the unofficial signs of spring's return, on one warm morning in April, the newspapers showed up on driveways again. It had been done this way for as long as anyone could remember.

The Sheriff tucked the paper under his arm. Deputy's brittle hips slowly angled across the driveway. The dog piddled with each step and was about done by the time he made the brown shrub, long ago killed with urine. "Ah, Deputy. Not on the driveway." Deputy sniffed the shrub and in a mighty effort, lifted his back leg two inches. Nothing. "The well's dry, old boy. Get on in now. Let's get us some breakfast." Deputy's ears went up at the word breakfast. The old lab sniffed at the frost on the leaves, then limped back up the driveway to the house. The Sheriff watched the old dog. *I'm gonna have to take him and a shovel out to the woods soon. Not looking forward to it, but he ain't going to make another snow.* "Let's get you some breakfast," he said. Deputy's tail swung to life and they walked into the warm house.

It was bacon-and-eggs Sunday for the Sheriff and his dog. Every Sunday, the menu never wavered: Thurgood would scramble six eggs and a half-pound of bacon. Deputy's cut was one scrambled egg and two slices of bacon on top of his kibble. The man and his dog ate noisily. The Sheriff finished off his portion with five cups of coffee and a cigarette from each pocket in his robe.

Most of the Sheriff's major-use clothing items held a pack of Camels in the right pocket and a pack of Vantage in the left. His robe was always stocked. His Sunday overcoat was another spot. As were the front breast pockets of his uniform shirt and his wool ice fishing overalls that still held a couple of forgotten packs from last New Year's Walleye Tournament sponsored by the Mutineer's Jug.

Sheriff Harris pushed away from the small kitchen table and went to the bedroom. There, bagged in back of the closet, was his dress uniform. It was no different from the three uniforms he wore through the week, except this one was taken out only on special occasions and dry-cleaned after each use. Best Thurgood could remember, the dress uniform had been dry-cleaned four times. After Amanda's funeral. After Charles Kuralt and his crew filmed the town for a nightly news special. After Doc Holloway, the Baudette dentist and his old duck hunting partner, passed. And after he posed for the front page newspaper photo with the wrestling coach, whose life he saved by pulling him from a burning outhouse.

As the story goes, the coach's wife had repeatedly, publicly threatened to "burn down that embarrassing, disgraceful old shithouse" if the coach didn't have it hauled away. But the outhouse had been in the family for three generations. It had sentimental value. The coach liked to say it ain't a family bathroom, it's a family heirloom. He ignored his wife's threats as idle. And on those occasions when the weather and his mood aligned, the coach would stroll out, comb through the stack of hunting magazines dating back 40 years, pick out a favorite, and have a lengthy sit-down. His wife would come out and beat on the door with an old stick so he couldn't have any peace. It was pretty much a standoff, the both of them being stubborn Lutherans.

One evening, she nailed the outhouse door shut so no one could get in. In the garage, she got a jerrican of gasoline, doused the base of the outhouse and put a match to it. The coach thought the pounding was nothing more than the usual harassment, so he quietly ignored it until smoke began filling the outhouse. He quickly tried the door, which wouldn't budge. The coach started screaming a blue streak, which set his wife to screaming because she thought the outhouse was empty. Lucky for them, Sheriff Harris was out walking the neighborhood. He put a crowbar to the door and got the coach and most of his magazine collection out with no time to spare. The next day the coach in his wrestling sweats and cap, his wife in her Sunday best, and the Sheriff in his dress uniform were photographed next to the ash heap. The 300-word story in the local paper told all under the banner headline: Outhouse Turns To Smokehouse!

Sheriff Harris pulled on the dress uniform and smoothed it down along his immense chest and stomach, previewing it in the mirror. He cursed the wrestling coach under his breath because he thought he detected the faint odor of smoke on the uniform. Actually, he had one thing right: the odor of smoke. But on account of the Sheriff's prodigious smoking habit, every item of clothing in the house smelled like that.

His pinned on his brown nametag, T. Harris, and took a further look at himself in the mirror. He was not impressed. At six foot six, he was closing in on 285 pounds. It had been an eternity since he'd seen the buckle of his holster belt. His hair was still mostly brown, but at age 48, he felt closer to 68. The veins in his nose and the splotchy red hue to his cheeks made him appear to be more of a drinker than he actually was.

He studied his mangled left hand. The field surgeon in Korea had done all he could, but that wasn't saying much. The tip of his big toe was sewn on above the knuckle where the thumb had been severed. His index finger was intact. He had a prosthesis that did an adequate job of filling in the next two missing fingers, and his pinky was stout from constant use. The artificial fingers looked real enough from a distance, and mostly kept strangers from staring.

Sheriff Harris phoned the coroner and told him to be at city hall at 8:30 sharp. The coroner had to transport the body out to the Blackholm farm before driving up to Lake of the Woods. He let it be known that he wasn't happy about spending his Sunday like this. The Sheriff simply said he heard the service at Bonaducci's Grocery was particularly good, and maybe the coroner could put his wife on the phone so they could trade notes. End of bellyaching.

With some time to kill, the Sheriff and Deputy took a walk around the block. It was a wonderful fall morning. The snap in the air shook some of the melancholy out of the Sheriff's disposition. Deputy stayed on heel without command. He would occasionally stop and consider a chase when he saw a squirrel making for a tree. A younger Deputy would have looked up for permission, waiting on one small forward movement of the Sheriff's hand before bolting after it. But these days, Deputy didn't bother. He'd just stop for a moment, seem to contemplate the futility of the act, and then continue his arthritic shuffle at his master's heel.

HomeSky was awakened by Joseph sitting on the edge of her bed. She sat bolt upright. "What's wrong!" She was breathless.

Joseph smiled. "'Morning, Mom. Just bringing you some coffee."

"You scared me half to death. Don't be doing that to your poor old mother."

HomeSky didn't look her 33 years, except, on close inspection, around her eyes. Those small lines told of laughter and hardship. She had Joseph at age 20 and planned for a large family. But there were complications during delivery that led to a hysterectomy. The elderly surgeon, who was white and a long-time area resident, didn't consider the removal a loss of any magnitude. There were enough unclean Indians running around like jackrabbits already.

A woman never fully recovers from such a surgery. HomeSky always carried a knot of sorrow crossed with guilt for not filling the farmhouse with children. She often dreamt of a sunny driveway lined with wild daisies, where her children, each a head taller than the next, raced down the gravel.

She took a sip of the coffee and looked at her dear Joseph. "I guess it's not all bad, you taking up coffee. Now I won't have to suffer the cold floor to make it myself." She smiled at her boy. She so loved him, it frightened her. She couldn't live without him. It was unimaginable without her husband, but that loss left her more bound to Joseph.

"I suppose you're too big now to give your mother a hug in the morning?"

"Not a chance," Joseph said scooting over and wrapping up his mother.

"Geget inga-izhichige?" HomeSky asked.

"Yeah, I'm sure," Joseph said, squeezing her tighter.

She enjoyed the moment, but worry seeped in. "What time is it?"

"It's okay, Mom. You've got plenty of time."

"No. I mean, how long have you been awake? Did you have trouble sleeping? I hope you slept." She squinted at the alarm clock on the bureau. "It's six o'clock, Joseph. How long have you been up?"

"Mom, relax. I've been getting up with Dad at five for over a year now. That's when I always wake up. I like getting up early."

"Did you sleep okay, honey?" she asked.

"I slept better than okay."

She took a long look at him. Studying around his eyes, examining him, quietly.

"BWAAA!" he blurted out, to scare her. He couldn't resist the opportunity.

She jumped. A splash of coffee spilled on the bedspread. "Joseph Blackholm! You'll turn my hair white as a snowdrift!"

"I'd still love you. White hair or not." He gave her his trademark, full-mouth smile and dabbed up the coffee with an untucked shirttail.

"Joseph, use a towel!"

"Too late." He stood. "I've got to get some stuff done outside. I'll be in by eight when Father Pat gets here. You drink your coffee. What's left of it."

"Breakfast at eight sharp. Don't keep me waiting," HomeSky said, watching her boy move lithely through the doorway. Her husband had moved fluidly, too. She sat holding her warm coffee cup, trying to remember how her husband moved, trying to see him. She felt panic rising in her chest. She felt out of place, unsure. She couldn't recall his face—what did he sound like?—how could she forget so soon?—and then, a comforting presence was in the room. She calmed. She could imagine him perfectly. She remembered his smell, the hardness of his body, his eyelashes, the calluses her finger would trace on the palms of his hands. She savored the detail of him, feeling strength and confidence fill her where anxiety had been.

"Thank you, dear one," she said aloud. "I'm still going to need you from time to time."

HomeSky made the bed. The floor was cold from the October night. She pulled open the shades to a clear sky. There will be sunshine, as it should be, she thought. The service deserved the witness of warm sunlight.

In the bathroom, she hung her nightclothes on a hook as the little shower spritzed out a crooked stream of hot irony water hardly substantial enough to soak through her hair. Slowly, the shower stall warmed and she felt her body relax and soften. Usually she wouldn't linger because there was only so much hot water for the three of them, but today she allowed herself the luxury of an extra minute. She listened to her breathing as the soapy water rinsed down her legs. She felt herself getting stronger, happier. She felt herself smile. She reached for the water taps and twisted them tightly, ready to face the day that would see her bury the only man she ever gave herself to.

Joseph was out in the barn checking the larger shovel blade he'd put on the tractor. The frost had driven down a good four inches. He would need the big blade to break the earth. He grabbed a long-handled spade to take up to the ridge with him.

Backing out of the garage, Joseph swung the tractor toward the front field. The morning sun was bright and low. Joseph pulled his collar up and his cap down as he slowly bounced through the plowed-under cornfield that led to the pasture. Bowling-ball-sized clods of frozen black dirt broke under the tires. It was bumpy going, less so when he got to the pasture. Then he went up the slow rise, cresting the ridge with the grove of ironwood and oak trees that overlooked the entire farmstead. This was the high spot of their land.

There was a place there, of tall prairie grass, next to the sliver of woods, that stood long-protected from the prevailing westerlies. His father had left this place untouched by human tool. Here they would sit and eat lunch or watch the storm come in or clean birds they'd shot. This place was where Joseph knew he should cut the grave. It wasn't to be a sad place. It was a place of strength, of protection, of peace, of long views. A place that reminded Joseph to live boldly today because tomorrow is just a superstition. Joseph didn't find this threatening; he and his father lived fearlessly of tomorrow's uncertainties. Do not count on tomorrow. Do not save for tomorrow. Do not live for tomorrow. Never barter with today. Today is the gift. Life is there, under your nose, and few ever recognize it until it's too late. But not Joseph. Thanks to his father, he revered the present.

As Joseph's tractor moved along the tree ridge, the sun baked the back of his coat. He shut his eyes and felt the ground bump through his body, swaying him in the seat as the steering wheel played back and forth in his hands. The stone braided in his hair tapped behind his ear, confirming.

He was in the one place, for as far as the eye could see in all directions, where there was good shelter from the wind. This ridge humped out of the vast flatness, creating a high spot with its grove of trees. Just off the lee side of the tree line, the bluff dipped, cupping a half-acre of wild grassy flats. Here the wind lay down to catch its breath. Here napped the westerlies before gathering strength and galloping down the rise, into the pasture, into the flatness, to more flatness, and more. Anyone who came to this high spot and listened to the wind cascade through the leaves of the trees above couldn't help but be overcome by peace. This was where Joseph's father would lie. This halcyon place. The native grass would grow over him come spring. The wind would stop here for a short rest, and then move on, carrying nothing on its back. Light. Strong. And always there to blow your hat off when you're too serious.

Joseph poised the iron tractor blade over the earth that had never once been cut by man's machines. The ground was concrete-frozen, but in time, Joseph broke through the frostline to the soft earth. The rest would be rightfully dug by hand.

Afterward, Joseph stood off in the adjacent grass and looked across the vista at the smoke spiraling from the farmhouse chimney. The songbirds had migrated, but a few chickadees and nuthatches flitted loudly in the branches above. The sun was warm, and the sparkling white frost began to vanish, the grass greening by the second. Joseph approached the grave. He cast a long morning shadow across the gaping rectangle. Joseph considered the moment. The earth torn open where his father would be laid, Joseph's shadow filling over it, the next bridge. To feel a purpose in life. To know a path, shining. To understand how you fit and proudly make your way. To leave something behind that is lasting not because it is forever, but because it connects to something honest and unafraid. This sense of himself gave Joseph such hope and strength. He smiled at the sky and knew what few people ever know: he was important. He knew he was vital to what came before and what would come after. So many people are looking to start over. Nothing could have been further from Joseph's aspirations. He was in love with his part of something longstanding. He was as calm as this windless place.

Joseph finished squaring off the grave with the long-handled spade. It was unusually warm, surrounded on four sides by dirt; the earth's temperature exceeded the air's.

He stood in his father's grave, closed his eyes, and lowered his head.

His watch read five of eight when he climbed back on the tractor, fired it up, coaxed it into gear, and drove to the trees, leaving it tucked out of sight. Joseph could run over the frozen fields to the farmhouse much faster than the tractor could take him. That, and he needed to run. He tucked his hat into his coat pocket and ran down the bluff, into the knobby pasture, through the plowed field to the farmyard. He went boldly, not wildly, so as not to turn an ankle in a varmint hole. Wind in his face, black hair streaming in the sunshine, the stone behind his ear, he was happy to be alive. This was his father's only significant request of him.

On the Rez, Father Pat stepped out of the shower noticing the water smelled particularly of iron. He felt needed. His morning six-miler had cleared the cobwebs, and he was ready for his biggest day yet in his new parish. More accurately, in his extended parish.

He looked at the long underwear laid out with his clothes for the day, but decided against it. He dressed in the traditional black slacks, black shirt and white clerical collar. With his wide shoulders and trim waist, he cut a memorable figure in the mirror.

Pat's hair was sandy brown, thinning. He had cutting blue eyes, a clean jawline, and just enough crook to his nose to indicate an interesting past. But the feature few saw immediately, but no one forgot, were the eyelashes on Father Pat's right eye: they'd gone completely white. The left eyelashes were dark, but the right were long and curled and white as winter's frost. It was a different kind of scar, one Pat preferred to forget.

Turning to leave the bathroom, he caught a glimpse of his profile. Undoubtedly, he was a handsome man. It troubled him that he cared about such superficialities. Pat began to chew a fingernail. He pulled it away, examining the row of fingernails that were the barometer of his emotional condition. His nails were chewed down closely to the fingers, but not to the point of bleeding, so he was doing pretty well. Only once in his adult life could he remember enough inner serenity to actually need a fingernail trimmer: the afternoon he sat on his single bed before graduation ceremonies from the seminary 14 years ago. The image he caught of himself in the mirror that day, dressed in his official undervestments, on the bed's edge, trimming his nails over the wastebasket—this priestly image was forever fastened to his memory. He would recollect it in times of ill temper or depression to even his keel.

Father Pat walked to the large saltwater aquarium in the living room where he kept his fish. He enjoyed the peacefulness of the tropicals, how they moved, bright-swimming jewels. He tapped the top of the tank and they rose to the flakes of food. The aerator bubbled with calming regularity. Absentmindedly reaching for the phone, he sat with the receiver in his hand watching the fish until the phone began to signal it was off the hook. He dialed Monsignor Kief.

"Good morning." The Monsignor answered his phone on the third ring.

"Frank, it's Pat."

"Good morning, my friend. Have we another car wreck to report?" Monsignor Kief laughed sufficiently for both of them.

"Not today. I've been staying between the shoulders. Say, I was calling for two reasons. One, I trust I'll see you at the Blackholm farm at nine?"

"You surely will. I just heard from the Sheriff and we're set like cement."

"Fine. The other thing, I went along with your idea and invited the Blackholm family to your residence for supper tonight. HomeSky thinks it's important to get the boys together. Joseph is especially excited. But I told them I still have to ask Cory's mother. Hopefully, she'll agree it's important they meet and have a chance to talk."

"I do hope so. But the stress of these days may leave her wanting to hold her family tightly together. Not see anyone. We have to be prepared for that."

"I suppose you're right," Father Pat said in a resigned note. "But if she does say yes, we're on for your place, right?" Father Pat allowed his spirits to lift again.

Monsignor Kief couldn't resist a chance for a little mischief. "Well, Pat, I tell you what. I need you to get on the phone with my housekeeper and see if you can talk her into it. She says her job is to cook for one. She's holding a hard line. Could you help me? Should I put her on?"

There was an extended silence on the phone. "Frank. I'm not going to fall for any of your shenanigans. I'll take that as a 'Yes, Pat, we're good to go.'"

"Ah, you're no fun," Frank said. "Nobody likes a fast learner."

"Good. I'm sure you've passed along that HomeSky and Joseph are strict vegetarians?"

"Vegetarians!" Monsignor Kief gasped, "We're planning a pot roast, I'm quite sure. I can smell the broth simmering—"

"Gotcha!" Father Pat said into the receiver. "That'll teach you to pick on the new guy."

"Touché, for now, my boy. But in the famous words of MacArthur, I shall return." Monsignor Kief hung up the phone smiling. He liked this young priest. He felt good about going out on a limb and recommending him despite his checkered past. During the interview process, the Monsignor was asked to review a few letters written by Father Pat's ex-superiors. In Frank's considered opinion, Pat just had a run of tough luck. He sent for Father Pat's complete file and it seemed like tough luck was a close companion indeed. His mother left when Pat was a teenager, and his father didn't appear to make much time for him based on the volume of juvenile offenses. They moved often. Young Patrick was expelled from high school and appeared headed down his father's path until, like a bolt out of the blue, at age 18, he showed up on the steps of the seminary saying he had been called by God. He turned out to be a natural leader and a hard worker. Alcohol and quick temper were the words underscored in his file.

In the 14 years since graduating the seminary near the top of his class, Father Pat had been, frankly, somewhat of a bust as a priest. His passion to be a positive force and induce change in the community came out more like being argumentative, short-tempered, and outspoken. When he ran into failure, which was common in the business of saving souls, he took it extremely personally. Alcohol was his balm. Mostly he drank quietly, with melancholy, behind the heavy closed door of the rectory. But his inclination for alcohol occasionally found its way into public life. There was a particularly ugly incident at a church softball game where the heat, the beer, and Pat's short temper got the better of him. He invited a loudmouthed third baseman from a rival parish to step off the diamond after repeated unsportsmanlike play. The third baseman readily agreed and was promptly taken to the hospital with a broken jaw and multiple facial lacerations. Father Pat was better with his fists than anyone imagined a priest had cause to be.

But what most tarnished Pat's record, and left him a different, more troubled person was the suicide. There was a teenage boy in Boston whom Pat had befriended. They'd become close, spending hours shooting baskets in the rectory driveway where they'd put up a hoop and backboard. The boy confided in Pat that he'd gotten his girlfriend pregnant and they were going to a clinic for an abortion the following weekend. Father Pat and the teenager had an earlier agreement that what was said between them stayed that way. It was their bond. But Pat was deeply anguished because this decision involved another life. He got the boy's and girl's parents together for an intervention. Somehow, the young couple caught wind of it, and disappeared before the meeting could come together. Everyone thought they ran away. They hadn't. The boy and his girlfriend drove to the empty stall of the rectory garage, pulled the door down behind them, and left the motor running. The couple and the unborn child died of asphyxiation. The following day one newspaper printed the spectacular front-page headline: Suicide Priest? Although the story went on to exonerate Pat, the name stuck like a plague. Seemingly everywhere he went, that moniker would come whispering out of the woodwork and undo all the good that he'd done.

Monsignor Kief sat in his kitchen contemplating Pat's trial of faith that day, and many times from then on. The Monsignor himself had faced down a mighty test, the loss of his eyesight to a degenerative retinal disease, but had come out of it, slowly, stronger. But what this young priest must have endured! In the six years and four parishes since the suicide, his luck didn't seem much improved. So when the archbishop asked Monsignor Kief if he wanted to give Father Pat a go up on the Rez, he said, enthusiastically, yes. And when asked a second and a third time if the Monsignor was sure—had he read the *whole* file?—he got angry at the inference. "Yes, for the third time I have read his file; it was transposed into braille and I think the Blind Priest and the Suicide Priest are going to get along just fine." He then hung up.

As Father Pat pulled up to the Blackholm farmhouse, he looked at his watch. It was 7:45. He stepped out of the car into the morning air. A long string of geese noisily made their way south. As they moved away, the sound of the tractor working just over the ridge filled in. Joseph, he thought. Sweet boy. Pat shuddered thinking what it would be like to cut your father's grave. Certainly he'd fantasized about such an act as a youth smoking cigarettes in the cemetery, but to do it out of *love*, my God. Perhaps, though, bad as it was, with it came a sense of closure, a transference from dependent to adult. Father Pat wished he were up there, but knew Joseph would be okay. If Pat were any judge of character, in fact, this boy was going to be much more than okay.

The door of the farmhouse swung open. "Good morning," HomeSky said, stepping out onto the cold sun-streaked porch.

"Good morning. How are you?" Father Pat turned toward her. She put her hand over her eyes, shielding the sun, looking up at the ridge.

She spoke, scanning the bluff. "Joseph shouldn't be but a few more minutes. He … he's getting things ready." HomeSky dropped her hand and looked at the priest. He, too, watched the ridge, listening to the distant tractor. Father Pat looked strong in his black slacks and buffalo plaid jacket, the wind mussing his hair, the sun on his face, the eye purpled and blackening, giving him a rugged edge. "Can I get you coffee? How's that eye of yours? It looks sore."

"It's embarrassing. As for the coffee, yes, please. So, how are you today?" he repeated.

"I'm okay," she said, nodding her head to help convince herself. "It's quite a day we've been given," she said, squinting into the sunlight.

"Your husband must be well connected with my Boss," Pat watched for her reaction as he came up the porch steps.

"My husband wasn't a religious man. Not in the conventional sense."

They sat in the small kitchen of the farmhouse, warmed from the oven. Something smelled delicious. Was it potatoes cooking?

Ham? Father Pat felt the effects of the morning run; he realized just how famished his body was.

"How about Joseph?" Father Pat asked. "Is he a practicing Catholic?"

"Yes and no," HomeSky answered. "He's been baptized. He goes to church with me maybe once a month. But in his day-to-day living, he's a shining example of Christianity. Considerate, unselfish, kind. His father instilled a deep spirituality in him, a great love for the outdoors and life. I would say Joseph's religion is a little less structured than mine, but more structured than his father's. Does that make sense?" HomeSky looked intently at Father Pat. She hoped he wasn't disappointed.

"I understand completely. We all have to find our own nook in the hand of God. There is no one right way."

HomeSky smiled. "I'm frankly surprised to hear you talk so liberally. Most of the priests I've encountered were by-the-book fire-and-brimstoners."

Father Pat leaned back in the old wooden ladder-backed chair and shook his head. "There is far too much rigidity and intolerance in our Church. It drives people away. Can you imagine anything more ironic? The ultimate symbol of community erecting barriers. It makes me wonder sometimes."

HomeSky looked at the priest, sensing his struggle. He had lowered his mask for a moment. Just then the front door banged open. Joseph stood out of breath at the threshold.

"Joseph! What is it?" HomeSky stepped quickly toward her son.

"Mom, please, I'm fine. I ran in from the ridge. That old bucket of bolts will shake itself apart if I go too fast across the fields. Hey, Father. Hope I didn't hold breakfast up too long. What are we having, Mom? Smells great!" The boy's undaunted spirit was just what the room needed.

"Sorry, you're too late," Pat said. "There just wasn't enough for three. It was delicious."

Joseph sparked at the chance to kid around. "That's nothing. Mom forgets to cook dinner all the time. Puts me to bed with two crackers. I'm used to missing at least a meal a day."

HomeSky wasn't going to stand by and just take it. "Oh, I'm sorry," she said very sincerely. "I didn't realize you two were planning on breakfast. I just made enough for myself. But I think there's some cornmeal left in the pantry and some bacon drippings in a can over the sink." Silence ensued.

Joseph and Father Pat looked at each other, wondering. She didn't mean it? She couldn't.

Joseph went over and opened the squeaky oven door. He turned around smiling. "Looks like a big omelet, bacon, and toast. You didn't fool me," he said, unconvincingly.

HomeSky smiled. "You go wash up, and Father Pat will lead us in grace."

They all gathered on the ridge for the nine a.m. service. HomeSky felt light-headed each time she looked at the gaping hole in the earth. She focused instead on Father Pat. There were a dozen men and women from the Rez, more than HomeSky anticipated. Sheriff Harris fidgeted uncomfortably in the background, watching the ribbon of highway half a mile away, worried that a nosy local might stop and inquire about the goings-on. But there were few drivers, and those there were, noticed little. Unblinking eyes, vacant as the landscape. Not thinking. Not looking. Not wondering. Driving. Point A to point B. Not so much as looking up to acknowledge the brilliance of the day.

Father Pat stood below the last amber and yellow leaves left on the oaks. Mixed in, the small, gnarled ironwood trees were stripped bare. Severe and angular, they scratched at the high-blue sky. Joseph, next to HomeSky, held her hand. He looked considerably older in a necktie and coat. Monsignor Kief had taken up a spot in the back, but Father Pat asked him if he would join him graveside. Pat addressed the small group in a strong, compassionate voice.

"I'd like to say a few words about RiverHeart on behalf of his loving family. I never had the honor of meeting him, but HomeSky and Joseph have given me their thoughts; also I've talked with some of you.

"It's obvious, RiverHeart was a man of unusual gifts. He believed there was no stronger bond than blood, and no closer blood than family. He came from noble warrior heritage, his great-grandfather's father riding alongside Hole-in-the-Day.

"The name RiverHeart was bestowed on him soon after his parents witnessed his indomitable spirit. If RiverHeart saw something that interested him, he'd kick until he was put down. He'd crawl through briars to reach it.

"As you all know, much the same can be said for his adult life. Where there were rocks, he went over them; where there was a forest, he bent around it. His heart, like a river, was undeterred by obstacles, stirring powerfully, yet on the surface, he was peaceful.

"When a man is taken at a young age, it makes us all, myself included, question the plan of the Creator. I don't know much. I don't know as much as many of you, and I certainly don't know as much as RiverHeart did, but this much I know." Father Pat looked into the faces of the gathering. "There is a plan for each of us and in due time it will make itself known in such shimmering simplicity, we will laugh at the earlier mysteries that confounded us. It is for us to go forward, proudly, honorably from here, from what is a terribly sad moment, and live the gift of that plan joyfully. To go over the rocks and bend around the obstacles. We will have the spirit of RiverHeart guiding us, at times so profoundly, we will actually *feel* his presence."

HomeSky and Joseph broke out in goose bumps because each of them had felt RiverHeart at their elbows. How did Father Pat know this? Had he, too, felt him?

"Today reminds us that the great gift of life is given with only one caveat: it can be taken back at any moment. RiverHeart, more than most, knew this and lived each day edge to edge, getting the most from it. Don't fill your days with such planning and worrying that you neglect to live them.

"Remember also that this young family will occasionally need your help. Do not be too distant to offer, or too proud to accept a nearby hand. A mother and a boy are whole, but they are incomplete. Call on them as friends."

Pat then unfolded the tributes written by Joseph and HomeSky. As the wind blew at the corners of the paper, he read in a strong voice, trying to let not a word crack or be lost in the emotion of the message.

"Lastly, I ask the Creator to bring peace to all here on this beautiful, living, fall morning. Please, Lord, along with the wind that frequents this farm, bring some quieter times, some happier times, some carefree times, some abundant times. Bring new strength to this foundation of old strength. Amen and God bless you all."

The small gathering shifted on their feet.

Father Pat continued. "There will be coffee and rolls back at the house. Please come and join us." The small crowd milled about the grave, dropping in feathers. No one was quite able to make the first move toward the farmhouse. HomeSky, sensing this, broke and began walking, soon joined by the other women. Father Pat was left shaking hands with some of the guests while Monsignor Kief walked along the high edge of the ridge with Joseph, his hand on the boy's shoulder to guide him.

"Tell me what you see," the Monsignor said. "The sun tells me we're facing east."

"Looking this way, you see the quiet pasture. The front pasture we just call the front pasture, but the back pasture we've always called the quiet pasture because the wind's usually out of the northwest. This bluff shelters it. There's a creek dividing the pastures that runs high in the spring. When Dad was my age, he and my grandpa floated logs down it to carve the border totems that mark our land. It's quiet enough by the creek to hear the brook trout rise to slurp whatever insects are hatching. The pasture is mostly blue stem, wild grass, and sorghum volunteers. We cut it every other fall and sell the seed. What's up here goes untouched by blade. This time of year it's not much to look at, but come the spring wild-flowers, you've got every color in a paint store."

Joseph continued. "Now, facing this way you're—"

"South," the Monsignor interrupted.

"South it is. The creek runs north-south, the length of our property, goes under the highway, and cuts through the state forest opposite the road. There's a little bridge on the highway, where the creek runs under, that iced up the night of the snow when Father Pat put your car in the ditch. We pull a half-dozen cars out of that ditch every year. Dad was killed on the road there, right where the gravel intersects the blacktop. I'll carve a totem for that spot that sings my dad's song up to the sky."

"Very nice. Very nice tribute," Monsignor Kief said quietly.

"Then this way is west. Over the ridge, down the bluff there's the front pasture, then the plowed corn and bean fields, then there's the house. Off to the side is a low spot ringed by cattails—there's a duck pond back there. We take a few mallards and teal out of that spot in early fall; late season, a big northern goose or two. Once I shot a huge Canadian that sailed on me and landed buried in the snow, five feet from the front door. It was the day before Thanksgiving. Mom walked out in her boots, dug around in the hole and found it stone dead. Had it with stuffing and sweet potatoes the very next day. It's great having that pond. Come winter, I keep it scraped for skating. I skate out there almost every day. Hockey's my sport."

Monsignor Kief interrupted. "Your dad was quite a basketball player in high school, did you know that?"

"Yeah. Mom showed me some old clippings from newspapers. He had really short hair. His hair was always long since I can remember. I couldn't stop laughing at the pictures. Dad with a flat crew cut." Joseph put his hands up by his head to emphasize the flatness of his father's hair, looked at Monsignor Kief, and realized the futility of the gesture. "Did you see him play? I mean, you being blind now, were you blind then, too? When my dad played in high school?"

"I was blind, but yes, I would say I saw him play, in my own way. As the superintendent of the school back then, I got to sit right on the floor with the coach and the bench players. I never missed a game, home or away. Your father was an outstanding, outstanding person to whom God gifted many talents, not the least of which was a deft touch from the perimeter."

"I'd have given anything to see him play." Joseph got quiet.

"Tell me," the Monsignor asked after a moment, "what's to the north?"

"Canada," Joseph said without missing a beat.

Monsignor Kief laughed, "Canada, sure enough!" The laughter escalated and soon the two of them were going pretty good. It was a much-needed release. Father Pat walked over to them as the last guests made their way down toward the house.

"And what's so funny over here?"

"Oh, nothing," Monsignor Kief answered. "I'm just beginning to learn that Joseph has his father's sense of humor."

Father Pat looked at the two of them and shrugged his shoulders. "I've got the keys to the pickup. What do you say we go to the house?" The three of them, side-by-side, walked toward the truck. Monsignor Kief had his hands on their shoulders. The sunshine dropped down warm on them.

"I have to fill the grave," Joseph said flatly.

"Of course," Pat said. "We'll wait. We'll all go down together."

Joseph removed his suit coat, folded it, and set it neatly on a rock. He climbed onto the tractor and fired up the ignition. It made for a striking picture, Joseph in his dark pressed pants and crisp white shirt, sitting high in the iron seat, wind blowing his tie back, set against the hard blue sky. He ran the tractor up to the mound of earth at the foot of the grave, lowered the shovel, and waited. Father Pat could see the boy had closed his eyes, tears squeezing out, running down his cheeks as the tractor rumbled in neutral. Joseph's lips moved as he talked to himself. After a moment, he looked forward, found the shifter with his right hand and rammed it into gear. The engine roared to life as he began pushing the dirt into the hole. The first shovelful made ugly audible thuds raining down on the casket. Father Pat grit his teeth and looked away. He noticed Monsignor Kief was crying. He put an arm around the old priest's shoulders, and rubbed his back. "Hell of a day, if you don't mind me saying."

Frank Kief wiped a tear away and shook his head. "Some days really test you."

GOING NORTH FOR CORY.

When Joseph, Monsignor Kief, and Father Pat pulled up to the farmhouse in the pickup, Sheriff Harris was half sitting, half leaning on the hood of his brown and maroon cruiser. Deputy lay on the ground in the sun, sleeping, next to a few fresh cigarette butts.

"I'll be with you in a minute," Father Pat said to the other two. The Monsignor put his hand on Joseph's shoulder and they went into the farmhouse to join the small group. Pat hooked over to the patrol car.

"Don't mean to rush you, Reverend," the Sheriff said sarcastically, looking down at the Vantage he was lighting. "You've got important work here and all, but let me remind you we're due up at the big lake in little over an hour. It's all of that and then some from here." He lit his cigarette, cupping it from the wind.

Father Pat stepped in close to the Sheriff. Their shoe tips were almost touching. His temper rising, he continued glaring until the

Sheriff finally glanced up from his lighter to meet the jolt of Pat's blue eyes. "God bless you, Sheriff," he said. "Now pick up those damn cigarette butts." He walked slowly up to the farmhouse.

Inside, HomeSky was busy with the guests. Mingling with his cup of coffee and donut, Father Pat was repeatedly complimented for his words on the ridge. Eventually he made his way over to Monsignor Kief.

"Frank, I'll be on my way to get the Bradford boy now. I hope to see you around six for supper. I'll call if there are any snags."

"Sounds like a plan. And say, excellent job up there today. Just excellent." The Monsignor found Pat's hands and squeezed them.

"Thank you for saying so. It means a lot hearing it from you."

"Don't worry about anything back here. HomeSky, Joseph, and I will keep things moving. Good luck with the boy … Cory, is it?"

"Yes."

Frank then leaned in and whispered. "And don't you fret about the Sheriff. He's full of prunes, mostly. Some day, I'll tell you the whole story and all of it will make sense. Meanwhile, just remember, there is no greater wisdom than kindness."

Father Pat thought about that for a second. "I'll do my best," was all he could manage.

Pat made his way through the crowd toward HomeSky, feeling conflicted for disliking the Sheriff as he did. What did Frank mean? What secrets did the Sheriff harbor that excused such caustic, uncompassionate behavior?

"You look a little lost," HomeSky said with a tenuous smile.

"Oh," Pat said. "Lost in thought, I guess. How are you?"

Much to his surprise, not to mention that of those around them, HomeSky gave Father Pat a long, strong hug. "Much, much better," she said into his shoulder. "Thank you for all you've done. You've been dropped straight from heaven."

Father Pat tightened under her embrace. He didn't know how to react. "HomeSky," he said pulling back, "I'm going now with the

Sheriff to get Cory. I hope all is still on with you and Joseph and dinner at Monsignor Kief's?"

"Yes. I think it's important the boys meet, don't you?"

Father Pat looked her in the eyes. "I think it's *destiny*. It's nothing short of God's will. Please tell Joseph goodbye for me. I don't want to pull him out of his conversation."

On his way out the door, Father Pat stopped for a goodwill gesture. He chose the plumpest, sugariest, strawberry bismarck from the donut plate. If this doesn't work, Pat thought, stepping into the brilliant sunlight, the Sheriff's plain hopeless.

"Mind driving?" Sheriff Harris asked, as he tossed the keys to Father Pat. Pat nearly lost the donut making a one-handed stab.

"I guess not," he said. "Never drove a police cruiser before," he went on, watching intently to see if he could catch the Sheriff off guard. "But I've spent a fair share of time in the back of them." To Pat's dismay, no shock registered on the Sheriff's face. He simply deadpanned, "Yeah. I know." Then he helped his old, smelly lab into the back seat before sliding into the front. He looked at the seatbelt, but couldn't bring himself to buckle it.

Father Pat slipped off his jacket in preparation for the drive, and climbed behind the wheel. Of all the fancy gadgets and equipment cluttering the dashboard area, two items particularly caught his eye. The Remington 12-gauge shotgun locked into the center console. And the jeweled rosary hanging from the rear-view mirror. They made an odd pair, not unlike a priest and a sheriff.

The Sheriff spoke up. "A right out the drive, follow the gravel to the blacktop, Highway 2 north to Lake of the Woods. Let's go. We're behind schedule."

There's no greater wisdom than kindness, Father Pat reminded himself. In front of them was a life-changing task. He took a deep breath and put the cruiser into gear. Concentrate on Cory, he told himself.

They drove. They were silent. The police radio was silent. The road was silent. All there was was the hum-drone of oversized tires on blacktop.

"Oh, I almost forgot. I brought you an olive branch." Father Pat handed the donut and napkin across the front seat.

"What makes you think we need to make peace?" the Sheriff asked, coyly. "I didn't realize we were at war."

"You're a smart one, aren't you?" Father Pat chuckled, watching the road. "Just as Monsignor Kief told me, 'A fox, that Sheriff of ours.' Your fumbling with scraps of paper, your toe scratching at the dirt, the small-town-rube act, it's pretty good. But you know and I know you've been working me overtime since the second I stepped into your office two days ago. You were on me when we sat in Lu Ann's diner. You were probably on me before that. You've probably been on me since you heard the Rez was bringing in a new priest. Why is it, Sheriff, that you've been on me like stink on skunk?"

"Easy there, Father. It doesn't look good for a police cruiser to be going 85 in a 55 unless the cherries are flashing. Let's just slow down, you and me." The Sheriff set aside his donut and fingered his two pockets, deciding on a Camel. He pushed in the dash lighter and they both waited for it to pop, like a bomb ready to detonate.

"I'll take one of those," Pat said, nodding at the pack of cigarettes.

"Well, shake the bushes and what flies out?" The Sheriff grinned, tapping another cigarette loose from the pack. "I could have sworn at Lu Ann's you said you didn't smoke."

"You don't miss a beat, do you?" Father Pat took a cigarette and lit it.

"Let me tell you something about me, Father. It's my job not to miss a beat. Yeah, I'm suspicious of people. It's my job to be suspicious. Of everybody."

"C'mon, Sheriff. Don't hide behind that righteous 'my job' crap. What a crock. You're suspicious because you get a charge out of it. It makes them bad and you good. What are *you* hiding in those bushes of yours? C'mon, you can tell me. It's *my* job to listen." The cruiser touched ninety miles per hour.

Father Pat had come to the end of his rope. He'd had it with the Sheriff's prejudices and bullying. He heard the low rumble of temper rising in his head, like the sound of water just before boiling.

"Padre. There's only one person in the immediate 100-mile radius with any secrets to listen to, and you know who that is." The Sheriff took a long pull from his cigarette.

"Okay, I'll bite. What's my secret?"

The Sheriff waited a dramatic length of time. He stubbed out his cigarette for added effect. "Do the words 'Suicide Priest' ring a bell?"

Pat stomped on the brake as hard as he could. The back tires locked and squealed, the rear end fishtailed violently, the Sheriff's chest went hard into the dashboard, knocking the wind out of him.

Outside, the cruiser's rear tires gave off plumes of blue-white smoke. The quiet of the surrounding woods was abruptly shattered. Three large crows went wheeling out of the pines as fast as their large bodies could get aloft, cawing an alarm. The car skidded sideways for 90 feet, rubber screaming against blacktop, and came to a stop bisecting the centerline of the highway. There it sat, rocking on its shocks.

The Sheriff looked at the priest, then at the shotgun racked between them, then back at the priest.

"Do you have a fucking pin loose! Endangering the life of a police officer is a felony offense!" The Sheriff was pale.

Father Pat stared at him. It was his turn to put on a show. He took a long pull of his cigarette, and let the smoke curl up into his nostrils. Surprisingly, Pat's hand was steady, something both he and the Sheriff noticed as he slowly put his cigarette out in the ashtray. The car remained idling, the hot engine ticking. "Sheriff Thurgood Harris," Pat said, clenching his teeth, "the loss of those three beautiful lives is a tragedy that you have no right to speak to. You hear me? I don't care of the felony consequences. If you disrespect their memory like that again, I'll drag you out of this car and keep coming at you until one or the other of us can no longer stand."

A semi came around the bend 300 feet ahead and was bearing down on them fast.

"Get out of the middle of the road, boy, that's a truck coming."

"Is that clear, Sheriff Harris?"

"Get out of the road, now. That logging rig has a full load."

The truck sounded its air horn as it began to brake.

"Is that *clear*? You will not disrespect the loss of those three lives." Father Pat wasn't looking forward at the truck closing in on them. His eyes were locked on the Sheriff.

"Yeah, damn it! It's clear. Now get the hell out of the road!"

Father Pat quickly looked at the road ahead. The trucker was trying to keep his skidding rig from jackknifing. Smoking air brakes shrieked. The Sheriff flung his arms straight out to the dashboard, bracing himself for the impact. Father Pat threw the cruiser into reverse and screeched back onto the shoulder just as the truck skidded past. Then he cranked it into drive and roared around the rig down the highway.

"You're fucking nuts!" the Sheriff said, still stiff-armed to the dash.

"Let me tell you something about me," Father Pat said quietly. "My job is to love unconditionally, and I'm still working on the unconditionally part, as I venture you've guessed. But I loved those kids and that unborn baby and I thought I was doing the right thing. But now, those kids are gone. They're gone. And what remains for me is a hole three times larger than the one I prayed over this morning. It takes a long, long time for something like that to fill. I don't need you scraping away at it."

The Sheriff unglued himself from the dashboard. He fumbled for and lit a Camel, overruling his traditional rotation which called for a Vantage. He smoked quickly. The cruiser made its way down the sun-dappled highway. All was quiet. Had it not been for the skid marks left on the road, a person would find it hard to believe that this serenity was ever disturbed.

"We all got our holes we're fillin'," the Sheriff finally said to the windshield. "That gives you no permission to nearly dig two more of 'em back there." They sat quietly. Out either window, they were fenced by green pines. The black two-lane stretched thinly ahead.

"Got another of those cigarettes?" Father Pat finally asked.

Sheriff Harris patted both of his shirt pockets. "Camel or Vantage?"

"What's with the dueling packs, anyway?" Father Pat asked.

"The Camels satisfy the nic-o-tine and the Vantage satisfy the rou-tine."

"Make it a Camel."

The Sheriff shook a cigarette out of the pack. While taking it, Father Pat shifted in his seat and said, "One more thing, now that we're baring our souls." Father Pat took the silence to mean the coast was clear for the question. "What is it with you and cars? I mean, you walk everywhere in town. You've got me behind the wheel, and I've watched you make the sign of the cross before you step into the street."

A thin smile came across the Sheriff's face. He remained looking straight ahead. "Well now. Looks like you've been doing a little police work of your own." The Sheriff paused to let the irony sink in. "I tell you what, it's a long story. But if you stick around, I just may bother to tell you."

On they drove in silence. Father Pat reached under his legs and retrieved the bismarck from the floor mat. "A little worse for wear," he said, inspecting both sides. "Good thing you keep a clean vehicle." The priest handed the donut across, and lit a cigarette. An unspoken truce had been declared as the cruiser powered north under a cloudless sky. The Sheriff chewed. Somewhere ahead, through this old-growth forest, Cory Bradford and his father's body were waiting for them. Father Pat couldn't get there soon enough.

At Monument Bay Resort, approaching the largest of the log buildings, Father Pat and Sheriff Harris heard what distinctly sounded like applause. They stopped short of the main lodge and looked at each other with furrowed brows. The heavy front pine door had been propped open with a rock to let the fresh fall air blow through the screen door. Sheriff Harris stepped forward, Pat flanking him. They peered inside, undetected for the moment.

A group of at least 20 were around three large harvest tables, centered in the dining room. All were clapping except for a smallish blond-headed boy seated in the middle of the first table. He was smiling. Sheriff Harris noticed his hand was bandaged.

"That'd be our boy, Padre," the Sheriff whispered out the side of his mouth. "I'll bet you dimes to nickels."

Someone at the table turned and noticed them. Little by little, the clapping sank away and soon the whole bunch were craning their necks at the Sheriff and the priest. A now uncomfortable quiet in the room indicated they'd interrupted something special between comrades. They were outsiders. "Say something." The whispering Sheriff nudged Father Pat ahead.

Father Pat pulled open the screen door, and walked directly across the creaky, fir-plank floor to the table where Cory sat. All watched him as he looked down at the boy.

"How do you do, Cory. My name is Father Pat O'Rourke and I sure am glad to meet you." By the look on everyone's face, they were expecting a sheriff, but not a priest. Especially not a priest with a black eye.

"Hello, Father," Cory said. "I hope you guys are hungry."

One by one, Cory said good-bye to each of the fishermen. He dazzled them with his ability to keep their names straight; many of these men had met numerous times over the years but only knew one another's faces.

The large dining room finally cleared out, leaving Father Pat, Cory, Sheriff Harris, Stu, and Darlene. Sheriff Harris asked if he could have a moment with the resort owners. Cory and Father Pat went down to the dock.

The Sheriff cleared his throat and looked at Darlene and Stu. "I've just got a few questions for you two and then we'll be on our way." He fished a folded square of paper from his pocket. "I'll need to look at the body. I assume you've got it put up someplace?"

Stu answered. "The last cabin out front along the lake. Number nine. I've got the heat off in there."

"I plan to take the kid back and then send my coroner for the body. I don't think he needs to spend any more time with the corpse. From what I got over the phone from your wife, the kid spent the better part of two days with that body already."

"Cory," Stu said.

"How's that?" said the Sheriff.

"Cory. The kid has a name. It's Cory. He's one hell of a boy," Stu said, riled.

"Sure, sure. Look, I'm just doing a job here." Sheriff Harris fumbled with his piece of paper, consulting notes which were scrawled in every direction, front and back. "Have you two looked at the body? Did you notice anything unusual? You know, suspicious?"

"Sheriff! For the love of Jude, what could you possibly mean?" Darlene spoke louder than she had intended. "A 13-year-old boy has lost his father. It was a tragic accident. He should be reunited with his mother as soon as you can get him there. There's nothing suspicious to it."

"With all respect, ma'am, it's my job to determine that. If I don't have a few routine questions answered, this story could start seeding more questions. You don't want that. That kind of publicity could be hard on business."

"Business!" Darlene all but shouted.

Stu put his hand on Darlene's. He looked across the room, out the window. "Two of my men and me took him in from the boat and put him in the cabin there where I told you. He was wrapped in tarp, to keep him from the weather. I took off that tarp—out of respect. I didn't look too hard, but I didn't see nothing." The Sheriff scratched a few notes in the corner of the paper.

Stu continued. "Can you imagine how it had to be for Cory? He had to leave his father's body out all night like that. Through the grace of God, he found a cabin to spend the night. He pieced together how to get back here, and rowed it. He told me he couldn't go off and leave his dad on the rocks. Hell, Sheriff, imagine what it took for that boy to get a man of 200 pounds back into a boat, let alone row across one of the most unforgiving pieces of fresh water in the country—through a snowstorm on top of that. There's no more to it. That don't sound suspicious to me. That sounds like grit. Something grown men would be hard pressed doing. You tell *that* story to whoever's listening. They ought to pin a medal on this boy, but you know what? He'd have none of it. He just wants to get on. He wants to go back to being a boy again. But it's too damn late for that. He separated with boyhood a couple days back."

Darlene got up and rubbed her husband's shoulders. He sat, staring blankly out the window.

The Sheriff stood. "I'll go have a look at the body. Oh, just one other thing. The kid—Cory—he has that left hand of his wrapped up pretty good. Is it broken?"

"I ain't no doctor, but I'd say one finger is," Stu said.

"Did it happen in the accident?"

Stu wasn't sure how to answer. He knew it was self-inflicted. Cory had his reasons, however misguided they may be. But did the Sheriff have to go digging around in all that, too?

"Sir," the Sheriff repeated, "I asked you how the hand was hurt. Because I agree with you. It's a feat for a boy to get a full-sized adult into a boat and then row across this lake. It'd be a near miracle for him to do it with a busted-up hand, wouldn't you say?"

Stu looked coldly at the Sheriff. "You'll have to ask Cory about that. Is there anything else?"

"I'll be in touch." And with that the huge Sheriff lumbered out the door and made his way down the worn footpath to the last cabin in the row.

"Cory," Father Pat said, as the two of them stood at the end of the long pier, looking at the October rollers building, cresting, on their perpetual march across the big lake, "is there anything you'd like to talk about? I don't want to rush you, if you don't feel like talking, but if you do …"

Cory squinted at some object seemingly far, far away. The wind blew through his tangle of blond curls. "I just want to know what killed my dad. Then I want to stop talking about it. I want a doctor to tell me, 'Cory, it was so-and-so.' If you can help me get that answer, I'd be grateful." Cory looked up at Father Pat. The priest had a slightly wistful look about him, like he had a secret, something more heavy than light.

"Has anyone ever told you that you look happy and sad at the same time, Father?"

"Well, no. Not quite like that."

"Hmmm," Cory said.

"Hmmm," the priest replied, smiling a bit. "You're a thinker, aren't you?"

Cory stood there, transfixed by the big water. "I guess so."

"I'll try to help you get your answer. Don't you worry about that. Would you like me to say a prayer over your dad while we're here?"

"It's a little late for that, Father," Cory said. "My dad wasn't much for prayer. He said religion was for the weak-minded."

Father Pat was caught off guard. "And what do you think?"

"I'll have to get back to you on that one."

"Fair enough." Father Pat put his hand on Cory's shoulder. Suddenly a current of déjà vu shot through his body. He was with Joseph, listening to the wind chimes, looking at the night sky. Father Pat blinked a few times and shook his head.

"You okay, Father?" Cory asked, squinting up at him.

"Have you ever had déjà vu, Cory?"

"Sure. I don't understand how it works, though. Did you just have it?"

"Yes. Quite strong. Whew, strong as I can ever remember. Cory, there's a boy named Joseph Blackholm back by my parish. I want you two to meet. I was going to wait until the drive back to tell you about him, but if it's okay, I'd like to tell you now."

"Is he the kid that you just got déjà vued with?"

"Yes. Can I tell you about him?"

"Sure. Why not."

"It's not a happy story. And I think it may involve you."

"That's kinda tough, Father, since I've never met him."

"Well that's what makes the story so … unusual."

"Okay. Let's have it."

Father Pat looked at Cory. He was considerably smaller than Joseph, even smallish for a 13-year-old. He had strong gray-green eyes and curly light blond hair. His body had a tension, an intensity, an athleticism to it.

"Before I tell you Joseph's story, I want to ask you a question. It may seem odd, okay?"

"All right."

"Your favorite sport is hockey, isn't it?"

Cory looked surprised. He broke into a rare smile. "How could you tell?"

"The boy I want to tell you about, Joseph, hockey's his favorite sport, too. I think you two are a lot alike, even though you're different. He's a Native American—you know, an Indian."

"How else are we alike?"

"You're 13, right? Well Joseph is 13, too."

Cory nodded for him to continue.

"And here's where it gets … unfathomable, I guess." Father Pat searched for the right way to broach the subject. Cory's eyes told him to jump right in. "Joseph's dad and your dad both died two days ago. His dad was in a car wreck. I believe—and I'm not trying to get overly religious on you—I think you two were destined to meet. It's God's will." Father Pat looked closely at Cory, watching to see how he'd absorb these words.

Cory was put off balance. "Oh." He shook his head like he wasn't hearing correctly. "His dad's dead too?" He sat down on the dock, pulled his knees up to his chest, and began thinking. "The same day?"

Father Pat sat on the dock next to him. "Are you all right?"

"It's not what I expected, Father."

"I know," he said, sitting cross-legged beside Cory. "I don't fully understand it myself. But I do have a deep, deep feeling that we've been sent a message. I don't know the whole message, but part of it is you and Joseph are meant to know each other, and I'm to bring you together."

Cory was pulling at the dressing on his injured finger. "Does this stuff happen to you a lot? Is this what it's like to be a priest?"

Pat shook his head. "No one ever told me about days like this in the seminary."

"Man." Cory looked at the priest. "His dad really died two days ago?"

"Yes, he did."

"And he's 13?"

"Just like you. How does all this make you feel?"

"Kinda afraid to meet him. But excited still."

"Do you think it's the right thing to do, meeting Joseph?" Pat asked.

"Yeah. Like you said, we've got a lot in common."

"Then trust that."

"Does Joseph know about me? About my dad and all?"

"Yes he does. I told him I was coming up here."

"Does he want to meet me?"

Father Pat put his hand on Cory's shoulder. "Very, very much."

"This should be a movie or something, Father. Except, no one would believe it." Cory frowned. And just then, right in front of the dock, a fish jumped. They both looked at each other like, *did you just see that?*

CORY AND JOSEPH.

The drive back was quiet. Father Pat was at the wheel. The Sheriff had started scratching some notes before nodding off. Police work, it appeared, wore the man plumb out.

As they crossed into Baudette County, it was as though some internal alarm was tripped. The Sheriff sat straight up, quick-like, hoping no one had noticed his nap.

"Welcome back to the living," Father Pat quipped.

"I wasn't sleeping, was I?"

"Sheriff, I haven't seen anyone sleep that soundly since last Sunday's homily."

"Yeah, yeah," the Sheriff said gruffly. "How's our transport? You still back there?" The Sheriff grabbed the rear-view mirror and trained it on Cory. He was sitting up straight, looking out the window.

"All present and accounted for," Cory said. Deputy had his head in Cory's lap and would groan with pleasure whenever Cory scratched under his collar. Next to Cory's feet was one of the two pine seedlings he had dug up from the island. The other one he planted with Stu out back of the main lodge. They twined it up with a stick, but Stu wasn't too sure it would take in the different soil. Cory was invited to come back next summer and see. Take a job for a few summer months grunting minnows, cleaning fish, gassing boats, doing a little guiding.

The Sheriff cranked the mirror back where it belonged and got on the police radio. By the sound of it, Cory's mom and sisters were at the Dew Drop Inn on the edge of town.

"So, Sheriff, here's what I was thinking," Pat said. "HomeSky said she'd drive Monsignor Kief home after the funeral and leave my car. A cousin would follow her in, and see to it she gets back to the farm. HomeSky," Father Pat said, craning back to look at Cory, "is Joseph's mother. I'm proposing we go to Monsignor Kief's, Cory and I get my car, and I'll take him to the motel to meet up with his family. I don't think we need all the commotion of a police cruiser in the hotel parking lot. Sound all right by you?"

Father Pat expected something negative, but the Sheriff just grunted and lit a Vantage. "Dinner is at six at the Monsignor's residence. You'll be joining us, won't you, Sheriff?"

"Go ahead and set a plate. But you never know with police work."

"What are you expecting, a threat to national security at the Baudette bowling lanes?"

Cory cracked up in the back seat. Father Pat couldn't help but laugh himself.

"Sure, laugh away. Sheriffs are a big joke 'til one night you're on the phone at two a.m. and you need something. Suddenly, things aren't so damn funny."

"Don't get sore. Just a little levity to make the trip go faster."

"Sheriff?" Cory asked from the back seat.

"Yeah, kid."

"You examined my dad, right?"

"I did a preliminary exam. The coroner will bring him back for a full work-up. Why do you ask?" The Sheriff sounded suspicious.

"When I see my mom, she'll want me to tell her what happened. I'd like not to go into all the stuff about crashing into the island. She'll freak. I was hoping I could just tell her Dad had a heart attack fishing, and leave it at that."

The Sheriff pondered this option. "That'll do for now," he said, with a hint of uncharacteristic softness. "How you going to explain your hand there?"

Cory looked down at the splinted finger. "I'll just say I took a fall and got the finger pinched between some rocks." The Sheriff started to ask something, but let it go. For now.

"We need to get that x-rayed," Father Pat spoke up. "A doctor needs to make sure it's set correctly."

Cory tried to move his finger. It hurt like hell.

"The sooner we get it looked at the better. That thing will be crooked forever if you're not careful," Father Pat added.

Cory turned his splinted finger in the sunlight, considering it. Crooked forever. For the rest of his life, never able to entirely straighten it. He watched out the car window as the first buildings of Main Street came into view.

"Father …" Cory broke the silence, now in Father Pat's car. They'd been dropped off by the Sheriff and were headed to the motel to see Cory's family. "I feel funny—nervous—about seeing my mom and sisters. It seems like they're, I don't know, a long way away. Like cousins or something."

"A lot has happened since you saw them. You're not the same person, and that's not a bad thing. But you need to let them know you're okay. They're terribly worried about you. Plus, they're nervous, too. It'll feel different at first, but then things will normalize again."

"But they won't be the same, either. Will they, Father?"

"No. I suppose not."

"Okay. I think I got it now." Cory sat up straighter.

As way of assurance, Pat added, "You've shown you can handle just about anything. Don't forget that. What you did the last few days is, well, as far as Stu and Darlene could remember, nothing like that has ever been done before."

Thoughts raced through Cory's head. He stopped at one in particular: when he remained hidden in the brush to let the boat pass instead of running out to the end of the dock and waving it down. Why? Why didn't he just run and scream for help? He wanted to talk about it with Father Pat, but he was ashamed to. He'd have to think on it a while first.

"Father, once I've talked to my mom and sisters, I think you're right. We should go have this finger straightened out. I might want to talk to you about some things then. Maybe like a sorta confession or something."

Father Pat pulled onto the pea-gravel parking lot of the Dew Drop Inn.

"Let's talk when you're ready. Now, do you recognize your mom's car anywhere?"

"Down there on the end." Cory pointed at the tan station wagon in front of room number eight.

"Father, I'll go in alone right now, okay?"

Father Pat put the car in park and looked at Cory, the sun streaming through the window, rim-lighting his face. The boy wasn't cute; he was better described as handsome. He would obviously grow into a man who would stand out. There wasn't a weak feature to his face. His was a face that was hard to forget.

"Sure. I'll go check on a few things in town I need to do. How 'bout I stop back out in an hour? That'll make it fourish."

"Good." Cory checked his watch, his face now serious, preparing himself. He stepped out of the car with his seedling. The window shades parted in the hotel room and Father Pat could see a woman with Cory's light hair look out. She appeared fragile.

Cory rapped on the car window. "Thanks for everything," he said as the window lowered. "I'll mention to my mom about supper at the other priest's house." Cory turned just as the door to room eight squeaked opened. Cory stood by the car. His mom and two sisters stood still in the doorway.

As would be his way from this day forward, Cory took the first step.

At four o'clock sharp, Father Pat pulled back into the motel parking lot. He was eating an apple. It was the tail end of the season and the fruit was wonderful. He carried a small bag of groceries to the door and knocked. Realizing he had a half-eaten apple in his hand, Pat winged the core toward the bushes. Cory opened the door just in time to see Father Pat's release. "Nice arm," Cory whispered with a faint dash of dimple. Then he put on his serious face, turned to the room, and led Father Pat in. It was obvious that Cory's mom had been crying.

Cory handled the introductions. "Everybody, this is Father Pat O'Rourke. He's the priest I was telling you about." Father Pat set the bag of groceries on the dresser trying to recall how Cory knew his last name. He walked over to Cory's mother, who stood up from sitting on the corner of the bed. "This is my mom, Melissa Bradford."

"I'm so sorry for your loss." Pat lightly shook her cold hand. "May I call you Melissa?"

"Please do, yes. Thank you so much for everything you've done for Cory. This whole thing is such a … out of the blue … I'm not going to cry. I promised Cory I wouldn't."

"Mom, do what you want. I don't care if you cry. Father, these are my two sisters, Amy and Sara."

The two girls came over and shook the priest's hand. They looked like they straddled Cory in age. The older one was quite serious upon shaking Father Pat's hand. The younger one appeared, more than anything else, curious.

"I'm Amy," she said. "I'm five. Do you wear your priest suit to bed?"

"Amy!" the older sister chastised.

Father Pat got down on his haunches to get closer to the beautiful, young towheaded girl. "No, Amy," he smiled, touching her cheek. "I wear pajamas. Just like you."

"With butterflies on them!" she said, thinking of her favorite pair.

"C'mon, Amy," the older sister scorned, as she picked up the little girl. "Let's go outside and look at the ice machine."

"Nooo!" Amy squirmed and kicked as her sister carried her out the door. "Noooo! I want to touch the white thing on his collar."

Father Pat straightened up. "Melissa, you have three wonderful children."

She seemed not to hear him. "Cory," she said. "Can you give Father Pat and me a few minutes alone?"

Cory looked at Father Pat. He wondered what secrets he might reveal. But he trusted him, or at least liked him. "Yeah. But you don't need to be worried, Mom."

"It's not that," she said. "I just need to talk with him by myself."

"See you in a little bit." Cory grabbed his jacket and left the room. Out roadside, he pitched rocks at the mailbox across the highway. There was no sign of his sisters. They were probably out for a walk.

"I don't know where to start, Father," Melissa confessed, tears streaming. "I'm so lost. I don't even know where in God's name I am, up here in the boonies. Oh, Father, what am I going to do?"

Pat came over and gave her a hug, a little stiffly. For him, this part of being a priest never came naturally. He was clumsy around pain; would rather avoid it. He sought to be alone with his sadness, and had to learn and relearn that others weren't necessarily the same. She cried for a few minutes and then tentatively regained her composure.

"Sorry, Father. It's all a giant shock. Giant, I tell you. How am I going to take care of three children? How am I going to provide for them alone? I'm a housewife …"

"I know this is daunting right now. But you're not alone with these children. God is with you. Have faith He will help."

"Oh give me a break, okay, Father?" Melissa walked to the window to watch her son throw rocks across the blacktopped highway. "God is the one who put me in this mess in the first place. How am I supposed to believe when I've got a husband to bury? Tell me that? *What* am I supposed to believe?"

She looked weakly at Father Pat. He went to the bag of groceries he'd brought in and took out a bottle of orange juice. He took a cup off the dresser and unwrapped the cellophane.

"Here, drink this." She promptly drained it. He filled another cup and she drank half of that. "Melissa, you're right. God did put this hardship in front of you. But I am absolutely certain that there is a way over the pain. It will take time. God has blessed you with three healthy children to help the healing. God took your husband for reasons we don't understand, but He didn't take Cory for reasons absolutely clear to me. Cory is here to help you. To help hold this family together so it can persevere and grow strong again. You must have faith in that. Look at that boy. He's your faith. He's what you're supposed to believe."

Melissa came over, very close to Father Pat, and looked into his eyes. "Is he okay, Father? Did what he go through out there, what he saw … is he really okay?"

Father Pat didn't hesitate. "Yes," he said, revealing none of his uncertainty.

Everyone was back in the crowded motel room eating apples and cheese and chocolate bars. The group was starving, including Father Pat.

"Mom?" Cory asked between bites. "Did you and Father Pat talk about having dinner tonight with Joseph and his mom?"

The youngest sister, Amy, piped in, "I want to go. I want to see Father Pat eat."

Cory's mom shushed her daughter. "He mentioned it. But I'm not sure it's a good idea. Father, what does the other boy's mother think? What's her name?"

"Her name is HomeSky."

"What kind of name is that?" she asked a bit too abruptly.

"She and Joseph are Indians. They live on a farm just north of me. She was apprehensive at first, like you. But she thought it would be a good thing. And her son, Joseph, is an outstanding, outstanding boy. Maybe Cory and he could become pen pals. Maybe more."

"I think we'll pass, Father."

"I'm sorry, what?"

"I think we'll stay in tonight and get an early start on getting home tomorrow."

"Ah, Mom!" the youngest daughter complained. "I want to eat with Indians."

"I'm not comfortable discussing it any further," Melissa said. "Thank you, really, for all you've done, but I think it's time we all started moving away from this."

"Do Indians use forks, Mom?" Amy continued.

Cory sat in stunned silence. But he could see his mom's mind was made up. Why argue? She'd just start crying and Cory'd had enough of that for one day. He walked over to Father Pat. In a voice that sounded louder and stiffer than normal to Pat, he said, "Thanks again for everything, Father Pat. I've got your phone number. When we're back in St. Paul, I'll give you a call to let you know how we all are. Until then, I guess this is good bye." He looked up and shook his hand. And unless Father Pat was mistaken, Cory gave him a little wink, too.

By 6:30 at Monsignor Kief's residence, they decided to go ahead and eat. All were seated and the only sounds were that of silverware and the chewing of pot roast. They hadn't cleared away the four place settings for Cory and his family, just in case they changed their minds.

Joseph was very disappointed when he learned Cory wasn't coming. On the contrary, HomeSky was slightly relieved. She'd had a long day with the funeral and the gathering afterward, and the thought of meeting new people, the energy it called for, put a knot in her stomach. She was glad to just be among familiar faces and the strong smells of dinner.

Most hard-hit by the news, and doing a poor job of disguising it, was Father Pat. He knew it was his place to bring the boys together and was devastated by Cory's mom and her adamance about keeping the boys apart. As he left the hotel, Pat came very close to speaking his mind, but caught himself. This woman, away from home, who'd lost her husband and was just reunited with her son, didn't need a sermon from a hotheaded Irish priest. (Even if he was right!) Instead he drove home, dug out the rake he had misplaced in the garage two days earlier, and worked until his hands bled. Then he went for a five-mile jog. By the time he got in the shower he was really mad. He broke the soap rack.

Sheriff Harris sat to the right of Monsignor Kief and was on his best behavior. Friendly, almost. No cracks about Father Pat. No racist commentary. In fact, he and Joseph talked duck hunting and the Sheriff promised to show him a secret spot or two in the following weeks when the northern mallards and bluebills migrated through.

The table hardly had room for another dish. What with the pot roast and onions, potatoes and squash, beans and carrots, salad and Jell-O, plus popovers hot out of the oven. Monsignor Kief's housekeeper had nearly put herself in the hospital getting it all ready; including the best china, pressed white tablecloth, and a Waterford wineglass for those interested—which seemed mostly to be Father Pat.

"Pass the wine, will you, Sheriff?" Pat said, with a bottomful remaining in his glass.

"Everything is just wonderful, Monsignor," HomeSky said, putting her fork down on her plate.

"Heaven forbid, don't tell me you're finished already?" the Monsignor said, hearing the fork settle on the china.

"No. Just taking a rest."

"Sheriff. The wine," Pat repeated.

"How about you, Joseph?" The Monsignor asked. "Are you resting yet?"

"No sir," Joseph said with a mouthful. "Just getting warmed up."

Father Pat tried not to be sullen and withdrawn, but he couldn't seem to snap out of it. He filled his wine glass to the top.

"It's all music to my ears," the Monsignor said with a big smile—and a little winter squash on his face. "The sound of lots of silverware on lots of plates. I adore it like spring rain on the rooftop."

Before long, everyone had set down their silverware and watched—or in Monsignor Kief's case, listened—in amazement as Joseph had thirds and fourths of everything. He was well aware that he'd become a spectator sport, but he didn't let it slow him down. He was a well-tuned eating machine.

"Save room for dessert," Monsignor Kief warned. "We've got warm apple crisp with cinnamon-vanilla ice cream."

"I didn't get much to eat today," Joseph said, polishing off his milk, showing the first signs of being full.

The doorbell rang.

Three differently pitched tubes played a nine-note tune. Everyone looked over at the door as the last note rang out. The grandfather clock ticked. The fire snapped in the hearth. Ice settled in a water glass.

"Joseph," Monsignor Kief spoke up. "Would you mind getting that?"

Joseph looked across the table at the empty place settings. A smile spread across his face. He pushed eagerly away from the table and crossed the room to the large oak door. He swung it open.

On the stoop stood a boy in an oversized canvas field coat. He was smaller than Joseph. They inspected each other in silence.

"Is this the Monsignor Kief residence?" the boy under the porch light asked. Joseph continued his study. The boy had blond curly hair. His cheeks were smudged red. He noticed a finger on his left hand was splinted. He looked stern.

"You're Cory, aren't you?" Joseph asked.

"You must be Joseph," Cory said.

Joseph extended his hand to Cory. "Sorry about your dad."

The boys shook hands. "Yeah. Me too about yours." They sized each other up as they shook. Cory couldn't believe the size and grip of Joseph's hand. Joseph had never seen eyes as intense as Cory's.

"Father Pat says you play hockey," Joseph said as their hands separated, there at the threshold.

"Best damn player in the state," Cory replied.

LANDING

No one gets up same as he fell.
You become what was jarred loose on impact.

— *Father Pat*

PART ONE

Autumn 1978

OCTOBER 15. CORY.

Cory was on the linoleum kitchen floor of his family's apartment, halfway through his fifty-third pushup, when the phone rang. His first thought was *screw it,* but 50 was all he was shooting for, so he rose, sweating. I'll get 55 next time, he assured himself, taking up the phone.

"Cory Bradford speaking," he answered, slightly winded. Now that it was his senior year and the college hockey scouts had begun calling, Cory took phone calls formally. He instructed his mom and sisters to answer simply, "Bradford's."

"Mr. Cory Bradford?" a deep voice inquired.

"Speaking."

"*The* Cory Bradford? The shoo-in for prep hockey player of the year?"

"Who is this, please?"

"Yank! You never say please. You thought I was a recruiter, Cory-boy!"

"Christ, Joseph. Aren't you a little old for prank calls?" Cory didn't enjoy being fooled.

Joseph continued laughing. "Easy there, big shooter. Repeat after me: humor is good. So, how are ya?"

"I'm okay. Just got 53 pushups. How many are you up to?"

"You don't want to know."

"Let me guess. Seventy?"

"Sixty-five," Joseph said, lying. He was really up to 75, but he didn't like upstaging Cory; that made him more silent and serious than he already was.

"Really?" Cory asked. "Sixty-five? I'll have that by the start of hockey. Mid-November at the latest. What are you benching?"

"You know I don't screw around with weights. All natural! All fiber! All—"

"B.S." Cory finished. "Weights can give you an extra step."

"Cory-boy, hockey is a fluid game, not a solid game. You got to go with the flow. Weights slow you down, man. You got to skate like a river."

"Last week, I thought I had to skate like grass in the wind."

"That too."

Cory returned to more tangible subject matter. "I'm benching reps with 250 now. Sets of 10. Swear to God, my back's stapled flat to the bench. No cheating."

"That's big-time. But I didn't call to check up on your workouts."

"Yeah. I figured that." Cory said, his voice flattening.

"Five years ago today. Can you believe it?"

"No. Not really."

"Five years. Just like *that*. What are you thinking about today?"

Now it was Cory's turn to lie. He knew it worried Joseph when he dwelled on things, especially his dad's death. "Not much. Working out. It's football Friday tomorrow night. We had a pep rally in the gym today with all the bullshit. The school's frothing at the mouth. Gives 'em an excuse to get ripped and swing at somebody in the parking lot after the game. Stupid. Football."

"Why play?"

"It's pretty cool running back punts. The rush. Anyway, how about you? How are you and your mom doing?"

"Fine. Mom's mostly fine. Today's rough, but we went up to the ridge and sat in the quiet there. Brought a lunch. It's real nice up here today. I bet it's 65 degrees. Banana-growing weather for these parts."

"Have you seen Father Pat?" Cory asked, concerned.

"I finally got him out running last week."

"How is he?"

"Not too hot, but better than in the hospital for sure. Monsignor Kief says it'll take a while."

"Is he staying with the Monsignor?"

"For now, yeah. He doesn't talk much, about any of it. He says he doesn't know what he'll do. Stay or not stay. Weird, you know?"

"No shit."

"Have you called?" Joseph asked Cory.

"Three times. First the nurse said he wasn't taking calls. I told her to say it was me, but nothing. Then when I called back a couple days later, they said he went home with Monsignor Kief. I left a few messages with the housekeeper. Still nothing back."

"I'm not surprised." Joseph switched subjects. "So you're still playing the barbarian sport, huh? When are you going to wise up?"

"Punts are a legalized riot. You'd like it. You just look up the field, find some daylight, and let it fly. The hitting's great. The coach says I've got too much contact in me to save it all for hockey. The rest of the game, I leave for the idiots."

"Just don't get hurt. Remember our deal," Joseph said.

"I know. Hockey is college."

"Hockey is college," Joseph repeated.

"Time to switch," Cory said.

"Okay," Joseph hung up.

Cory also hung up. He then dialed Joseph's farmhouse. Cory had them doing phone calls like this now—half and half—so when their mothers got the long-distance bills, each call appeared only half as long as it really was.

The phone rang in the kitchen. It was still the only phone in the farmhouse. Joseph hiked himself up on the countertop and picked the receiver off the wall in one smooth motion. He'd catch hell from HomeSky for sitting up there; his size made the whole counter wobble. Just months into his senior year of high school, Joseph was 6-2, 225 pounds. Nobody even considered messing with him.

"How are your mom and sisters doing?" Joseph said, the conversation not missing a beat.

"Fighting like cats and cats," Cory said. "I don't understand girls. If they've got a gripe, why not take it outside and settle it?"

"Not everyone solves things like that. You should brush up on your diplomacy."

"Yes, mother. Oh, hey," Cory said, "did you get your fields harvested? I'm bummed I couldn't come up to help and hunt the duck opener. I had … shit, just too many—"

"Punts to return," Joseph kidded.

"Things got crazy. It's nonstop. I've got sisters and a mother crawling all over me in this little box. Don't get me started. But speaking of punts, I ran another one back all the way," Cory's tone cheered.

"How many does that make?"

"Three. Five's the school record. I'll have that by the end of the month."

"That's cool. Get the record, just watch your knees. Football eats knees for breakfast."

"Yeah. I'm on it. I've been in the pool a lot, and doing my squats. My legs are bulletproof. So, what's the deal on the fields?"

"The corn's still standing, but the beans are in. Kinda sad, really. This time of year. Empty dirt under the sky. We had a good crop …

but I can't stand the sight of fields empty. Reminds me of the funeral. All that. But what can you do. Harvest is harvest."

"Fall is overrated, if you ask me. Everything withering up and people can't drive out there fast enough with a picnic lunch to get all ga-ga. I don't get it."

"The colors are pretty. People don't have much pretty in their lives. For us, it's different."

"Yep," Cory said. "Leaves drop, then the puck drops."

"Nothing better, is there?"

"Not where I'm coming from. We waited a long time for this. Seniors, finally. A lot of our starters are coming back. Should be good."

Joseph asked, "You guys going to be as good as everyone's saying?"

Cory deflected, "Are *you* guys going to be a good as everyone's saying?"

"Time will tell, my boy," Joseph said confidently.

"Always has, always will," Cory returned, cockier yet.

The two of them laughed. Quiet long-distance static waited on either end of the line as each of them thought about the other. *How is he really doing? The fifth anniversary of our fathers' deaths.* Cory broke the pause. "Well, we better get off before we get chewed for the bill."

"Suppose you're right. You're good then?"

"I'm cool. I miss him though. You too, I bet," Cory said.

"I dream about Dad a lot. Then I go a patch and don't. Most times when I dream, his face is real close—like he's right next to me, like he was when I was little and he came in to check on me and pull up the covers. I'll wake up in the morning, and those covers will be up tight and neat. You know me. I sleep like a wrestling match. But not on those dream nights. You dreaming much about your dad?"

"Nah," Cory lied. Neither said anything. The long-distance static crackled.

"Well, I just wanted to call, Cory-man. Just remember, you're the best friend I've got in this world. You know that, right? You're my spirit brother."

"We can't be pulled apart, me and you. A guy could live a hundred lives, and never find a better friend."

"Hey, you're sounding very Indian. I'm impressed."

"I feel part Indian. Sometimes I wish I just lived up there with you and we could skate on the same line and play our way to the pros."

"One more year. If all goes right, we'll be playing college together. It's a test to see how badly we want it. If it were easy, it'd be worthless."

"You're straight on that," Cory agreed. "Well, time for me to get rolling. Thanks for the jingle."

"It's your start next week."

"I'm on it. Talk to you then."

"Giga-waabamin," Joseph said goodbye.

"Giga-waabamin," Cory replied.

With the receiver in one hand and the index finger of his other pressing down the hang-up button, Cory sat quietly, looking at the crooked reminder of his father's death. That finger. Its tip permanently flattened. The fingernail never completely right: smaller, gnarled. The nerve-damaged tip forever deadened.

Cory rested the receiver back in its cradle. It felt lousy lying to Joseph. What could he do, though? His Dad dreams were ruthless. He didn't want to think about them, let alone talk about them—not even to the one person he had no other secrets from. It would anguish Joseph hearing it, weigh on him. Plus, what was Cory going to say, anyway? "Yeah, Joseph. I do dream about Dad. Pretty much every week. It's great. Dad leans in, right in, really close, right over my face, and says, 'Hey, fuck-up, you're a disappointment. You let me down.'"

OCTOBER 15. JOSEPH.

Joseph hung up on his end. Something wasn't right with his friend. Cory put up a good front, but Joseph had an uneasy feeling. Unconsciously, his hand slid back to the long braid of hair that held the small river stone behind his ear.

In his bedroom, Joseph went to the dresser and pulled open the top-right sock drawer. It had become the nesting ground for all of Cory's letters. A large rubber band held them tightly together so they wouldn't spill over the top.

When he felt out of sorts, Joseph went to the letters. They helped him return to the solid ground of brotherhood and mutual need. Usually, Joseph was very happy. Inspiringly so. But occasionally his stomach would draw up. He'd feel a slight disorientation, a disquietude. Cory's letters were a balm. Joseph would randomly pull a few from the stack, lay on his stomach, and go back in time. This retracing helped him rediscover his course. He took the very first letter off the bottom of the stack, dated two weeks after the accidents, October 30, 1973.

Dear Joseph,

I got your letter. Thanks for writing. Man you write a long letter!! I know we said we would but I didn't know if we meant it or if we said it to make everyone at the table at Father Kief's happy.

It sounds like you're doing good. I'm doing good, except everybody at school is looking at me weird. Is it happening to you? They look at you scared, like you're really really really sick and you might drop at any second so they're extra nice. It makes me want to puke!! I just want to get back to normal. Like when everyone pushed each other around. Now they're afraid of hurting my feelings. Maybe things will be different soon, but I don't know. Does any of this make sense or am I just a retard?

Joseph stopped reading. He thought back to his first days back at school and how he was getting looked at, too. He remembered writing Cory back and telling him he knew exactly (underlining it so many times he wore through the paper) how he felt. Joseph continued reading.

I'm sure glad we met and all. It's good having somebody to talk to that knows this stuff the same way. When Father Pat asked me about meeting you I said sure but I wasn't. My mom is still mad about me hitching a ride over that night but I told her I had to and she let it drop. Man that was cool, meeting all of you.

Did you like me right away? I liked you. You were funny all the time.

I hope we get to see each other this winter once in a while. I talked to Father Pat on the phone last week. I told him I wanted to come up and teach you Baudette pansies how to play hockey…ha ha. My mom doesn't know it, but I was thinking about maybe coming up Thanksgiving when we have school off if your mom and you thought it was a good idea. Is your pond safe for skating by then? What would your mom think? We could skate all day if you wanted.

It's OK if you can't. Write me back about Thanksgiving. Don't be a turkey…get it?

Your new friend,
Cory Bradford

Joseph smoothed the letter down onto his bed. He thought back to that first Thanksgiving holiday when Cory took the Greyhound up to visit and how he and Father Pat met Cory up at Scalzo's gas station. He stepped off the bus with his skates on his hockey stick and a duffel bag over his shoulder and a fierce intensity in his eyes, just like the first night they'd met. Cory's eyes, Joseph thought, always had an inner glint, like he'd just been shoved and he was ready to shove back.

The weather had been clear and cold, and there were four inches of good hard ice on the duck pond. Cory and Joseph and Father Pat skated until Father Pat got blisters so bad he couldn't turn anymore. They all went in for hot cider, but Joseph and Cory came back out for more. They worked on their stickhandling, playing keep-away. Then they practiced passing and pretended they were on the same team. They had to be dragged in for dinner. The next day, Father Pat chopped two holes into the far end of the pond, pounded in two-by-fours and set up a sheet of plywood. He had cut five different slots the size of Kleenex boxes in the plywood and gave each target a different number. They would skate the length of the pond and alternate between wrist shots and backhands, trying to shoot pucks through the slots. Skating, stickhandling, shooting. In that order, Father Pat would tell them. Work through all your drills, but remember, the secret to hockey is skating.

For Thanksgiving that year, Father Pat, Monsignor Kief, HomeSky, and the boys made five for the feast. They had squash and beans from the farm, wild rice, goose and duck that Joseph had shot himself. Joseph told fantastic, winding stories about flushing grouse from the overgrown edges of logging trails and belly-crawling along river banks to jump shoot sunning wood ducks. The stories ended in a pact: the "men" would go hunting next year.

Thanksgiving on the farm became a tradition for the group. Father Pat would be there, skates slung over his shoulder, lugging an old straight-blade hockey stick he liked to say was older than both of the boys. Hopefully, Joseph thought, this Thanksgiving would be no different and they'd all be back together. Hopefully Father Pat would be better. They'd drag that weathered piece of plywood out of the barn with its years of chips and puck marks around the target holes. Only difference now was that he and Cory could rip the pucks through those slots from 30 feet, forehand and backhand. Joseph had to smile. Even though Thanksgiving was over a month out, he was already looking forward to it. The way the house warmed from bread baking, the scent of browned loaves just out of the oven greeting them as they tromped in after hours of skating. How they'd stay awake far too late, talking in the dark, making plans to play college and pro hockey. Man, that Cory could play. Joseph just hoped Father Pat could make it this year.

Joseph pulled a second letter from the stack. This one was dated more than a year later, January 15, 1975, when the boys were in eighth grade.

Joseph,

Two kick-ass goals tonight! Our traveling team still only has one loss and that fluke the refs screwed us on. Tonight's first goal was a three. The other was a backhanded five.

Joseph thought about the scoring system they used on the duck pond goal: a three was the hole on the upper right, and the five hole was the low opening between the goalie's legs.

It was soooooooooooooo sweet. A few of the girls from school showed up just in time to see yours truly put the game winner in the back of the net. One girl is so hot she isn't allowed near the ice. I hear she's going with a sophomore who plays varsity, but you wouldn't have known it by the way she and her friends were hanging around us after the game. All our games are indoors now, but we still practice outside. You guys have to get an indoor rink up there in the boonies. No more frozen feet. And the puck echoes like crazy indoors. If you shoot wide it booms off the boards like a cannon. Sometimes in warm-ups we purposely miss the net just to rattle their goalie.

I'm getting pumped for high school next year. I'm not going to quit until I'm skating JV. The coach told me I better put on 10 pounds this summer if I want to play for him. Man, the guys are huge. You're lucky to be big. But I plan to go back to Darlene and Stu's this summer and work my butt off swimming and rowing. I'm going to be in the best shape of anyone trying out. Being smaller won't hurt me too much. I can skate circles around those stiffs. I bet you'll play varsity as a freshman. That'd be so cool even if you get your head taken off. You'll have plenty of ice time by the time we meet in the state tournament as seniors (never say never).

Write me back and tell me how many points you've got so far. How's your mom and Father Pat and Monsignor Kief? I've got homework to do but it's so simple it puts me to sleep. Hope you don't miss your dad too much and are doing good. Keep your shot down and your head up, buddy boy!

Best friends always,
Cory

Joseph rolled over on his back, looking at the cracked ceiling with the dark yellow water stain where the roof once leaked. His hand reached blindly to his side, searching lazily on the bedspread for the thick hardcover. He was reading Steinbeck now. And Kant. He was reading Hemingway and Twain and Lewis. He was reading anything he could squeeze in. Monsignor Kief had opened a door and Joseph walked into a world that became more fascinating by the step. He'd never seen books like he saw at Monsignor Kief's the night he and Cory met. Each hardcover he tipped out of the tight-packed shelves was a little box of leather-bound art. At first, he was drawn to books as objects, beautiful to handle. Inside, they were bewitching, with their scrolled initial capital letters, their typeset words neatly justified. Monsignor Kief insisted he take two home with him, and continued to send out handpicked novels by way of Father Pat every other month. Joseph was hooked. He loved to drop into the words. To live with the characters. He read each night until he slept, and his first act of the morning was to read as many pages as he could before the call of nature won out. Reading meant he had to do morning chores that much faster, and his homework suffered, but those sacrifices were minor.

So much had happened in the five years since his father died. He and Mom were keeping up better now. Each year they got by, somehow, but they still owed a lot. They both survived on six hours of sleep. Joseph's body begged for more, but with chores before school, sports after school, homework, and evening chores, plus the reading, there was no time. Sometimes, like tonight, he wanted desperately to close his eyes before dinner and steal a nap. But there was a tractor transmission to fix and the pages of Steinbeck calling.

Joseph slid off the edge of his small bed, lowering himself slowly to the cold pine plank floor. "No sleep for you, Good Thunder," he said. "Early sleep is for dogs," one of his dad's favorite lines. Joseph lay on his bedroom floor thinking about his chores. Then he smiled; why worry? They weren't going anywhere. From the floor, Joseph started a set of sit-ups. When he got to 58, HomeSky walked into his room.

"There you are. Dinner's about 45 minutes away. Can you wait that long?"

"Sure. I'll just gnaw on my wrist."

"I'm sorry. Work in town keeps me later and later. Who was that on the phone?"

"Cory," Joseph said. "He's doing fine," he added, anticipating her next question.

"Have you talked to Father Pat today?" she asked quietly.

"No. He'll call, though," Joseph said with certainty.

He started another set of sit-ups. "Mom, do you realize we don't have a couch?"

HomeSky looked at her full-grown young man, effortlessly snapping off sit-ups. "Of course. You and your father never sat down long enough to need one. Why?"

"I was just thinking. Did Dad ever have a couch growing up?"

"I'm sure he did. I don't know. Why the sudden interest in couches?"

"I'm making a decision. I'm going through life without a couch. Maybe I'll be famous for it. Joseph Blackholm: Mr. Couchless. I'm going to ask around school. See if any other kids don't have couches."

HomeSky's brow wrinkled. "Are you feeling okay, with today and everything?"

"Yeah."

"You're positive?"

"Positive," Joseph said, well into his second set of sit-ups.

"In that case, you will *not* be asking about any couches in school. You'll get social services pounding on my door."

Joseph stopped and jumped to his feet, cat-like. "I'd just tell them you're the best mom in the entire world, and say to them, 'Please, make yourself comfortable on the floor while we discuss it.'" In one quick move, Joseph wrapped his arms around his mom's waist, picked her up, spun her around, and set her down. "Are you gaining weight?" He cocked an eyebrow in mock seriousness. "I detect an extra few pounds."

"Just because you're bigger, doesn't mean you're tougher." HomeSky lunged at Joseph. One smooth sidestep, and he was out of reach.

"Those extra pounds might have cost you a step," Joseph said back to her, laughing as he ran.

"You *better* run." HomeSky chased him around the corner into the kitchen.

Joseph head-faked one direction; HomeSky bit, but he cut the other way, staying easily out of her grasp. "Getting older, too, I see," he said, grabbing his jacket off the peg as he reached for the door.

"Old? OLD!" HomeSky picked up an orange from the kitchen table and launched a fastball at him. There was a burning instant, as the orange streaked directly for Joseph's face, when she thought, oh, no!

Joseph's hand came off the doorknob and snatched the orange just in front of his nose. "Thank you," he said. "This should hold me through chores." Joseph's laugh could be heard through the door as he closed it behind him.

OCTOBER 15. FATHER PAT.

Defeated, Pat set the receiver back in the cradle and let his head fall, chin to chest. He had dialed all but the last number, but he couldn't finish. He needed to talk to Joseph; no anniversary of RiverHeart's death had passed without the two of them speaking. But he couldn't get past the possibility of HomeSky answering.

There, on the edge of the bed, dressed in his loaner jogging sweats, bare feet on the carpeted floor, Pat sat. He studied the pair of running shoes under the window, waiting like a loyal dog. The last of the afternoon sun paced patiently on the windowsill, hoping Pat would finally endeavor out. He looked at the phone. He looked at his hands. He looked at the wooden Fontanini crucifix on the bare wall through particles of dust sparkling in a shaft of light. Pat closed his eyes and upon reopening them, glanced out the window of Monsignor Kief's third-story guestroom. He was eye-level with a magnificent silver maple; sun was cupped in the colored leaves.

"You transition so elegantly," Pat whispered jealously to the October leaves.

His hands told the story. The fingernails—or more accurately, the raw, red skin near where his fingernails should have been—were so chewed, the exposed skin was alternately scabbed or bleeding. "I ought to have my priest's license yanked," he muttered, repeating an accusation overheard by one of the firemen that night.

That night was two weeks prior. Father Pat had been drinking. Hard. He passed out in his chair with hotdogs boiling on the stovetop. He dreamt he was in hell, and awoke to find the water had boiled off and the hotdogs were in flames, which spread to the window curtains behind the range, leaping up, igniting the ceiling.

The kitchen was all fire; he couldn't get to the phone and didn't want to risk going upstairs to call the fire department from the other line. Outside, stumbling through the dark, he got an extension ladder from the old pole barn and climbed on the roof with the garden hose. All while hopelessly drunk. Pat was lucky not to have severely injured himself when the fire-ravaged rafters broke underfoot.

There was nothing else to do but drive the quarter mile to the nearest neighbor and call the Rez volunteer fire department. There was no answer, so he called the Baudette county fire department. By the time they arrived, it was a battle for containment. The rectory was too far gone.

The story buzzing through Lu Ann's diner the next day was that Father Pat was a Rez priest in every sense: unreliable, dangerous, and thirsty. No wonder the Indians took to him, they said. Mostly, the story was fanned along by Sheriff Harris, who was quickly on the rectory scene. He said Father Pat reeked of alcohol, couldn't walk a line, and admitted he'd passed out, causing the fire. Sheriff Harris had tried unsuccessfully to wake up the tribal police chief. He gave it ten rings before he overstepped his jurisdiction and arrested Pat for reckless endangerment and driving intoxicated to the neighbor's to report the fire. A jail cell was fine by Pat. His home was ashes.

The next morning, back on the grounds, looking at the smoldering black fractures of cinder rising out of the foundation block, Father Pat was pressed to his knees by shame. In desolation, he knelt, shivering in the wind, for how long he didn't know. He was unable to pray. He was unable to seek forgiveness. He was unable to lift his eyes.

A parishioner drove in hours later. Pat had been kneeling so long he had to be helped to the back seat. Pat asked to be taken to the hospital. His every life possession, every photograph, keepsake, and knickknack, gone. *I am no one*, he thought.

Priests weren't supposed to be like this. Priests were supposed to be vital and wise and witty and inspiring. They were put on earth to be givers, not receivers. Father Pat felt like going to sleep. He wanted to close his eyes to all of this indefinitely.

For two days he remained at the hospital. Monsignor Kief came to visit, morning, noon, and night. Pat refused him. What could he possibly say to Frank? How could he face that warm, melodious voice? He'd betrayed his confidence. In Monsignor Kief's blindness, there was a capacity to see Pat for what he really was. Blindness isn't fooled by a handsome face. Blindness sees to the core. Pat could not withstand such inspection. Frank had spoken out ardently, recommending him for this parish. And how had Pat repaid the Monsignor? Go look at the rectory now. *Please,* Pat implored. *No visitors.*

Finally, after the second day in the hospital, Pat broke down on the phone, telling Frank everything. He confessed his feelings for HomeSky. Frank listened quietly and simply replied that tomorrow, Pat was to come stay with him. He had more than enough room. The two of them, he said, needed to get busy on a plan to rebuild the rectory. They had work to do, Frank said, and his home was just the place to headquarter such an undertaking. He told Pat he'd arrange for someone to handle his masses for the next month or two, to give him time to sort through it all. We have much to discuss, Frank said, but not now. Right now, there's work to do.

Joseph had tried unsuccessfully to get Father Pat to return his phone calls all week. Finally, early Saturday morning, he took matters into his own hands. At eight o'clock he rang the rectory doorbell and was greeted by Monsignor Kief. "I'm here to see Father Pat," Joseph had said. "I knew you'd show up sooner or later," was Monsignor Kief's reply. "I could use the help. Up both flights of stairs, second door on the left."

When Father Pat opened his bedroom door, there stood Joseph with a rolled-up brown grocery sack. "Running gear," he said tossing the paper bag to Father Pat. "I got some sweats and stuff from the gym's lost and found. I think the shoes will fit. We're about the same size."

Pat handed the bag back, said thank you, but he wasn't in the mood right now. Joseph said he'd wait in the hall until he was. "I'm patient," Joseph said. Pat softly shut the door.

Fortunately for Joseph, Monsignor Kief had loaned him a new book: Mark Twain, with no shortage of pages. He leaned his back against the wall, sliding down until he sat on the floor. A few hours later, Pat had to use the bathroom. He wasn't surprised to see Joseph still there, reading. "I appreciate what you're doing," Pat said, "but my energy is off today."

"You've got to make energy to have energy," Joseph said. "Nothing gets you running like running." He smiled his pure gap-toothed smile, eyes dancing, cracking his knuckles. "What do you say?" Pat used the bathroom and went back into his room and closed the door.

Monsignor Kief brought up sandwiches. Pat answered the rap at his door, said thank you, he wasn't hungry. Joseph was. He ate all four. Then, at three in the afternoon, Pat opened his door, looked at Joseph lying on his back, reading Huck Finn on the hallway hardwood. "Let's see what you've got in that bag of yours." Pat pulled on the red Adidas sweat pants, the Baudette varsity football sweatshirt, stuffed his size 12 feet into size 11 tennis shoes, and down the steps the two went.

They stretched wordlessly and ran likewise. Joseph led the way out of town along the soft shoulder of the highway. Joseph found his rhythm quickly, the stone braided behind his left ear drumming softly, connecting him so tangibly to his ancestry. There was something in the motion of running, much like riding a horse, that brought the swing of the stone down with a pronounced certainty.

On the other hand, Pat, with every stride, was feeling considerably less euphoric. His toes raked against the tips of the undersized tennis shoes. Each footfall came with a little shot of pain. Blisters, Pat concluded, were just a down payment on the debt he owed.

Joseph asked nothing of him. Just to run. They ran past the coin-operated laundry, past the Ben Franklin with its Halloween decorations already up, across the iron suspension bridge above the Rainy River, past the empty VFW park, past the motel mailbox—the last mailbox as you left town. After a few miles, he offered Father Pat snippets of high school senior stuff. Pat listened to stories about cliques, bad teachers, fights in the gym, popularity contests, drinking, and a girl, Sadie, who made Joseph feel clumsy for the first time in his life. Joseph also talked about Cory and how he was getting straight A's in school and scoring touchdowns running back punts. Pat ran and his blisters bled through his socks. He said little, except that he appreciated the run and hoped they'd find time in the next few days to get back out again.

Joseph didn't mention the farm. That would have introduced the subject of his mom. There was an unspoken understanding that HomeSky was outside current conversational limits. For her part, his mom hadn't spoken of that night, either, or of the words she and Father Pat had. She said only that she needed to talk with Father Pat soon, but would wait until he was ready. Joseph could read the pale tautness in her face; it wasn't for him to ask further. He didn't need to know. To Joseph's great credit, it wasn't in his constitution to think he needed to know everything. His mission was simple: enjoy today. And to help Pat find his energy. The rest would explain itself.

All of this is what put Pat in Monsignor Kief's dusty third-story guestroom on Thursday that afternoon, the fifth anniversary of the accidents. He walked across the room, laid his hands down on the bureau, leaned in, and looked closely in the mirror. He searched his bloodshot eyes for some of the worth and goodness Frank said was so bountifully there. Nothing. All he saw was a nose crooked from a high school punch, the white eyelashes over his right eye, and the small scar left from the rollover he had the day Joseph disappeared. He thought about Frank's counsel regarding "re-telling his story." About not privileging the negative in a life, but presenting the positive. He thought, clenching his jaw, how Frank had listened to him, uninterrupted, into the night when he arrived at the rectory from the hospital. How Frank had finally said, "Don't misunderstand me, Patrick; I'm not suggesting impunity, but right now you need to leave all that behind. You need to go forward with faith. Only God is fit to judge, and He does not judge in the past tense. Hear this, if you heard nothing else from me since the day we met. Who you are, not what you've been, is all that matters. If an angel put her hands on your shoulders today, right now, and lifted your chin and looked into your eyes and saw you for what you are at this very moment, *that* is how you are judged. The past is forgiven for those who live kindly in the present. The past is merely the grist required to make you better. Ask yourself, what would an angel see in this moment's embrace?"

Pat took a step back from the bureau mirror. He looked down at his blistered toes, raw and red. His fingernails were chewed to nothing. "What a mess," he uttered. "But it's a modest start, I guess."

Over at the bedside phone, he dialed and stretched the corded receiver to his ear. He imagined the farm kitchen through the ringing. The table with its mismatched chairs. The white swirled-horsehair plaster walls. The front door that wouldn't shut without putting a shoulder to it. The checked gingham dish towels hung on the oven door handle. The canted window frames.

After the fourth ring, the phone was picked up.

"Hello?" the voice said.

"Hello, HomeSky. It's me."

There was a pause.

"I'm sorry—" they both said at the same time.

OCTOBER 15. HOMESKY.

What only HomeSky knew was exactly *why* Father Pat drank a quart of whiskey the night of the rectory fire.

On top of her endless parade of responsibilities on the farm, HomeSky had taken a job at Lu Ann's diner in town. What a blessing that decision had been. She and Lu Ann got along famously. Both single mothers, it was as if they could read each other's thoughts. They were fast becoming like sisters.

In stature they couldn't have been more different: HomeSky being 5-11 and Lu Ann at 5-2. But they did share uncommonly good looks. They'd laugh and dismiss all the attention and flirting they received, but honestly, it was appreciated, harmless, and it plain felt good.

So Lu Ann's, the unofficial social hub of Baudette, grew even more crowded after HomeSky's hiring. The reputation of the best food and the prettiest waitresses (not necessarily in that order) spread to the outlying towns.

More and more young men seemed to find their way to the counter. Carpenters, route drivers, salesmen, realtors, factory men, bankers—a couple times a week, minimum, would show up and blush when they asked for more coffee.

To HomeSky's surprise, one man caught her eye. A salesman from Minneapolis working with the expanding McKnight Forestry Products plant in town. He sold manufacturing equipment and was in the diner weekly, buying lunch for one or another of the product managers. Other days, he'd come in alone, read his newspaper, and do the crossword, talking mostly with Lu Ann. He'd tell funny, involved stories, and usually somewhere along about the middle, Lu Ann would give up standing and take up a chair across from him. The tales usually had something to do with a snafu involving the locals. Careful not to name names—but revealing just enough about the enterprising backwardness of small towns—he'd get Lu Ann laughing so hard she'd have to pee.

To put it mildly, both women were surprised when he asked out HomeSky. He said his name was Roger Burke and he'd be in town straight through the month. Would any night work for taking in a movie or dinner somewhere, he wondered? HomeSky said she'd have to think about it. She was busy with a lot of things, she claimed. Maybe they could talk tomorrow. Really she was stealing time until she spoke with Lu Ann. She wasn't going to jeopardize their friendship for one silly date. Although he *was* handsome, she thought. And funny, too, it seemed. But HomeSky hadn't had much cause to talk to him in the weeks he'd been coming in. Usually, he sat in Lu Ann's section. Other than the times when things were crazy busy, it was always Lu Ann who turned over his cup the moment his butt hit the chair.

"He asked me out," HomeSky said that evening before the dinner rush.

Lu Ann's face brightened as she grabbed HomeSky's arm. "Who?!" It was like they were in high school.

"Roger Burke," she said, carefully monitoring the reaction. Lu Ann's face went slack. Her smile drooped, but she worked the edges back up. "Ohhh," she managed.

"I didn't say yes or anything. I'm not sure I want to, especially, you know, if you're interested." HomeSky looked into her friend's brown eyes.

Lu Ann blinked away her shock and shook her head no. "Don't be silly, honey. Really, fair's fair. Just you be careful if you do say yes. That man can make your head spin with words." Lu Ann patted her on the forearm and stood to leave. She sat back down fast in a heap. She grabbed HomeSky's hand. "Am I ugly, HomeSky? Tell me straight. I know I'm not as beautiful as you, but am I just an old muskrat?"

"You've got to be kidding," HomeSky said. "You're the prettiest woman in town. Everybody says so. You have men walking into tables when they come in here."

"But now that I'm 32, and the twins almost in high school, I feel so *old*."

HomeSky took Lu Ann's hands. "You're a long way from old. You could have any man in town you wanted."

"Except Roger Burke," she said.

"Who's Roger Burke, anyway? Just a smooth-talking salesman, probably. I'm not even sure I'll go out with him."

Lu Ann perked up. "Oh, you have to. He's real nice. And what, it's been forever since you've been on a date. The only man I've ever seen you as much as sit and talk to is Father Pat, and that doesn't count."

HomeSky frowned. "What do you mean it doesn't count?"

"Well, silly, he's a priest. Priests have to talk to everybody. It's their job to be nice. You should see how you fare with Roger the Dodger, if you know what I mean." Lu Ann raised her eyebrows.

HomeSky laughed and shook her head. "I don't even know if I'm slightly interested," she said, standing. "I've got silverware to do."

"Sure. Just leave an old woman here to rot," Lu Ann said. Then she smiled and waved HomeSky away.

HomeSky felt a prickle of nerves when she thought about Roger Burke. But quickly, her attention flipped back to Father Pat. Was it true what Lu Ann said? Did he spend so much time with her because it was his priestly duty? She considered them true friends. They shared so many things. But maybe Lu Ann was right. Maybe the best thing for her was to go out with this Roger Burke character. What could be the harm?

So she did. And as much as she secretly hoped he'd be a flop, he wasn't. He was funny and considerate and handsome, and he could listen as well as he could talk. They had dinner one night. A week or so later they drove 23 miles to the closest town with a theater and saw the dumbest Burt Reynolds movie, but they both laughed and added dialogue until they were shushed to the balcony. They had a really nice time. Nothing earth-shattering. They were cautious. Then, just like that, his work finished, he was gone. Things returned to uneventful.

Some three weeks later, late one Friday morning at Lu Ann's, he suddenly walked through the door. HomeSky looked up from cleaning menus at a back table and felt her ears getting hot. She was nervous. Roger looked at her, smiled, exchanged a friendly hug with Lu Ann, and came her way. HomeSky remained seated, not looking up, wiping her menus. He took a small wrapped present from his coat pocket and set it on the table as he joined her.

"Happy October," he said, sliding his arms out of his brown leather jacket.

HomeSky looked up. "What's this?" she asked, staring at the gift like it was ticking.

"Only one way to find out," Roger said. "Go ahead. It won't bite." He pushed the wrapped box a little closer to her.

"I don't understand, Roger …"

"It's nothing. Just a silly gift. Open it up. I saw it and I thought of you."

Unbeknownst to her, Father Pat had just walked into Lu Ann's.

"I'm not used to gifts out of the blue, is all," HomeSky said.

"Well, if it helps, I'm not much used to giving them out of the blue, either," he smiled. "But I wrapped it myself and I must say,

I'm glad to finally see that old paper out of my house." He smiled a little more, nudging her foot under the table. "C'mon."

HomeSky shrugged as if to say, well, all right then. She brushed her black hair aside and offered a little smile. What could it be, she wondered?

Pat made his way through the tables toward HomeSky's section. He wondered who she was sitting with. He didn't recognize the man's back.

She reached for the small box. It was wrapped in paper that looked left over from Christmases past. The ribbon was red. The wrapping was clumsy—Scotch tape everywhere. "So it won't bite ...?"

"Cross my heart." Roger watched her.

"Here goes nothing,"

"Hello—?" Father Pat said, arriving at the table just as HomeSky unbowed the ribbon.

Everyone looked at each other. Eyes darting from one to the next. Smiles tightened on their faces.

Then Roger saw the man's clerical collar in the open V of his jacket. This seemed to break the standoff. "Hi," he said, standing, smiling his all-star smile. He shot out his hand. "Roger Burke." The men met eye-to-eye in height, Roger with 20 more pounds of "the road" softening him.

"Oh, excuse me—you haven't met ..." HomeSky said.

Pat let the salesman hang for a beat with his hand outstretched. He just looked at HomeSky and that small box in her hands. She set it down quickly on the table.

"Father Pat O'Rourke," Pat said, looking finally at Roger. "Didn't mean to interrupt." He gave the man his best handshake. It was obvious Roger wasn't ready for that grip—not from a priest.

"Oh, well, no ..." HomeSky's words couldn't find traction. "Really."

"Would you care to join us, Father?" Roger asked, a little confused by the tension.

"Thank you, no. I can't stay. Just came back to say hello."

HomeSky finally found her voice. "Please, Pat, eat something. I need to get back to work anyway." She began to stand.

"No thanks," he said, putting a hand on her shoulder. "I'm off to Bonaducci's for some supplies. My cupboards look like Old Mother Hubbard's. Maybe next time." Pat took a final glance at the gift. "Roger, will I see you at mass on Sunday? I'm out at the reservation church."

"Sunday … hmm, I'm not sure where I'll be Sunday, Father. I'm over at the pulping plant, helping them get some new equipment in. It could be a few days, could be a few months." Roger held up his hands and shrugged his shoulders. "Life of a salesman." He flashed his white teeth.

"See you Sunday?" Pat looked at HomeSky.

She could see he was itching to leave. "Yes, of course. Sunday."

On his way out, Pat slapped a few backs and shook a few hands, but he couldn't get out of Lu Ann's soon enough. His skin was ready to ignite. As he reached for the door, Lu Ann shouted from the counter, "Father! What in blazes? Where you off to so fast? I thought you said you were starving."

Pat froze at the door. He knew Lu Ann's voice could pierce metal, so surely it had made its way back to HomeSky and her salesman. His options were: Make some crack about the food quality, like Monsignor Kief was famous for. Or wave and say something had come up. Either way, seconds dragged on like minutes. Pat felt eyes boring in on his back. He went for option three: yanking open the door, he left without looking back.

All afternoon, Pat smoldered. Why had he acted the part of the pimply faced adolescent at the high school mixer? He was a priest! He'd behaved like a fool. Yes, he was jealous. He'd pretty much had HomeSky to himself. Their friendship went unchallenged. Who was this Roger Burke? Giving her gifts? Why hadn't she spoken of him? Pat stopped himself. It was none of his business. HomeSky didn't report to him. She was a single adult woman. Back and forth he went.

By evening Pat had run out of patience with himself. He needed to go out to the farm and apologize for the way he'd behaved. He picked up some charcoal, hot dogs, buns, an onion, mustard, a box of chips, and a six-pack of beer. He had no right to act jealously, he thought. It was silly, really. He'd drop by and they'd get the grill going. He even grabbed his running gear in case Joseph wanted to get some miles in. Pat had eaten dinner at the farm so many times, but couldn't remember when he'd last cooked. Tonight he'd be in charge of dinner.

He pulled his Toronado into the gravel circle drive at around six. It was a beautiful fall evening. There was an hour or better of light left but the heat was retreating quickly along with the sun. All was quiet on the farmstead. Father Pat slammed the car door, announcing his arrival. This usually brought Joseph's dog, Lick, running. Lick, a good duck dog but a lousy watchdog, counted it as his duty to lick any trespasser until he had no recourse but abandon the property. But there was no sign of the dog. Pat walked to the barn; no Joseph. He looked in the house, in the machine shed; no HomeSky. No nobody.

Father Pat fired up the coals and cracked a beer. He waited as the sky oranged. The coals were going well so he went inside, laid open the onion, put a bag of chips in a bowl, uncapped the jar of mustard, and stuck a butter knife in it. Setting the table, he heard the porch groan under the weight of someone approaching. "In here!" he called out, wiping his hands quickly with a dish towel. Pat went to see who was home. "Well, Lick," Pat said to the yellow lab. "Looks like you've been running deer." The dog used his little remaining energy to jump up on Pat and lap at his chin. "Let's get you some water and me another beer while we wait. Where's your family?" Pat asked, scratching Lick's ribs. "Huh, boy?" Lick's tail and tongue responded. The lab was too spent to jump up. He was happy licking Pat's pant leg.

They sat together and watched the sunset. What a spectacular finish. Orange to red to pink to purple. "Glad I had someone to share that with," Pat said, rubbing the meat between Lick's shoulders. Lick's tail thumped the wood porch and his tongue lapped at the air.

After it had gone completely dark, Pat put the rest of the bag of coals on the grill. He sat on the porch step. He sat on the porch swing. He sat on the car's trunk. He sat back on the porch step. Just as Pat was beginning to worry, headlights pulled into the circle drive. Pat waved to HomeSky. His hand hung in the air, frozen by a second car that pulled in behind her. Before Pat could confirm it, he knew who the driver was. The car came in under the yard light, with Joseph in the passenger seat. The sight of Roger Burke made Pat drop his wave. His hand struck the porch step, and found another beer. He opened it as HomeSky scooted out of her car. He took a long swallow. The rest remains a bit surreal:

HomeSky: "What a nice surprise. I had no idea."

Father Pat: "I thought we'd barbecue, is all. I should have called."

HomeSky: "No, of course not. I've always said you should just drop in. Let me get a jacket."

Joseph: "Father! We went bowling. Get down, Lick. I got a 225!"

HomeSky: "The table looks great." She grabbed the bowl of hot dogs, determined to salvage the barbecue.

Joseph: "They serve burgers right at the lanes. Hey, how come the coals are going?"

Roger: "I'm Roger Burke. From this morning."

Father Pat: "I was going to grill you guys up some hot dogs ..."

Joseph: "I could still eat."

HomeSky: "I've got the hot dogs. The coals look perfect."

Roger: "Remember? I'm doing some work with the guys at the factory. That last beer spoken for?"

Father Pat: "I should be going. You guys have already eaten."

HomeSky: "You should still eat. Really."

Joseph: "I'll eat one or two easy."

Roger: "By all means, eat."

Joseph: "Lick! Down!"

HomeSky: "Please, stay."

Roger: "Yes, it's okay. Really."

Something inside Pat let go. He swung his eyes to Roger Burke, speaking quietly, directly, making a fist in the darkness. "No one's looking for your okay about anything happening here. You got that?"

HomeSky stepped in closer. "Please, Pat. Joseph, you and Roger go on in. Father Pat and I will be in in a minute." She was still clutching the bowl of uncooked wieners. "Would you both just please."

"Okay, Mom," Joseph said, confused by Father Pat's behavior.

"Yeah, sure." Roger said, returning a look of his own; a look that clearly said, *careful, now.* It was how a man looks at a man, or how a dog looks at a dog. Not how a man looks at a priest. "Sure, let's head in, Joseph," Roger said, still watching Pat.

Pat started toward his car. "I'm sorry, HomeSky. Bad idea."

She walked quickly after him. "Why are you acting like this, Pat? Why don't we just eat?"

"Bad idea," Pat repeated. "Live and learn."

"Pat. Can you slow down a minute? You fly out of the restaurant this morning, now this. What's going on with you?"

Pat turned and faced her. His eyes sparked. "What's going on with me? I'm jealous, okay?"

HomeSky was confused. She took a step back. "How do you mean, you're *jealous*?"

"What part of the word don't you understand?"

"But you're a priest. You're my friend. How can ...?"

"HomeSky, I have feelings for you that go beyond being a priest. I know that's confusing, believe me, I know. Yes, I am a priest and yes, I am your friend. But there's more."

HomeSky looked up at Pat, her mouth slightly open, her brow furrowed. "There can't be more," she whispered with certainty.

"You've never felt more?" Pat asked, looking at her hard in the half-shadows of the yard light.

"Pat. You're a priest. Our faith says that's the beginning and the end of it. There can't be more."

"Sorry to disappoint you," Pat said, reaching for his car door. "But for me, there is."

HomeSky didn't know what to say. She watched as Pat started the car, and then looked at her, waiting for her to say something ... anything.

"You should take these," HomeSky said, finally, handing him the bowl of hot dogs. "You haven't eaten."

That night, at home, about three-quarters through a quart of Canadian Club whiskey, Pat stumbled out to his car and picked those hot dogs off the floor mat where he'd flung the bowl. He set them to boiling, continued drinking, and passed out. The rest of the story is Baudette legend.

Three weeks later, Pat was on the phone from Monsignor Kief's upstairs guest room talking to HomeSky for the first time since he nearly drove over her foot leaving the farm.

"How are you?" HomeSky asked carefully.

"I'm fine ... you know. Say," he changed subjects, "I'm wondering if Joseph is there. How is he getting through the day?"

"Like the champ he is. You know Joseph." She laughed a little, trying to break the tension between them.

Pat asked, "And how are you? Today, I mean."

HomeSky considered his question. "Today is fine. The last three weeks, not so fine." She paused, "Pat—"

He interrupted. "Let's not go into it now. I just wanted to say hello to Joseph. You and I, we'll be okay. We'll talk. Is Joseph there?"

The fact was, HomeSky had been doing a lot of hard thinking in the past three weeks. While working the chores, while walking fence lines, while absentmindedly putting plates of food down in front of the wrong customers. There was a recurring question: was she completely honest that night? Was there truly *nothing* more?

"Yes, he's here," HomeSky said. "Let me get him."

CORY.

The dark shape spiraled downward out of the high night blackness. Caught in the spray of stadium lights, the brown leather, its white stripes, its spinning laces, were now illuminated. Cory had judged the arc of the punted football precisely. He waited a heartbeat, bit down on his mouthguard, then his cleats dug into the turf, taking those first, powerful, critical strides forward so he'd be fully sprinting upfield as he caught the punt. The boy was greased lightning.

NINE-YARD LINE. Tearing turf up with his spikes, Cory went hard up the gut of the field, clearing his head of all thoughts but one: school record. One more return for a touchdown, and he'd have six, setting the new mark. His legs powered easily through the outstretched arms of the first tackler. You had to put a shoulder flush on Cory Bradford to have a chance of taking him off his feet.

TWENTY. He sold that he was going near-sideline, then cut

across field, leaving the overanxious tackler empty-handed except for fistfuls of grass. Cory's body was getting fluid, musical.

THIRTY-FIVE. Cory got to the right sideline and instinctively shifted the football to his right arm to protect it. This was his favorite sideline to run because it was where the teams stood. He could hear his boys jumping and shouting. School record! School record! His forward wedge of blockers flattened everything that moved in front of him.

FORTY-FIVE. The opposing team came pouring toward the sideline like someone had tipped the field. Cory's peripheral vision caught their coach screaming at his boys to stay home, don't overpursue! Straight ahead was jam-stacked with tacklers and blockers, pushing and heaping on the grass. Cory broke for open field like a drowning man surfacing for air. He cut hard off his outside leg, exploding toward the middle of the field, shifting the ball to his other arm. The tacklers had had made the classic error; they had overpursued. Cory's lower body found the next gear, knees pumping high in the air, green turf somersaulting in his wake. Not a step wasted.

FIFTY. Cory, jetting out of the swarm, crossed midfield and entered the opponent's territory. Only the punter had stayed back. He was all that remained between Cory and the record. The punter, a cocky trash-talker who Cory also came up against in hockey, was back-pedaling, trying to guess which way Cory would cut. What a mouth this dickhead had on him. Whether it was football or hockey, he was always jawing. Last year he had deliberately run Cory's goalie, breaking his collarbone and putting him out for the playoffs. Cory could easily torch the punk with an inside-out move.

THIRTY. With the whole student body on their feet, Cory did what he had to do. He bore down, straight for the punter's numbers. The punter, now comprehending his immediate future, squared to face Cory, lowering his helmet. Cory too lowered his. With 80 yards of momentum behind him, he sprang off his feet and hit the boy with every bit of force he had. The last thing the punter remembered seeing was a thin smile spread across Cory's face.

TEN. The helmets' impact echoed through the stadium like the sound of butting rams in a canyon. The punter flew back, arms and legs rag-dolling. Cory sailed over top of him. According to high school rules, one knee touching the ground marks a player down. Cory spun in the air from contact, one foot landing on the turf. The punter was laid out flat behind him. Cory's second foot came around, tangling up with his planted leg. He tripped. He put his hand out, trying to hold balance.

THREE-YARD LINE. Cory's knee struck the turf and he somersaulted into the end zone. The crowd went berserk, but the referee signaled frantically, blowing his whistle. No touchdown. Dead ball. Cory set the football in the end zone and jogged toward the sideline.

The official stood over the splayed-out punter, waving to the sideline for assistance. "What in hell, boy?" the ref said, dismayed, as Cory passed.

Cory's coach walked out on the field. He met Cory, putting his hands on his shoulder pads. "What in hell, boy?" he said.

"That's what the ref just said," Cory replied, looking up at his coach, his eyes sparkling with dangerous energy.

The coach shook his head, studying Cory. "You could have cut it into the end zone for an easy six. What's going through your brain? That boy's rolling around out there like he's been gutshot."

"He had it coming." Cory unsnapped his chinstrap and spat his mouthguard into his hand. It was pink with blood, the coach noticed.

"One lousy juke and you had the damn record."

"Old debt, Coach. You got the ball on the three. Put it in the end zone, make them punt on their next possession, and I'll have that record." Cory jogged the rest of the way to the sideline. His body fizzed from his scalp to his toes. He pulled off his helmet and spat blood. His team swarmed him like they'd won the championship. The crowd stood in applause. The punter was helped off the field, talking nonsense about not stealing twenties out of his mother's purse.

With the opponent's second-string kicker filling in, the punts for the rest of the night were short line-drives. Made to order for running back. By game's end, Cory had the school record plus one. He got the game ball and the shadow of his legend stretched further.

Already, he was the most famous kid in high school. Cory Bradford, the boy who had rowed for days, a week, three weeks (depending on who was telling the story) after his dad had a brain aneurysm, tried a double suicide, was decapitated by a boat prop. Cory Bradford, the walking mystery. The school's most interesting boy because he didn't say much, but what he did say, he followed through on. Everybody knew him, but no one *knew* him. He was a two-sport standout and a straight-A honor-roll student, but really, who was he?

Of his many talents, the most exceptional was his memory. He could see a math equation or a physics formula or a word's spelling just once, and remember it like he authored it. Since early childhood, his memory had been a point of conversation. When Cory was just over two, he watched his dad decorate the Christmas tree. His dad showed Cory each ornament, called each by name, and then hung it. With forty-something ornaments on the tree, he called in the family for the show. He said, Cory, where's the reindeer? Two-year-old Cory toddled around the tree and pointed to it. Where's the little boat? Point. Where's the dove? Point. And so on.

Named captain of the hockey team as a junior, he became quite popular. He was everyone's buddy, but no one's best friend. He went to school, practices, games, and parties alone—and left alone. In between, he mingled, but never engaged. He preferred listening to talking. He set up clear boundaries. People hung around him, but couldn't get close. No one really tried anymore. He was given his space, like royalty.

Most of all, Cory was a relentless worker. He hardly sat for a minute. He had no tolerance for wasting time. When he did sit, he became quickly agitated, like someone was tapping his forehead saying that the time could be better used.

On top of the sports practices and training, he bagged groceries and washed dishes to help his mom out with the bills. His mom, it was no secret, was a basket case. They had rent on the apartment, clothes for Cory and his sisters, a car to keep up, food, and tuition. Cory had to step up. His father would have had it no other way.

All of this gave heft to the Cory Bradford mystique. And the record-setting night on the football field furthered it. In shag-carpeted living rooms where players' parents gathered to drink highballs and flirt harmlessly with one another's spouses, in cozy, aromatic pizza joints where fans had post-game slices, in smoky corner bars where ex-jocks bought each other frosty mug after frosty mug, in cars out front of post-game parties where students guzzled beer they pretended to enjoy, the subject of the conversations was Cory; what he did, and *why* he did it. That punter, they agreed, was all mouth. He was the hack that put our goalie out last year. Cory let him have it; they smiled, they raised their glasses. In the living rooms, the pizza joints, the corner bars, the parked cars, there was collective agreement: that Cory Bradford doesn't screw around. Man, did he put that kid in his place. *Then* he got the record. In that order. They shook their heads in admiration. He was what everyone wanted to be. Everyone except for Cory himself.

Back in the locker room, the coach tried to chew Cory out after the game, but his heart wasn't in it. He barked out Cory's last name and waved him over to his office as the team was slapping backs and stripping down to shower. For good theatre, the coach let Cory enter the office first, then rattled the door closed behind them. Mostly he told Cory that a stunt like that could have seriously hurt somebody, not to mention embarrassed the team, the football program, and the school. He said he'd most certainly be fielding angry phone calls, including, you could be sure, one from that punter's parents. What am I supposed to say, the coach asked, when those calls start coming in? Cory shrugged. He told the coach to tell it how it was. Football is a contact sport. If a kid can't take a hit, then he should clean out his locker, hand in his jersey, and go sit in the bleachers with a blanket and hot chocolate. Cory looked straight at the coach with those radiant hard gray-green eyes, and the coach just shook his head and grinned, thinking, this kid doesn't budge.

"Did you have any fun out there tonight?" The coach called after Cory as he went to leave the office. "You set one hell of a record on that field. I didn't see you smile once."

Cory turned to the coach, bare-chested, ropy, well-defined, every muscle group cut, wearing just his football pants and a towel looped around his thick neck. "You should have seen the smile I had on right before I scrambled him, Coach." Cory smiled some, reliving the moment, then gave the coach a wink, the first sign of humor the coach had seen from him in weeks. Then he twisted the doorknob and made for the showers.

There was an after-game party at one of the popular girls' house. Her parents, like always, were out of town. Cory borrowed his mom's station wagon and pulled up in front of the solid-brick St. Paul three-story. There were cars lining the curb for a block and a half. Cory wasn't much for this scene. A bunch a drunken idiots dry-humping on the basement couch and puking mom's lasagna in the shrubs. But he'd promised he'd show, so there he was, coming through the front door in his letter jacket, curly sandy-brown hair halfway over his ears and just touching his collar. High-fives. An underclassman who didn't know any better offered Cory a beer off his ring of six Special Exports. Cory just shook his head no and walked by. Cory didn't drink. Everybody knew that. Another guy punched the underclassman in the arm after Cory was out of sight. Cory made for the kitchen.

Athletes walk a certain way. It's more magnetic than graceful, but it's both. There's a little hitch, a catch in the stride, something just out of alignment. The residue of a badly sprained ankle that never healed just right. A knee that's favored just slightly from an old injury. A bad hamstring. Something that flawed the walk just enough to make it captivating.

People watched as Cory made his way in. He said his hellos.

A crowd slowly gathered in the kitchen around Cory, hoping a little of him might rub off. Hiking himself up on a counter, he swigged a Coke. He was only 5-8 and always felt uncomfortably small at parties. His teammates towered on his right and left. Big, loyal teens with taped-up fingers wrapped around cans of beer. They were happy just to get close, maybe have a laugh with him. The mascaraed girls in soft sweaters slid sideways through the cracks of the crowd to get closer, smelling of perfume and mint gum and alcohol. The underclassmen were forced to the outlying areas of the kitchen, to the doorways or, worse yet, to the adjacent dining room.

Cory's good looks, his physical gifts, his success tonight—the avenging of the old hockey debt—were all part of his attraction. But when Cory told a story, in the school lunchroom, at a party, in the parking lot after practice, it was his recollection of things that most drew a crowd. He was uncanny; that was the best word for him.

"Tell us how it went down, Cor," the quarterback spoke up, his arm loosely around the small waist of this month's girlfriend. The room quieted as the stereo thumped in the background. All looked at Cory, sitting on the counter. "Yeah, tell us something," a nearby girl flirted.

He took another swallow of Coke. "When I walked the field before the game," Cory started in, "the wind was blowing out of the north—left to right—so I set up right of the center hash marks for that first punt. Shithead kicked it. When it left his foot, I knew he got all of it. I went back and the ball disappeared out of the stadium lights and that's when you have to trust you've got it measured. I knew I was in good shape when the lights caught it coming back down.

"Shithead over-kicked his coverage. That got me 10 yards in the clear before number 85, their wide receiver, arrived. He's one fast dude but he couldn't tackle my little sister. I left him face down on the 20. Number 25 had the best shot at me, but all he hit me with was arms. You should have seen his face. Either he was trying to grow a mustache or he had a runny nose." The kitchen broke up laughing.

"Sixty-eight and 72 got clocked by Sully and Beef. That gave me the sideline." Sully and Beef banged their beers together in a cheers.

"And Ted, you smoked that big number 55. Nick, while I was tight-roping the sideline, I saw you pull off your helmet and yell at me to get burning. Everybody in the stands was chanting 'school record.' It was pretty cool.

"Their whole team bites left and I see their coach screaming, 'stay home!' and it's clear as a sunny day what to do next. I cut it up the gut and by the time I cross the fifty, I know I'm home. I see shithead back there, dancing around like he's got ants in his jock, trying to guess which way I'll go. Hell, I knew on the bus ride over if I broke one open and it was just me and him, then we had old business to square. He danced left. He danced right. Finally it occurs to him what's on my mind. He gets his feet set and lowers his helmet just as I blew out his candle. He hit the turf and I was thinking, stay up. Was close, too. But I spun, and my second leg got me hogtied. The ref made the right call. My knee hit on the three. That's it. I'd say shithead has something to think about before he runs one of our guys again." The kitchen erupted. Players guzzled. Everybody clapped Cory on the shoulder and wanted to shake his hand. The girls just hoped for a look in return.

The party was picking up steam but Cory had a headache that wasn't going away. He angled toward the door. One of Cory's trademarks was flipping a silver dollar in the air and catching it as he walked or stood and shot the breeze. It occupied him. Walking wasn't enough; he had to be doing more, working on his hand-eye coordination. He could flip the coin and catch it with either hand equally well, never falling out of stride. As Cory moved through the living room, Nick, the quarterback of the team, snatched the coin out of the air.

"Hey, where you sneaking off to so early?" Nick said, squeezing the coin.

"It's my bed time, big man," Cory replied.

"Exactly," Nick gave Cory a conspiratorial pat on the shoulder. "Why don't you, me, Lisa, and Julie get out of here and go bed down in Lisa's basement. Her parents won't bug us down there."

"Julie? I hardly know her," Cory said. "Why would she go?"

Nick smiled. "C'mon, dude …"

"What?"

Nick looked at Cory in disbelief. "You're serious? Shit, she'd go because you're Cory Bradford. Any girl at this fucking party would go with you. In a heartbeat."

"Nick," Cory smiled, "you are, and always will be, completely full of shit." Cory slapped him on the shoulder. "That's what I like about you. Now give me my coin. I'm out of here."

Nick was amazed. "You're really going home?" He pointed over to the corner of the party where a group of girls were laughing and drinking beer. Lisa and Julie waggled their fingers and smiled. "You've got that lined up, you broke a record that's been around since, like, the time of leather helmets, and you're going home to bed?"

"Now you're tracking."

Nick shook his head, disappointed. "Jesus."

"Not that it's any of your business," Cory looked up at him hard now, "but I start stocking shelves tomorrow at eight a.m. A.M., as in *ante* fucking *meridian.* The grocery store's a zoo all day Saturdays. I won't get out of there before six. Then lift, then swim. After that, my mom wants to go to the movies. And my little sister, too. They said I promised. When that's done, how about I give you a ring, you send Julie over, and I'll accommodate her."

"Hey, Cor," Nick said defensively, "don't get jacked at me. The girl's Lisa's friend. I said I'd bring it up. She likes you, man."

Cory was going to say something else, but he held back. Nick was a good guy, easy-going, a guy who never really applied himself to anything. He made it on looks, personality, and natural talent but would likely end up playing a few years of junior college ball before blowing out a knee and taking over his dad's liquor store. He'd have season tickets to the Vikings, he'd over-coach his kids through sports, he'd spend nights drinking too much and spilling on his yearbook. Cory backed off. Nick was harmless.

"You take care, man," Cory said with unusual softness. "Good game tonight." He gave him a little shove.

As Cory reached for the doorknob, Nick called to him. "Over your left!" The silver dollar flipped high through the air. As it came over Cory's shoulder, into his peripheral vision, he moved his left hand just so. It landed in his palm.

"Heads," Nick called.

Cory looked at the coin sitting tails up in his hand. "Heads it is," he said back to Nick, closing his fist around the coin.

Too wired to sleep, when Cory got home he went upstairs, told his mom he was in ("What are you doing home so early?") before going to the kitchen for a glass of milk. At the table, he looked at the blank sheet of paper. It was too late to call Joseph, but he had to tell him about the game. In neat handwriting he wrote about why he smoked that punter and about the school record. He dropped in a few lines about the party and the girls. Cory knew his antisocial side worried Joseph, who was everybody's best friend, so he didn't say much about how stupid it all felt to him. Joseph was too damn emotional, Cory thought, stamping the letter and putting it in his coat pocket to mail in the morning. That was Joseph's Achilles' heel.

In his room, Cory flopped down on the bed with an apple and his two shoeboxes of letters from Joseph. How many, it was hard to say. Maybe 70. He had read them all countless times over. The pages were wrinkled and softened from handling.

In the first shoebox, on top, serving as a paperweight was the small Welcome Home needlepoint he'd taken from the cabin on Lake of the Woods. He turned it over in his hands, tracing the threaded words, feeling the bumpy ornate border. He set it aside. One of his favorite letters, from back in eighth grade, was near the top. It was from when Joseph's hockey team played the rival town, International Falls, in the regional playoffs. It was dated February 13, 1975. Cory bit into his apple and read.

Hi Cory,

Thanks for your last letter. Sounds like hockey is going good. We had our playoffs last night and guess what? It was 44 below zero! Without windchill! I swear. Our coach tried to reschedule but their coach said no way. So we played. Each line would skate a shift, but instead of going over the boards and standing in the snowbank, you'd head straight to the warming house. When the next line came in, you'd head back out and skate another shift while the other guys warmed up. It kept going back and forth like that, but pretty soon it was taking everybody longer and longer to warm up. That was fine by me because I never get very tired and the cold doesn't really get to me.

The coach just kept me out there. I skated the whole second period except for coming off once because I couldn't feel my toes in my right skate. Our team's lucky. We're sponsored by the city maintenance department. They drive the big snow-plows and sand trucks right down to the rink and Mom and Father Pat and all the other parents climbed up and squeezed into the cabs and watched from there. Mom says the heaters could melt your pants and they sit up so high, the view of the game is much better than standing on snowbanks.

In the warming house before the third period, some of the guys were rolling around on the ground and even crying because their toes and fingers got frostbite. I can't wait till we get an indoor rink like you guys. The coach asked me if I could skate the whole third period. We were short because a few parents said that's enough and dragged their kids off the ice. I was rubbing my toes and they went from being numb to being on fire. I said I'd give it a try. I wasn't going to lose to International Falls. They think they're so bad!

Our guys who couldn't play anymore put on their boots and climbed up in the snowplows to watch. Mom said it killed them but the parents said it's 50 bleeping below and the game should be cancelled. I was glad it wasn't because we were getting beat two-zip. I scored right away in the third. Upper-left corner (a number 2). The plow drivers laid on their horns and turned on all their flashing lights and I warmed right up like you couldn't believe. Something must have happened because I started feeling better and everyone else seemed like they didn't. I scored 5 straight goals and we won 5 to 2. The newspaper made a story out of it, and it feels kinda dumb reading it, but Mom bought a bunch of copies so I cut one out and sent it along. I got black blisters on all my toes from frostbite and the tips of two fingers are numb with the skin peeling off. It's just like a burn, so it'll heal up fine. It doesn't hurt as much today as yesterday anyway.

We all got big trophies and had pizza after we won. You should have seen our team in those snowplows coming down Main Street with the lights flashing. It felt like the Stanley Cup. I wish you could have been there. I know you would have lasted the whole game too. Pretty soon we'll be playing in college together. Hope you like the article. It's pretty funny.

Your best friend and future linemate,
Joseph

Cory looked at the old yellowed newspaper clipping that had been folded up in the letter.

FIFTY BELOW CAN'T STOP BLACKHOLM AND THE BAUDETTE MUNIE BLACKHAWKS

Joseph Blackholm, skating most of the second and all of the third periods, almost single-handedly beat the unbeaten International Falls Cougars in Friday's single-elimination playoff championship. Blackholm had 5 goals, 4 of them unassisted. All of his goals came in the third period when as many as one-third of the skaters could play no more. "The kids' toes and fingers were like icicles," said Blackhawks coach, Dennis Toomey. Before the puck dropped, Toomey wanted to reschedule the game on account of the bitter conditions, but International Falls refused. "[Their coach] used some language not fit for print. Essentially what he said implied our jerseys should be pink. The guy's

> dumber than potting soil, always has been," said Toomey at the afterparty at Carballas Pizza. "I used to skate against him back in high school."
>
> Joseph Blackholm was named team MVP at the party and quipped that it was short for Most Valuable Pizza eater. He went on to prove it by eating a large pepperoni with extra cheese all by himself. This is one reporter, who after watching the hockey clinic Blackholm displayed on the rink earlier, thought he'd seen it all. Let me tell you, folks. You haven't seen anything until you've watched this kid eat.

Cory lay back on his bed with a tennis ball. He tossed it in the air, just high enough to skim-touch the ceiling, and caught it with one hand when it came down. Over and over and over, always working on the hand-eye. Left hand. Right hand. Left hand. Right hand.

He thought about his best friend Joseph and about those years after the accidents and the tradition of going north to the farm for Thanksgiving break to play hockey. And, in the summers, how he went and stayed with Darlene and Stu in July and worked at the resort. The fishermen he was paired with always looked skeptical when they saw they were getting Cory as a guide. "He's just a kid," they'd complain. But Stu's rebuttal was always the same: "If you don't limit out, the boat, the gas, and the guide are no charge." Cory never had a disappointed customer. He knew the hot spots, he worked them hard, and he kept the beer cold. And he never wet a line himself unless they needed a few more fish to limit out. "You do the catching, I do the netting" was his motto. At the end of the day, he'd clean their catch and put the fillets on ice.

All the lifting, hauling, and gophering—and Darlene's cooking—helped Cory put on some much-needed hockey weight. He missed jogging, because you can only run so far on an island, but he made up for it by swimming every day and rowing a couple hours every other night.

At first, Cory wasn't much of a swimmer. He'd thrash the water, but after about 60 yards he'd blow out of steam. Darlene got in the water with him and forced him, over and over, to learn the proper technique for the freestyle stroke. As Cory advanced, she'd paddle a canoe off his side, belting out instruction. By the end of his five-week stay that first summer, Cory was the best swimmer she'd ever seen. He put his mind to it and was utterly relentless. His legs, his back, his shoulders and his cardiovascular strength made tremendous gains. Cory could freestyle swim for a straight hour by the time he left, and even now, four days a week, he did his hour of laps at the YMCA.

On the nights that Cory rowed, Stu would sit in the bow of a beat-up aluminum 16-footer with a trolling spoon rigged on heavy Dacron line and a stout rod. Cory pulled on the oars for 60 to 90 minutes, depending on when the mosquitoes drove them in. Stu would strip out 20 yards of line and that lure would flutter behind them as Cory followed the shorelines of the islands and bays. They landed a few muskies over 40 pounds that way. But mostly Stu would stick the rod under his leg, light his pipe, and tell stories about the great days of hunting and fishing when he was Cory's age. *Come fall, the sky would get so black with ducks you wouldn't see the sun for days. In spring, the spawning fish in the warm-water bays got thick enough to walk across without so much as a drop of water getting on your boots.* Cory would pull hard, using his legs and his upper body, listening to tales in rhythm to the cries of the oarlocks. The sun would quietly duck behind the western horizon, lighting the underbellies of huge cumulus clouds loafing across the sky. It was the closest thing he knew to contentment.

The descending tennis ball bounced off Cory's hand, rolled off his fingers, and dropped to the floor. End of game. Once you miss it, that's it. He grabbed his half-eaten apple off the shoebox top and dug into the stack for another letter. This was one of the first he'd received, dated December 15, 1973.

Cory,

It's going to be sad without Dad for Christmas. I had an idea that I guess backfired. We hadn't cut our tree yet because Dad always took us on the tractor to get just the right one. He'd drive us close and then pull our hats over our eyes and take us on the toboggan through the woods and when he stopped and said okay, Mom and I pulled our hats up and would be looking up at the perfect tree. Dad always found them and this year I knew Mom wasn't up to it. So yesterday when I went to catch the bus, I went into the woods and skipped school. I had put some tools and the toboggan down by the creek. I looked for hours and finally found the perfect tree. I cut it and dragged it out and still had some time before Mom was off work so I put it up and decorated it and everything.

When Mom got home, I told her hockey practice was canceled and I had a surprise for her. She covered her eyes and I led her into the family room and when she uncovered them she just stood there really quiet and cried. I tried to make her laugh by asking did she think I picked a Charlie Brown Christmas tree but that didn't work. So anyway, Christmas is going to be tough. I hope yours will be good. Maybe with having sisters in the house it won't seem as empty.

You asked in the last letter about the dream vision I had about you the day my dad died. No I don't think it's weird. There are many stories about stuff like that happening in our history. I think you and I were introduced early by the Dream Spirit so that when we met at the door, we were already friends. My dad said when people meet and like each other right away or even feel like they've met before, they have. I better get going on my math. Do you know the square root of 144? What's a square root? Is that a root that's very uncool? Ha ha. Merry Christmas and talk to you next year.

Your best friend,
Joseph

Twelve, Cory said, in answer to the square root question. He knew it then, too. Now in his senior year, he could get an academic scholarship to most any college he cared to, but he was going to go to college on a hockey scholarship and so was Joseph. They had decided that the first Thanksgiving together out on the pond. That was their vow. Cory could no sooner go back on that than he could ask his dad for advice.

The University of Minnesota had recruited Cory, hard. He asked the recruiter if they knew of a Joseph Blackholm up in Baudette. He said sure, but he's an Indian. He wouldn't fit into our program. Cory hung up. The recruiter called back and asked what happened to the connection. Cory left the receiver off the hook. The head coach called a day later. Said they were extremely interested in Cory. Talked the talk. National championship heritage. Tons of exposure. Ice time as a freshman. The whole song and dance. Cory asked about Joseph. The coach said he had heard of him, but had never seen him play. He said the program only had so many scholarships. Cory had the last one if he wanted it. Cory told the coach that he and Joseph looked forward to beating him in the future.

In the bottom of the shoebox, Cory hid his recruiting letter from the University of Minnesota. He didn't want his mom to see it. Her hope was that he'd stay close to the apartment. Close to her and his sisters. They needed him, his mom said. Especially your little sister. No hockey program was closer to home than the U of M's. Cory lied and said they hadn't made contact. Finishing his apple, Cory looked at their recruitment letter.

Dear Cory,

I've been notified that we've spoken to you about playing hockey for the Golden Gophers and you've expressed to our staff that you're only interested in further conversations if we include another player in them.

Son, I admire your loyalty. Hockey is a team sport and it's good to see a player thinking beyond himself. But a team is only as strong as the individuals and it's time you thought more about yourself and your future. The education and exposure you will get from the University of Minnesota is second to none. It will open a great many doors, now and after graduation. I urge you to reconsider. My head coach has informed me that this other player you speak of is a fine player, but there isn't a spot for him on our scholarship list. I give you my word he will be given every possible chance should he try out for the team as a walk-on.

Let me reiterate, this is about you right now, and your future. You'd be in very good hands at the U of M. Please feel free to phone me anytime so we can discuss it further. Good luck this season and God bless.

Tom "Buzz" Sager
Athletic Director, University of Minnesota

What a bullshit artist, Cory thought. He put the letters away, spun around and tossed the apple core across the room into the wastebasket. It was almost one a.m. and he had to be up in six hours for work. His body had finally settled down from the game. His neck was stiff from the hit he put on that punter. He looked at the game ball on his desk next to his physics text. He wanted to go to bed. He was tired now. But there was one loose end.

The punter's name was Mark McDonnell. His father was a prominent trial attorney and that was part of the reason the kid had such a mouth on him. On the rare occasions when his dad was around, he was ceaselessly blowharding about some case or another. The kid learned from the best how to run his mouth. On top of that, his dad gave him everything he wanted to compensate for being a no-show parent.

Cory found their address in the phone book. It was over in a wealthy suburb west of Minneapolis. Cory had been to a party in the area once before. With Cory, being there once was all it took. He scooped up his mom's car keys and tucked the game ball under his arm, careful to shut the door softly.

Cory stood on the McDonnell's stoop, shuffling foot to foot. He was about to ring the bell for the fourth time when the overhead light came on and he heard someone unbolting the lock. A man with gray hair and a satin robe opened the door. He looked, Cory thought, like Hugh Heffner.

"What is it?" Mr. McDonnell asked. "Has there been an accident?"

"Who is it?" a woman's voice squeaked from the top of the stairs.

"Sir, is Mark home?" Cory asked.

"Debra, see if Mark's in bed," the attorney barked at the stairwell. Then he faced Cory and looked at the football. "What's this about? Are you on Mark's team?"

"No, sir, I'm not."

"Honey, he's not in bed," the wife yelled from the upstairs landing. "What's happening?"

"Who are you?" the attorney asked, coming fully out of his sleep, deepening his voice, straightening his posture, eyeing Cory.

"My name is Cory Bradford. I brought your son tonight's game ball."

"Jonathan?" the wife ventured down the first few stairs.

"I thought you said you weren't on Mark's team."

"I'm not. I'm on the team that played Mark tonight. I was given the game ball, but I thought he should have it."

A looked crossed the attorney's face. A look of *oh, I see what the fuck this is now.* His voice raised, but cracked, which shamed him some. "Hey. It's one fucking thirty in the morning and you're on some dangerously thin ice here."

"Jonathan, should I call the police?" his wife asked, hearing her husband's rising tone.

"What's your name, smart guy?" The attorney glared at Cory.

"I've told you, sir. Cory Bradford."

Further recognition came over the attorney's face. "You're the punt returner. You're the asshole who nearly put my son in the hospital."

"I'm calling the police," Mrs. McDonnell said, now fully to the door, wearing a matching satin robe.

"Probably not a good idea, ma'am," Cory said. "They'll likely get here just about the time your boy pulls up drunk in his Corvette or Firebird or whatever car you've undoubtedly bought for him. He'll get a DWI and I'll probably just get the game ball back." Cory looked at them both. A moth fluttered near the overhead light, throwing strange, large shadows.

"Get out of here," the attorney spat. "Go back over to wherever you live, climb back in bed with your sister or whatever it is you people do over there and stay off my property."

Cory's hand was a blur. The attorney's eyes hardly had time to widen before the game ball was shoved into his soft midsection. Cory heard an oof! of air come out of him. "Tell your son," Cory said slowly, "I'll be seeing him on the rink. If he doesn't clean up his act and play the game right, tell him that little hit I put on him tonight was just a teaser."

"Get the hell off my property!" the attorney wheezed.

Cory put his finger to his lips. "Shhh. Please, sir, this is a respectable neighborhood. People are trying to sleep." He turned and walked away.

The McDonnells stood in disbelief on the threshold of their brick tudor watching Cory drive off in the rusted-out station wagon. "Fucking lowlife," the attorney hissed. "Doesn't he realize where he is?"

Cory tossed and rolled through the black morning hours and dreamt football dreams. Physically, he was his current size, but his abilities were those of a young boy, maybe seven. He and his dad were at the park they frequented on summer nights to work on Cory's sports. In his dream, his dad kicked punts high into the wind and Cory weaved under them. They came down in his hands, ball after ball after ball, fumbled. His dad would lay into him: *C'mon! You should be able to handle those.* Cory felt the same way. He should. As the summer evening wore on, he tried and tried, but he never caught a single one.

Finally, the day just ran out of light.

JOSEPH.

Joseph crouched in the drizzle with his shotgun. His dog, Lick, kept his eyes on the gray skies, eyebrows twitching, watching for any movement above the six mallard decoys bobbing on the water. Father Pat sat alongside, his mind elsewhere, thoughts piling up, trying to find a place to start. How, he wondered, do you tell a boy you love that you love his mother? *How does a priest do this?*

These were the last days of October, and you could feel the intention in the air. Soon the drizzle would crystallize, then snow. By sundown, Joseph knew, snow would surely come.

For Pat, undoubtedly, it had been the worst month of his life. The Boston suicides had convinced him he could go down no further, but this latest incident—and its aftermath—proved him wrong. Had it not been for Monsignor Kief's support and Joseph's persistence, Father Pat would have just tucked up in a ball.

What a blessing, Joseph. Coming to take him running three times a week. Dragging him out to watch the high school football team get beat on Friday nights—Monsignor Kief at his shoulder. These friends on either side of him. Joseph doing his comic version of play-by-play as the Baudette boys got hammered into the turf. Monsignor Kief, asking for ever more detail: who has the ball now, Joseph? What yard line are they on? Is our quarterback still picking his nose?

Three weeks earlier, Joseph hunted the opening weekend, but he did so alone. Father Pat was still refusing phone calls and Cory had a football game. They hadn't, as a group, missed an opener in the last three years. Joseph and Lick found themselves with too much room in the duck blind.

"Double coming in," Joseph whispered abruptly to Pat. Lick's body went on alert; his nostrils flared at the anticipatory note of Joseph's voice. Two mallards, 60 yards out, cupped their wings and dropped through the mist toward the decoys. "You want them both?" Joseph asked. "I've shot plenty this season."

"I'll take the drake on the right," Pat said, quietly, pulling his hand out of his jacket pocket, finding the gun's safety. The ducks sailed in.

"Take 'em," Joseph said. Both men shouldered their shotguns and Joseph fired quickly, missing. Pat swung steady on his drake and folded it with one shot. Joseph pulled the trigger again and missed with his second and final barrel. "She's yours, Father!" Joseph said. Pat swung. The hen was rising fast above the decoys. He got his barrel over the duck, leading her, and squeezed off the final shell in his double barrel. The hen cartwheeled and landed heavily behind them in the cattail muck. "Great shot, Father!" Joseph laughed. "Lick!" Joseph commanded. "Dead bird! Fetch!" Joseph hand-signaled the lab in the direction of the fallen hen, and Lick followed the line out, disappearing headlong into the wall of cattails. "What a double, Father! Nice shooting!" Father Pat was beaming. He hadn't taken a double like that since he couldn't remember.

"I think that hen came down hard," Pat said, nodding, excited. "I don't think it was a cripple."

"Boy, she was up there, but that bird's dead, sure." Joseph smiled big and wide. A few moments later Lick came powering out of the slough with the hen.

"Look at you!" Joseph praised. "Good fetch." Father Pat added, "Lick, good boy!" Lick, after retrieving the hen, swam out and mouthed the second mallard, which he also fetched to Father Pat. With both ducks at his feet, Father Pat felt better than he had in weeks: the rain dripping off the bill of his cap. The residual adrenaline. The wide open of duck slough and surrounding fields. It sure beat the tight, painted walls of Monsignor Kief's guest room. Joseph couldn't stop smiling. Lick trembled for more.

"Coffee?" Joseph asked, setting his gun down and reaching for the Thermos.

"Please, yes." Pat listened. The rain had begun to sharpen its pitch as it struck their coats. "That rain's changing its mind, Joseph."

"Sleet then snow, you can bank on it. The ducks should be flying low so keep an eye peeled." Joseph uncapped the Thermos.

There was a prolonged silence as he poured Father Pat a steaming black cup. It filled their nostrils briefly before the wind stole it away.

"Joseph, there are a few things I need to say … to talk about with you." Pat looked up from his coffee. "Maybe now's as good a time as any." He squinted through the sleet watching for Joseph's reaction.

Joseph heard the tension in Pat's voice. "Sure, Father. But you don't owe me any explanation or anything. Just so you know."

"I appreciate that." Pat looked the young man in the eyes. The air's moisture, rather than fogging the moment, magnified it. "But it's more for my sake than yours … so we can get restarted."

"How do you mean?"

"I mean we can't go back to being how we were before the fire."

Joseph began to interrupt, but Pat put his hand up, then let it fall on Joseph's shoulder. He looked at him with a glint of urgency.

“It’s not a bad thing, us restarting, going forward. You’re o[illegible]ously not a boy anymore. But that’s how I originally saw it. A boy, coming out of the woods, mourning his father, needing *my* help. I’ve now come to realize it was you who were sent out of the woods to find me. Tumbled in the ditch in Monsignor Kief’s car. You pulled *me* up. I had things backward. Exactly, perfectly, ironically backward. Long ago, Joseph, I had a dream that I helped a young boy in great sorrow. It was this dream that called me to the priesthood. When I first learned of your dad’s accident, and you, vanished, I assumed the boy was you and I was sent here to help. Now I realize I was the boy in that dream and it was you who held out your hand. You’ve picked me up from this disaster in my life. It was you who waited in the hallway, literally and figuratively. You pushed me back into the community. You even missed that duck there to give me the chance at shooting two. In more ways than I’ve counted, I’m sure, it’s you.”

Joseph looked at the priest. He loved the man like a brother and like a father. He’d been there so much for Joseph in the past five years. It was hard to see him so pained. “Here’s where I come out on things, Father. Actually, here’s what I know. No real friendship is as simple as you’ve just put it. It’s not you’re down and I’m up. It’s not boy and man. Even father and son don’t remain so one-sided, one giving, one taking. At any time, anyone can pull the other up.

“When my dad was a boy,” Joseph continued, “he had many friends and a few enemies. He told me about a kid who lived over on the reservation that was about a year older. This kid was meaner than the dogs he kept chained to a stake in the yard. One day in spring, my dad had his canoe out fishing in the river that wound through the reservation. The water level was very high from the snowmelt and the rapids swamped him. Dad was swept downstream. He yelled and yelled but he kept getting towed under by that raging river. He said he didn’t think he’d live. All of a sudden, in front of him on the swollen bank, was his enemy. The kid he’d had rock fights with, the kid he’d made fun of and cursed and ridiculed. This kid threw my dad a loop of rope. He pulled him in. On the shore, my dad was completely ashamed. My father's lesson from that day, the lesson he told me to never forget, was don't think you know so much about a person. Don't judge him or live by the foolish belief you've figured him out. Because that person may be the one to throw you the rope. Unexpectedly. On the bank. When you most need it.

"As far as I see it, Father, it hasn't been you being pulled or me pulling or like that. We've both been in that river some. We've been on both ends of the rope."

Pat just smiled at Joseph. Joseph couldn't help but smile back. He was wired to smile, it was hair-trigger. His smile, wide and crooked, his front teeth gapped, what an absolute beauty that smile was.

They sat there, grinning, as four mallards came dive-bombing out of the low smudge of clouds, and then peeled up and away as the men scrambled for their shotguns.

"We blew them," Joseph laughed.

"Joseph," Pat started again, "there are two things I want to tell you about me and about what happened a month ago. The first is I've finally come to accept that I'm an alcoholic. I've joined A. A. and I'm trying to live a sober life. My dad is a big drinker and a real mess and I think—I know—I'm not built for the consumption of alcohol. It started with a long talk with Monsignor Kief. He told me if I didn't quit, right now, he'd have to recommend my transfer. This is my last chance up here. Monsignor Kief already went out on a limb getting me here. We talked about the troubles I've had in the past, and alcohol has always been there. I'm through with it." Father Pat looked unflinchingly at Joseph.

"I'm glad to hear it, Father. I don't drink either. I've seen what that poison does on the Rez." Joseph clenched his jaw. "The fights, robbery, rapes, child abuse, unemployment—I hate it. I have no desire to associate with it. It's pollution."

Father Pat nodded. "The second thing is about your mother. I'm not ashamed of this, Joseph, I just don't know where it leaves me, and you and me. You see, I love her. I have for some time, I've come to realize. Not only as a priest, but I love her as a man. When I saw her with Roger, all of that came to a head. I told your mother how I felt. Our faith—or at least the Roman Catholic Church—doesn't allow for such a possibility. The law of our Church is I'm to commit to God. I've made a celibacy vow to Him. We're told it's our gift back to God, and it's unconditional.

"Your mom was rightfully upset and confused that night. I went home and the drinking started and that led to the fire that took the rectory." Pat hung his head.

Joseph whistled low through his teeth, unguarded, honestly. "Whew. That's … that's a lot. I don't … what does Monsignor Kief say about you loving Mom?"

"He says I have a decision to make."

"And what do you say?"

"I say, I love them both. I love the Church. And I love her. I say I'm stuck. I'm waiting for a sign. Joseph, it's important for you to speak honestly and openly to me about this."

Joseph thought about it, not for long. "It's for you and Mom. The laws of the Church have no more place in this than the laws of the government had in telling us where to bury Dad. Laws are for people who don't know better. You two are to judge. Why would the Great Spirit have brought you together? It's for you two to find the reason. In the end, all I know for sure is I'm your friend."

Father Pat buried his head in his hands and wept. It was like a truck had been lifted off his back. He felt he'd deceived Joseph, even though he hadn't. The relief, the guilt, the self-loathing, the confusion, it all poured out to be left there in the duck blind, piling on his boots along with the sleet. Lick rested his head on Pat's knee.

After 10 minutes, Father Pat was shaking. He wiped his face and tried to draw a few deep, steady breaths. His reserves were drained. The cold had no mercy.

"I'm done hunting if you are," Joseph said. "I've got a week's worth of duck hanging in the barn and you have two fresh mallards for you and Monsignor Kief. If you like, there's some wild rice back at the house you could take with your birds. Monsignor Kief would be in heaven."

"Agreed. But I don't know about getting the rice. I'm not quite ready to see your mom yet."

"No worries. She works 'til six."

"Joseph, how lucky I am to have a friend like you. You are my blessing. Is there anything—you know—anything you need to ask of me? Any questions? Just ask."

Joseph thought. He furrowed his brow. "Yeah. How did you know I missed that duck on purpose? I thought I did a good job of missing it."

Pat smiled thinly and Joseph laughed. "Joseph, you're too good a shot and too lousy a liar. That's your cross to bear."

For that night's dinner, Monsignor Kief was indeed in heaven. Wild rice with peach-stuffed mallard wrapped in bacon. Broccoli. A loaf of fresh-baked pumpernickel. On more than one occasion, Pat's right hand reached out for the wine glass and found water in its place. A pleasant surprise. The room was warm and comforting in its quiet; Pat breathed deeply. He felt himself finding some measure of cadence, a slowing down, a rhythm resetting.

"How nice it must have been to be back hunting today," Monsignor Kief said between bites.

"Frank, that Joseph, he stuns me. For a boy still in high school—any age for that matter—he positively stuns me. He's a miracle. I told him today of my alcohol addiction and I confessed my conflicted feelings for his mother. How does a priest say such things to a boy? I've struggled with that question for days, months, maybe years. You know what he said when I told him?"

Monsignor Kief put down his fork. "No, I'm sure I don't."

"He said, it's for you two to decide, not him to judge. He said he's my friend. He said you never know who's going to throw you a rope."

"I'm sorry. I lost you there. Who's going to throw whom a rope?" A puzzled look took over the Monsignor's face.

"Joseph believes we're all thrown a rope, symbolically speaking, that pulls us from troubles. And that rope may come from someone we'd least expect."

"You're right," Monsignor Kief agreed. "The boy is a miracle. Sometimes it's so obvious. His connection to divinity is so direct. We're lucky to have him."

"Lucky to have him, *and* you, Frank," Pat added. "It gives me faith, the proximity of you two. Knowing I'm no farther than rope-throwing distance."

"Thank you for saying so." Frank was noticeably moved by Pat's words.

"Frank, I think I might be ready to take over Sunday mass again. I would like to face my congregation, if nothing more, after mass, to try and explain what happened and how we're planning to rebuild. I'm not sure I'm ready, but by the same token, I'm not sure a person's ever fully prepared for turning points until he's there, turning."

"I agree fully. Part of your healing process will come in seeing those people you care for. They care for you too, Pat. They're anxious to see you back, healthy and happy. You'd be surprised how much they need to hear from you again."

"I feel I let them down so." Pat studied the blind man's face. His serenity was displaced.

"Pat, if you let them down, it's your responsibility to help them back up. Isn't that what Joseph has taught us? They have always admired your strength. In good times and in bad. As have I."

"But I don't know where I'm headed. I can't mislead them and say otherwise."

"You'll never find out where you're headed by remaining still. You need to take a step."

Pat finally arrived at the center of the issue, the area he had been tiptoeing around, but hadn't the courage to address directly.

"Am I fit to preach, Monsignor?"

"Pat, people need to hear the word of God. We all have our private struggles. The altar would be empty were it only taken up by perfect priests. Let your faith guide your life instead of vice versa. You have been called to save a child's heart from despair. This you know. There is no greater calling. Hear me say this," Frank's face, now beguiling, without a wrinkle, "you will surprise yourself yet. I know it and it gives me great peace saying so."

Pat wondered, not unsure of the veracity of his Calling Dream, but what was the meaning? Was he to help or be helped? At the quiet dinner table, he sat, empty fork hovering above his uneaten food.

That night at the farm, Joseph too cooked mallards and wild rice. He wanted to surprise his mom by coming home early from the hunt and getting dinner on the table. He found the few good dishes she kept put away in the bottom drawer of the pine bureau, and set the table. Found the candles tucked away, too. They had one dinner's melt from them, certainly a dinner long ago with Dad. They were wrapped in tissue. Joseph placed them on the table. He felt good, fortunate. There was no emptiness.

"Something smells very, very good," HomeSky said, pushing the door shut, leaning on it with her shoulder, stomping the snow off her shoes, hooking her car keys on the peg and hanging her coat over them. The long day, the wind-whipped cold, the sudden warm rush of the kitchen and its aromas, oven baking, brought such instant radiance to her face; her beauty was further pronounced.

"Hello there," Joseph said with a grin. "Wash your hands for supper and be fully prepared to grasp what it's like to be the luckiest woman on mother earth—or the luckiest mother on woman earth."

"What is it I smell?" she asked, going quickly to the kitchen sink to wash her hands. Joseph almost pointed out this breach of her own rules, but there was no reason to detract from the moment. She dried her hands absentmindedly as she moved toward the oven for a peek inside.

"Uh-uh!" Joseph wagged his finger. "No looking. Just sit and be served, madam."

HomeSky sat in the dining room candlelight. She watched through to the kitchen as her child, all six feet two, 225 pounds of him, spooned hot cranberries into a serving bowl. He fixed two plates, careful to keep his body between her sight line and the entrée. "Okay. Close your eyes," Joseph said, bringing in the ducks on their beds of wild rice. The skin of the mallards had browned and crisped perfectly. He set HomeSky's plate down before her. "All right. Open."

"Oh my goodness! It's a sight to behold. And on the good plates." Joseph relished her excitement. "What have I done to deserve to be treated like the queen of Sheba?"

"I finished hunting with Father Pat early, and that last corn field's too wet to go into, so I got domestic. Doesn't it look tasty?" Joseph asked, like Lick, hopeful for more scratching.

"It looks so wonderful I could cry." HomeSky felt such overwhelming tenderness, she though she just might.

"Don't do that. You'll get my rice soggy. Dig in already. It'll get cold. Especially those cranberries."

As they ate, they talked about HomeSky's day at Lu Ann's. Mr. Swenson's meatloaf was overcooked (he said), Ruth Kippin complained about the drafty seat she was given (she moved three times), and Larry and Kent asked if Joseph had gotten his deer yet (yes, with a bow, first day).

HomeSky ate two-thirds of her duck before she edged back to the subject of Father Pat. Joseph, long done with his, was on to scraping together the last of the cranberries and rice onto his plate, making a medley. HomeSky said she was full and gave Joseph what was left of her duck.

"How is Father Pat doing?" she asked, quietly. "How is he, really?"

"I think he's going to be good. He shot a double today. He's getting back to his old self."

"Did he say anything? About him and me, I mean?" HomeSky watched Joseph stir his rice-cranberry hodgepodge.

"He said a lot about you and him, Mom. But that's between us, right? Just like our conversations are just between you and me."

"It's a little different, Joseph. I haven't been able to talk to him since the fire. I don't have any idea how he is."

"I just told you. He's good. He took a doub—"

"A double. I know. That doesn't give me much. Can't you tell me anything more without jeopardizing his trust?"

Joseph looked at his mom, tenderly, and bit his lip. "Nope. Sorry. Why don't you call him? There's this ingenious invention called the telephone."

"Seriously, Joseph," HomeSky said, a bit abruptly.

"I am serious, Mom. Call him. Everything will be clear as a brook."

She looked at her boy and couldn't help but smile. "You're not going to tell me a darn thing about what happened out there in that frozen duck blind, is that it?"

"Mom, talk to him. Or talk to me. But don't talk to him through me."

HomeSky thought for a second. There truly was nothing she couldn't discuss with her son, she knew that. He was an adult, but this was difficult. Friendship and religion and loneliness and love made for quite a tangled knot. Maybe talking with Joseph would begin to unravel it.

She began. "Father Pat told me, the night of the fire when you and Roger and I went bowling, he said he loved me. Not just spiritually, but more." HomeSky looked at Joseph, as if watching for something to fracture. Joseph looked back at her, unblinking. HomeSky exhaled and continued. "I said that can't be. The Catholic religion doesn't permit such a relationship. But he was sure about how he felt. I told him I couldn't have such feelings. That's the last I've seen him. I'm worried sick. I've overheard things Sheriff Harris said at the diner about the fire, and a night in jail, the hospital, and moving in with Monsignor Kief. I know you've seen him a few times, gone running, but you haven't said much about that. I need to know he's all right. That's why I'm prying." HomeSky looked at her son for help.

"You need to call him, Mom. You need to see him, for yourself. He's okay. Really. He's getting better. I think he's both ashamed and unashamed of his love. I imagine that's an incredibly hard place."

"Did he tell you he loves me?" HomeSky finally raised the courage to ask.

"Yes he did."

"What did you say?" HomeSky held her breath.

"I said I love you, too."

HomeSky could only shake her head. "I just never expected this, is all."

"Here it is though. Right, Mom?" Joseph smiled.

"Here it is," she replied, with a just a trace of a smile. A sad smile.

"Mom?"

"Yes."

"Ready to talk about something else for a minute?"

"Yes!"

"Cory's coming for Thanksgiving. I think Father Pat and Monsignor Kief should come like always, too."

"I thought we were changing the subject."

"We are, sorta. This is about Thanksgiving."

"I think it's great that Cory's coming. I think Father Pat and I will have to work out the other chairs at the table. I don't even know if he wants to come. And Monsignor Kief, what he must think about all of this."

"My vote is we invite them all. Get things back like they should be. So you talk to Father Pat. Just remember, Thanksgiving is coming fast, so you better make that call before it gets too late and they make other plans."

"Are you pressuring me?" HomeSky asked, suppressing a smile.

"Me? Pressure? Mom, c'mon." Joseph tried his best to keep a serious face. He waved a hand through the air, "I'm but a humble cook. What would a kitchen worker know from pressure?" With that, Joseph got up to do the dishes. Actually, he got up to turn toward the sink with his plate. He didn't want his mom to see the smile on his face.

"Humble cook my eye," HomeSky said, tossing her napkin at him. "I'll do those," she said, sliding back her chair, picking up her dishes. "You made supper. Go relax. Read."

"No, no," Joseph said. "From what I understand, you have a phone call to make."

HOMESKY.

Stroking the length of her hair with her grandmother's maple-handled brush, HomeSky met her dark eyes in the mirror for an honest conversation. Long stroke followed long stroke. "This is one of the few luxuries I allow you," she told her reflection. "But you do have a phone call to make, so enough stalling." Her reflection was stunning, but this was lost on her. Her smooth, tan skin. High cheekbones. Long slender nose with a thin, hardly perceptible scar across it from an icicle she knocked off the roof as a girl: she was admiring her snowball accuracy and failed to move quickly enough as a piece of the icicle struck her. For the most part, she appeared regal, except for her dry, callused hands and her swollen feet. Hers were the hands and feet of a peasant. But the long smooth of her night-black hair, the curving line of her lips, how she held her head, there was a royalty about her.

"HomeSky," she prodded, "you can't sit here forever."

Across the cold pine floor, she walked barefoot into Joseph's room. He lay on the floor, next to his bed, too big to read comfortably on the single he'd long since outgrown. "What are you reading?" she asked, crouching down to see. "Dylan Thomas. I'm impressed."

"I'm ..." he looked at his mom and rubbed his face, "in over my head. I think I like it. Monsignor Kief said it's worth the struggle."

"Is there anything you need?" HomeSky asked.

"What do you mean, Mom? Like a new tractor or something?" Joseph smiled.

"Like a hot chocolate. You know, anything?"

"Nothing I can think of."

They looked at each other.

"Well, maybe I'll call Father Pat then."

"Sounds good."

"Okay then."

"Okay then," Joseph returned, on the brink of laughing. His mom was usually so sure of herself.

HomeSky went to the phone in the kitchen, exhaled fully, and picked the receiver off its hook on the wall. She started dialing Pat's number, but then remembered his home no longer existed. She opened the cupboard. At eye level, her finger traced down the list of phone numbers neatly written on notepaper taped to the inside of the door. She dialed Monsignor Kief's. On the third ring, Pat answered. "Mount St. Olivet residence, Father Pat speaking."

"Hello, Father," HomeSky said.

"Well, hello to you," he said back. She instantly felt relieved at the sound of his voice. The tone. The brightness. He sounded himself. He sounded good. She hiked herself up on the countertop, disregarding her own rule, settling in for a talk.

"We had duck here tonight," Father Pat opened, fairly safely. "Birds Joseph and I shot today. With a bit of your wild rice on the side. The Monsignor was beside himself. He's out in the study squared off against the largest bowl of toasted almond fudge I've ever laid eyes on. Why he doesn't weigh 300 pounds, it's the greatest mystery since water into wine."

"Joseph made duck for us, too. It was delicious." She struggled with how to continue.

"HomeSky, let me just say how sorry I am for the way I've acted. I don't know what to say. I've really put you in an awkward position."

"Let's not do this on the phone. I just wanted to hear your voice right now, hear for myself you're okay. We should be face-to-face when we talk. I should have said more that night. I'm so sorry I couldn't."

"Don't apologize," Pat said. "Please don't do that."

"What are your plans for tomorrow?" HomeSky asked.

"Tomorrow. Let's see. I'll be out on the rectory grounds most of the day, meeting with a builder. I'm playing general contractor these days."

"How's the project going?"

"We're trying to pull together the money for the framing materials. That will get us off the ground. It'll take close to twenty thousand to get things buttoned up and roofed before winter. Then I'll do a lot of the inside stuff myself. There are a few plumbers and electricians out here that have offered to pitch in when I'm stuck. Maybe by late spring, assisted by a number of small miracles, we'll get everything right again."

"How much will all that come to in the end?"

"Somewhere in the neighborhood of thirty thousand."

"But thirty thousand!" HomeSky said. "How will you manage?"

"I'm working on a plan as we speak. It won't be easy, but I'm not prepared to take no for an answer."

"Can I come out and see what you've planned?"

"By all means. I'd love to show you around." Pat took a quick breath. "I must ask, did Joseph say anything to you?"

"What do you mean, exactly?"

"About our hunting conversation."

"All he said was we needed to talk in person."

"I couldn't agree more. There's this … wall between us. That can't be."

"No. It can't."

"We'll catch up on everything when you come out. Just be prepared. It's a tough sight, seeing it all in ruins."

"Don't you worry about me. Buildings can be replaced. Most everything can."

"Most everything," Pat said, wistfully. "Let's say 10 a.m.?"

"How about noon? Then I can bring lunch."

"HomeSky, you don't have—"

"I'd like to. I'd like to help, somehow. I feel partially responsible."

"That's good of you, thanks. But don't believe for a second you're at all responsible for that mess. It's the work of one man. I'll humbly accept as many helping hands as are willing, but that's my handiwork."

"I'm glad you're accepting help. And a little surprised, to be honest."

"All this has forced me to look at some things. I've got more to rebuild than the rectory. Symbolically, though, it's a perfect undertaking. Me and the rectory, we're both at square one. Monsignor Kief tactfully pointed it out." Pat chuckled. "Anyway, the rebuilding begins. We'll catch up on that and a few other surprises later."

"Other surprises?"

"Yes, for later. Noon, you said?"

"With lunch in tow."

"I very much look forward to seeing you then."

"Me too," HomeSky said, more than a little nervously.

The following day at 11:30, as Pat was in the pole barn taking an inventory of the tools, he heard a car door slam. Must be HomeSky, he thought, pleasantly surprised she was early. He came out into the sunlight holding an old hammer and was greeted by the sight of a smirking Sheriff Harris leaning on his squad car up on the driveway. "Piss," Father Pat said, under his breath, slowly climbing the rise. He'd put himself on a limited ration of curse words and wasn't sure if "piss" counted against it. HomeSky was due in less than half an hour, with lunch. Nothing would make Sheriff Harris happier than reporting *that* get-together to the locals. He was a king-sized gossip, and the townies leaned into his voice like they were hearing music. Inevitably, HomeSky would have to deal with the long looks and whispers from the patrons; that infuriated Pat. "Cool down," he said under his breath.

The Sheriff watched the priest ascending the hill. He noticed Father Pat appeared to have his strength back, his sense of stride. He also noticed Pat held a hammer in his hand. "I hope you're of better disposition than the last time we were standing here." The Sheriff chuckled, reaching into his right shirt pocket for a Camel.

"What can I do for you on this fine day, Sheriff?" Pat squinted into the sun, sidestepping the small talk.

The Sheriff forged ahead, digging for a truffle of gossip. "I hear you turned over a new leaf."

"How's that?" Pat asked, the muscles in his upper back tightening.

"Robinson who runs A.A. His sister bowls Thursdays with my secretary. Hell, it's all over town. You're dry as a bone, is the word."

Father Pat could do nothing but laugh. "You are an old woman, aren't you, Sheriff? There's nothing you like better than finding a spot on someone's laundry. Yeah, I'm going to A.A. You'll find me on a folding chair in the gym Saturdays eight to ten. And if you feel a continued urge to talk about it, speak with God. I could use the prayer."

"Ah. That's between the two of you," the Sheriff said, inhaling his cigarette, the irony totally lost on him.

"Then let's leave it there, okay Thurgood?" Pat said, meeting the Sheriff's eyes. The Sheriff coughed out, surprised to hear his first name. The priest continued to face him, but he appeared different. Calmer. That confrontational spark in his eye was subdued. He looked more ... what was the word the Sheriff was struggling for? Priestly. That was it.

Pat checked his watch. Ten minutes to twelve. "Sheriff, I'd love to stand in the sun and gossip the afternoon away, but as you know, there's a lot of work to be done. Is there something on your mind?"

"Monsignor Kief asked if I'd shoot out. Worries you're too busy. Asked if I'd look in on you. Maybe see if I can help some way. I told him I'd be happy to."

"Well, I sure would appreciate a hand with things. We're going to be swinging hammers next week, once we convince the lumberyard we've got the money to start the project."

"How's it all coming?"

"None too fast. We need twenty grand to get going."

The Sheriff took a long, contemplative pull on his cigarette. "Those lumber men are thieves." He scratched his chin, thinking. "Maybe I could talk to them about eating their mark-up on this one. Otherwise, there might just be a code violation or two on their property." The Sheriff smiled slyly.

"I'd appreciate whatever you could do. I've got to make this right for the reservation before I—" Pat stopped himself. "It needs to be made right here."

The two men looked at each other. *Before I ... what?* the Sheriff wondered. Uncharacteristically, he let it drop. "I'll see what I can do at the lumber yard," he said, crushing the cigarette butt under his steel-toed boot. "They love to fleece people from off."

"From 'off'?" Pat asked.

"Yeah. Non-locals. You don't need them treating you like a tourist."

"Appreciate it," Pat said.

Surprisingly, a fledgling camaraderie trickled between them.

They kept their distance, both glancing down, watching the butt come apart under the hard rubber tread. "I can reach you over at the Monsignor's, then?" the Sheriff asked.

"Yep. There or here."

"Good enough," the Sheriff said, shifting his sizable weight. "Good luck out here."

"Thank you, Thurgood," Pat said, looking up at the big man with his hard eyes and his large, soft face and his short, neatly clipped brown hair, still kept at military length. The autumn ruddiness flushed his cheeks.

"Sheriff will do just fine, Father. Most who called me Thurgood are gone now. I prefer to keep it that way." He looked at Father Pat with an intensity that could galvanize metal.

"Thanks for the visit." Pat extended a hand.

The Sheriff took it, and with unexpected lightness, clasped and shook.

Pat sat on a stump in a rectangle of sunlight, feeling the hard-worn smoothness of the old hammer's ash handle, thinking of the many hands that had taken it up before him, putting it to swing. Who before me, he wondered? Building what? The skills, the frustrations, the dreams of the hammer's keepers inspired him. They would be at his elbow.

He was beginning to feel less alone than at any time since he'd arrived at the reservation. He bowed his head and let the sun warm his neck, his shoulders, his wrists, his hands. His long, strong fingers rubbed the handle. It gave him peace doing so.

A car turned into the L of the long wooded drive and rolled to a stop near where Pat was sitting on the stump. He looked up. Behind the wheel was HomeSky, her dark hair pulled back. She smiled tentatively at him and he waved as his stomach tightened. He sifted for the primary emotion he felt upon seeing her. It was melancholy. Would he never get over this ache?

"Hi," she said, a little forcefully, stepping out of the car. "What a beautiful day."

"Snowing one day, sunny the next," Pat said, remaining seated, feeling safe on the warm stump.

"A man and his hammer," she said, approaching him. Her black hair was back in a ponytail, held in a loop of her own hair.

"Found it in the pole barn. It's got a few years on it. Made me think about all the hands that have taken it up." Pat let his thumb ride down the handle's length. "I hope it won't be too judgmental about its newest foreman." He looked up, smiled through the bright sun at HomeSky, and stood. They remained apart. The nuthatches flitted in the tree above. A squirrel was busy putting up winter rations. A wind blew lightly across their backs.

"I'm not sure where to start," Pat said.

"I've got some pickled beets and cheese and crackers. Maybe we start there?"

"Pickled beets?" Father Pat wrinkled his nose. "You really must be mad at me."

HomeSky smiled, this time fully, unrestrained, beautifully. "You haven't tried my sugar beets, so don't be so sure."

They stretched out a wool plaid blanket and sat. They talked about canning beets and buying bigger jogging shoes, the waning fall colors and Lu Ann's adding strawberry apple crisp to the dessert menu. The conversation was careful, like stepping out on early-season ice.

Then Pat lunged. "I said some things to you that I've been thinking about a lot."

"So did I—that I've thought a lot about, too."

Pat took a deep breath, some catching in his throat. "I've decided there are a few things I need to change in my life," he said, watching carefully for her reaction.

She squared her face and studied him. He looked tired, she thought. His hair thinner, his white eyelashes more pronounced; maybe it was the darkness under his eyes. But his eyes told another story. They were as dancing blue as ever—maybe more. He had the look of a man with a secret. HomeSky loved that look. When a man was brimming with the possibilities of something—it gave you a glance of him as a boy, catalytic, full of what-ifs.

Pat continued, looking back at her earnest face. "I've decided to quit drinking. I've joined A.A. I've gone three Saturdays and I hope to make it stick. It's a tight-knit group. Incredibly so. Forthright. Everyone there has lost so much to alcohol. We're all trying to fill a void, and we know more drinking's not the answer. I can tell these people things I've never said, even in the confessional."

"I'm so glad to hear it," HomeSky said quietly. "Alcohol ruined my father; I never told you that, did I?"

"No."

"It's a long story for another time. You said there were a *few* things to change. What else?"

"I'm taking a second job, or at least trying to."

"A second job?"

"I'm trying to get on at the McKnight plant, eleven 'til seven. That gets me back for my daily eight a.m. service. After some sleep, I can work on the rectory."

"If I count right, that's three jobs."

"I can't really count the rectory; that's spare time. But when you put pencil to paper, there's more than enough time. I could easily find eight hours a day for here. Except Sundays."

"What does that leave for sleep? You do need sleep, you know."

"Service is over at nine. Sleep 'til one or two. Pound nails 'til ten. Be to work at eleven. It's very doable."

"Pat, you'll work yourself sick."

Pat looked at her with more of a smile in his eyes than she was accustomed to. Usually, when he was challenged, his eyes fired in defiance. "No. I *am* sick. What I'll do is work myself healthy. I'll carve out time to run. I'll take care of myself. I'll wear my scarf and eat my vegetables." He laughed and took a big bite of a beet. "Whoa. This clean living won't be easy."

"Hey!" HomeSky smiled. "My beets have won ribbons."

"Help yourself then," Pat said, handing her the canning jar.

"Why all the work, Pat? Really?"

"Why?" he said, astonished. "In case you missed, there used to be a terrific two-level rectory standing over there with windows and carpet and nice appliances and a doorbell that played out a tune. That's going to take thirty thousand dollars to replace, *if* I do as much of it myself as possible."

"Thirty thousand!" she shook her head. "Where will you find that kind of money?"

"I've got eight thousand in savings and Monsignor Kief has ten. I told him absolutely not, but he said it's just sitting in the bank for a rainy day, and the way he sees it, it's coming down cats and cows. Of course I'll pay him back, with interest, but it's going to take a long time. There's only a ten-thousand dollar insurance reimbursement on the rectory because they've determined the cause of the fire was negligence. Frankly, they're right about that."

"Could you fight them on it?"

"After the attorney fees and whatnot, I don't think so. Worse yet, it would be like stealing. I'm at fault here."

"Don't let the insurance guys hear you say that or you might not get anything." HomeSky frowned. "Those people have no qualms about stealing as long as it's them doing it."

"If I get work at the plant, I can make up the difference and start paying Frank back."

"Joseph and I have a thousand, maybe thirteen hundred—"

Pat held up his hand. "No. Thank you, but absolutely not. You two have worked around the clock for what you have. I won't have a hand in that being compromised. I'm up to this. I'm going to live on the thin edge of a dime for a while, but so what? I'm indebted to my friends and this community to leave this place better than I found it."

HomeSky paused, digesting what he'd said. "What do you mean, leave?" she asked, startled.

"Oh, I don't know. I mean, whenever. We all leave eventually." Pat looked down at the blanket. He put his palm on the sun-warmed fabric and let the heat rise up through his hand, spreading throughout his body.

"Are you leaving us?" she asked.

He whispered, closing his eyes, feeling the warmth inching. "I'm considering leaving the priesthood. I don't know from there. I'm listening every day. I may stay as well. All I know for sure is I'm close to something. I must get stronger, make reparations, rectify friendships. This church, these sacred grounds, all of you deserve better. I'm going to make it better, make me better, and then I will, with an unclouded heart, make a decision. I'm not holding the answer behind my back. I don't know what I'll do. All I know is I'm on the path to finding it. And the path, I am glad to report, is not as straight and narrow as the Roman Catholic Church would have us all believe. We who stumble along its weedy ditches, we'll be okay." Pat opened his eyes and looked at HomeSky. A tear slid from the corner of his eye. She reached over to him and wiped it with her thumb. She let her hand linger there for a moment. Pat took her hand and squeezed it and gently set it back in her lap.

"I'm sorry to have dragged you into this," Pat said.

"You haven't *dragged* me into anything. I'm a grown woman. We got here together. I've been thinking, too. Maybe some of this is my fault. Maybe I was sending out mixed messages. I don't know. All I know is that I care for you. You've been nothing short of wonderful to me and Joseph. All the time you've spent with us has not just been as a priest; you've been a much-needed male presence. For us both. I honestly don't know for sure anymore. I just feel I abandoned you when you needed me most. I just didn't know what to do or say. You could have died in that fire ..." HomeSky looked at Pat like she might be seeing him for the last time.

"HomeSky, no. You didn't abandon me. Don't ever tell yourself that. *I* added the complexity to our friendship. I'm not ashamed of my feelings, but they are inappropriate, or maybe, I don't know, unfair. I could control them no more than I can control this beautiful day."

"What did you mean, exactly, that the path isn't so straight and narrow?" she asked.

"Oh, that. Well, all these years, I've worked under the assumption that I had to become good enough for the Church. I had to qualify for God's affection. That I had to learn to walk right down the center of this narrow, unbending path, or not at all."

"I've felt the same way."

Pat sat back on the blanket with his hands behind him, looking up into the yellow-orange crown of the tree overhead. "That's plain foolishness. God knows we're human. Failings, foibles, weakness, lousy attention spans, bad days, short tempers, all of it. It's all part of the package He designed. So why on earth would the path to Him be narrow? So just the few could join Him? I seriously doubt there's an occupancy limit in heaven. The more the merrier. Not to be confused with being reckless or hateful or unkind or endlessly self-centered. We do need to be people who make God proud. But straight and narrow … ridiculous."

"I admit. I'm a little confused," HomeSky said, lying down on the blanket, watching leaves drop-tumble toward her as the early November wind bullied its way through the treetops.

Pat lay back, opposite her. "That's okay. God also takes the confused."

They lay there, basking in the final shimmering, chimeric remnants of autumn. This was the last of it. The wonderful parting fringe, winter's prologue, the long goodbye that hesitates in the doorway before turning away for good, and is then long missed.

"Oh, before I forget, I have a favor to ask," Pat said, staring up at the sky.

"Hmmm," HomeSky said, eyes closed, edging toward a nap.

"You know your boyfriend, Roger, who I met a while back?"

HomeSky's eyes snapped open. "He's not my boyfriend."

"He told me he works selling equipment at the plant."

"He's just a friend, an acquaintance. He comes into Lu Ann's." HomeSky was flustered.

"If you could, please ask him, the next time he's in the plant, to have the honchos pay special attention to my application; maybe work it to the top of the stack. I need the job and would be grateful for his help."

"Okay. *If* I see him. I'll probably see him at the diner. I don't know."

"Or you could ask him when you two go out for bowling night." Father Pat chuckled.

HomeSky picked a half-eaten beet off her paper plate and lobbed a perfect toss that landed splat on Father Pat's forehead.

"Hey!"

"We only went bowling once, for your information."

Pat picked the beet off his forehead and tossed it into the leaves. "I pity the creature who finds that little morsel."

HomeSky, up on one elbow, looked across the leaf-sprinkled blanket at Pat, who was stretched out, eyes closed, a boy's smile across his face.

"It wasn't easy for you, was it?"

"What's that?" he said, eyes still closed.

"Asking me to ask Roger."

A furrow came across Father Pat's brow. He didn't know HomeSky was watching him. Then the frown cleared and a peace settled back across his face.

"Ah, it wasn't so bad." Pat said, exhaling, breathing in again, calm. "Although I'd prefer you don't ask him on bowling night."

"Well, I have a favor to ask you, then," HomeSky said, still watching him.

"Shoot."

"Will you and Monsignor Kief have Thanksgiving with us? Joseph, Cory, and me? Like always?"

"That I'll have to think about."

HomeSky's heart dropped an octave.

"I've thought about it," Pat said, a grin filling his face. "As long as you don't serve those beets, we're there."

THANKSGIVING.

It was noon, and what a noon it was. A fresh quilt of white lay across the flat fields of the Blackholm farm, rippled by the undeterred winds of the plains. Every direction hurt to look at, an unsullied white.

From out on the farmhouse porch, she could hear the distant voices, the thudding of hockey pucks, the laughter coming in on the stiff wind. HomeSky stood in her moccasins, looking at once tall, beautiful, at peace, happy, but chilled as she wrapped her arms around herself, the wool sweater insufficient. These were her Thanksgiving sounds, and she inhaled them to be forever stored. Breath plumes escaped and vanished as she exhaled, listening there, shuddering in gratitude, to the mock cries of foul, to the shrieks, to the joy of the distant pond's song. Joseph, Cory, Pat. Hockey.

Monsignor Kief greeted her from his chair as she came back inside with a few pieces of split oak from the porch pile. "Did you have to fell it *and* split it?" he asked, alluding to the length of time she was out of the house.

"No. It's right there off the door. I just had to listen to those boys playing. As long as I live, I'll never tire of that sound. You should hear them razzing one another."

"Can I do something, HomeSky? I'm afraid I haven't been much help sitting in this chair."

"No, Monsignor. I just need to add these in the stove. I can't seem to chase the draft out of the living room." Using an old glove to open the hot iron door, she loaded the oak into the potbellied stove. "Nothing to do but wait while the bird cooks." She paused, summoning her courage. She hadn't yet talked to Monsignor Kief about Father Pat. She didn't know how he viewed her role in all of it. "Father Pat seems better," she said to the fire, playing the opening card in the conversation.

"Much better, yes. The Alcoholics Anonymous group, the rectory reconstruction, the services, and the night shift have him hopping. He seems to very much enjoy it, though."

"I hope he doesn't wear himself down."

"Patrick O'Rourke is one of the most determined individuals I've ever met. But I do share your concern. And about you, my child? How are you?"

It was the genuine, kind tenor of those two words—my child—that undid HomeSky. She felt tears behind her eyes.

"Are you very much disappointed with me, Monsignor?" she asked, her voice cracking.

"What is it?"

"I'm usually not like this, but lately …"

"Please now, HomeSky. Tell me what's on your mind." Monsignor Kief stood from his chair and walked over until his hands brushed her. He took hold of her hands. "My goodness, your hands are ice."

"Monsignor, I'm so worried that you think badly of me. Of my friendship with Father Pat. Of its potential inappropriateness."

"Here now," he said. "Let's sit down a minute. Where is that chair?" he said, frustrated, waving his hand through the air.

"It's here," HomeSky said, dragging it over.

"You sit, now," Monsignor Kief said. He stood in front of her. "I've talked at great length with Pat. I know nothing inappropriate transpired. Pat loves you and he loves God. But our Church doesn't allow for such a division in allegiances. Pat is searching for the answer. You can't give it to him, and neither can I."

"Monsignor, I don't know what I feel anymore. I always thought I would grow old with RiverHeart. I always thought our pictures would be the only pictures on the walls of this home. He and I. He and I and Joseph. I took one down the other day; it felt wrong, but not entirely. I don't know. He's been gone five years. When do I let go of the only man I've ever loved?"

"Is Pat accelerating your thoughts on this subject?"

"I can't honestly say. Maybe. Up until a few months ago, I never thought of Pat as anything but my best friend and trusted priest. Now, I don't know how to characterize my feelings. I've hardly seen him, he's so busy lately."

"He's been going nonstop, especially with the overtime at the plant. It pays time and a half."

"Monsignor, would you say I've sinned in God's eyes?"

"I most certainly would not. You are a blessing on this earth. I'm sure God counts you among His finest friends."

"Sometimes I feel God will be angry with me and take Joseph like He took RiverHeart. I couldn't survive it."

"God didn't take RiverHeart away from you as a form of punishment. RiverHeart was a gift that God gave us, you especially, for a time, and then brought back home. We need to be thankful for that time. Like a beautiful day, like a great piece of literature, a good life ends too soon no matter how long it lasts."

HomeSky nodded, so grateful for Monsignor Frank Kief.

"I'd like you to come out on the porch and hear something," she said, taking the elderly priest's hands. She wrapped a scarf around his neck and led him out on the porch where they stood quietly. Off in the distance, down below the gentle slope of the pasture, was the sound of hockey being played, a dog barking, laughter, skate blades against ice, taunting, pucks slapping. HomeSky watched the gentle face of this inspiring man absorb every sound and react to them like prizes.

"What a time they're having," he said softly, so as not to disturb the air. A smile stretched across his face. "That's pure love we're hearing. Thank you for this."

At dinner, the men and HomeSky took one another's hands and bowed their heads. Father Pat, as was custom, led them in grace. They basked momentarily in the gathered smells of roast goose, squash, beans, loaves of bread, wild rice, stuffing, and wood smoke.

"This circle, united, is a source of boundless peace and strength. Our Creator has chosen to bring us together, from vastly different places and backgrounds, for reasons unknown. We are here not by accident, but through accidents. This circle was drawn by the hand of God and I am forever thankful for my inclusion. I bring to my dear friends here my shortcomings, for which I am sorry, and my strengths, which are yours for the asking. I'm thankful for HomeSky and Joseph's hospitality. For bringing Cory here with us for another Thanksgiving. And for Frank's infinite patience. Mostly, I'm thankful to witness and participate in the true gift of companionship. God has smiled upon us. Let us thank Him daily by smiling back. Amen."

"Amen," everyone said, with the exception of Cory. He quickly let go of the hands he was holding and picked up his silverware. Joseph noticed Cory's discomfort, how he retreated during Father Pat's blessing. Cory's foot tapped ceaselessly on the floor.

"Beautifully done," Frank said to Pat. "I'd say *masterfully done*, but why would those words be less apropos? Joseph?" Monsignor Kief, who had been feeding a steady stream of books to Joseph, liked testing his prized pupil. Everyone started passing food and loading plates.

"Hmmm," Joseph considered. "Masterfully verses beautifully … I think either word works fine. The distinction," Joseph said, feigning haughtiness, "escapes me."

"Cory," the Monsignor continued, "what do you think?"

Cory held the squash bowl and looked over at the blind priest. "You chose not to use masterfully because it would imply less spontaneity."

"Oh, now we're getting somewhere," Frank beamed.

"I'm not sure I'm tracking," Pat said.

"Me neither," HomeSky chimed in.

"I remain neutral," Joseph declared, crossing his arms in mock defiance. "Either word is adequate. Adequate, how about that, Monsignor?"

Frank nodded. "Cory. Do you wish to further your opinion on the distinction?"

Cory wasn't interested. But he could see the others were enjoying themselves, so what the hell. "Mastery implies study and repetition. Father Pat's prayer was extemporaneous—like open-field running versus something practiced until it's mastered."

Frank addressed Joseph. "Joseph, your rebuttal?"

"Cory got the brains, I got the looks, remember, Monsignor?" Joseph laughed.

Cory interjected. "Actually, Joseph is the smart one. While I've been talking, he's made a good-sized dent on his first helping." Everyone laughed. The passing of food continued.

"How will your respective teams be this year," Father Pat asked. "Is there a chance you'll meet in the state tournament, Cory?"

"Baudette, thanks to the big horse here, is ranked fourth in the state. We're ranked second. So it's possible."

"There's a lot of hockey to be played before the tourney," Joseph said. "But it sure would be fun to come to the Twin Cities and show you young ladies how to skate."

The two of them locked eyes and smiled at each other. "Yeah, yeah," Cory said. "That's what you've been threatening for years. Who knows. Maybe you'll get your wish this year."

Pat asked, "Would you boys look forward to it? The chance to play against each other?"

They looked at one another, and quickly pointed. "I wouldn't want to be him," they said simultaneously.

HomeSky jumped in. "I for one hope to never see it. How many high schools make it to the tournament?" she asked.

"What do we have, Cor, eight teams that make it out of how many?"

"There are four divisions, thirty-something teams per … better than a hundred forty in all."

"It just could happen," Monsignor Kief said, excited. "You two warriors, on TV, crossing swords."

"Monsignor, please," HomeSky said. "Crossing swords? They're just playing a game. Right, you two?"

"I'd go easy on him, Mom." Joseph winked at Cory.

Cory winked back. "I promise to bring him home in one piece, give or take a few."

"The warriors have spoken," Monsignor Kief gleefully provoked, forking into seconds of wild rice. The table grew quiet with eating. Silverware tinked. Bowls circulated. Compliments were handed out to the cook and the hunter.

As dinner was winding down, Joseph kicked Cory under the table. Joseph looked at Cory, his eyes lit up as if to say, *Go on. Tell them!*

Cory frowned a little. *Right now?*

Yes, now! Joseph's eyes said in return. He further implored, *c'mon.*

The nearness of everyone around the table, almost elbow-to-elbow, made Cory uncomfortable. Despite how much he cared for them—he'd do anything for them—he felt smothered. More and more, Cory had been taking his meals alone. At home, what with work, late practices and the like, he rarely ate during normal hours. And many mornings he was up, had breakfast, and was out the door to swim laps before anyone was out of bed. He was retreating at school as well. Many days, he'd simply wander into an empty classroom to eat while he studied. The policy was no eating in classrooms, but because it was Cory, teachers looked the other way.

Now, especially after being outdoors skating all day, the small farmhouse dining room was stifling. Cory's foot jittered on the floor. He cleared his throat and proceeded.

"I've got an announcement to make," he started, looking at the tablecloth. "It concerns Joseph and me."

Everyone stopped eating.

"What is it?" HomeSky asked.

"You all know it's been our goal to play college hockey together. And with money being the way it is, we'll need scholarships to do it. We've received recruitment letters from some quality schools. Some want Joseph. Some want me. A few want both of us. Last week we agreed to visit the University of Wisconsin, Madison. They've got a great program and they say they have two full scholarship slots set aside for us."

"Praise the Lord!" Monsignor Kief clapped his hands together and raised them heavenward.

"Congratulations, boys!" Father Pat added. "It's nice to know all those nights of extra prayers paid off!"

HomeSky was quiet.

"Mom?" Joseph said.

"It's great, honey."

"You don't look like great," Joseph said.

"No, it's not that. It's just you'll be moving away. I mean, I always knew you would, but now it's almost time."

"Mom, it's not for practically a year."

"It's just hard to think we'll all be sitting around this table in a year and you'll have been gone." HomeSky could see the mounting concern on Joseph's face. "But enough of that. Madison isn't so far. I hate to be a wet blanket."

"We'll make road trips," Pat tossed out, trying to resuscitate the mood. "Not only home games, but the Twin Cities and Duluth. We can shoot over there easy."

HomeSky put on a smile. "Tell us more of the details."

The boys tore into the particulars like kids on Christmas morning. They planned to visit the school, walk the campus, see the rink, meet a few players, the coaches, see the dorms—and the dining hall, Joseph was quick to add. If they liked it, they'd need to come back with their mothers and sign letters of intent.

"What are the scholastic strengths of the school?" Monsignor Kief asked.

"Hockey," Joseph teased, flashing his gap-toothed smile.

"I've been looking into it," Cory said. "Liberal arts, communications, biology, and the natural sciences."

"What will you boys study?" HomeSky asked.

"Girls," Joseph tossed in. Cory glared at him. It was no time for kidding with his mom already upset. But with Joseph, there was no such thing as no time for kidding.

"I might study forestry," Joseph said. "Or PE."

"I like biology and chemistry. Maybe pre-med, but that's tough sledding when you're trying to play winning hockey. We'll see."

HomeSky tried to rally her excitement, but couldn't get there. She couldn't imagine her boy gone, studying, playing hockey, having dinner, and her not there. She imagined how quiet and isolated the farmhouse would be without him. What would she do? Sell and move to town? She'd so miss the vast openness of the property if she did that. There was something about the scale of the land that kept things in perspective, kept her from feeling too big or too small. She fit out here. She knew her place. Her mind raced.

"So, what's for dessert, Mom?" Joseph asked, his attention bounding to the next subject.

"What's that?" HomeSky said, her thoughts coming out of the land, back to the table.

"Is there dessert?" Joseph repeated.

"Oh. There's rhubarb pie and hot cider. Remember how you two used to go through the cider over Thanksgiving break? All that skating, then into the house to warm up. Then back out there again." HomeSky felt close to tears. "I'll bring dessert in."

"Let me, Mom."

"I said I'd get it." Then HomeSky softened her tone. "Really, I'll be just a minute." She pushed quickly away from the table.

Father Pat got up after her. "I'll see if she needs a hand," he said to the table. Everyone nodded.

In the kitchen, she stood at the window, looking out, as she so often did, at the front pasture cloaked in the night. Her intimacy with the land allowed her to feel its contour through the blackness, the slight rise and fall. She could almost trace her hand across that land, like smoothing a quilt, like she had all these years making Joseph's bed.

"Are you okay?" Pat asked, her back to him.

She looked at his reflection in the window. "It's going to be so quiet. I'll feel lost. Not even sure where my home is. Can you imagine that?" She turned to look at him. They stood close together.

Pat considered the question. "Yes, I suppose I can."

"You can at that, can't you?" she said, recalling his situation. She wiped her eyes with her hand. She wanted to reach out for him, to feel his strength, his presence. She needed something solid as all else was spinning away. "Are you leaving, too?" she asked.

Pat studied her face. Her eyebrow, that wonderful, thin, arched black eyebrow that rose slightly in question, waited, poised for his answer.

He held her. And she him. Tightly. They stood there, holding one another against the night, against progress, against odds, against everything that told them to do otherwise.

"It's in God's hands," he whispered.

That night in Joseph's bedroom, Cory lay zipped in his sleeping bag on top of a blanket to keep him off the cold floor. Was Joseph asleep yet? he wondered. They were both tired from the day of skating.

"You awake?" Joseph asked.

"I was wondering if you were."

"You were quiet at dinner. Is everything cool with you?"

"Sure," Cory said nonchalantly. "I get claustrophobic around all those people."

"All what people? Cory-boy, there's five of us."

"It's just uncomfortable for me. I pretty much eat alone."

"Why?"

"Let's just drop it."

"Tell me. Why eat alone?"

"What are you, my shrink?"

"Don't be like that. Why?"

"Weird schedule with practices and work. I'm gone all the fucking time. Plus our apartment is so tiny, I can't stand being cramped in there with my mom and sisters scampering around like mice. I just have to get some space to myself. That's what I love about up here."

"That's it. That's the whole story."

"Whole story."

"How come you sometimes lie to me?"

Cory was sideswiped. "What do you mean? I don't lie."

"Remember when you told me on the phone you don't dream about your dad? I could tell you do, but you weren't telling me. Just like now."

Cory closed his eyes. He rubbed them until he saw dots. "Everyone's got their shit to deal with. You don't need mine on top of yours."

"We're best friends. Best friends dump shit on each other. Think of it as fertilizer. You know what fertilizer does?"

"Yeah. It reeks."

"No, city boy. Fertilizer helps things grow."

"I'd rather not think about cow shit right now," Cory said.

"Quit trying to divert the subject."

"Ooh, *divert.* You are eloquent these days."

"Don't be a prick. Just because you're smarter than 99.9% of the senior class, doesn't mean we're all idiots."

"I know. I was just greasing you. Let's talk about something else, okay?"

"No. Not okay." Joseph got up on his elbow and looked over, trying to see Cory's face in the darkness. "You gotta be straight with me. That's our deal. No secrets. How many times did we agree to that?"

"That was a child's agreement," Cory whispered into the darkness.

"Don't belittle it, man. That's nothing to mess around with."

"I know. But things change."

"How much have I changed? How different am I, really, since our dads died?"

"You're like the rock behind your ear. You don't change. But we can't all be you."

"If we have a bunch of secrets between us, we lose each other. Secrets are fences."

"Okay, already. My dreams about Dad … they pretty much suck." Cory could feel his stomach tighten, causing it to roil and growl audibly in the quiet bedroom. "Dad's nocturnal visits have a prevailing theme," Cory said in a mock German accent. "Failure. Either I failed him or I'm going to fail. They all sit in that territory."

"Have you talked to anyone about them?"

"I'm talking now, doctor."

"What do you do when you wake up from a dream?"

"I lay awake."

"For how long?"

"Until morning."

"You go on no sleep."

"Sleep is overrated."

"Cory, you should tell Father Pat. He maybe could help."

"C'mon, Father Pat is just a cup of water away from drowning, himself."

"He's seen a lot. He knows about things we don't. Talk to him."

"How is he going to help?"

"I don't know. But he was put here to help. Us, I mean. You gotta believe that. The guy shows up here from where, Boston? Boston to Baudette isn't exactly a direct flight. His being here is no fluke. Don't you believe that after all that's happened?"

"Yeah. And no. Who knows what to believe. But I'll think about talking to him. That's the best I can do. Now let's talk about something more pleasant. Like taking one in the cup from a slapshot."

"Ohhhhh," Joseph groaned. "That hurt so good."

Cory laughed.

"Ohhhhhhhh, yeah," Joseph groaned louder.

"Easy, there, perv. You'll wake your mom."

Joseph grew quiet. "She took it rough. The scholarships."

"Yeah."

"Gets quiet out here. It'll be hard for her."

"What do you think she'll do?" Cory asked.

"Maybe move into town. But neither of us wants to lose the farm. There's a lot of history here. Sweat and good times. Plus this property might be worth something. You know that hand pump we have in the yard?"

"Yeah."

"Our land's on a giant aquifer. We could drive that pump anywhere on the property, my dad used to tell me, and get water. He said his granddad used to irrigate that way. They said we're on maybe the largest aquifer in the whole state."

"Cool. Is that worth anything?"

"Probably. We never talk about it or do any land surveys because that'll bring white men sniffing around. No offense."

"No, that's smart."

"But if things got too tight, Mom and I always said we'd move. I don't know. That was always *we*. But now, crop prices are a little better and there's been a few good years. The farm is doing fine."

"What if she just went into town for the winter? We could help her out. Take an extra job on campus, send some money."

"You already have one mom to take care of."

"It wouldn't hurt. We could send a little this way."

"I feel lousy for leaving."

"I know. At least my mom has my sisters, but she lays it on pretty thick. But you can't stay here. You were born to play hockey. Everybody who sees you skate says so. Plus, you know she wouldn't let you stay."

"Yeah. But it still feels shitty."

"We'll work it out. We'll make them proud. Your mom's tough. Mine—shit, she's one chipped dish away from another prescription."

"Is she doing any better?"

"Nah. Mom's convinced she got the short straw and everyone else got the picnic. None of her situation is her fault. 'If your father and you just hadn't gone on that damn fishing trip,' she says to me, 'we wouldn't be stuck in this stinking apartment.' I hear it monthly, about the time the bills are due." Cory laughed. "Mom. She has me bring her home those fancy interior decorating magazines from the grocery store. She keeps scrapbooks. I guess she blames both of us. We messed up her floor plans."

They lay still, quiet, spent from the day. The hard November wind painted the old farmhouse. In the living room's pot-bellied stove, the oak would shift and drop as it burned down. They each listened for the other's breathing to get regular, but sleep stayed at bay.

"If we get to the state tournament ..." Cory said, pausing, waiting for Joseph to speak. The only reply was Joseph's steady breathing. Cory whispered, "You sleep now, Good Thunder. If we get to the tourney, how will I skate against you? How could I look at you the way I look at opponents? We belong in the same color jersey. We were teammates since the beginning."

But what Cory sensed late that night, what he was becoming more and more afraid of, was that he'd started down a path. Or, more accurately, down a steep hill. And as much as he wished otherwise, Joseph wasn't his best friend in the world anymore. Something unstoppable was put in motion, and all of the momentum of his situation was hurtling him toward his one true loyalty:

Winning.

PART TWO

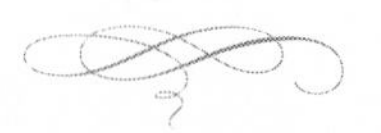

Winter 1978

FATHER PAT.

Going into the Christmas break, neither Joseph's nor Cory's teams had lost a single game. The possibility of their meeting down the road had Father Pat and Sheriff Harris talking over a cup of coffee at Lu Ann's. "*This* could get very interesting," Pat said.

"And what possibly could be very interesting in these frozen parts?" HomeSky quipped, coming up behind them with their breakfast.

"The good Padre was just telling me the boys might be banging heads in the state tournament," the Sheriff said.

"I didn't put it quite like that," Pat quickly interjected.

HomeSky merely frowned and left them to their food.

"That was graceful," he said to the Sheriff.

"What did I say?" the huge man complained, spinning his plate so the four over-easy eggs would be the first victims.

"She doesn't like the idea of the boys playing against each other."

"Ah hell. It'd be fine. Those two have been joined at the hip since the passings. They can handle it."

"You know how competitive they are. Somebody'd have to lose." Pat stopped to ponder that thought, syrup dripping off the wedge of French toast suspended in front of his mouth.

"Somebody always has to lose," the Sheriff said, mouth full, spraying a little egg white. "That's life. If anyone learned that it's them two."

Pat took in the French toast, ruminating. "Maybe so."

The Sheriff asked, "And how is it you managed to get the morning off? You've been more scarce than ten-dollar bills in the collection plate."

The Sheriff had been walking past Lu Ann's front window when he saw Father Pat being poured a cup of coffee. He figured he'd go in and prod a little. Provoking people was his favorite sport.

Father Pat turned to him. "I'm at the plant Sunday night through Friday night. Saturday's my day off. So here I am. Guy's gotta eat."

"From what I hear, you don't take a day off and you eat about as often."

"Why all the interest, Sheriff?"

"Now don't go gettin' huffy on me. I'm just making small talk."

You do nothing small, Pat was tempted to say. Instead he took a mouthful of hash browns. "I was getting lumber and whatnot. Lu Ann's Italian sausage patties popped into my head and refused to shoo."

"How's things going out there? Ran into Swenson. He said he was helping put in windows week before last. Said it's going up faster and straighter than he'd ever guessed."

"Going good. Better than I'd have guessed, too." Pat hunkered over the last bites of French toast and shoveled them in like a freed POW.

HomeSky came back over with coffee refills. "Sheriff, I hope you're letting this man eat in peace."

"I'm a keeper of the peace, ma'am. Wouldn't know any other way." He smiled wide and false and brushed his hand across his right shirt pocket, opting for the Camels. She refilled his coffee, too.

"She's mighty protective of you, Padre. Noticed she filled your cup fuller." The Sheriff lit his smoke and gestured to the cups.

"Thurgood, I'll make you a bargain." Pat looked the Sheriff in the eyes. "You stop with the Padre this and the Reverend that, and I won't call you Thurgood anymore. How about that?"

"You sure are touchy."

"Do we have a deal, Thurgood?"

"Yeah, fine," he grumbled, pulling deeply on his cigarette.

"I could use a hand out on the church grounds today. What do you say?" Pat was already standing, finishing his coffee with one hand, looping the other through his coat sleeve.

"I've got plenty to tend to here in town, Father."

"The Lord's work is never done. Come out for a few hours and drive some screws. Sheetrocking alone is as close to eternal damnation as I hope to tread."

"I may stop out for a spell. My back's been acting up lately, though."

"I'll go easy on you. Can't have the town go lawless were you to be laid up." Pat rapped his knuckle on the table for good luck as he made to leave.

"Hardy-har," the Sheriff said, stubbing out his Camel. "And by the way," he said to Father Pat's back as he moved toward the door, "you shouldn't eat so fast. You're skinny enough for a mail slot."

"Don't worry about me, Sheriff," Father Pat shot back. "You keep buying me breakfast, and I'll fill out in no time."

"What!" the Sheriff sputtered.

"Thanks again." He saluted the Sheriff. The Sheriff just shook his head.

HomeSky intercepted Pat up by the door. "Did you even bother with chewing?" she asked.

"Idle hands ..."

"He's right, you know," nodding toward the Sheriff. "You're a split rail."

"Clean living does that to a guy." He looked at her, then out the plate glass window, through the gold letters reading Lu Ann's backward. He dared not look at her too long. She weakened his resolve. She made him want to pause, to stand still, to reach. He had to keep moving.

"Will you join us for supper at the farm? Come out early and have a run with Joseph. While you guys clean up, I'll put a venison stew on the table that will pad those ribs." She playfully stuck him in the ribs with her finger.

Pat was surprised by her nonchalance. "I better check with my roommate first," he smiled. "See if the Monsignor has anything planned for us. I'll call you here if I have a conflict. If you don't hear from me, what time should I be?"

"About five-thirty. Counting for the run, that'd have us eating a little before seven. Is that too late for you?"

"Suits me. Let me talk to Frank, see if I'm forgetting something. It seems once a week we're eating with a family in town or the ladies' auxiliary or the rotary or something. Frank drags me along." Pat shrugged his shoulders. "It's been fun, actually, meeting more people in the community."

"Okay then," she said, looking at him. She smiled slightly.

"Okay then," he repeated, and stepped around her.

HomeSky brought the two tickets to the Sheriff's table. "That was nice of you," she said, patting the bills as she set them down, smiling slyly at him.

"I should haul him off to jail for running out on his check." Then his face brightened. "Would, too," he paused, theatrically, "except the food's better there."

There was something spiritual about it. Being alone with the wood. The smell of it. The knotty pine and cedar. So new and raw and straight and unblemished. Father Pat had been feeling this way quite a lot lately. Contented. Talking to the 2 x 6 framing studs. Whistling while routing the electrical. And then, at the end of the day, lying down on the plywood subfloor, putting a tennis ball under his shoulder blade, and working out the muscle knots. He loved the solitude. The progress. The hearty cold of winter construction. The heft of a hammer and a tape and nail pouch around his waist. Scooping up sawdust, letting it sift through his callused hands. This was work with immediate results. It was so unlike faith-building, which so often had an intangible impact. No wonder Jesus was a carpenter, Pat thought. It helped him through those long patches when his work was invisible.

Carpentry was something at which Pat was moderately accomplished. Over the years, his parishes had participated in outreach projects: they built and remodeled homes in impoverished urban areas. A few of the parishioners involved were carpenters and contractors, and over time, they taught Pat enough to get by. The rest just took trying. Pat wasn't fast, but he got the job done.

The rectory shell, now with the windows and doors in, was buttoned up tight. A few propane heaters made the inside work very tolerable. Pat was putting up headers for the kitchen and living room doors when Sheriff Harris stomped in like a Clydesdale, getting the snow off his boots. He looked around, his orange deer hat swiveling.

"Son. Of. A. Biscuit. Place is coming right along." The Sheriff, wide-eyed, was noticeably impressed. He went to light up.

"Uh-uh. Not in the house. I want it smoke-free, considering the demise of its predecessor." Pat thumbed, "There's a coffee can on the southern exposure. My plumbing sub says that's the best spot to smoke."

The Sheriff waved a hand through the air. "It can wait. How much of this did you do yourself?"

"All of the inside work, except the plumbing. I don't mess with plumbing. Outside, I was the fourth in the crew that put her up. The fireplace rock I subbed out. The roof I did."

"What'll it cost ya, all told? If you don't mind saying."

"Let's see. Carpet, appliances, bathrooms, 33,000 and change."

"Not bad, Padr—" the Sheriff caught himself. "Not bad. Did those lumber barons come down on their numbers after my little talk with them? They're as slippery as butter on the griddle."

"Yes they did, and I meant to thank you for that. Hey, get hold of the other end of this, would ya?" The Sheriff came over and helped Pat with the door frame.

"Where'd you learn all this?"

"My parishes got involved in some low-income housing. I met some very talented people. I've always liked working with my hands ..." Pat stopped himself. It was thoughtless of him to say that in front of the Sheriff.

"Ah, don't worry about this," the Sheriff said, waving his left hand. His artificial fingers were a poor imitation. "I'm used to the gawkers. Can't say as I blame 'em."

"How'd it happen? Do you mind my asking?"

"Shit. Just an overanxious kid in Korea with a faulty piece of hardware in my hands. Browning automatic. Blew out the barrel, took my fingers with it. Lucky it didn't take the whole hand."

"I'm sorry to hear that. That had to be life-changing."

"Guess so. Third day over there. Lost two fingers and most of my thumb. A digit a day. Got sent home and tried to disappear. My Amanda wouldn't hear of it, though. She got me back playing the piano again, of all things. Good therapy, in a lot of ways. First, just the duets. I didn't want to go near the damn thing. One good hand, one good woman, all a man needs. That's what I used to tell her. We'd smile about that, yes sir. Got so as I could muddle through. Mostly playing the easy stuff."

"I wouldn't have pegged you for the piano, Sheriff," Pat said, smiling. They moved over to the next door frame.

"We all hold our surprises."

"We do at that. Are you still tickling the ivories?"

The big Sheriff shook his head. "Tickle." He laughed at the thought of a man his size tickling anything. "No. Not since my Amanda passed seven years ago now."

"I'm sorry for your loss." Pat looked at the man. For all his gruffness, he had soft features. His skin had a youthfulness to it. And his cropped brown hair, absent a strand of gray.

"You do good work, Father. Maybe I pegged you wrong, too. I never would have guessed the guy I hauled off after that fire would be standing here with a hammer in his hand and a roof over his head come winter. The beaver knows which way to run when the tree starts to fall."

"I don't follow you."

"I just thought we saw the last of you after the fire."

"That fire, that mess, that was the best thing that ever happened to me. I didn't know it then, but it was a blessing. I needed to go back to square one. It brought everything down around me. I lost it all but my vehicle, did you know that? My every possession fueled that fire. Now, every penny I ever saved is gone. And I can't remember a happier time. This is what I got. This new start. This new frame. That fire was my second baptism."

"Does that mean you're staying? The rumor around town is your toes are pointed toward the road."

"Which rumor? How do you keep them all straight?"

The Sheriff scoffed and waved it off. "It ain't nothing. People talk. They're mostly lonely, so they latch onto other folk's troubles for company. It makes them happy knowing they ain't the only ones messing up. Doubly so when it's a priest. So, what is it: are you staying?"

"I can't honestly say. With A.A. having me take things one day at a time, all I know is tomorrow I'll say mass at nine and eleven. I'll pound nails. I'll sleep some. I'll clock in at eleven. And if the Lord speaks to me, I won't greet his voice with a hard heart."

"You must have some inkling of what you're going to do."

"No sir, I do not. My crystal ball went up in flames with the rest of it. Just going to have to wait until tomorrow and see." Father Pat smiled, looking around the building. "But short of falling dead off a ladder, I will finish this rectory. That much I know."

"Well, I should mosey. I got a dispatch on the way here. There was a dustup at Wendell's Truck Stop east of town. Seems he's put up a petting zoo to help pull in more business. A grandmother from the cities was bending down to feed a baby goat when a deer bit her in the rear. Her son says he knows a lawyer back home mean enough to make babies cry."

"If it's not one thing," Father Pat said.

"You can say that again." The Sheriff straightened his orange hat.

Pat looked at the big man, shuffling to stay warm, appearing rather forlorn. "Let's get together one of these Saturdays and eat. I come in for my meeting, but it isn't 'til eight. Do you play cribbage?"

"I'll gladly give you a lesson on the finer points any time you like," the Sheriff said confidently. "Just look for me at Lu Ann's. That's about the extent of my Saturday night."

"I'll give you a shout."

"Do that," the Sheriff said. "A-yep." He had one more look around as he stepped toward the door. "You'll be done here before you know it. Be a shame to see you go … after all the work you put into it and all," he qualified.

"It's out of my hands, Sheriff. Whatever happens will be for the best."

And that left Pat alone again with the wood. It felt right. There, framing up the door, with the pounding of the nails reverberating around him. He felt on the verge of something. Close to some clarity, now. Nearing an answer. Then he came down on his thumb with the hammer but good.

By 5:15 it was already as dark as the inside of a cow. At least that's how they described it in Baudette. Pat's Toronado sliced through a night that seemed abandoned of any other form of life.

Next to him on the passenger seat, his running shoes, sweats, towel, change of underwear and socks were in a rolled-up Bonaducci's grocery sack. Pat's thoughts ricocheted as he drove to the farm. Did she blush at Lu Ann's? Did she, or was it my imagination? Pat could have sworn that in parting, there was a force between them, something HomeSky acknowledged by blushing. Nah, he thought better of it. Probably just me. *What if I asked her*, he thought. "HomeSky," he said aloud to the grocery sack, "am I mistaken, or did you blush as we separated in the diner?" Pat smiled. "Yeah, right," he said, looking out at the infinite blackness framing the car's high beams. "Not in this lifetime."

At the farm, Pat knocked on the door, feeling as he imagined Joseph might on prom night. "Easy," he said to himself. "How about you quit acting 17."

HomeSky called "come in!" from the kitchen. She had her back to him, kneading bread dough on the heavy cutting block. The house smelled of loaves already baking. The aroma was good and clean and how Pat had imagined family might be.

"I can't believe your feet don't freeze like that," he said.

She took her hands out from the dough and swung around to greet him. He looked tired, but strong. She felt a jolt. She recognized his look, but from where? When the answer cascaded inside her, she almost lifted her hand to her mouth.

"What is it, HomeSky?" Pat asked, concerned by her frown.

"I'm sorry, what?" she asked, trying to settle down. "Oh, my feet. Just a habit. Since I was a girl I've gone barefoot. You're right though, let me get my moccasins." She hurried out of the kitchen, leaving Father Pat standing there alone. She looked like she'd seen a ghost.

HomeSky sat on her bed, moccasins in hand. She had seen her husband in Father Pat. Was there an actual resemblance, or had she willed it? Something about the way he entered the house. Something in his tone, in the resolute tired in his eyes.

"Hey, Mom," Joseph poked his head around her doorframe. "We're going to hit the road. See you in 45. Okay?" Joseph took a step closer to her. She sat on her bed, holding her moccasins on her lap. "Mom?"

"Yes, fine." She looked at her son. "You guys have a good run. And go easy on him. He looks tired."

"Easy on him, nothing! He's been running me into the ground lately. He's a deer out there."

"Just take it easy. Both of you. There's no moon up yet."

"Loud and clear." Joseph gave his mother a goofy face and went out to the kitchen where Father Pat had a leg pulled up behind him, stretching his quad.

"Mom says I shouldn't push you too hard. You trying to get the jump on me?"

"Hey, big man." Pat said. "I don't know what's gotten into her. She looked at me funny the minute I came in."

"Women," Joseph said, like he knew what he was talking about.

"Tell me about it," Pat smiled, nodding. "I need to change into my stuff."

Once outside, their eyes adjusted as they stretched a little more at the end of the driveway. They started slowly up the gravel, careful not to turn an ankle in the dark.

"Can you see, Father?"

"Hardly. But it's too cold to stand around."

"My eyes are getting better now. By the time we hit the highway, we'll be good."

"Your eyes are younger than mine. We'll see about those legs."

One of the advantages of living in such an uninhabited part of the country was that a person could run in the middle of the highway at night, especially in winter, using the yellow center dashes as a guide, and not worry about encountering a single vehicle. Deer, yes. You had to watch for those. But they wouldn't do any harm beyond nearly frightening the pee out of you when they bolted out of the ditch, snorting, their hoofs clopping and slipping on the winter-hard asphalt.

The two found a good seven-minute-mile pace and let the night do the talking. The stars seemed audible as the constellations hummed in the black-violet sky.

The wind swept through the tops of the Norways, squeaking them like rusty gates. Hoot owls got busy bragging over warm field mice filling their stomachs. Pat felt his hamstrings warm and stretch, easing the work from each stride. Joseph listened as the stone behind his ear softly thudded against the collar of his wind shirt. The rhythm was hypnotic, entrancing, peaceful, transporting. He transitioned to a new level of contentedness. Athleticism was his drug.

"So, how's school treating you?" Pat asked, sweat beginning to ice below his temples.

"School is school. Nobody takes it seriously. All my buddies think about is getting out, grabbing the first five-dollar-an-hour job around, buying a truck, and knocking somebody up. Only two of the twenty-six in my graduating class are talking college. Me, and this one guy who's a pathological liar. Last month, he was going to move to Hawaii after graduation to be a surfing instructor. He's never seen a wave bigger than a July whitecap, and he's going to open a surfing school." Joseph laughed.

"Do the teachers challenge you?"

"You got to be joking. After the bell rings, they challenge us as to who will get out of the room faster. The only teacher-type who has challenged me is the Monsignor. If he hadn't started pumping me full of books five years ago, all I'd have is hockey. Mom pushes me, too. And I've learned a lot from the farm. Making the crops pay. Deciding when to go to market and when to hang on for a better price. Inventory and interest rates and mortgages, working through that with Mom has been good homework. Keeps my brain active. Stuff like that."

"Are you excited about college?"

"I absolutely can't wait. To play hockey with Cory. To travel to all those cities and play on those beautiful sheets of ice. Hotels with pools and color TV you can watch from your king-size bed. Just to get out of the tin barn we skate in. Do you know what other schools call our rink?"

"The meat locker."

"You know why?"

"Because it's so cold. You can't watch you guys play without long johns."

"They call it the meat locker because during deer season, the owner and his son-in-law hang their bucks in there. One time they forgot to move them before figure skating practice and one little girl saw 'em hanging with their tongues sticking out. She's played basketball ever since."

"Doesn't seem to be slowing you guys down."

"We use it for motivation. But ever since Cory and I visited the University of Wisconsin, and saw that arena, and sat up in the warm stands in numbered seats watching the team go through pre-season drills—when I saw all that—I realized that little extra motivation we get from the meat locker is overrated. Don't get me wrong, I'd lace 'em up anywhere. But if the rest of the guys saw what they were missing, I don't know what they'd do. Hockey here makes you love the game. You're certainly not in it for the glory.

"Cory and I wandered that campus for hours, sneaking into the huge empty classrooms, the libraries—you should see the books, Father! You're fenced in by them." Joseph changed subjects. "The dump road is right up here. Do you want to turn around?"

"What have we gone, three?"

"Maybe a little more."

"Sure. Let's head back. Don't want to keep your mom waiting too long."

"Mom's not all gung-ho on me leaving, is she?" They turned around and headed back. Both of them spun their hats backward, their sign the run was half over.

"It's a big step for you both. But I know she's so proud. She's always wanted college for you."

"But that doesn't make it easier."

"Not a lot, but a little. She is happy, though, that you're not going off to open a surfing school in the Pacific."

They smiled at each other in the blackness. Pat gave Joseph a little shove.

"Watch it there," Joseph replied. "I might have to retaliate. In college hockey, if you don't retaliate, you're labeled a marshmallow."

"There are various ways to retaliate, Joseph. Somebody pushes you, you could turn him inside out with a move and score. Or introduce him to a clean shoulder later."

"Or just pick up the pace a little," Joseph said, grinning, putting his stride into the next gear.

Father Pat stepped it up. "*That* would be another way."

They pushed it hard down the center of the road. With the moonrise hours away, the darkness was unrelenting. You had to trust there was nothing in front of you but emptiness. The road was dry and in good shape. Because of the darkness, because you couldn't really see anything to judge your progress against, it was like running on a treadmill under a ceiling of stars.

"What about girls?" Pat asked.

"What would you like to know? Ask me anything."

Pat laughed. "I meant is there anyone you especially care for?"

"I'm friends with them all, but nothing more than that. I'm not exactly the best-looking guy, Father, in case you hadn't noticed."

"No. I hadn't. What do you mean?"

"With the girls that my size doesn't scare off, my face usually does."

"I'm still not tracking?"

"Pimples. I've got 'em like cocklebur. No killing 'em."

"Every kid has acne in high school."

"Father, it is what it is. I'm not worried about it. I didn't get my mom's good looks. That's what my buddies tell me."

"It'll clear up."

"Until then, Father, girls are going to prefer me in this light. I'm their pal. Which, seriously, is fine by me."

Pat looked over at Joseph. His shoulder-length hair bounced off his collar. His silhouette was powerful. Long, smooth, thick, hooked nose. Full chin. And his head, demanding the adjustable cap be snapped fully open, and it was still too tight. But his 225 pounds he wore, somehow, lightly. He moved quicker than a rumor.

"Don't sell yourself short in the looks department," Pat said.

"I can't change me on the outside. I live from the inside out."

They ran along, feet slapping the frozen blacktop. It was invigorating to be in Joseph's company. Pat was learning to live from the inside out, too. Funny how long it took him.

"How good is your team, really?" Pat asked, as they got close enough to home to smell wood smoke.

"The state ratings have us at four, but I don't think we'll stay four. This team is different. I can't explain it, but we get better every week. Somebody picks up their game, and it stays at the new level. In the past, a guy might have a great night, but it was a fluke. The next night, we'd be back to our old ways. Everybody's feeding off each other now. We're on a mission."

When they crossed onto the gravel utility road leading to the farm, they slowed to a light jog.

"But you really didn't answer my question. Just how good are you?" Pat breathed hard into the cold night. He looked at Joseph, who seemed almost unfazed by the run.

Joseph, walking with his hands on his hips, looking straight ahead, smiled and shook his head. "I don't see us losing, Father."

SUNDAY TRAINING.

Damn if it didn't make him free. Away from his mom and sisters and the sniveling and the cloying looks of schoolmates. Away from coaches, full-contact, full-pads, clipboards, practices. Away from those fucking whistles. Away from indoor ice that always had an unnatural warm cloak hanging over it. As much as Cory loved the game, a part of him resented its hold on him.

But this was his Sunday morning. His couple of hours. Free from the small apartment, the responsibilities, the mindless jobs, and, worst of all, the expectations. The weight of his life was thrown off here. Even though it was a bone-chilling February morning, Cory couldn't wait to skate. He always skated outdoors on Sundays. No stick. No puck. Just pure skating in sweats with a ball cap turned around and a few old sweatshirts of his dad's hanging down to his upper thighs. Crossovers. Figure eights. Transition footwork to backward skating. Stop and gos. Drills, drills, drills to make his skating stronger. The key to being a great player was being a great skater. It was a principle most players overlooked.

Cory didn't skate on the public hockey rink, which, inevitably, was full of rink rats with red cheeks playing pick-up until it was too dark to see. That's where Cory got his start, where he fell full in love with the game. On Sundays, he skated instead on the large boardless general rink where he needed only to avoid the occasional figure skater or a mom with her three-year-old on double blades.

Mostly on cold Sunday mornings, he had the general rink to himself. Until Shara arrived. Then he'd skate with her. But first, for those 50 minutes, he'd just skate. Alone. Me, myself, and I: one word for each power stroke. Like a man just out of prison, he'd skate.

While on the ice, he tried not to think about the question even strangers hounded him with. It was mid-February, and everyone, Cory included, was beginning to believe the burgeoning story.

What had first appeared as a small filler column in the St. Paul newspaper seemed to be on its way to making headlines: Cory and Joseph would be meeting in the Minnesota State High School Hockey Tournament, barring some catastrophic team breakdown or injury. Of the nearly 150 varsity programs in the state, Cory's team was ranked first, and Joseph's had moved up to third. Just three weeks remained. Certainly, anything could happen in the sectional playoffs, but it looked as though their two teams would be among the eight vying for the state championship.

The obscure newspaper story was sparked when a sports reporter caught wind of something in the stands during a game. He happened to sit next to some parents who were talking about Cory, and what an inspiration he was, especially considering what he'd been through. They went on and on about how hard the upcoming tournament could be on him.

Hard? thought the reporter. He and his newspaper were of course familiar with Cory; Cory was the state's leading scorer. His picture and story had been in print numerous times. Why would it be so hard, he wondered? So he introduced himself to the parents, apologized for overhearing, and asked about it. They explained that Cory and his best friend, Joseph Blackholm, were almost a sure bet to meet in the state tournament. They talked about the boys' shared catastrophe. How could friends like that go up against each other?

The reporter was taken both professionally and personally with the story. And the little newspaper piece he wrote, as these unusual stars continued to align, created a groundswell of public interest. As a follow-up, the reporter was assigned to interview Cory, and then travel to Baudette to talk to Joseph on his home ice. The paper wanted to get the boys photographed side-by-side. What a story, the editors agreed. If the boys' teams made it to the tournament, the human interest was sure to sell papers.

But on this cold, gray Sunday afternoon, there were no reporters and no questions about facing his best friend. Cory did think on it, though, rounding the ice, his powerful strokes automatic, pushing him against the stiff wind. What would it be like to throw his body into Joseph's? Could he? The way the tournament sectionals were aligned, both teams would have to win two games before meeting in the championship. Hell, odds are, one of us will get knocked off by then, Cory thought. But what do odds have to do with us, he wondered?

Cory switched over and worked on backward crossovers. He could skate backward as fast as most players could forward. All the swimming, running, squats, and skating had paid off in legs that were a rare mix of power and quickness. Most players were one or the other. Cory, careful not to bulk up his legs too much, knew speed was his number-one asset. But if you're not strong on your skates, you get killed in the corners. Despite being only 5-8 and 175 pounds, Cory was feared as one of the biggest hitters in high school. He'd go into the corner giving away 30 to 40 pounds, and still come out with the puck and on the better end of the check. Running back punts the last two years had definitely toughened him up. His body had come to crave contact. He loved to see the flashing white jolt that major contact sent behind his eyes. He was fearless. He was fast. And if that wasn't enough, his capacity to split-second process what was happening on the ice was simply unrivaled. He had all the tools, no doubt. Everyone knew it and respected it.

As he skated, his body found its rhythm. The anger inside him burned like high-performance octane. Athleticism took him to a clean place, an unrestricted place. This alone was where Cory experienced happiness.

A van from across the street honked twice as it pulled over. Cory geared down and waved. Reality returned. It was Shara and her dad. Her father got out and went around to the doors in back, taking out her wheelchair, unfolding it as the wind blew through his thinning hair.

In Baudette, Sundays started early for Joseph. At 5:30, he was out the door to run. Sunday was the day, the only day, HomeSky stayed in bed. She did so because Joseph wouldn't have it any other way. He wouldn't have thought twice of putting a lock on her door, and she knew it. Joseph called it Sleep-In Sunday. Her attendance was not optional.

HomeSky appreciated the rest, needed it, but worried about Joseph, who somehow got by on six or fewer hours of sleep a night. She knew better. She knew his body needed more. But he would just smile and pinch her under the arm. When she let out a yelp, he'd say, see, you're the runt of the litter.

His energy reserves seemed inexhaustible. HomeSky could hardly remember ever seeing him yawn. It just didn't happen. Of course, he was in amazing condition. He ate plates, as in two, of vegetables a day. One in the morning, one at night. He ate pocketfuls of nuts throughout the day. Fruit didn't last the week in the refrigerator. He drank skim milk, over a quart a sitting. And except for the occasional duck or goose, his meat intake was low-fat venison and fish. For the last year, he had stayed away from most breads, but would eat pasta two times a week. Mixing-bowl-sized servings.

His playing weight was 225 pounds, and he was something to look at. In the last year he had actually lost fat, gotten leaner, but gained pounds in muscle. He was built like a bank safe. Joseph didn't lift weights—wouldn't touch them. He said they dulled quickness—not only through endless repetitions, but because they were so flipping boring. Push-ups, sit-ups, pull-ups, and farm work carved his upper body. Plus, his strength was naturally off the charts to begin with. He threw hay bales around like boxes of Kleenex and would grab 80-pound feed bags, one in each hand, and walk across the farmyard whistling like they were empty. His hands were strong enough to crack walnuts. He could jump up, grip two joists, and do fingertip pull-ups.

Sundays always began with a run. Fifty minutes—actually, seven seven-minute miles—with a Duluth pack on his back holding skates, gloves, shin pads, shoulder pads, breezers, and his helmet. He always ran with the weight equivalent to what he played in. Joseph wanted his body adjusted to the additional pounds. Recently he'd taken to dropping a rock in the pack every week before the run. He had over a dozen in there now along with his equipment. Just for fun, he'd say to himself, dropping one more in.

Joseph had adjusted to running in the morning's dark with the big pack strapped on his back. Actually, had come to crave it. Striding down the middle of the road, not a car, not a person to be seen. His braided stone tapping with each footfall, urging him forward. *Run to the daylight,* his father's spirit had told him. Even in the dark, he would find the brightness, the wide blue skies over green pastures. Athleticism took him there. *Hockey is college*, he'd tell himself over and over, the mantra he and Cory repeated countless times in their heads as they trained through the years. They both knew this was their shot. Cory had always said so. Now it was coming true.

After his run, Joseph showered and started breakfast for himself and his mom. It was five minutes to seven. Most kids his age were just stirring, pulling the covers over their heads for a few more hours of sleep. But like every day on the farm, Sundays were wall-to-wall. After breakfast, he and Mom would go to Father Pat's 9:00 mass—but Joseph still needed to squeeze in a chore or two first.

The nine-egg spinach omelet bubbled up on the stovetop in the large blackened iron skillet. Two sliced potatoes fried in canola oil.

Joseph got down on the drafty floor for 80 push-ups followed by 80 sit-ups. He cracked them off as easily as some folded laundry. During the fill of any day, Joseph spontaneously broke out into push-ups and sit-ups. In the machine shed, or on the grass next to the truck waiting for his mom, or just after using the bathroom, wherever there was enough room to stretch his large frame. He could be talking to someone at school, and while the person answered, he'd hammer off a quick set. No one thought anything of it anymore. They knew Joseph had a plan.

HomeSky came out dressed for church, stepped around her exercising son, and flipped the omelet. "Smells wonderful. We could use you at Lu Ann's."

Joseph finished his push-ups and rolled onto his back. "Not pretty enough to work there," he said, catching his breath.

"Flattery suits you. Keep it coming."

At mass, Pat's homily was particularly forceful. In the first months after the rectory fire, his voice had lost all traces of crisp certainty. But much of it was back as he talked today about never reducing people to a stereotype because it robbed them of their uniqueness, their mystery, their soul. He said only the foolish and proud have the arrogance to declare someone 'figured out.' By classifying someone, you judge them. Joseph recognized that some of these thoughts were inspired by their conversation in the duck blind. Shaking hands after mass he told Father Pat that his words hit home. There the two of them stood, in front of the pipestone church, strong hands clasping, clear-eyed, healthy, unfazed by February's icy bluster.

Cory waved at Shara's dad as he guided her wheelchair carefully down the steps to the rink. She tucked the blankets around her legs. They both waved back. Shara smiled big as could be. She lived for Sundays.

Before breaking her neck skiing her sophomore year, Shara was just another high school girl to whom Cory paid no particular attention. She'd always been pretty and loud and popular, but the accident ended the loud and popular aspects. People didn't know what to do around her. She made them silently uncomfortable. Cory had the opposite reaction. He was drawn to her. Her isolation was kindred.

He would put his books on her lap and wheel her through the halls at school. Neither said much at first. But by the end of their junior year, Cory was running her down the hall, her hair waving behind her. She could almost touch her memory of speed. They would laugh as classmates darted out of the way, banging into the lockers saying, *Hey!* It surprised everyone. *What's with Cory?* they said. He was always so serious. He's running around with Shara like he's stoned.

During his junior hockey season, Cory got an idea. He knew Shara was cooped up inside all winter. He decided he'd take her skating. Let her feel the speed. At the library, he checked out a few woodworking books and, in his tiny bedroom, he slowly built a beautiful maple skating chair. It was high-backed for Shara to lean against, had a safety belt, and it was firmly upholstered. Every inch was beveled, stapled, sanded and varnished to Cory's exacting standard. It was much the same dimensions of her wheelchair, with handles for Cory to push. The skating chair's legs were slightly straighter versions of rocking chair legs that functioned like runners. They had an eighth-inch exposed metal blade running their length to help the chair bite into the ice and ride true.

Cory had brought the skating chair over to Shara's for Christmas. Christmastime was hard on him. The apartment got smaller. Not having your dad for Christmas makes you walk around feeling like you've forgotten something.

Shara's dad had answered the door that Christmas day a year ago. Cory had the chair in the yard with a Santa Claus helium balloon tied to it, tugging in the wind. He asked her dad if it'd be okay to take Shara skating. He'd made her this present, he said. Her dad looked at the chair and his eyes welled up.

The moment at the door turned over an old memory for Cory. On Christmas days past, his dad would drive him to the local rink.

Cory would cross the street, skateguards on his skates, too excited to stop and go to the bathroom at home or in the warming house. He'd hold it for as long as he could while his dad slid around on his black rubber overshoes, kicking pucks out to him to shoot forehands and backhands. It was the same park he was at now.

"Hello you," Cory said to Shara. Her father wheeled her down the last step, before setting the brake and going back to the van for her skating chair.

"I'm not going to let you off easy today," Shara said, smiling a week's worth of smiles in their moment alone. Her dad handed Cory the skating chair. Cory turned his skates sideways and braced as Shara switched chairs. Her dad almost dumped in the exchange.

"Whoa, Mr. Callahan. You need to get yourself some boots. Those steps are treacherous."

"Yeah, Dad," Shara teased. "I'm not letting you out of the house next time in those shoes. And a sensible hat." She beamed, settling into her skating chair. Her face transformed, alive, hopeful.

"Yes, parents. I promise."

"You want to go the full hour today?" Cory asked. "The wind's nasty, and it looks like snow."

"Yeah," she said. "Unless *you* can't hack it." Cory and Shara's dad looked at each other and shook their heads. The fresh air always brought out the spark in her.

"See you in an hour, Dad."

He patted her hand wistfully. "Okay." He nodded at Cory. It was the nod of unspoken camaraderie.

Cory took a few strong strokes backward, pulling Shara's chair onto the rink. He skated around her, to look after her, closely. "Hi," he said quietly, looking into her large, pretty eyes. He pulled her hat down a little lower over her ears and tucked in a loose blanket end.

"Hi to you." Shara smiled at him like no one else ever had, or could ever have.

They pushed off and quickly gained speed. Shara's dad lingered on the steps. He knew he was intruding. Only a few seconds more, he told himself. His beautiful little girl's face filled with life. He watched as the chair went around in a wide oval, Cory and his Shara, gliding. He watched as a few long strands of her straw-colored hair were teased from her hat to stream in the wind. She was his one true love. She was why he rose in the morning and swallowed what he swallowed from life. She leaned back, bit her lip, laughed, throwing her head back. And so began the one single hour of the week that Shara prayed would tick by as slowly as God could see to it. Her dad waved, and left them. Around they went. Like in a music box.

Their ritual was to sprint hard for five minutes, then go easy for five so they could talk. Cory was breathing hard as he slowed down.

Shara looked over her shoulder. "Well, well. Someone's got some garbage to incinerate. You better go first. What did you dream about this week? Anything new?"

"Mmmmmm, don't remember."

"C'mon, now," she prodded gently.

"It was the same one, I guess."

"Which same one? The hockey same one or the dad same one?"

"Both. How about you?" Cory asked.

"I had the weird one."

"The school weird one or the running in place weird one?"

"The school weird one. But there's a new twist."

"Let's hear it."

"You'll think I'm deranged," Shara warned.

"Already too late for that." Cory squeezed her shoulders.

"Okay. I dreamt I was walking, and naked, like always. Late for a test I hadn't studied for. I couldn't find the right room. I ended up in the gym, which was empty. Suddenly everyone jumped up from behind the bleachers and yelled, 'Surprise!' The whole crappin' school. I tried to cover myself with my books but I kept dropping them. Everyone whistled and laughed. I'd try and try and try but they kept falling. Finally I looked down to see why the books were so slippery and they were tiny newborn babies—you know when they're slick with all that gunk right after delivery? I kept dropping those little babies and everybody just laughed and laughed harder and harder with each poor little one." Shara shook her head. "Pretty messed up, huh?"

Cory let the chair glide free as he skated around to the side to look at Shara. "That's what you get for eating a bag of potato chips before bed." He winked, and pulled her hat a little lower yet. "You warm enough?"

"Let's go, soldier!" she barked in her best Hollywood drill sergeant impersonation. "We got miles to go!"

Joseph was skating up the Rainy River. Technically, it's up because he was headed toward town and the river runs away from it. That being a moot point in February when the currents run quiet under the thick ice.

To pick up the river, Joseph walked a mile south of their land. There on the riverbank, he'd lace up his skates and go the 10 miles to Baudette. Ever since he was in the fifth grade, he had skated to and from school in winter.

On weekends Joseph trained on the river. His best time to town and back was just under an hour, a little better than a 20-mile-per-hour pace, a speed most would have trouble sustaining on a bike. What made the feat more phenomenal was the river's many twists and turns, which slowed him down. He'd make up lost time on the straightaways.

The stretch of the Rainy River he skated rarely got wider than a two-lane road. Joseph blurred up it, surrounded by trees. The river carved its way though the quiet forest, occasionally meandering parallel to Highway 2. Then it would duck back under the pines and birch, disappearing from the sight of the road for miles. Occasionally the river would squeeze down so narrow, the trees would canopy overhead. It was like racing through a magnificent tunnel. Joseph had read a book about the Normandy invasion on D-day in which soldiers marched down narrow hedgerows where trees from either side touched and knotted overhead. He thought about those soldiers, hardly older than himself, as the sun winked through the stark winter treetops, his body flickering past. Up the river he powered.

Joseph had a simple goal. He wanted to be strong enough to skate hard for a full 60 minutes. He wanted his body to know it could do that. Then when a game called for extra shifts of ice time, no doubts would weigh on him. A high school hockey game is 45 minutes. By skating 60, he was more than ready.

As the river neared town, it paralleled the highway. A quarter-mile ahead was the familiar iron suspension bridge crossing into downtown Baudette. Large green grain elevators that Joseph had driven to countless times boxed in the horizon. A car honked at the familiar sight of the town's beloved hockey star striding upriver, ice shavings sparkling off his blades. Joseph waved and the horn bleated twice more.

Under the bridge, he cut hard to circle back for home. A bumpy patch took his skate edge off the ice, and Joseph's feet went up in the air. The side of his head came down first. His cheek and temple bounced off the hard ice. A flash of white ripped through his head. He lay on the ice, stunned. *Oh, shit no!* he thought. Something's broken. It's over. Injury is always the number-one assassin of a great season. Joseph cringed. He managed to shake off his glove. Behind his ear, he felt for the stone. As pain radiated all directions, he squeezed his eyes shut. His head throbbed and his shoulder shot pins down his arm. I can't be hurt, he said over and over, ten times slowly. I can't be, I can't be. Slowly the pain reversed. He felt it move back through his limbs, back toward his face and shoulder where the initial contact was made. The pain left his body, back to the contact point on the ice. He lifted his head. Right before his eyes, the ice there cracked, splintering out slowly and regularly from the impact point. A symmetrical star-shaped mark was left in the river ice.

"Thank you," he said. He stood up slowly, looking down at that star fracture on the dense ice. Then he pushed off hard, making for home. He was good. He couldn't be hurt. Around the bend of the river, into the forest—and like that, he was gone.

When Cory and Shara's hour was up, her dad's van pulled up across the street. He honked a few short beeps. Cory stopped the chair and glided around in front of her. He squatted down on his haunches so they were close, eye level. It had begun to snow. The light, dry, cold-weather flakes swirled and twisted, occasionally finding updrafts, before a few quietly settled on Shara's eyelashes. He looked at her delicate features, her brown eyes twinkling now.

"I need to ask you something," Cory said, quietly.

"No. I will not marry you," she joked.

Cory, serious now, put his hand down on hers. "A reporter wants to do a tournament story on Joseph and me. He says he'll write it next week, if we each win our sectionals. Front page."

"That would be so awesome."

"The angle on the story is, you know, the whole Cory-Joseph thing, blah, blah, blah."

"It's an amazing story, Cory. Don't—"

"Okay, whatever. But what the reporter wants is a photo of us getting ready for the game. He knows both of us have worked hard on conditioning. The lead shots he's talking about are side-by-sides of us training: Joseph up in Baudette. Me here. He knows about my regimen, except for how you and I skate here on Sundays. I wanted to know how you felt about me telling him. I think if he knows about our skating, he'll want to photograph it. Right now his plan is me at the pool. He thought that'd be interesting."

"You at the pool. That could be real hunky."

"Seriously."

Shara looked at Cory as the flurries came down around him. His hair curling out from beneath his ball cap, frosted and iced from sweat. The scar below his lower lip where a puck had opened him up. She was infatuated. She couldn't help it, even though she knew she was fooling herself.

"What do you think?" Cory watched for her reaction.

"Why do you want the picture with me?" Shara finally asked, quietly. "It's not some pity thing, right?"

"You know better than that." Cory frowned. "I don't know, maybe because hockey is always shown just one way."

"This is private, us skating."

"I know. That's why I didn't say anything. But I got thinking, maybe it'd be cool if it wasn't so private. Why not? It's not like we're doing anything wrong. Maybe our picture belongs on the front page. What the hell."

Shara smiled at the thought. At Cory's intensity.

"Don't answer right away," Cory said. "Think about it. Talk to your dad."

Shara looked at him. Her breathing quickened. "I don't want to talk to my dad. I have to ask for almost every thing I do. I'm sick of asking. Let's go for it. The girls at school will miss three days they'll be so jealous."

Cory smiled at her. "Remember, it's up to the reporter. But I'll tell him."

"You guys almost done?" Shara's dad hollered through his cupped hands, standing next to her wheelchair on the steps. "I'm freezing my bootless-hatless butt off!"

Cory stood, brushing the snow from his black nylon skating sweats. "We're coming."

Shara buzzed inside with the thought of being photographed with Cory. She loved him. She knew he didn't feel the same way; how could he? Yes, he was infinitely kind to her, but he didn't treat her like a fragile heirloom. She hated when people did that. But now, to have a moment with him that everyone could see. Something forever. Nothing could take that away.

Cory stopped the skating chair at the rink's edge. This was the part she most loved. These eight precious seconds. Cory bent down and she put her arms around his neck and he picked her up and took her the last stride to the steps. This was the only way to get her to her wheelchair. She was so grateful to those ascending steps. She loved the feel of her arms around his solid neck. The smell of him. The closeness. His breathing.

Shara's dad watched his daughter's face as she was lowered back into her wheelchair. He winced, to watch her try to keep her smile alive as Cory set her down. She would let go of him, and re-grasp the reality of her situation. She put on a good face.

"See you at school tomorrow," Cory said, watching her shrink into the wheelchair. Shara's life was one big letting go. It wasn't fair. He and Shara had talked about it. That was why they were able to trust their way into this friendship. They both were broken. The only difference was no one could see Cory's wheelchair.

THE ARTICLE.

"Hello?" HomeSky said into the receiver, out of breath, having dashed in from outside. A few months back she and Joseph wired an outside ringer so phone calls could be heard in the farmyard. She'd nearly broken her arm slipping on ice the other day getting to what turned out to be a wrong number. This morning, as she helped Joseph load silage into the trailer, HomeSky wondered who could be calling at this hour on a Saturday.

"HomeSky? That you?"

"Yes. I just—"

"I'm looking at it. I'm looking at it! Hot off the press. I've got it spread out."

HomeSky could hear the rustling of paper on the other end of the connection. "Pat?" she said.

"Of course it's me! I've got the article on the boys. Front page in the *St. Paul Pioneer Press.* Man, you should see it!"

"Slow down. Take a breath—"

"It takes up almost three pages, beginning with the bottom half of the front page. It's got ... well, I'm not going to tell you. You have to see for yourself. I'll be there in two and a half hours."

"Two and a half what? Where are you?"

"In a phone booth in Duluth. I drove here after my shift let out. I bought 30 papers. The writer did a super—"

"You drove all that way? You should be in bed, sleeping."

"Bed! Are you nuts? I'm too wired to sleep! Don't move. And make sure Joseph's there. Wait 'til you guys see it! The writer really did a bang-up job."

"Why didn't you wait for our delivery?"

"What? And wait a whole day for the city edition? Don't move. I'll be there in a jiff!"

The phone line went dead. HomeSky, receiver in hand, shook her head and smiled. When was the last time she had heard Pat this fired up? Maybe never. She hung up and sat for a moment in the drafty kitchen in her winter coat. Her instincts hummed discordant. The tournament was next week. The boys were going. She didn't like it. She was proud, but she didn't like it one little bit.

"Who was it?" Joseph asked, forking silage into the bed of the pickup now that the trailer was loaded.

"Father Pat," she said, picking up her shovel.

"What's he doing awake? He said never call before one on Saturdays."

"He's in Duluth."

Joseph stopped his chores and looked at his mother. His mind raced: Was he hurt? Was he leaving? Was he back drinking?

"Don't worry," she said in response to his look. "He went there to get the newspaper. You know what day it is?"

"Saturday," Joseph said, bewildered.

HomeSky smiled a wan smile. "Today's the day the whole state of Minnesota gets to meet my magnificent boy. The newspaper article is out and Pat drove to Duluth to buy a bunch of them up."

As Joseph was delivering the silage to the dairy farmer two sections over, HomeSky sat and thought with a cup of hot coffee. This day's been coming for a long time. You can't keep a light as bright as Joseph's hidden under a bushel basket. The world deserves to know there are people on this earth as special as the one God gave her. She just wasn't ready to share him. She was 38 years old and she knew how to spot meadowsweet, good for indigestion, she could find her way around the carburetor of a '54 John Deere, she knew to plant rye after the harvest so it'd overwinter as ground cover to be plowed under for fertilizer come spring, she could beat half the men in town arm wrestling, but she didn't know how to share her son with the world. He was seconds away from a new life. She was 38 and about to be the lone tree in a pasture.

HomeSky walked into her bedroom and looked at the hand-tooled jewelry box her husband had made when they were courting. She traced her hands over the smooth walnut edges. Inlaid in the lid's center was a round piece of quartz, surrounded by six grooved lines radiating outward. She had asked him why six lines. He said because every person lives six lives: Child. Adult. Parent. Loner. Savior. Thief. Once you've lived out those possibilities, you become something else. A plant. A bird. A tree. All living things, except humans, are content with a singular life. This is why no dog wants more than one bed and no wildflower covets colors other than its own. It's why fish can happily eat their young and the lone tree in the pasture is not lonely. That's what HomeSky remembered him saying, about the single tree, and it brought her to the jewelry box.

She opened it. There was one raised shelf lined in velvet, divided into four small compartments. They had joked about it. That's all the jewelry space HomeSky would ever need; she presented herself modestly. In two of the compartments were pairs of earrings, although the holes in her lobes had long ago closed. The fourth held an opal ring of her grandmother's. The third space held nothing. Odd, she thought. She had never noticed how empty that bare space appeared.

In the mirror, HomeSky found a few more gray hairs every day. According to the Indian wives' tale, for each gray hair plucked in vanity, another beautiful girl was born to catch your husband's eye. HomeSky frowned at the notion as she looked at herself. Ever since she was 14, people had stopped to watch her. Men and women alike. She had a distracting beauty. The high eyebrows. The long angular face. The coal-black eyes. The long sweep of eyelashes. She came to resent her looks when she was in her late teens. She just wanted to be ordinary.

As her figure began to fill out, things worsened. Men were rapt, girls were jealous. And for HomeSky, it was always the same question: if someone liked her, was it about who she was inside, or was she just an object of desire? Did anyone ever see beyond her physical beauty?

Now, in her early twilight, as the first hues of age crept in along the edges, she knew her answer would come soon enough. In the darkness of age, as in the darkness of a room, we are left only with inner beauty.

HomeSky slid off her thin wedding band, set it in the final empty compartment of the jewelry box, and closed the lid.

Father Pat, Joseph, and HomeSky sat at the kitchen table, each with their own newspaper. Joseph's appetite for books made him the fastest reader of the three. He finished the article and then started again. HomeSky lingered over the words, often frowning. Father Pat had read it four times already. He studied the large side-by-side pictures of the boys skating on the front page. Joseph, with his heavy backpack, blurring down the sun-streaked Rainy River, his shoulder-length black hair streaming behind him. Cory, pushing a girl in a wooden chair on an open rink, a smile transforming her face, as Cory's eyes augured into the camera with a look that Father Pat thought was best described as certain. The caption under the photos read:

Joseph Blackholm (left) skates 10 miles to and from school with his hockey equipment carried on his back. Cory Bradford pushes his paralyzed friend, Shara Callahan, for an hour every Sunday around his neighborhood rink.

The article read:

THE GREATEST STORY EVER IN MINNESOTA HOCKEY?
BY NICK COLLINS

Cory Bradford lives in a cramped three-bedroom apartment in Minnesota's capital city of St. Paul.

Joseph Blackholm lives on 160 acres in a third-generation farmhouse near a wind-swept speck of a town called Baudette, Minnesota.

Both are high school seniors. Both are their team's best player and captain. And both are headed for this week's state tournament.

Oh, and they'll tell you they're best friends, too.

What, you might wonder, brought these two 18-year-olds together from 350 miles apart? Unfortunately, this isn't an entirely happy story. Five years ago, the unexpected deaths of their fathers united them. As fate would have it, Joseph and Cory's dads passed away on the very same day.

"We met a couple of days after," Joseph said before hockey practice last week. "I lost my dad. I got Cory. We've been brothers ever since."

"Joseph is the most together guy I've ever met," Cory says. "Whenever I need someone to talk to, it's him."

But now what? They're headed for the same prize. A prize to which they've dedicated untold amounts of blood, sweat and dreams. Yet despite everything these boys share, they can't share the championship trophy.

"Cory is, in the opinion of most, the state's best player," says his coach, Paul Ryan. "I could see it in the early grades when I watched him skate. Even then, his hockey smarts were a couple levels ahead—in the body of this little guy. He'd hit everything that moved. He's always been fearless, but smart fearless. I've never seen anyone like Cory before or since."

Joseph's coach tells it like this. "Joseph is our team. He's our offense when we're behind and when we're ahead in a tight one, I put the pads on him and put him in the net. He's our best goalie and our best forward, but his natural position is defense. He's the picture of composure on the ice. I've never seen him rattled. He tells me to calm down in the big games, and [expletive], I've been at this 31 years."

Joseph goes 6-2, 225. They call him Good Thunder.

Cory goes 5-8, 175. They call him Captain Kid.

"I'm quite a bit stronger than most kids my age," Joseph admits when pressed. "It's kind of embarrassing."

"They made me captain my junior year," Cory says. "My teachers joked it's the only C that I ever got in high school."

What would happen, I asked them, if the puck was in the corner and both of you went after it?

Joseph (smiling): "Have you ever seen a cow cookie after a tractor rolls over it?"

Cory (pensive): "What period is it and what's the score?"

And if that isn't emblematic of these two, nothing is. Cory considers. He deals with things by absorption, taking the problem apart, and then coolly dispatching it. Joseph grins. And proceeds to romp over it with athletic abandon.

When I interviewed these two, I had no idea how lucky I was for the opportunity. The more I learned, the more struck I was by how utterly special they were. Yet despite the tragic similarities in their lives, I've never met two people so different.

Cory comes into the tournament leading all players in scoring. In this 28-game season, Cory has 38 goals and 36 assists. That puts him on the ice and involved in almost 75% of his team's scoring.

"Cory's a sniper," Joseph says. "Every Thanksgiving he comes up to our farm. We play pond hockey. We shoot for hours at an old piece of plywood with slots cut in. You should see him hit the holes. Forehand and backhand."

"Joseph has always loved Bobby Orr," Cory says as we sit in the warming house on a Sunday at his local skating rink. "He has 17 unassisted goals this year. Seventeen. I looked it up. The state high school season record was six. Imagine, 17 times, Joseph has taken the puck himself and beat everyone on the ice. He's the next Orr."

They go on about each other. And they have some big ambitions after high school. They've both signed letters of intent to skate for the Wisconsin Badgers. "Playing college hockey has been our plan for years," Cory says. "In all the letters we wrote back and forth, we always talked about pulling on the same color jersey."

But before that dream is realized, the question I keep coming back to is this: what if that puck is in the corner and they both want it? Say the score is tied in the third and that loose puck is just sitting there. What then?

Cory considers. Joseph grins. And we wait. I don't know what will happen. I'm not sure I want to. How do you write the ending to what could be the greatest story in the history of the game?

Or is this just the beginning?

"Pretty good," Joseph said, finally breaking the quiet in the kitchen. "Little melodramatic and the writing's occasionally clumsy, but all and all, not bad."

"Not bad? It's great," Pat said excitedly. He folded back to the front page, to the pictures of the boys skating. "What a neat picture of you both. Look at that, HomeSky." His voice trailed off, noticing she remained quiet about the story.

"What do you think, Mom?"

"I pray you two don't face one another. I'd rather see you lose than that."

"Mom, take it easy." Joseph put his feet up on the table and locked his hands behind his head. "It's just a game. Cory and I go deeper than that. If the game goes down, it's going to be fun."

"HomeSky," Pat chimed in, "they worked so hard to get there. It'll turn out fine."

"I just have a bad feeling about it."

"Mom! Don't say that," Joseph swung his feet to the ground, looking into her eyes. "C'mon ..."

She realized she should have kept her worries to herself. "I'm overreacting, I know. That's what mothers do. Cory is like a son to me, too."

Pat yawned. "I need sleep." The full weight of the week's work had begun its avalanche. Along with the overtime at the plant, all the church activities, and services on the Rez, he was stretched to the limit. Plus he was going hard on the finishing work inside the rectory. He hoped to move back in and complete everything by early summer. Yet despite the overwhelming work, Pat's life had returned to regular rhythms. One day at a time, he was getting stronger.

"I'll walk you out then," HomeSky said.

Outside, the cold, bright, early March day showed all the signs of the lion the month is famous for; March comes in like a lion and goes out like a lamb, the saying goes. With temperatures around zero and five inches of new snow on the ground, it felt like spring was just an optimist's suspicion.

"Brrrr. I've had it with winter. When will it give in?" HomeSky squinted through the sharp farmyard sunlight bouncing off all the white. Her eyes watered.

Pat stopped to face her. "Here," he said, reaching for her coat zipper. HomeSky's hands were buried in the pockets of her jeans. He zipped up her coat. "You northerners. Complain about the cold, then walk out of the house with coats wide open."

"Thanks," she said, looking into his blue eyes.

He looked away, at the machine shed roof covered with snow. Prolonged, direct eye contact from HomeSky was harder for him to withstand than the blinding white. "Those zippers are a remarkable invention. You should try one sometime," he added, lightly.

"No. I mean thanks for going to get the newspapers and coming out and sharing it with us. I wish I could have been more excited for Joseph. I'm glad you were able to be. I know you're worried, too."

"Yes and no. I've quit trying to believe my wishes have any bearing on the final shape of things. For a long time, that arrogance left me holding an empty bag." He looked back at her now. Her dark eyes, her long eyelashes. "It's liberating not trying to control the universe," he joked. "Your hands are free to zip someone's coat."

HomeSky said, "The outcome of the day is for time, not me, to chisel away."

"I remember that," Pat said. "That's from the tribute poem you wrote for RiverHeart."

"That's what he said when I fretted too much over things."

"Good advice."

They stood next to Father Pat's car. On the fringe of the field, crows clawed and pecked at the recent covering of snow, snow that had started as rain before the temperature dropped. It had crusted over, making it hard for the birds to forage.

"I was thinking about RiverHeart today. I felt he was trying to talk to me."

Pat looked at her. "What did you hear?" He was holding eye contact now. The blue sky hung above them, cloudless. The wind stood quiet, listening.

She smiled faintly and took a deep breath. "He told me to move on."

THE GAME.

Eight teams had made it to what is unquestionably Minnesota's most prestigious high school event. Not only is the state hockey tournament covered on television and radio, the three-day event draws over 100,000 screaming, stomping, face-painted spectators. For three days in March—Thursday, Friday, and Saturday—everyone's talking hockey. You can't open the sports page, watch the news, or stand in line at the movies without being in range of the topic.

So far the tournament had been all Cory Bradford and Joseph Blackholm. Both skaters had led their teams to the championship game. In fact, both teams breezed through the quarter- and semi-finals with hardly a scare. It was like this game was predetermined.

The amount of media attention the boys received would have muddied the focus of any other high schooler. Every regional news channel wanted some tape to send home for the evening news.

What had started weeks before as a newspaper article had become a full-fledged media free-for-all. Even *Sports Illustrated* was there to cover the boys in the championship game. The story of them coming together for 45 minutes of hockey had reached beyond the game itself. This was human interest in every simple, unpredictable sense of the phrase. Everyone wanted a piece of the action.

Cory and Joseph were sick of it. For hours before and after the first two games, they had one insatiable journalist after another looking to hear the story again. The boys just wanted the puck to drop.

For tourney weekend, teams and their families stayed in a well-appointed downtown hotel within walking distance of the arena. Neither Cory nor Joseph had ever stayed where there was a pool *and* room service. They were trying to relax, have fun, and make the most of it, but the distractions made it impossible.

The championship game was set for Saturday night at 8 p.m. Both teams had played two nights straight and they were dog-tired. The coaches had imposed curfews and told the kids to sleep in late on game day. Just rest until the pre-game skate.

Cory and Joseph had a slightly different plan. They agreed to meet early Saturday morning at the pool to swim out the sore muscles. They kept it quiet and arranged to meet at eight.

Father Pat, Monsignor Kief, Sheriff Harris, and most of the town had gotten a block of tickets to come down for the game. Baudette pride would be there in full force. The joke was that the last person out of town was to turn off the lights.

Because Cory went to school in St. Paul, the tourney's host city, their entire student body would be on hand, along with most of the parents. The championship game was always sold out, and tickets on the street went for three times face value. It was the biggest crowd and biggest game of their young lives. While their teams slept in, the two captains snuck out of their rooms and met at the pool.

"Hey man," Cory said, shaking Joseph's hand.

"What, no hug?" Joseph kidded, pulling the smaller Cory into him and giving him a giant bear hug.

"Man," Cory pushed him away. "Not with swimsuits on."

"Watch it, or I'll toss you in," Joseph warned.

"Like hell," Cory said. "You big hick. Careful you don't end up wetter behind the ears than you are already."

They smiled and Cory dove in. They had the pool to themselves. Cory went an entire length underwater.

"Get in here, you big puss." Cory backstroked effortlessly through the water. Joseph eyed the diving board. He proceeded to send can openers splashing all over the pool deck while Cory did laps with flip turns.

Before getting out, both of them spent the final 15 minutes just stretched out, gliding underwater, letting the warm pool water loosen the aches and pains. With all the ice time they'd logged, they were banged up but good. The water worked its magic.

Afterward, they sat poolside with their legs in the water, talking quietly.

"It's going to be weird out there tonight, Cory-boy."

"That's an understatement. I watched you win yesterday. You were running guys left and right. I was thinking, tomorrow night, I'll find out what that truck feels like."

"I don't know, Cory …" Joseph said tentatively.

"Don't give me any of that crap." Cory glared at Joseph, wet hair slicked back high off his face. "When we pull on the jerseys tonight, those 45 minutes, we're not friends. That's our agreement."

Joseph was silent.

"Right?" Cory insisted.

"I guess," Joseph said. "But it's just a game."

"Joseph, I can forgive you knocking me on my ass a few times tonight. But I can't forgive you *not* knocking me on my ass. We owe it to our teams and ourselves. Somebody wins, somebody loses, that's life. Then it's behind us and we go wear Badger red next season. All right?"

Joseph looked at Cory. "Are you nervous?"

"Shit yes. It's only natural. The whole state has been watching us like circus animals."

"I'm not," Joseph said, putting on an act.

"Bullshit artist," Cory said, slapping him on the back.

Joseph winced. Cory had hit a spot where Joseph took a stick in last night's game.

"Sorry about that," Cory said.

"Ahh. Just a stinger."

The two stood up and walked to the poolside chairs where they'd left their towels and sweatshirts.

HomeSky, who'd earlier seen the boys talking by the pool, had started down to say good morning. As she approached from behind, she saw them in their swimsuits. The sight of it stole her breath. The bruises and welts. Ugly purple and red. On their ribs and arms, the backs of their legs, their sides and backs, all that pain hidden under clothes and never a word of it. She wanted to stop it all right there. To call off the game. To hug them both like little boys. Something fierce and maternal wanted it ended.

Cory turned around, wrapping his towel around his waist. "Oh, morning, HomeSky," he said, smiling at her with a fat lip. He came over and gave her a hug. "Something wrong?"

"You two look like you've been kicked by horses," she said. "Look at those bruises."

Joseph quickly pulled on his sweatshirt. He came over and threw and arm around her. "Don't be such a mom, Mom." He gave her a strong squeeze. Cory hurried into his t-shirt.

"They look worse than they are," Cory assured her, his arm around her other side so she was sandwiched in between.

She tried not to be charmed off the subject. "Why couldn't you two take up track?" she asked.

The boys looked at each other and smiled. At the same time they said, "Because hockey is college."

Five minutes before the game, one of Cory's linemates puked in the corner of the locker room. Cory looked at his coach and the coach nodded. Cory stood up to speak.

"Looks like McFarland had ... what is it? Spaghetti for lunch," Cory said, breaking the tension. Everyone, including McFarland, laughed. Cory walked to the center of the room. Except for his helmet, he was dressed for the game. His gray-green eyes sparked. Everyone went silent.

"Hockey's a team game," he began. "Each one of us is going to have good shifts and bad shifts tonight. Every individual in this room is going to screw up. But when you do, someone on this team will pick you up. We have the best team in the state. This team has scored the most goals and this team is rated number one." Cory's eyes flashed around the locker room. "There's been a lot of talk about who's the best player in the state. Fuck that! Last time I checked, hockey was still six on six. Our team's better than theirs. Our year's been better than theirs. We've scored almost twice as many goals this season. If we play like we always play, we'll win—by about twice as many goals. Two to one. Four to two. Six to three. How's my math, Beef?" Cory eyed the team's worst student. Everybody loosened up as Beef shrugged his wide shoulders. "Look around this room. They don't have this kind of group across the hall. They have one great player surrounded by a bunch of average. One guy can't beat this team. Forget the hype."

There was a rap on the door, and a referee looked in. "It's showtime, gentlemen," he said, and ducked back out.

The coach stood up. "Okay, everyone in." The team huddled in the center of the room and got down on one knee. The coach led the prayer: "Lord, let us have a clean, healthy game tonight. Give us the strength not to let down our school or our parents." The team responded together: "Mary, Queen of victory, pray for us!"

All heads went silent and turned to Cory. Again, in an effort to loosen the guys up, he cracked, "Good and gracious Lord, please forgive us for what we're about to do to these ladies from Baudette."

"YEAAAH!!" the group yelled, standing, slapping helmets, grabbing their sticks and making their way down the walkway to the ice.

Cory, as was his superstition, was last to leave the room. With the locker room door open, he could hear the deep murmur of the packed arena, waiting for the teams to hit the ice. The referees came skating on first, greeted by a smattering of boos from the student sections. As the first of the boys came through the runway and stepped onto the ice, the crowd erupted. The band cranked up. The high-pitched screams of the high school girls climbed above all. Cory just needed those first explosive strokes under him. His stomach was unsettled, but as soon as he touched the ice, he'd be home.

With his teammates circling the ice in front of him, Cory quick-stepped out onto the brightly lit sheet of ice and his legs responded. An extra burst of applause went up when the familiar number 10 blurred up the boards, jersey rippling. A chill ran through him and with five quick steps, he rocketed into the circle of skaters, slapping each other's shin pads with their sticks. He was with his team. This was family. It was finally game time. No more talking. No more interviews. He wanted to get that first hit under his belt. The tension began to evaporate. His body vibrated. Underneath the face mask of his helmet, he smiled like a boy who'd never known a worry.

Joseph and his team heard the sudden peak of crowd noise swell through the walls of their locker room. They knew Cory's team had taken the ice. There was a loud knock on their steel door. "You're up, guys," the last linesman barked. The whole bunch stood when Joseph did. They were silent. They were tight. They were 360 miles from home. They were about to take the ice against the number-one team in the state. "Huddle up," Joseph said. The guys' helmets came together; they made a tight circle. Their hockey gloves united as they joined hands.

"If we're within three by the third period, we can win. I give you my word. Don't get intimidated. Let's just slow these guys down at first and not let them get too much early momentum. Lay on 'em in the corners. Tie 'em up. Stay in their face. Hit 'em hard. When they get up, hit 'em again. By the third, they'll be gassed. Then leave it to me." Joseph looked around at his circle of friends. They hung on his instruction. "Now let's go say hey to those city boys." He grinned his classic smile and the tension in the room broke like a fever. The team shouted and yelled and laughed and from behind Joseph, they came down the hall and flying onto the ice, pumping their fists. The Baudette band fired up and the students with their hair dyed school colors jumped up in a frenzy. Father Pat, Monsignor Kief, and the normally unflappable Sheriff Harris leapt up, too. HomeSky remained seated, saying a prayer. "Don't let either of my boys get hurt out there today," she whispered. "I beg of You."

Pat sat down next to her. They could hardly hear over the din.

"You okay?"

HomeSky nodded yes, looked at him, then shook her head no.

Pat smiled at her, took her by the elbow and helped her to her feet. "Look at those boys," he said to her. "Would you just look at them." His eyes teared. Below on the ice, the boys circled and stretched their legs. They were in overdrive. She looked for number 5, her Joseph. He moved on the ice like he was born skating. He and his team jostled around, slapping each others' helmets. She looked to the other end of the ice; Cory, number 10, his stick behind his shoulders, stretched out his upper body. The referee blew his whistle and the teams lined up for the face off.

"This is going to be one hell of a dog fight," the Sheriff shouted.

"Saints preserve us," Monsignor Kief returned.

"I need a drink," Father Pat joked.

"Tell me when it's over," HomeSky added, covering her face with her hands.

The crowd sat down in tense anticipation of the puck finally being dropped.

"Bob, this game has been dissected every which way to Sunday," the TV play-by-play announcer said. "I don't know what I could add other than to say I'm as excited as a five-year-old at a sleepover."

"I couldn't agree more, Al," the color commentator chimed in. "This game was on everybody's wish list and here we are, along with a standing room crowd of over 35,000 to see if it can live up to the billing."

"Oh, would you look at this!" the announcer interrupted. "Ladies and gentlemen! Before the referee could drop the puck, Joseph Blackholm has skated in from his position on defense, pulled off his glove and is shaking hands with Cory Bradford at center ice!"

The crowd erupted in applause as the two boys delayed the dropping of the puck.

"Bob, that's a first for me. Have you ever seen that before?" the announcer asked, rubbing off goose bumps.

"Absolutely not. What a gesture. You hate to see either of these kids lose."

"They've been the class of the tournament all week, no doubt. Okay, everyone's squared up and the puck's about to drop."

Televisions from Baudette to the southern border of Minnesota were tuned in for the big Saturday night clash. Cory and Joseph's faces and names had become recognizable from all the media coverage. Households across the state were divided as to whose team they were pulling for.

Early in the first period, the play was tight and tentative. Passes misfired on both sides. Nobody was finishing their checks. It was like both teams were waiting to see how Cory and Joseph were going to play it out. At seven minutes of the first period, they got their answer. Cory, a center, made an outlet pass to his winger on the boards. The winger shoveled a soft return pass that Cory, skating full speed, had to look back for. Joseph instinctively stepped in at center ice and lowered his shoulder. Cory got his head up just in time to throw his weight forward at the oncoming Joseph. The two came together in a tremendous collision. Cory was knocked backward onto his butt, and Joseph lurched, falling to one knee, but kept his other skate under him. Joseph slid forward on the ice, found the puck caught in his skates, and as he stood to advance it, one of Cory's defensemen piled into him. Stunned, both Joseph and Cory angled for the bench for a line change.

"Let's score on these bastards!" Cory screamed at his team as he climbed over the boards onto the bench.

"C'mon!" Joseph yelled, climbing over into his bench. "Wake up and play hockey!"

The game was on. Back and forth, up and down the ice. Cory had a great chance a few shifts later and rung one off the post. Joseph twice skated the length of the ice with the puck but couldn't get off a clean shot because of Cory's relentless back-checking. The first period ended 0–0. A moral victory for the underdog Baudette team.

In the locker room Cory was ready to erupt on the inside, but he kept calm. He grit his teeth and talked slowly. "Guys, we need short, crisp passes. Move the puck up ice fast. They're trying to slow us down. And we're being too cute, stickhandling or going for long bomb passes. Quick, sharp passes. Open up the ice. Don't fuck around trying to get on the highlight tape. Move the puck. Get the bricks out of your breezers!"

Nobody said anything. They just looked down at their skates.

"Johnny?" Cory said.

"Short passes," he answered, looking up.

"Skinny?" Cory said.

"Move the puck," he replied, meeting Cory's stare.

"Dino?" Cory said.

"Bricks out of breezers," he said. Everybody laughed.

"All right," Cory said. "That's more like it. Let's loosen up and play our game."

Over in locker room B, they were devising a plan. Joseph, sweat running down his face, said, "Barry, you've got to shadow Cory. Get inside his jersey. Don't let him breathe. Where he goes, you go.

You two are officially married. Your job isn't to score, it's to not let him score. I'm going to start taking double shifts. If Cory stays out for a double, Zack, you got him on shift two. The rest of you just keep doing what you're doing. We've got them running around like Christmas puppies. Tom, watch for my breakaway pass. When I circle around the net I'm going to be looking for you coming across the middle fast, behind their defense. When they pick it up after a few tries, we'll put it away 'til the third. This is our game now. We've got them thinking instead of playing."

Not even a minute into the second period, Cory put his team on the board with a goal as pretty as any you'll see. Cory's linemate drew back for a slapshot, Joseph closed to block it, but the winger read it nicely and dropped the puck back to Cory. He caught the pass with a full head of steam, faked a shot, dropping the other defenseman to his knees, cut around him, deked the goalie to his forehand, drew it across to his backhand, and put the puck up in what he and Joseph liked to call the sock drawer. Upper corner. A number two. The crowd exploded. The band was too busy hugging and jumping to play music. The red goal light flashed as Cory was mauled by his line in one big scrum behind the net.

Five minutes later, Cory's line scored again. This time on a perfect pass from Cory across the crease that his winger tipped in. Suddenly it was 2–0 and Baudette was on the ropes.

"Baudette is a cotter pin away from the wheels coming off, Bob," the announcer said. "They need to slow down and regroup."

"Al, I don't know. That just might be too much firepower out there for the Baudette kids," his broadcasting partner added. "They've battled gallantly, but I don't know."

Joseph, sensing his team's avalanching nerves, took over the game for Baudette. He became a one-man show, stickhandling, pounding any offensive threat that stepped over his blue line, and ripping some slapshots that put the goalie back on his heels. After his team fell behind 2–0, Joseph never stepped off the ice for the rest of the period. When the horn sounded ending the second, they had stemmed the tide, and were within two goals. Cory and his teammates noticed that Joseph seemed to get stronger as the period went on.

"The son of a bitch doesn't get tired," one of Cory's teammates said, throwing his stick as he entered the locker room between periods. "He's not human."

Cory dropped onto the bench, pulled off his helmet, and unlaced his shoulder pads. This was their third straight night of hockey. It was taking a toll on everyone. Except Joseph.

"We got them down two-rip. Don't freak, you guys. Joseph is one guy and he's going to tire before the third is over. Just keep coming at him. He can't keep it up."

"Man, he hits hard," one guy admitted.

"Don't let him get that cannon off," the goalie spoke up.

"Easy, guys," Cory interrupted. "If we keep moving the puck, we'll wear him out."

Joseph sat up straight up in the other locker room. He had a towel around his neck. He rolled the braided stone behind his ear in his fingertips. His guys were slumped on the benches; a few lay flat on the ground. He spoke quietly and forcefully. "This is our period. A whole season in fifteen minutes. They thought they'd be up by four or five by now. Two goals. They're frustrated. We can get those two back no sweat. You gotta believe, guys. They're losing it. It's switching on 'em like the wind before a storm." Joseph's voice remained strong, but it cracked slightly in the emotion of the moment. "Let's show the entire state that where we come from, there's no quit." Joseph smiled big and sure. Around the room, the boys' postures straightened like flowers to the sun. It was like the entire room started to hum.

In the third, Baudette took to the ice like a team possessed. They had five quick shots on goal, and Cory and his boys couldn't seem to break the puck out of their zone. Then the puck squirted out, Joseph strode into it and ripped a shot that tore into the lower right corner. The goal light flashed. The fans went wild. Baudette had become the underdog favorite as the crowd sprang to their feet. It was deafening on the ice as Joseph's teammates piled into him after the goal. Cory watched from center ice. He was worried. He could feel the momentum reversing. It was palpable.

"Bob," the TV announcer said. "If I'm not mistaken, Baudette has put the number one team in the state back on their heels."

"Boy, have they. I don't know what was said in that locker room between periods, but they've found another gear. They're winning the race to the puck, their passes are right on the tape, and that shot of Joseph Blackholm's, have you ever seen anything like it in high school?"

"There are kids in college who can't shoot the puck like that," the play-by-play announcer said, genuinely impressed. "He's everything they advertised. I don't think he's left the ice since early in the second period."

Joseph felt himself getting stronger. He was having fun, skating with the puck, making good passes, and hammering anyone who dared to cross his blue line.

Cory was centering the first and second lines, then taking a short break while the third line just played defense. Then he was back out, double-shifting again. He felt the incremental weight that tension loads onto your game. He was tentative, but nowhere near as much as his team. They were clinging to a one-goal lead. They knew one shot could bring them down.

Now the game was all Baudette. Every shift, they had good scoring chances. The crowd was big behind them; it's hard not to love an underdog. It was just a matter of time before Baudette popped one in—everyone could feel it.

Cory closed his eyes on the bench, catching his wind. *You have to turn this around. This is your responsibility. Go do it now.*

The lines changed on the fly and Cory's skates hit the ice. He felt a tidal surge of adrenaline—the kind that only comes to a desperate man about to execute a plan.

Joseph, striding powerfully from behind his net, weaved deftly around a defender and bore down hard on each stroke, streaking across his blue line.

Cory strode, at full sprint, straight from his bench, accelerating at a breakneck pace. He bit down on his mouthguard.

Joseph stickhandled up the ice, catching something coming out of the corner of his eye, but it was too late.

He and Cory met at mid-ice. The collision could be heard all the way up in the nose-bleed seats. It was like an explosion in slow motion. Joseph staggered four steps back, his stick, caught between them on impact, splintering above their helmets, pieces in all directions. Cory felt the wind go out of him as he was sent back, nearly out of his skates.

"OH MY, WHAT A HIT!" the announcer screamed.

Joseph felt his legs deaden, his arms pinwheeling, trying to stay on his skates. He landed on his butt like someone pulled a chair out from under him.

"That was almost too much to watch!" the color analyst added.

Cory landed flat on his back and his helmet whiplashed down, slamming the ice. The puck slipped unattended toward the boards.

"Both kids are down," the announcer said, his voice thick with concern.

All skaters stopped. The referee held his arm up signaling a penalty on Cory. The benches of each team stood, stunned, like witnesses at an accident scene. Cory's body nearly convulsed with pain, but he slammed the door on it. He would not accept it. He willed himself onto his skates.

"Two minutes, number 10, charging!" The referee pointed at Cory.

"Charging?" Cory barked, skating toward the ref in protest. "That's complete bullshit!" His teammates skated over and pulled him away. They didn't want him tossed from the game.

"What the hell kinda call is that!" Cory screamed over his shoulder as he headed toward the penalty box. "You're a joke!" The more Cory yelled, the more his teammates filled with energy. Cory slammed shut the penalty box door, then opened and slammed it again, the bang echoing like cannon fire through the quiet arena. The referee spun around and pointed at Cory, plainly warning: one more and you're tossed.

Cory's team on the bench started beating their sticks against the boards, screaming *let's go! let's go!* They felt the life return to their dead limbs like a valve had been opened. Joseph, still on his butt, stood and skated wobbly-legged over to his bench to get a new stick. He was shaking his head, trying to get the cobwebs out. All voices were muted, like his ears needed to pop.

"Can you skate?" his coach asked him.

"Blue," Joseph replied. He'd never been hit so hard in his life. It was like getting slammed in the chest with a battering ram.

"You better sit this power play out," Joseph's coach said.

"What?" Joseph said, leaning on the boards as the arena rocked around him.

Cory's hit, and the subsequent posturing with the ref, had worked. His boys came back from the dead. They had two great short-handed chances, but the puck just wouldn't go in. They were playing inspired hockey again.

Joseph slowly felt the aftershock from the hit leave his body. He stood by the bench, testing his legs. He paced, jumped up and down, felt his focus return. He stepped on the ice just as Cory's penalty expired. With three minutes left in the game, Joseph was back and, frankly, pissed off.

Cory, on the other hand, was not at all right. From the moment he'd sat down in the penalty box, he knew something was wrong. Inside him, he knew it. He bit down on his mouthguard and tried to ignore it.

Cory's line was playing like their old selves. They were moving the puck all over the ice and had set a higher tempo. More and more of the game's play was now in their offensive zone. They were putting the heat on the Baudette goalie, with shots bombing in from all directions.

Joseph intercepted a centering pass and came flying out of his zone. He led the charge down ice, but the backchecking slowed him down while two defensemen sandwiched him, freeing the puck. Cory was a few steps behind the pack. Uncharacteristically, he couldn't keep up with the flow of the game, which left him open for a breakaway pass going the other way.

A perfect pass sprung Cory. He crossed over the blue line, moving in alone on the goalie. He tried to focus on the net, thinking about the five targets he had spent years hitting: upper left, upper right, lower left, lower right, between the legs. Those were the high-percentage shots. Which one would he go for? He tried not to listen, but he could hear it. Inside, it was like something was leaking. *Score*, he thought. *Score and put the game away.*

Twenty feet from the net, Cory collapsed.

He was in the water, swimming.

The crowd gasped, rising to their feet.

The lake water was the opaque algae-green of late summer.

Joseph dropped his stick and gloves, skating fast to Cory.

Lake of the Woods had him.

Joseph took off Cory's helmet.

He felt the water leak in him.

A doctor, pulled by two players, skidded on his dress shoes to Cory.

He was filling up.

Joseph told everyone to get back.

He felt his body getting heavy.

The doctor put his ear to Cory's mouth.

The warmth of the surface water dissipated.

The doctor waved frantically to the men with the stretcher.

He was sinking, cold.

They rushed him off the ice.

He saw Joseph's dog, Lick, shaking water off his back.

LANDING

The paramedics ran the stretcher up the ramp.

He saw the green pasture vanish into the endless blue sky.

The ambulance doors waited, wide open.

He saw HomeSky's loving face below through the leaves of the climbing tree.

They shoved the stretcher through the rear doors of the ambulance.

He saw RiverHeart walking through the veil of tractor dust to take his lunch.

The doctor climbed up next to him.

He sank and rolled away from the light.

Cory lifted his hand, to the doctor's amazement.

He saw the light growing faint.

The ambulance doors slammed shut.

He watched the last bubbles rising away from him.

Cory's hand remained outstretched.

He was filling, filling.

There was pounding on the ambulance door.

He felt his fingers tingle cold.

There was shouting at the ambulance door.

He felt his hand getting so heavy.

The doctor opened the door.

He saw the last languid light rippling away.

Joseph, in his socks, climbed into the ambulance.

He felt himself rising.

Next to him, Joseph took hold of Cory's hand.

He felt himself rising now.

RISING

Only angels fall from grace.
The rest of us fall toward it.

— *Father Pat*

PART ONE

Autumn 1980

SOPHOMORE SEASON.

The team was screwing around on the ice. Joseph, as always, was in the thick of it. Cory gave him The Look: intolerance mixed with disappointment mixed with *the coach is going to have your ass.* The team picture was an hour late being snapped. The head coach would be out on the ice any second. The team's media director tried to gain some aspect of control but got the respect accorded a high school substitute teacher.

The photographer looked at Cory like, *can you please pull these dumb puppies together?* The final 26-man roster was on the ice, the season was a few weeks off, and they needed to get their team poster shot. Off by the net, Joseph was mock-fighting, taking on three at a time, pulling their jerseys up over their heads, wrestling them to the ice. The jerseys were new, washed, and pressed just for the photo. They were on their way to looking slept in. Great, Cory thought.

Joseph, laughing, caught Cory's look. "All right," he said, "let's pull it in." The guys started heading for mid-ice. "Look presentable," Joseph said to Stevens, completely messing his combed new haircut. Stevens, a soda straw freshman who could fly on skates, loved the attention from Joseph, last season's WCHA Rookie of the Year. "A team this good-looking owes it to our public. Let's show 'em our best side," Joseph commanded.

"That'd be you standing backwards," his teammate, Chevy, barked out. The boys loved it. Joseph thought it was funny, too. For him, funny was funny, no matter at whose expense.

The head coach came out on the ice for the photo. The rink got noticeably quieter. So far, the day had been a disaster. They'd had a grueling, mistake-riddled, three-hour practice. That led to two hours of non-stop drilling in the meeting room on offensive and defensive schemes. And that concluded with the coach kicking over his chalkboard. About that time, the photographer came in and said they were late getting dressed for the picture.

As everybody moved toward center ice, Joseph peeled off and glided to the bench, where he filled his hockey glove with something while no one was paying attention. No one except Cory.

"All right, ladies, let's look pretty and get this over with," head coach Waldron yelled, tipping up his university ball cap, spitting something green from deep in his lungs on the ice. "Fucking virus," he grumbled. Meanwhile, as the players were shuffling into place, Joseph secretly handed out his latest gag to a few of the guys. Cory didn't know what was up, but he could see Joseph was doing everything possible not to bust up. Joseph snuck Cory something just as the coach hollered, for the last time, to get fucking lined up.

As the photographer got the big bodies to squeeze closer, a photo stylist came by for a last-second brush-up. She flattened down hair and straightened a few jerseys. Cory looked into the palm of his glove to see what Joseph had handed him. He had to smile and shake his head. "Jesus," he said softly.

The stylist got out of the picture and the photographer told everyone where to look. Joseph interrupted. "Count to three so we all get a good smile. I was disappointed with my smile last year."

"Since what century did you give a crap about that?" The coach squinted across at Joseph.

"Just want to make sure we represent Badger hockey in a fine fashion, sir," Joseph said.

"Everyone look here, now," the photographer ordered. "One."

A few players wiped their faces with their gloves.

"Two."

A few others made a quick move to their mouths.

"Three." The shutter opened and closed. Click.

Joseph and his six accomplices smiled big, exposing the large, fake buckteeth. They quickly closed their mouths between shots, always flashing the big plastic choppers at the three count. As immature as Cory found the whole idea, he couldn't help but go along. Joseph had that kind of magnetism. And sure enough, if you look closely at the 1980-81 team poster, which to this day is a collectors' item, for a few reasons, there are seven players with a special gleam in their eyes and plastic buckteeth in their mouths. In the years later, that poster was something people went back to and often looked at—teammates, students, coaches, sportswriters, and of course, Cory. What a year it turned out to be. What a magical group of players. Especially Joseph. Although Cory was developing into a young leader in many ways, Joseph was the heart of this team. And the team poster, in its own way, was permanent evidence of it.

After the photo, a few of the younger guys stayed for 20 minutes of extra skating drills—Cory leading the way. There was quite another agenda for the juniors and seniors. They were ready to shower and hit the bricks. It was Saturday night, and they'd practiced like dogs all week. The weekend beckoned. Hockey players at the University of Wisconsin carried deity status at parties. No waiting in line for beer or girls. It was time to go from grunts to gods.

Partying was the furthest thing from Cory's and Joseph's minds. They were entering their second season and had grander plans. Freshman year, they had come in wide-eyed and green. It was like night and day from high school to college hockey. They were playing against men now. Physically, Joseph was fine, but the mental demands of the game were like nothing he'd encountered. He used to skate a game without much thinking about it. Those days were over. Now he had to play defense at the Division One level, facing the elite of the elite. Almost any forward on the ice at any second had the skills to beat him. Joseph liked to joke as he pulled on his helmet that his was putting on his thinking cap.

As for Cory, he had always been years ahead of his peers mentally. He quickly adjusted, and renewed his mental advantage, even over most juniors and seniors. He hit the ice ready for every second of every shift. He constantly ran game scenarios through his head, so when they presented themselves, he was ready to capitalize just a nanosecond faster than his opponent. His most challenging adjustment was physical. At this level, hockey is, in a word, mean. His 5-8 frame took a beating. And the goaltending, it was like the nets had shrunk. In high school, Cory could score fairly easily, especially one-on-one. Now it was near impossible. But he kept crashing the net, taking good quick shots, busting his ass on every rebound, and the puck started going in for him. His first goal as a freshman came in the third period of his second game. That's when he thought, *Oh yeah. That's how you do it. I can handle this.* And he did and did and did some more. He ended up with 29 goals in his first 36-game college season—a WCHA freshman record, good enough to make him a second-team All WCHA selection. But it was Joseph who won Rookie of the Year honors.

This sophomore year, both were slated to see a lot of ice time. Cory centering the second line, with Joseph on defense. Both would see some power play minutes, too. The freshman jitters were long gone. They had a year under their belts, and some notable successes. Sophomore season can be magical because you haven't seen enough disappointment to be jaded, and everything's new enough for you to naively believe. Youth stokes confidence, a blind belief that can make you dangerous. Joseph and Cory were officially dangerous.

Joseph put in his plastic teeth and skated over to Cory. They were the only two left on the ice now. "How do you like my new mouth guard? I think it's perfect for road games." Cory smiled. Something of a rarity for him, except on the ice, bathed in adrenaline.

"You're lucky Coach didn't catch you. Man, something crawled up his ass and died."

Joseph spied a puck down by Cory's skates and fast as a cat, he dug it out with his stick blade and skated around him. "Mine!" he said through his plastic teeth. And the game was on. Keep-away. For 10 non-stop minutes they skated just as they had on the pond all those years, trying out new moves. Their stickhandling had grown so advanced, especially Cory's, whose hands were lightning; the puck seemed glued to his blade. But Joseph was no slouch either. When he deked Cory, he looked back at him and flashed those fake teeth.

They wrapped up by shooting. Working on accuracy. Slapshots, wristshots, snapshots, backhands, and breakaway moves. These two loved the ice. Playing together, wearing the same jersey, living their dream. Neither ever said much about what happened the one time they'd met as adversaries. They were as they were meant to be now: brothers. Most nights, the rink manager had to chase them off with the Zamboni.

"What's up tonight, Cory-boy?" Joseph asked as they showered. "I hear Chevy's house is the ticket."

"Surprise, surprise," Cory said. "You going?" he asked, remaining noncommittal.

"I think I'll take it slow with Nicole tonight. We might stop over before it gets too packed."

Cory shampooed silently, feeling, although he'd never admit it, jealous. More and more, his best friend was making couch pretzels with his girlfriend and it pissed Cory off. He confronted Joseph about it once, but Joseph just laughed. He said he and Cory spent more time together than a couple of old crows. He told Cory he ought to try a few new things, open up a little, get a girlfriend. There's a lot of life out there. But hockey and Joseph were life for Cory. Everything else bored him.

"I might go over," Cory offered. "Chevy's cool. But every corner of that house reeks of beer. That guy has a keg tapped seven days a week. I don't know how he skates."

"Hung-over," Joseph said, no humor in his voice.

Chevy was the senior captain of their team. Mike Chevalier, a French-Canadian who was as accomplished with the opposite sex as he was with the puck. He loved the beer, the late hours, and the game. Athletically, he was talented enough to get away with the list in that order. For a while.

Chevy was old for a senior because he'd played two years of Canadian Juniors after high school. Like many other Canadian players, he got some seasoning and toughening up before stepping onto college ice. A year or two of Junior hockey could get a guy up to 120 extra games, not to mention time for his body to develop.

Since the first practices of Cory's freshman year, Chevy had taken him under his wing. They were drawn to each other. Chevy played with fearless improvisation, which appealed to Cory. Cory played with fearless discipline, which intrigued Chevy. The qualities underdeveloped in each of them bonded them. As a result, Chevy was always trying to get Cory drunk, and Cory was always trying to get Chevy into better shape. Neither had been successful. But they appreciated each other's effort. And because both were very talented centers, they came into the year as keys to the Badgers' plans, with Chevy skating first line, Cory second.

Joseph was toweling off. "Why don't you and me and Nicole go to Chevy's together. We might split early, but we could eat something and then see what's happening. I'm starved."

"I don't think so. You guys eat too weird for me. I don't see how you keep any weight on eating all that tofu and grass."

"Vegetables, beans, fruits, nuts, fish, pasta, hockey. You're the smart one. You should know that's the food pyramid that'll keep you on top in the NCAA."

Cory thought about adding Nicole to Joseph's consumption list, but let it go. "Maybe I'll see you guys there. I'm going to hit the library first. Organic chemistry. It's tougher than it should be."

"Say what?" Joseph mugged. "Cory Bradford declaring a subject hard?"

Cory offered a thin smile, but said nothing. Silence was his most effective response.

"I can tutor if you need it." Joseph feigned concern. "We need you on the ice this season, Son. If I have to pull you through organic chemistry or astrobiology or nuclear reactions 101, I'm here for you."

Cory remained poker-faced.

"Ahh, you're no fun," Joseph said, tossing his towel at Cory's head.

The only place more vacant than a church on Saturday night is a college library. Cory sat alone devouring organic chemistry. It came easily. The suffusion of adrenaline made Cory's mind attack. He completed three hours of studying in 45 minutes.

At nine p.m. he stepped into Chevy's party. The house was already a zoo. Body heat swarmed him at the door. Windows were steamed. Speakers the size of coffins pounded out Springsteen from all corners of the living room. Not a stick of furniture remained on the floor; it was all in the backyard. Chevy liked to sell the most beer cups per square inch; couches and chairs didn't pay the freight. Students pulled off sweaters, dancing in t-shirts, mouthing every tenth word to the songs they pretended to know. You could feel the floor heave on the downbeats. *High school,* Cory concluded, squeezing through the crowd, *only drunker.* All those dads painting houses, turning wrenches, and climbing into garbage trucks on Saturdays so their kids could have it better with a college education. Here they were. Learning Springsteen lyrics and the physics of emptying plastic cups. Cory shook his head. *What a pile of fuck-ups.*

Ironically, though, he had no trouble playing hockey in front of them. He loved it. To bring the rowdy 8000 to their feet when he buried the puck in the back of the net. The din. It made his body fizz. Nothing else even came close.

Cory wore his colors into the party: the Badger red letter jacket with the large white W scripted across the front. All the hockey players did. One of the benefits of playing a winter sport was you had a reason to wear your heavy letter jacket in public. But the cold wasn't the true motivation for the coat. It was a flag. Make room, an athlete has arrived.

"Cory!" a group shouted from the corner where the stereo equipment was housed. His teammates were there, along with their gum-snapping groupies. Chevy was the centerpiece, sitting up high on the built-in wet bar they'd constructed. He lifted his beer glass to Cory. The bar was the only vantage point from which anyone could sit and see the whole room. Chevy called these the first-class seats. They weren't available to many. He shoved over and patted a spot next to him. "Get up here, Cor. Mikey, get the man a frosty one."

"I'm okay, Chevy," Cory said, hiking up next to him.

"Like hell you are. Mikey! Where's that beer!" Chevy pressed a full cup into Cory's hand. "Shit, man," a look of utter fulfillment spread across his face. "Wait 'til you see the tits bounce from up here."

Right there, at the door of her apartment, Joseph kissed Nicole like he'd just returned from fighting the Germans overseas. That's what she loved about him; his truthfulness permeated everything.

"Wow," Nicole said, unable to manage more than a three-letter word.

"I missed you," Joseph stepped back and smiled. "Since early this morning."

Nicole brushed her hair to the side. "It's nice to be missed." She took his hand and led him into her little off-campus apartment, which smelled faintly of candles and shampoo. She shared the place with one other English major. They had books everywhere. Stacked in corners with plants on top. Sticking out of full bookshelves. In the cupboards next to the macaroni and cheese. In the bathroom on top of the toilet. Joseph, since meeting Monsignor Kief, had grown to appreciate the magnetic pull of a closed book, with its wonderful secrets inside. Waiting, practically humming with promise.

They pushed a few books aside and sat on the couch. Nicole climbed on top of Joseph and tried to return a fraction of the passion he'd sent through her with that kiss at the door. They momentarily lost track of time.

Joseph, wincing, pulled a sharp-cornered book from behind his the back. "Anna Karenina," he said, looking at the hardcover. "Always the third wheel. Hey, I'm so hungry I could almost eat your roommate's pizzas."

"Oh, now that is severe." Nicole pulled Joseph up from the couch. "Quick, you must be preserved from preservatives."

Nicole was a year older than Joseph. She had originally laid eyes on him in a poetry class a year earlier. It was the first day of class and he arrived fifteen minutes late, looking lost. Her impression was that he'd stepped into the wrong room. Physically, he didn't fit in a poetry class. He looked like a football player, she told him later as they got to know one another, discussing Goethe. Jokingly, he said he was offended. To be dubbed an athlete, let alone a football player! That was low, he told her. They laughed about it. He decided to make no mention of his hockey scholarship. I'll have her meet me slowly, he thought. Like a poem.

One Thursday about six weeks later, in a group breakout discussion on meter, one of the students changed subjects and asked Joseph about the weekend series against the University of Minnesota. Nicole was in the breakout group. She and Joseph weren't a couple yet, but sparks were flying. Lunch, coffee, studying, calling out of the blue to go for a walk and a long conversation.

In response to the question, Joseph told the student it would be a huge couple of games because both teams wanted to set the stage for the season with this first weekend series. Plus you have to win your home games. Nicole listened as they talked. A few other people asked questions of Joseph. Finally it occurred to her. Joseph was on the team. And she was the only one who didn't seem to know it. She was upset. After class they usually went somewhere to study together, but she disappeared out the door before he could talk to her. The next day, outside, walking between classes, Joseph caught up with her. She strode purposefully ahead, not looking at him.

"Are you mad at me for some reason I should know about?"

She stopped. "Why didn't you tell me you were a hockey player?" She looked brightly into his eyes.

Joseph thought about her question. "Because of what you just said: 'a hockey player.' At this school, you get labeled. I wanted you to meet *me* first. Without any of the other stuff."

"Give me a little more credit than that, all right?"

He looked at her softly. "Do you remember what you thought the first time I walked into poetry class?"

Nicole racked her brain. "The first day?" She shook her head no.

"You said I looked lost and like a football player. That's what people do. I stick out. People compartmentalize."

Nicole looked at him. She had long thick waves of red hair. Her face was thin and angular. Her blue eyes sparkled always with such intensity. "I did say that, didn't I? Shit. I'm sorry. What an idiot."

"Don't get me wrong, I love hockey. But with you, I was happy we didn't start there. We started with words. With verses. With Whitman. That's never, ever, ever, *ever* happened to me. My introduction has always come in an athletic context. You never know if people are interested in you or the hockey player."

"I'm interested in *you*," Nicole said. Hearing it gave Joseph goosebumps.

He smiled at her, but was frozen as to the next move. Nicole filled the space between them. The wind blustered through the campus buildings, blowing back her hair. She stepped in and kissed him softly on the cheek. He smiled and his eyes teared up. *God*, Nicole wondered. *Am I falling for him?*

Yes, she was. And over a year later, as they walked from her apartment to their favorite Thai place, she knew she had met "the one." He was a gift.

The off-campus area was sprinkled with little restaurants and shops and bars. It was a cold night. Hand-in-hand, they went. Actually, hand-in-glove. The cold didn't bother Joseph. He wore a jean jacket and no gloves or hat. He was the only hockey player who didn't wear his letter jacket around campus. He wore it on road trips, to be part of the team, but at school he thought it tried too hard. "Why not just carry a sign? Hockey jock," he laughed. Cory, on the other hand, all but slept in his colors. He loved the sound of his arms sliding through the sleeves, the feel of his letter jacket settling on his shoulders. His hockey team gave him his identity.

Nicole asked Joseph as he ate, "So, where do you see us going?"

Joseph looked up from his vegetables and rice. "How do you mean?"

"You and me. As a couple. Where do *we* fit into *you*?"

"I love how you put things," Joseph smiled, "even when you're nervous."

"I am not nervous," Nicole smiled, kicking him under the table.

"The tops of your ears are as red as your hair. Dead giveaway."

"Shut up. They are not." She covered her ears with the hair that had been tucked behind them.

Joseph got up from across the table. They remained looking at each other as he took his chair and brought it over next to her. He sat so their shoulders were touching. She could feel his heat and he hers. They sat there feeling each other breathe. They aligned. Joseph closed his eyes and went into himself. He could feel her. He could feel the stone behind his ear. He could see the dust of his father's tractor. He could hear HomeSky's bare feet step lightly on the kitchen floor. He told her what he believed, just then, side by side, surrounded by the smell of curry and ginger and lemon.

"We should get married."

FRIDAY MORNING.

For over a year now, Pat had waited. Waited like a boy might, breathlessly, at a mailbox for a promised letter long overdue. Or as a sailor's son might wait, hands clenched, staring at the sea for a mast to break the horizon. Each day. Alert in the waiting. Still, nothing came. Every afternoon, he'd find a quiet moment. He'd close his eyes, lips parted as he turned an attentive ear, scanning. Oh, how he listened. But nothing.

On weekend mornings, he stretched. He ran. Afterward, sweat rolling off his face, he would hold out his arms. To his faith's credit, with no less certainty than the day before, he stood like a human antenna. He waited for the answer to find him. *Heavenly Father, what would you have me do?* He watched. He prayed. But nothing came. So he did as any good Irishman would. He disappeared in his work.

The rectory was completed. It looked fantastic. Everyone was frankly shocked by his building skills. His Sunday nine and eleven a.m. masses were overflowing to the balcony. Plus, still working the third shift at the McKnight Forestry Products plant, Pat had been bumped up to night floor foreman. He led his weekly A.A. meetings. And he wrote a letter every ten days or so to Monsignor Kief, who'd taken a 20-month sabbatical to work with the blind and impoverished in Guatemala. How he missed Frank's voice, his wise, face-to-face counsel. Pat could hear him in the words of his letters, but it wasn't the same.

Also, very carefully, he saw HomeSky. They kept a safe, unspoken distance. HomeSky, too, was waiting. The options discussed, what seemed like years ago, were clear: Pat would ask to be reassigned to a new parish; Pat would remain a priest and stay; Pat would stay but leave the priesthood. That's where they'd left it. The tacit agreement was to not discuss it further. Time would tell. Monsignor Kief, blessed with the patience of Job, had written: *What did you expect, Patrick? An overnight package at your door? God will provide absolute instruction, as He has for you before. The answer is unfolding before you, albeit slowly.*

True enough. Pat was living his call in the service of God. And things were better for him. Things were well. *Trust today's tranquility,* the wise old Monsignor advised in his letters. *Live the life in front of you. Tomorrow will be illuminated.*

Pat walked the vacant seven a.m. parking lot of the plant. In a short 30 minutes, the old pickups of the first shift would be wheeling in, listing on their springs, beer cans rolling in their rusted truck beds.

This, the dawn emptiness, Pat coveted. His frosted-over Toronado waiting. The quiet of the windless trees framing the lot. Only a handful of other cars between the painted yellow lines. Fewer birds singing now, in the sharp sting of autumn. He felt blessed.

A thought sprang on him from out of nowhere. *Maybe HomeSky and I could go see the boys play their season opener tonight.* Was that my idea, or His? Pat wondered. How he had tired of questioning everything. He scraped the frost off his car window. As the shavings curled away, his reflection appeared in the black glass. He looked drawn, but strong. Healthy. It was Friday morning. His workweek at the plant was over. For the first time since he could remember, he faced a Friday where all he had to do was say his morning mass. No appointment with a paintbrush, a gallon of stain, a miter saw; no family intervention, no fundraiser for the church organ, no first communion classes. His schedule was miraculously clear. *Miraculously?*

He noticed the dirt under his fingernails, smiling at the significance. Up until a few months ago, they'd been chewed raw. Now they could use some trimming. Progress for us all is measured in our own ways.

Joseph and Cory and the Badgers opened their second season tonight on the road against the University of Duluth Bulldogs. Duluth was only a couple hours' drive. It would be good to spend some time away. With HomeSky. The thought, the lack of sleep, left him light-headed. He pulled onto the highway, the rising sun pouring molten over the horizon. He would go see HomeSky. Her first reaction to this possibility would help him make his decision. If she was for it and could get someone to cover for her at Lu Ann's, they could leave after the lunch rush.

The neon coffee cup over Lu Ann's faithfully filled and emptied, the words Home Of The Bottomless Cup illuminating with each cycle. Pat walked under it and entered the diner to the familiar tinkle of the brass bell. The smell of breakfast slapped him heartily on the back. Lu Ann was at the register making a new sign for the community penny cup.

"Whadaya think, Father?" she asked, showing him her hand-lettered sign. It read: *Need a penny, take a penny. Need two, get a job.*

"That ought to clear up any confusion," he said.

"It just fries my bacon how the same people abuse it. It's always the same few."

"Crisp out there this morning," Pat diverted, not wanting to delve into the family histories of the offenders.

"Apple weather," Lu Ann said, cracking a roll of pennies into the till. "Sit wherever. We're just getting open." Lu Ann paused, giving Pat a tense look.

"What is it?" Pat said, sensing her struggle.

"Ah, nothing." Lu Ann kept busy at the till.

Pat looked at her. Lu Ann's face softened some. "My dad," she said. "You work with him at the plant, don't you?"

"In a way. Reg Cunningham, right?"

"That's the son of a bitch, forgive my tongue."

"He's getting off when I go on. But we've met. Your father's a hard man to miss."

"He's a first-class jerk is more like it. You know he ran off the father of my twins."

"I've heard that. That was a long time ago. Maybe it was a mistake that can be forgiven," Pat suggested.

"Father, there's only one asterisk stuck on the word forgiveness: you gotta be sorry. Forgiveness isn't tossed out like candy at a parade. My dad has neither shown nor expressed any regret for what he did. 'What's done is done,' is all he's ever said of it."

"But you miss him."

"Not him, really. The thought, or, the possibility of him, I miss. I miss having a dad. Reg Cunningham I don't miss."

"I think you've made a wise decision, I'm afraid."

Lu Ann was taken aback. "What do you mean, Father?"

"From what I've seen, you'd have to look hard for a redeeming quality. He has a terrible mean streak."

"It's more than a streak, Father. It's to the core. But he's okay, health-wise and all?"

"Seems healthy enough. Most people just back out of the way."

"Yep," Lu Ann said, looking off, rewinding to some memory. She shook it away. "Enough of that."

"Is HomeSky here?" Pat asked.

"In back. Helping with the potatoes. The dear. My cook is sleeping one off. He answered on the 15th ring."

"I think I'll poke my head in. Can I take a cup of coffee with me?"

"Help yourself," Lu Ann said.

Pat came through the swinging kitchen doors, unnoticed. HomeSky was seated, wearing her light blue uniform dress, head down, peeling from a hill of brown potatoes. Her hair fell over her face; a garbage can collected the peelings in front of her. *Integrity is what you do when no one's looking* is the aphorism.

Pat cleared his throat.

She looked up, startled. Pat saw what HomeSky would look like as a woman in her golden years. Strong. Without conceit despite her beauty. She smiled.

"Good morning," he said.

"Well, stranger." Her voice was deeper, not yet broken in by the day.

"Got another peeler?" Pat asked. "I understand Tim's running late this morning."

"You don't have to do that."

"I don't mind. I want to talk to you anyway. What better music than the strum of a potato peeler?"

"First drawer on the left by the sink," HomeSky said.

Pat pulled off his coat and brought a chair up across from hers. They both faced the garbage can full of peelings, scraped in silence, auguring out a few blemishes with the tip. "I had this thought," he said, looking at her. She stopped peeling and watched him. "It's Friday. Tonight the boys open up in Duluth. What do you say you get the afternoon and tomorrow off and we go catch a game?"

HomeSky raised her eyebrows. "Really?"

"As far as I'm concerned, why not? The rectory's done. There's no overtime this weekend at the plant. I got a paycheck burning a hole in my pocket. If I can get my morning mass covered tomorrow …" Pat smiled at the thought of such freedom.

"I don't know. Lu Ann might get caught short."

"Ask her. Only way to know."

"When would we leave?" Her eyes showed she'd started to believe in the possibility.

"It's a couple hours to Duluth. Say around three-ish."

"I've got to get some silage put away. They're calling for rain. Maybe snow."

"I can do it. The hill on the south pasture, or out in front?"

"South pasture. But I can't ask you. It's your day off."

"Are you kidding? It's only a couple hours' work. I've done it with Joseph. Just mash it and bin it, right?"

"Yes, but—"

"Piece of cake."

Just then, Tim, the fry cook, came banging in. "Sorry I'm late, HomeSky," he said, his eyes bloodshot, his flattened hair jutting off to one side. He didn't notice Pat as he looked behind the door for his apron. "Hell of a night up at the Mutineer's Jug. I musta got some bad ice in my drink 'cause man, my head's doing the two-step."

"Hey Tim," Father Pat spoke up.

"Jeez, Father Pat. I didn't know you was back here." Tim seemed still somewhat intoxicated.

"We've missed you at the meetings," Pat told him.

"Yeah. I've been awful busy, Father. Work. And deer hunting, you know."

"And going up to the Jug," Pat added.

"Yeah, well. Here and there. Maybe I'll catch you at next week's meeting. My mom needs me to help her with some stuff tomorrow."

"Next week would be fine. You want me to pick you up?"

"I don't know. I can get there. Hey now, you two scram. I'll have this place ready in two shakes." Tim put on an apron. His shaky hands fumbled with the ties.

"Next Saturday, then," Pat said, pausing at the kitchen's swinging doors.

"Yeah. 'Less I'm bow huntin'."

"Tim, you can't be taking deer at eight at night. That's shining. Sheriff Harris will have you hanging from a hook."

"I've never shined in my life," Tim boasted. "All my bucks been straight up. I know some who rifle shoot 'em and stick an arrow in the hole. Rotten bastards."

"We'll plan on next week," Pat went for the close.

Tim rubbed his temple with the heel of his hand. "Yeah. Maybe. There at the gym, right?" Thinking about the gym helped Tim. He thought of cheerleaders doing splits.

"In the gym. Same as always."

"Sure thing, Father," Tim said, doing his best to hide behind the potato he was peeling.

Pat sat down out front where the sun came through the window and ordered the ham and cheese omelet with melon. He added a side of hash browns, being that he was personally invested in the potatoes. HomeSky went over and sat down with Lu Ann, who was having a cup of coffee and rolling silverware into paper napkins. The women talked softly. Lu Ann looked over at Father Pat as they talked. She and HomeSky continued their conversation. A few local handymen came in and sat in Lu Ann's section. HomeSky went into the kitchen to check on Pat's food.

"It'll just be a few more minutes," she reported, refilling his coffee. "Tim burned the first wave."

"So," Pat asked, "what does Lu Ann think?"

"She says go. She'll call Mary Alice."

The two of them looked at each other. Slowly, smiles stretched across their faces. They looked like kids who'd just snuck out the back door of school.

"Well, that just leaves it to you then." Pat watched for her reaction.

"You're sure it's no bother to put up that silage?"

"None."

HomeSky's heart was beating a mile a minute as her mind tried, unsuccessfully, to pump the brakes. "I say we should go." She thought: *It's no big deal. We should. It would mean a lot to Joseph.*

Pat nodded. A part of him, too, was advocating caution, but it was a minority voice.

"The team probably traveled yesterday afternoon," he said. "I could try to reach Joseph and tell him we're coming. He'd arrange tickets. More than likely the game's sold out."

They took one last long look at each other, each giving the other a final chance to back out. The plan was setting fast around them. Neither blinked.

"What time do you think, then?" HomeSky said.

"I'll get out to the farm and be done by, say, three," Pat said.

They waited.

"Okay then," they both said at the same time, then laughed at themselves.

It was only 1:13. HomeSky couldn't remember the clock moving this slowly since Sister Mary Dictionary's third-grade class on sentence composition. HomeSky's plan was to work through the lunch rush—two-ish—get home, pack an overnight bag, and go. It had been a long time since she'd had something to look forward to. You don't realize how much you miss the lightness of that feeling until a prolonged separation points it out.

Quite honestly, she'd been waiting for the other shoe to drop for some time now. Pat had come out of the fire stronger, more comfortable with himself. She wasn't so sure about herself. Joseph was off to college. And home was as quiet as 100 candles: a quiet you can't help but notice. The quiet was there in the empty coat pegs next to her jacket. There in the refrigerator where hardly an item moved day to day. There in the towels still neatly folded and put up in the pantry. There in Joseph's unruffled bed and in the two mismatched kitchen chairs that moved mostly for the broom. She missed the surprise mess of dishes in the sink. Joseph doing push-ups after he'd shut up the barn for the night. She missed waiting for the shower to open up. Or coming home and meeting Pat and Joseph running on the highway, rolling down her window, tweaking them about the pace, leaving the window open the rest of the way. She lived now with windows shut. It wasn't like her. This life transition was taking her in the wrong direction. *Enough already,* she thought. One way or the other, she needed that other shoe to drop.

Pat had talked, almost two years ago now, about staying or leaving. He'd said he would listen for an answer. Little by little, they saw less of each other. Pat was wrapped up in two major rebuilding projects: himself and the rectory. But what about this man who'd once said he loved her? They'd kept a safe friendly distance. How was this morning's invitation to Duluth to be interpreted? Was it just an innocent, spur-of-the-moment thing?

"Hey, easy there, honey," a customer chirped as HomeSky absentmindedly almost put an egg salad sandwich in her lap.

"Oh, sorry, Mrs. Trimbil."

"You were a million miles away, sweetie." Mrs. Trimbil winked at HomeSky, picking a rippled chip off her lap. "We all should be so lucky to get that far." She laughed a smoker's laugh and passed a little gas as she squared off in front of her sandwich-and-chip special.

HomeSky rechecked the clock. 1:14.

Pat fired up the old John Deere and ran it out of the dank, cold barn into radiant sunlight. He thought about contrasts, the power of them. One moment he was dead-tired, walking out of the plant, the next he was smiling with HomeSky about the possibilities of a road trip. "Sometimes you're in the barn, sometimes you're in the sunlight," Pat confided with himself.

The trick to first-class silage is patience. Just run your tractor up and down and up and down and up and down the big corn pile, shucks and all, mashing it. Over and over until you've compacted it "tight as a fruit jar," as Joseph would say, into the below-ground storage bin. That way there's less air to decompose it.

Joseph had been selling silage to a few of the farmers in the area. He'd deliver, too. HomeSky's current arrangement was that she would store it on her property, but farmers would have to come by and pick it up. She sold on the honor system. Some days she'd get home and there'd be five ten-dollar bills held down by a rock on the front porch. The money helped, but she liked the silage more so because it kept her connected. Even if she never saw the farmer, it was nice knowing someone had been by.

When Pat finished, he turned off the tractor and sat a spell in the iron seat. All around, it smelled of dirt and old corn. Mighty autumn. The colors up on the ridge were almost audible. The afternoon sun leaned warm against him. He thought about Lick. He missed the old boy. The dog had gone off, to run deer, likely, and never come back. In this country that usually means someone shot him. For sport. Or hunters shot him because dogs running deer foul the hunt. What a waste. Pat listened to the wind, attentive for his message. Up the ridge, the long, tall grove of hardwoods cupped the property like a hand might, trying to keep a flame lit in the wind. He sat cradled below in the pasture's stillness. RiverHeart was there. Everything was good. Pat knew what to do now.

THURSDAY NIGHT.

Sheriff Thurgood Harris never cared for his first name. It hung on him like a summer cold. As a kid, it got him called Turdy. It got him called No-good. Why hadn't Thurgood gotten a normal name? Prayed to God Almighty for one. Mike. Jim. Steve. Why did his parents hate him enough to do this?

The beer sprayed slightly as he cracked open a can. "For flavor," he said to his second beer. He poured it into the mug next to his officer nametag on the countertop. T. Harris. T as in Tom. Tim. Ted. Thurgood shook his head.

He shuffled his frame into the living room to the puzzle table. Snapping on the table lamp with his good hand, he used his prosthesis to hold the beer mug up on the ledge of his stomach. He was working a 101 Dalmatians puzzle. He'd found it on the half-price table of Robertson's Card & Craft. He should have left the damn thing where it sat. It was a one-thousand piece exercise in self-abuse. All those spotted puppies spilling out of the auburn wicker basket. He'd been at it a month and there was still a hole in the center big enough to shoot a basketball through.

"All right pups," he whispered to the puzzle. "I ain't going to bed until I can I.D. the sex of at least three of ya." Thurgood soldiered on, taking a large draw of his beer. He let the carbonation nip at the insides of his mouth, swallowing just as the phone rang. The Sheriff conferred with his watch. Past ten o'clock. A Thursday. Can only mean one thing. Some parents are going to be grieving a teenager's car wreck tonight.

"Harris," he said gruffly into the receiver.

"Didn't wake you, did I, Sheriff?"

"Cory?" Sheriff Harris confirmed.

"Yes sir. Sorry about the hour."

"Ah the hell. It's a wild one here tonight. I'm on my second beer, staring at a puzzle that'll blind you faster than a welding torch. Where are you? On the road, right?"

"Yep. Just pulled into Duluth." Cory's foot was tapping unconsciously, methodically, on the carpeted floor of the hotel room.

"Pretty late for that, isn't it?"

"We always stop for dinner on the way. It takes a while to get the herd fed. Anyway, I was wondering if you thought any more about coming over for the opener like we talked about."

"Well, I haven't given it much further consideration. Been pretty busy up here," the Sheriff lied.

Cory knew the Sheriff had to soak in an idea like a crusted pan before the possibilities could loosen up. "It's your call," Cory offered. "Be a nice drive with the leaves. Maybe we'd go out after the game."

"I'm sure you'd have better things to do than that. When's the game start?"

"Puck drops at 7:30."

"Friday nights are tough for me. Lot going on," the Sheriff added dramatically.

"What about the guy from International Falls who's always hitting you up for favors. What's his name?"

"Halloran. Sheriff Halloran."

"Yeah. Couldn't he cover for you?"

"Suppose he could. He owes me like kin."

There was a pause on the line. Cory sensed the Sheriff was mulling over the drive, the city traffic.

"The Holiday Inn the team's staying at is just off the interstate," Cory said. "You could walk from here to the arena. Easy."

"I could take a room at the Holiday Inn," the Sheriff repeated, like it was his idea, "then I could walk over, easy as pie. That'd work, wouldn't it?"

"Sure would," Cory agreed. "Let me shoot you some directions."

At face value, Cory and Sheriff Harris were unlikely friends. But the more you examined it, the less unlikely their friendship became.

Both lacked a father figure, or much of a family for that matter. The Sheriff's dad spent most of Thurgood's life in a wheelchair professing that hardship rendered him unable to care for his boy. That left it to Thurgood to sort out for himself those perplexing situations parents are meant to help kids maneuver through.

Similarly, Cory's mom was a failure as a parent. She went from depending on Cory's dad to depending on Cory. He quickly ascertained that no one was going to take care of him but himself. So it was in the mutual singularity of these two men that a bond was given its chance.

And hunting. A few duck hunting openers had brought together Cory, Sheriff Harris, Joseph, and Father Pat. Cory and the Sheriff always paired off in one duck boat. There's nothing like the close confines of a duck blind, the way the hues of sunrises and sunsets massage unguarded conversation out of you, the long stretches of nothingness accentuated by the report of guns, the cartwheeling of a few birds, the reliving of it in the quiet after the retrieve—it brings men together. Cory and the Sheriff had talked about things in the duck boat; they acknowledged, without actually saying so, that they had more than a little in common.

Over the last few years they'd stayed in touch. Wrote an occasional letter. Made a habit of talking on the phone. All the while, Sheriff Harris kept a close eye on the boy's blossoming hockey career.

What forever solidified their friendship, though, was Cory's injury at the state hockey championship. It was a night of surreal confusion. The panic over Cory's condition as he was rushed out of the arena, along with the disappearance of Joseph—only his skates were found by the arena's exit door—was overwhelming. Unanswered questions multiplied, rumors ignited, paralyzing the two families who didn't know where to turn in the sold-out, stunned arena.

Sheriff Harris had been a blessing. He kept the group together, kept Cory's mom from coming entirely unglued, located arena security, went to their offices, contacted the St. Paul police, found out which hospital the ambulance was dispatched to, and got directions. In short, he was a good cop. His instincts, organizational skills, and commanding 290-pound presence were what the situation required.

Cory suffered a broken rib in the collision with Joseph. His right lung was punctured, bone-nicked, just a pinhole, but enough to slowly collapse. He was taken into emergency surgery while Joseph paced the waiting room in his stocking feet and hockey uniform. Sheriff Harris helped Cory's mother with the paperwork and spent most of the next day on the phone with insurance people working out billing. Cory's mom lived on vending machine coffee and bags of M&M's. As she pointed out repeatedly, Cory usually handled problems like this.

Cory was indebted to those 48 hours, to how Sheriff Harris stepped in when the moment called. And Cory never forgot a debt. He knew the Sheriff to be a lonely man. An outcast of kinds. Shortchanged. Cory went out of his way after that. He always made an effort not to disappear on the Sheriff. The Sheriff had known enough of that.

"So. What do you say I leave a ticket for you at Will Call?" Cory said. "Then afterward we grab some chow."

The Sheriff fiddled with the phone cord, wrapping it around his artificial finger. "If it's not too much trouble. But I'd think after the game, you'd want to be tearing the night up one side and down the other."

"Nah. I don't go in much for that. Plus, Saturday's typically the big night out. Sunday's our only day off, so after the full week, the guys let it fly come Saturday."

"Okay. I say we do this, then." The Sheriff's tone brightened. "What's the scouting report on Duluth?"

"They have a lot of seniors coming back. They'll be tough. It'll be a physical game. What the hell. I like our chances."

The Sheriff pressed the phone between his shoulder and ear and patted his pocket for a Camel. He was getting excited at the prospect of seeing the boys skate. He passed clear over the Vantage for a second consecutive legitimate cigarette.

"So look for your ticket," Cory said. "Then let's plan to meet up at the Holiday Inn afterward."

"Good," the Sheriff said, taking the smoke into his lungs. "Keep your head up out there. You're a known commodity now, not some no-name freshman."

"Yes sir."

"They'll be coming for you."

"I'll say hello for the both of us when they do."

The Sheriff chuckled. "I'm sure you will."

Thurgood hung up and lumbered into the kitchen for the third in his three-beer ration. "For relaxation," he said, pouring the beer into the glass. That boy, he thought, a twinge of melancholy riding in on the tails of the alcohol. I care for him as much as I could a boy not mine. Of the province of children, he knew little. Generally, Thurgood was put off by kids. He and Amanda had tried to conceive, but were blessed with nothing but disillusionment. Numerous attempts, numerous failures. This brings a silence to a couple. It brings unmentioned blame that a man and woman roll away from in the dark, their backs separating in bed. Questions go unasked; they come to your lips, but are swallowed. All's well. You grin and move ahead. So Thurgood came to resent children. He'd see the pained smile they'd leave on his Amanda's face as they skipped in front of her at the hardware store, hair braided, ribboned, freckled, miniatured, perfect. Or there she'd be, slightly open-mouthed, stopped in mid-chore, dusting rag held above the intended surface, staring out the bay window across the street where children wrestled like puppies. She carried her pain full term. From it, there was no deliverance.

But Cory's presence had softened the Sheriff's resolute heart. Slowly, Thurgood opened himself to the possibility of some closeness. He watched the boy from a distance, watched him take on his adult-sized responsibilities with unflinching composure. Not a bad kid, he'd allowed himself to say.

They'd talk about a thing or two if the situation seemed open to it—when normally, with others, they'd just let the silence close over. And more times than not, when Thurgood did risk an opinion, he found Cory agreeing.

Thurgood absentmindedly accordion-flatted the three cans on the cement back stoop. He tossed them in the garbage and thought about his Friday. He would call Sheriff Halloran and get the son of a bitch to sit for him. That's what they called it. Can you sit my town? As in babysit. Then he would make his way to Duluth. His reluctance to drive had diminished, but hadn't disappeared. Hell, he'd be okay. And if he got anxious, he'd do what he always did. Look for some out-of-state plates, flip on the cherries, and pull the tourists over. Transfer his fear. Like a game of tag. That's what he'd do.

HOMESKY AND PAT.

Her heart leapt. Father Pat's Toronado was parked in the farmyard. As HomeSky swung past it and looped around the gravel driveway, her home of almost half a life felt unfamiliar. Slightly off. It was as if someone had moved her landmarks just inches: the farmhouse, the big front oak, the outbuildings, the hand pump, all set down inches from where they'd always been. She saw the barn door was open. Pat, backlit on the John Deere tractor, was out in the south pasture. HomeSky stood by the car and smoothed down her waitress uniform nervously.

There was time to shower, HomeSky decided. The smoke and grease of Lu Ann's cloyed her hair, her clothes, her skin. She wanted a hot shower. She wanted to pack her overnight bag with wet, clean hair and bare feet. Oftentimes, what HomeSky wanted and what she did were merely passing acquaintances. But this afternoon, she would embrace what she wanted.

She was brushing back her wet hair when she heard the front door come closed.

"Hello?" Pat's voice asked the quiet house. HomeSky smiled at the sound of it.

"Back here," she said, looking herself over in the mirror. She took a deep, catching breath.

Pat came back and leaned against the door jamb of her bedroom. "Beautiful day out there," he said, face flushed with work and windburn. "The trees are amazing. I've never seen so many variations on the color orange. This property is a treasure."

"I love it." HomeSky said. "It would break my heart to ever sell."

"Hopefully it'll never come to that."

"Hopefully," she agreed. "I laid out a towel if you want to clean up."

The thought of a hot shower was inviting. He looked at his watch; it was going on four. "I'll do that. It'll save us the time later. I just have to get my bag out of the car."

Showered, clean, excited, they climbed into Pat's car. The doors closed; the two of them and the aroma of soap were sealed inside. A large distance seemed to separate them on the old, cracked car seat. In the seven years they had known each other, the distance between them had yawned and narrowed with the complexities of their friendship. At this moment, they were very close mentally, but physically, purposefully distant. Safely so.

The car crunched out of the driveway and the tension began to evaporate. HomeSky's hands left her lap, her shoulders loosened. Pat's grip relaxed on the steering wheel. His back found the seat to rest against. Unspoken between them was the certain knowledge, the certain feeling, that they were leaving one set of definitions and traveling to another. Here, they were widow and priest to those who saw them. There, they were … anything. Unknown. Undefined. Every possibility existed. But the last guess a person might venture was widow and priest. They would leave this driveway and they would return to this driveway—for certain. But would they return as widow and priest? The essence of this question hung for a moment in the silence of the car. Then they turned into the sun. The angled yellow light of the afternoon scattered all such thoughts. They drove and let time unfold like a hand unclutching an answer.

"How was Lu Ann's?" Pat asked. "They going to survive without you?"

"Yes they will, thank you very much for asking." HomeSky teased back, "And as for you? Do you miss your work gloves already?" They smiled at each other.

HomeSky suddenly frowned softly. "Lu Ann is a remarkable person. She's done so well with her kids all by herself. The restaurant. Everything. She hasn't had it easy. She never complains. She's so strong."

"Sounds like someone else I know," Pat said. He glanced over at HomeSky. She looked quietly out the windshield at the spray of fall colors, clinging, on the verge of letting go. She smiled.

They pulled into the Duluth Holiday Inn. They had an hour to check in, get dinner, and get over to the arena for the 7:30 start. The hotel was busy.

"I didn't even think about a reservation," HomeSky whispered as they set their bags down in the lobby.

"It's all set," Pat said. "When I talked to Joseph, he said this is where the team bunks." They approached the registration desk.

"Good evening, you two," the bubbly, round middle-aged woman said through her chewing gum. She appeared delighted to see them. Her eyes flashed. "After 22 years on the desk, I've got an eye. I know newlyweds when I see them. Am I right? Tell me I'm not right?" Her chubby hands rubbed in front of her face in anticipation.

"Sorry," Pat said. "Not this time."

"Anniversary?" the receptionist proceeded ahead, unfazed. "I never miss twice." Her little eyes twinkled and widened as much as they could.

"Strike two," Pat said, his voice tightening. "The name's O'Rourke—"

"Ohhhhhhhhho," the receptionist said conspiratorially, nodding her head slowly. "I see." She winked. "Your secret's safe with me. I'm like a bank vault."

"*Father* Pat O'Rourke," Pat emphasized. The woman's hand went to her mouth like she'd swallowed a bug. "Pardon me, Father ... It's just, the two of you—" Her voice trailed off as she got busy flipping through the reservation book.

"The other room is under the name Blackholm, first name HomeSky."

"Yes, Father," the woman said, her cheeks blooming crimson. "Sorry."

Pat looked at HomeSky. HomeSky looked at Pat. They couldn't help it. They burst out laughing. The receptionist looked up. She didn't know whether to laugh or cry.

Rooms 223 and 224 were just across a hallway of orange carpet from one another. Pat dropped his bag on the extra bed, shaking out the folded dress shirt on top. He'd brought his jogging stuff for an early morning run, a change of clothes, and his shaving kit. He sat on the bed, buttoned on his clean shirt, and said a prayer.

Across the hall, HomeSky stood in her bra at the mirror. She freshened her antiperspirant and put on just a trace of lipstick. She rarely used makeup of any kind. Never had she put it on for a man except RiverHeart. She looked into her eyes in the mirror. She went deeper and deeper into her reflection. The longer she looked, the blurrier things got. "Oh shit," she said.

There was a knock on the door.

SKATING LIKE BROTHERS.

Before the inaugural game of this 1980 season, the Badger players milled around the locker room where they were handed the season's media guide. The booklet had all the relevant player information so the media covering the game would know names, faces, jersey numbers, heights and weights, hometowns, scoring stats, and such. Cory remembered getting guides like this sent to him when he was being recruited. He'd flip through the pages late into the night, memorizing stats and faces. It was all he could hope that someday his picture would make it in, too.

Cory sat off in a corner studying his likeness in the guide. He had no opinion of the photograph. He retied his right skate. He checked the tape on his stick. All around him, the guys went through their routines, getting ready. The boom box blared. Some sat, staring a hole in the wall. Others threw tape balls at each other's heads. Cory studied his stats from last year. Twenty-nine goals, a freshman record in the WCHA. But Cory only made all-WCHA second team. Joseph was Rookie of the Year. Cory mentally retraced the posts he'd hit. Had a few more of those pucks gone in, he thought, it could have been me. Joseph was getting all the buzz. No-miss pro material. He was made for the NHL, scouts fed to the reporters. Born to it. Cory got down for push-ups.

On the other side of the locker room, Chevy, the team captain, got into a juicy story about a latest conquest: a blonde freshman waitress at one of the favorite campus bars. Chevy was the team's alpha dog and went unquestioned, especially on the subject of women. He was good-looking. He was funny. He was charming. He was well put together. And he wore the C on his jersey. That basically got him access to almost any campus dorm room, sorority house, even a teacher's bedroom or two. Of course he had a girlfriend, Hanna, and of course she was beautiful and everything a guy could ask for as far as being cool, but Chevy wandered. His live broadcast of those wanderings in the locker room, that was his way of taking off the nervous edge before a game. Chevy's Sex Symposiums, as he liked to call them. He stood half-dressed in his pads, leaning on his stick, lecturing, fielding questions.

"So Blondie has her hands all over me. I kid you not, her ass is better than a figure-skating flight attendant's. She says, 'I'm just crazy about your chest,' and I'm getting her turtleneck off thinking, *I know the feeling.* She's giggling drunk—and that's the phase you have to watch for, boys. Giggling drunk is put-the-puck-in-the-net time. Cut off the alcohol and get to work. Punch in, immediately, 'cause the following phase is spinning drunk and then she's sick and pretty worthless. Sometimes only one cocktail separates giggling from spinning. You have to monitor it like a surgeon."

"How do you know?" Twig, a lanky defenseman asked, riveted.

"Watch her hands. The hands tell all." Chevy left Twig hanging.

"The fuck," he said. "What about the hands?"

Chevy smiled like a tenured professor. "When she's giggling drunk, the hands are busy. Flying around the air when she's talking.

A lot of grabbing on you. If you're at a bar, make your move right there and get her to your digs. Hell, finish her drink if you have to because she's hotter than a fifty-dollar stereo. But one more drink, her hands get heavy as lead, and you're greased."

"What if she doesn't want to leave?" one of the other players asked.

"This isn't a democracy. You tell her you're out of there, you need some peace and quiet, a place where you two can talk. They love that. Tell her it's her call, stay or go, but you've made up your mind. Then you walk. Two times out of three, she'll catch you at the door. If not, it probably wasn't going to happen until after you went to church with her parents. Cut your losses. Hoof down the street to the next establishment and find yourself a new doubles partner."

"What if your girlfriend is around?" Cory tossed in from across the room. Cory knew Hanna. In fact, he liked and respected her. She had covered the team last season as a journalism major interning for a small Madison TV station. She did on-ice interviews after home games. She was awesome on camera. Smart, articulate, and a knockout, but the smart and articulate parts were lost on Chevy. She graduated after the season and took a job in Duluth doing some live reporting, especially for the sports desk. Hanna and Chevy remained a couple despite the distance. She was faithful. He was Chevy.

"Good question," Chevy answered with a mock seriousness. "When the girlfriend is around, that's what separates the men from the altar boys. This is key, so pay attention. Even though you're spent from the previous night's diversion, you have to really "miss" your girlfriend on date night. Sleep? Forget about it. She'll suspect if you don't perform. You got to suck it up like playoff hockey."

A few things about Chevy were beginning to wear on Cory. Sure he looked up to him, but he was starting to see that maybe Chevy wasn't what he'd first believed. For starters, Chevy's partying was affecting his hockey. He wasn't spending the necessary time in the weight room, on the bike, running stairs like the rest of the team.

He'd do enough to slip by, but he was the captain. He was to set the example. No doubt he could score goals, but how many pucks ended up in the goalie's glove because he stayed out too late and said yes to just one more? Cory had no time for people who weren't focused. On top of that, Chevy was constantly bagging women behind Hanna's back. She deserved better. She was one of the few females Cory could have a conversation with and not be bored after two sentences.

"My last tip," Chevy said, wrapping the wrist he broke in the off-season when his golf cart flipped, "is in the area of toiletries and linens." Chevy was always using language like this. It broke the guys up.

"Lemons?" one guy asked.

"Bed sheets, my good man," Chevy said. "There are two places you should never skimp. Bed sheets and toilet paper. Get the best of both for your place. Women don't want cheap toilet paper that feels like sandpaper. Think about it, form a mental picture." He paused for the crowd to visualize, "And they'll always reward you for top-notch sheets. Invest wisely." Chevy finished taping his wrist, "End of symposium for today, boys. We have some Duluth ass to kick. And I mean some big ass. I know, I've been with their women."

They guys all laughed. The music was cranked up. They finished lacing and taping. Cory and Joseph ripped off another quick 50 push-ups. Game time.

Joseph and Cory stepped onto the ice in the best shape of their lives. Cory had spent three weeks in August up at Stu and Darlene's place swimming, rowing, guiding, and putting on some much-needed weight thanks to Darlene's rations. Then he and Joseph spent the end of August and early September on the farm, baling hay and working out. They'd constantly interrupt what they were doing for push-ups, sit-ups, and pull-ups in the barn. Baudette had finally built an indoor rink, so they'd drive to town after dinner to skate. No sticks. No shooting. Just skating drills.

As they stretched during the pre-game skate, Cory looked over at the Duluth players. They didn't look as big and intimidating as they had last year. Cory felt solid yet anxious. He wanted to hit somebody to scatter the butterflies. That first hit gets everything on track.

Joseph glided around the ice effortlessly. His long, powerful strides gave the illusion that he wasn't going fast, but anyone who skated next to him soon learned otherwise. He cleared his head and calmed himself, visualizing the green pastures of home stretching out under the blue sky. Joseph was one of the enlightened few who understood the importance of staying loose while playing a sport at this level. There's a zone where your body functions optimally. Muscles don't optimize when overly tense. It wastes energy. Joseph skated faster, shot harder, stickhandled more deftly, and checked more powerfully because he never let the joy get squeezed from the game.

Mentally, Cory went to a different place in those few minutes before a game. He tapped into red anger. He thought about his dad. He heard his constantly needy mother. He thought about his mistakes; the missed goals, the fumbled punts. He thought about the cheap shots he took in front of the net. He thought about the whispers that said his team wouldn't have hung on to win the high school championship if Joseph hadn't left the ice to be in the ambulance. Cory piled it on like gas-soaked wood to a fire. He knew what he was doing. Cory was working *his* edge. Cory got mean.

During the game, the boys skated like brothers. They anticipated each other and worked the puck back and forth as if they were the only ones in on a secret. They were beautiful.

It brought a tear to Father Pat's eye, watching them skate. The crowd buzzed as Cory and Joseph moved together on the same line, passing, shooting. Pat had watched these boys grow together for seven years. He'd been there from the beginning, setting up that piece of plywood for them to shoot at. To see them now. It was profoundly moving.

Next to Pat, HomeSky clenched her fists and watched through squinting eyes as her boys gave and received body checks, battled for loose pucks, blocked shots. She cringed at the unapologetic violence of the game. Her jaws ached from gritting her teeth. "Why couldn't they just have played baseball," she muttered. But when the two of them skated up ice together, and the crowd noise stirred, the boys watching for each other, slipping passes to spots the other hadn't yet reached, she understood they knew each other like few ever do. It did her heart good to witness this, despite the hitting.

Unbeknownst to any of them, Sheriff Harris was no more than 10 rows over from Pat and HomeSky. The Sheriff's emotions ran surprisingly taut. He was nervous for the boys, especially Cory, who was among the smallest players. Every hit on Cory drew an expletive sandwich from the Sheriff: "Son of a bitch, crap, son of a bitch!" "Asshole cheap shot, number 15, asshole cheap shot!" And so on. Sweating through his plaid Sunday shirt, including necktie, Sheriff Harris received sidelong glares from the home crowd, but his physical stature silenced any direct confrontation.

When Cory netted the game's first goal, the three of them launched out of their seats, hollering, fists in the air. It was behavior equivalent to laughing at a funeral; that is, they stuck out like sore thumbs among the solemn home crowd. Pat thought he saw something out of the corner of his eye. Sheriff Harris could have sworn that his wasn't the only shout after the Badger goal. They looked over and saw each other.

"Harris!" Pat yelled.

"O'Rourke!" the Sheriff replied, glad to see an ally in enemy territory. The two of them shook their fists in the air.

"Sit down already," the home crowd jeered.

As it turned out, Pat, HomeSky, and Sheriff Harris were on their feet more often than the local faithful as the season opener went on. The game wasn't even close. Six to one, Badgers. Cory, with four points on the night, two goals and two assists, was the game's best player. Joseph was no slouch with a goal and two assists. Chevy, held to one assist, skated off less than delighted. He was none too happy to see his girlfriend, Hanna, pulling aside Cory and Joseph to tape an interview, either.

The camera rolled and the bright light shone on the two, helmets off, towels around their necks, sweat streaming down their happy faces. Cory's short hair was sweat-curled. Joseph's shoulder-length black hair was pulled back, away from his face. His adolescent acne had cleared, and some of his mother's looks were coming through. Each player's face carried just enough scars to flaw them to the point of being intriguing. No doubt, though, Cory was classically handsome. Crooked nose and all.

"Cory Bradford, Badger center, let's start with you," Hanna's interview began. "What a way to open the season. The game you played tonight, four points, you were everywhere. You have to be happy."

Cory nodded. "The puck went in for me tonight. It's a great start. Working hard in the off-season always gives you an extra step the first weeks of the year."

Hanna turned to Joseph. "Joseph Blackholm, Badger standout defenseman, a three-point night for you. You have to feel good about those numbers."

"Yeah. But I feel better about the numbers six to one. Our guys played great. It's not easy to come into this building and steal the opener. Tonight was an incredible team effort."

Hanna turned back to Cory. She had a rare mix of intelligence and sex appeal that drew a person out. Even him. "Cory, only one goal from what most consider to be a high-powered Duluth offense. How do you explain that?"

"My hat's off to our goalie, Tommy Jelnick. He stood on his head down there. And the defense, especially this guy," Cory elbowed Joseph a good one in the ribs, "kept the shooting alleys clear and didn't give up rebounds."

"Plus," Joseph interrupted, "our forwards got back and stayed on their guys. We laid on them in our zone. It was exactly how Coach chalked it."

Hanna shifted gears and smiled. "So how is it skating together, now as you go into your second year on the collegiate level? You guys are becoming a pretty famous pair. It's like you can almost read each other's minds."

Cory went first. "It's a dream come true. We always knew we'd play together. Now we're with a great program and we're going to go take a run at the national title."

"Joseph?" Hanna said, turning the mike to him.

"It wouldn't hurt if Cory would hustle a little more. He missed a couple assignments out there." Joseph remained deadpan. Then he reached over and smothered Cory under a huge headlock. Cory tried to squirm away. "Man!" he said.

What an unusual group they made for dinner. They went to Duluth's Juicy Pete's, a favorite local burger joint. Despite it being after 11, the place was packed with people up to their wrists in burger baskets. They squeezed around a table in back while Sheriff Harris went out on what he called "chair recon." He came back with two and they all sat: Father Pat next to HomeSky next to Joseph next to Cory next to Sheriff Harris, who took the equal of two spots. Both the boys wore their Wisconsin letter jackets, which got them some looks as they walked in. Duluth is a big hockey town and most of the customers knew of the shellacking that went down earlier. Joseph wore his jacket on the road only because the team did. He wasn't much for show, and quickly slid his off.

"So you guys didn't know the other was coming down tonight?" Joseph laughed. "It's a small world."

Father Pat jumped in. "Every time we scored, I just heard this bellowing like a calf caught in barbed wire. Finally, I looked over, there was the Sheriff."

Sheriff Harris shot Father Pat a frown.

"It's great, Mom, to have everyone here. Isn't it?"

HomeSky was delighted. "It just came out of the blue. Pat came by Lu Ann's early and said why not? Here we are."

Father Pat asked, nodding at the Sheriff, "Cory, how'd you ever get the big guy to hand over the keys to the town and take a night off?"

"It wasn't easy," Cory said. "When was the last time you put in for a night off, Sheriff?"

"Well, I can't rightly say," the Sheriff said, looking for the waitress. He was starved.

"Come on, Sheriff," Pat teased. "When, really?"

The Sheriff just shook his head.

"Ahh. You're just avoiding the question," Pat persisted.

The Sheriff looked Pat in the eye. It wasn't a mean look, like Pat used to get from him. It was more of an *it's unwise to ask too many questions you don't have the answer to* look.

"My last night off was when Amanda passed," Sheriff Harris said, letting his hands brush across the cigarettes in his shirt pockets. "Nine years now."

Everyone looked down at the table. Joseph broke the uncomfortable silence. He had a knack for it. "Man, Sheriff, that's a long time. Good thing we didn't lose tonight."

It took a beat, but Joseph's wit penetrated. The Sheriff was the first to laugh. Then Father Pat. Then Cory and HomeSky. Then Joseph on top of them all. The waitress showed up and she started laughing, too. It was contagious.

While they were eating, two girls got up from the bar and came over to the group's table.

"Hi," one of them said, more than a little inebriated. "We just had to meet you."

"Yeah," the other parroted. "Just HAD to." They both giggled, looking at Cory and Joseph.

"Yes girls?" HomeSky interjected as the two rocked slightly. "Can we help you with something?"

"No. But these two hunks can," said the one. The other shrieked with laughter.

"You're Cory and Joseph, aren't you?" the talker slurred, pointing from one to the other.

"They're so cute, they should be on the menu," her friend added loudly.

"We saw you way back in the state tournament and in the papers. We love hockey."

"Yeah, LOVE," the friend hiccupped. They both laughed and snorted at that. "You guys are like heroes."

"Hey," Cory snapped. "We're trying to eat, all right?"

"Don't be so tense, Cory," the talker said, putting her hands on his shoulders. "I can help with that."

Cory figured he'd have a little fun.

"I'm not Cory. He's Cory," he pointed at Joseph.

"Nah-uh," the talker said. "Really?" she blinked a few times. "I thought the little cute one's Cory."

"I'm Joseph," Cory continued. "And if you don't get lost, I'll have the manager throw you out."

The talker and her friend were astounded. Cute girls weren't used to being told off by guys. "Well," the talker said in a huff. "All I can say is I like Cory over there a lot better than you."

"Yeah, Joseph! You're stuck up," the friend chimed in.

Cory nodded his head. "All the girls like Cory better. Now hit the road." They swerved back to the bar, grumbling.

"There goes my rep," Joseph said. "Thanks."

"Good," said HomeSky. "Are girls always like that around you two?"

"Nah," Joseph said dryly. "They're not nearly that restrained when we win at home."

"Joseph!"

"Mom, I'm kidding. You know Nicole. She'd clobber me if I looked at another girl. Cory-boy, tell her I was just fooling." Joseph, in role reversal, looked sternly at Cory, who merely shrugged.

The Sheriff, having polished off his second burger basket, stretched. "Well, I better shove off. Got a long drive."

"What do you mean?" Cory asked.

"Yeah," said Father Pat. "You're not driving back tonight?"

"Yep," he said, lighting up a Camel from his right pocket.

"Didn't you get a room at the Holiday Inn?" Cory asked.

"By the time I got there, they were cleaned out. Didn't cross my mind to call ahead. No big deal. It's an easier drive at this hour."

"I've got two beds," Father Pat said. "Bunk with me."

"Nah. Good enough of you, but not necessary."

"Where's the sense driving back now? It's close to midnight."

"In law-enforcement time, that's early," the Sheriff said, straightening his posture.

"Sheriff, I know you're trained for hours of surveillance without food or sleep, but why not just bunk with me?" Pat crossed his arms, prepared to fight stubborn with stubborn.

Cory plugged in his two cents worth. "You know what happens to the incidence of accidents after midnight." Appealing to the Sheriff's professional judgment was the only way to crack the safe. "As you know, usually it's the other driver."

"Can't argue you there," he acknowledged.

"*And* you've had two of those," Pat said, pointing to the Sheriff's empty beer mug.

"At my size, that's a spit in the pond. But if you're sure it's no trouble. Least you can do is let me take half the cost of the room." The Sheriff shifted his sizable weight and wrestled his billfold from his back pocket.

"There's plenty of time to settle up later. I trust you."

On the way out of the restaurant, Cory and Joseph heard a whistle they knew belonged to Chevy. Chevy rarely called for a pass on the ice; he just bleated out a quick double whistle. The sound of it was as unique as a voice. The guys looked over and there was Chevy with Hanna. Chevy was a little glassy-eyed.

Joseph introduced his mom, Father Pat, and Sheriff Harris. "Well no wonder the boys dominated tonight," Chevy charmed. "You had a unfair advantage up in the seats." Chevy was a wonder at saying just the right thing to make everyone feel good. He slid closer to Hanna, picking up his beer. "Can you join us for one?"

Cory jumped in. "We ought to be going." He was comfortable

around Chevy and he was comfortable around Hanna, but uncomfortable around them together. He looked at Hanna. Was he mistaken, or were her eyes red from crying? The light wasn't great and he didn't want to stare, but he could have sworn. Chevy tossed his arm around her.

"Well that's too bad. I was hoping I could keep you boys out late. That way I'd have a chance at a few points tomorrow." Joseph smiled and gave Chevy a good-hearted shove.

"Cory, you're quiet," Hanna finally said. Everyone looked over at him.

"I don't mean to be," he said.

"He's all talked out after those interviews." Chevy tried to laugh it off as a joke, but there was an obvious trace of envy to the comment.

"The boy did all his talking on the ice tonight," the Sheriff felt compelled to say.

Cory just looked at Hanna. Crying. Definitely.

Back at the Holiday Inn, the Sheriff went to the cruiser to get his overnight bag. The night was blowing cold and his tie took to the wind. The Sheriff wasn't much bothered by cold. He'd known it all his life. Still he wished he'd packed a jacket. "Gettin' soft," he scolded.

Pat walked up to the rooms with HomeSky. They were quiet together now. It had been a long, wonderful, loud day and neither of them knew how to be in the quiet. But now the day was looking to end. Neither was sure what that meant. They proceeded down the hall. Father Pat chuckled.

"What?" HomeSky asked, looking over. He looked good. Relaxed. Especially laughing. The crow's-feet, his face wore well, she thought. He seemed to have found a peace in the last six months or so, like he'd made a decision. HomeSky was afraid to ask. She, conversely, had grown more anxious. "What's so funny?"

"I was thinking about the Sheriff. So determined to get back to crime-riddled Baudette."

"He's like a worried parent," HomeSky smiled.

"Maybe he just doesn't want me to see him in his pajamas." They both laughed.

At her door, she looked at him. "Thanks for today." She was looking into his eyes. Pat had a way of avoiding direct eye contact with her, but not this time.

"It was perfect. Being with you." Pat felt his resolve shifting, teetering.

"What's meant for us?" she dared to ask, barely audible. HomeSky began to lean in toward him, just so. She felt her hold on things slacken.

"THEY HAVE PING PONG!" Sheriff Harris bellowed, coming around the corner, seeing the two figures standing at the doorway. He held up the paddles as proof, his bag slung over his shoulder. "You just leave your driver's license there with them at the desk and you get the paddles and the ball." The Sheriff looked as excited as a kid reunited with his lost dog. "You got the key there, Father?"

Pat broke away from HomeSky's eyes. He found the key, crossed the hall, and opened the door as the Sheriff squeezed past. He went back to HomeSky. The quiet had poured back between them. They were as cordial as strangers in line at the bank. "Good night then," Pat said.

"Where the hell's that damn ball?" the Sheriff grumbled from across the hall.

"Good night to you," she said, biting her lip.

"Did I give you the ping pong ball?" the Sheriff barked toward the hallway.

HomeSky looked down, putting her key in the door. Father Pat was taken, just as he had been originally: her nose, her cheeks, her neck, her lips, her subtleties.

"THERE it is!" the Sheriff exclaimed. "Damn. Put it in my pocket." He closed and locked the door and came out into the hallway.

"Good night, Sheriff," HomeSky said, with a tenderness not lost on him.

“And good night to you, good lady. I’m going to teach the Father here a lesson in table tennis he won’t soon recover from.”

“You guys try to restrain yourselves. Children are sleeping.”

HomeSky, leaning on the door jamb, watched as the men went down the hall. The Sheriff stood a head taller and twice as wide. They made a funny pair. As they turned at the end of the hallway, she could still hear the Sheriff.

“I don’t want you conceding nothing because of the hand.” The Sheriff rapped the paddle against his artificial fingers. “I don’t accept no pity points.”

HomeSky closed her door, leaning on it out of habit like she did at home, wondering the exact thought that Pat, too, contemplated at the moment: was this God’s work? Did He keep them apart tonight by way of a six-foot-six, two-hundred-ninety-pound wedge wielding a ping-pong paddle?

THE INTERVIEW.

The dream season cruised along more perfectly than Cory and Joseph could script. They fed off each other's accomplishments in gulps, and just when it seemed impossible that they could jack their play up another level, one or the other sure enough did.

Cory's scoring touch was deft. He was leading the team in goals, a spot that Chevy had owned the last two seasons. No one had imagined his reign would be seriously threatened. Cory said his success could be attributed to being "ten pounds tougher." He mentioned that in an interview, it became a headline, and that was all Joseph needed. He started calling him Ten Pounds. Joseph kidded that Ten Pounds had a mystical Indian ring to it. The name stuck.

"As in ten pounds of you know what," Joseph ribbed him after reading yet another Cory story in the local paper. Even outside of Madison, Cory was becoming college hockey's most sought-after quote. The combination of dangerous scorer and rarified student offered a voice previously unheard in hockey ranks. The reporters ate him up. Cory grew more and more accustomed to the fascination.

Joseph just seemed to get stronger, faster, and more at ease quarterbacking the ice from the blue line. His defenseman's position made him the anchor of the team. When Joseph wanted to pick up the tempo of the game, he pulled up anchor, took chances, and carried the puck deep into the offensive zone. When he wanted to slow the game down, he stood strong on the blue line, played more conservatively, and bottled up the other teams.

They roared into Christmas break in first place in the WCHA, neck and neck with the powerhouse University of Minnesota. The two teams had been exchanging leads all season, with no more than two points of separation.

The U of M had vigorously recruited Cory in high school, but they wouldn't even look at Joseph. The influential white alumni preferred writing checks to watch clean-cut caucasian boys draped in the university's maroon and gold. Forget that Joseph was a native Minnesotan. Joseph Good Thunder Blackholm was a Native American. His shoulder-length black hair flying out the back of his helmet wouldn't sit comfortably with the well-heeled in their walnut-trimmed dens with their framed, yellowing U of M diplomas gathering dust on the walls.

Cory never told Joseph about the U of M's offer because Joseph would have insisted he go ahead without him. This slight to Joseph always motivated Cory when he took the ice against them. Cory would take a long look into the Minnesota bench and lock eyes with the coach. That coach remembered Cory's reply letter, to be sure. Cory just wanted to let him know nothing was forgotten between them.

As the season went into its final ten games, with the two teams almost deadlocked, Cory wondered if he should tell Joseph about the racially slanted treatment. Would it be motivating or deflating for Joseph? Up to now, Cory had thought it best to say nothing.

The way Joseph was playing, he hadn't needed any further incentive. But it was crunch time. They had to get past Minnesota to reach the national championship.

They had a two-game series on the U of M's ice to decide who would win the WCHA and gain first seed for the championship tournament. After the usual light Thursday afternoon skate, everyone had an hour and a half to pack, get to the locker room, check their gear, and get on the bus. It fell to the freshmen to carry and load the bags. Cory was glad to be past that job. Joseph still helped the newbies, but not this time. He was busy saying goodbye to Nicole.

On the floor, they lay side by side, eyes closed, barefoot, fingers entwined. When he was on his feet, Joseph's lower back was one constant, dull ache. The hard flat of the floor helped.

"Maybe you shouldn't go," Nicole said. "Or just don't suit up. A weekend off is the rest you might need for the playoffs."

Joseph smiled. "Guys who don't suit don't travel." He gave her hand a gentle squeeze.

She said, quietly, "Something just doesn't feel right. I have a bad feeling."

"It's nothing. I just need to realign."

"Nothing," she said getting up on one elbow. "Look at you. On the floor like a … like a …"

"You? A word short?" he kidded.

"Joseph. I'm serious."

"Like a kicked-over piano bench."

"What?" she frowned.

"On the floor like a kicked-over piano bench. That's how my inner poet would pen it."

"Joseph, can you, for one second, be serious, please?"

"The piano bench is a serious metaphor. It has many layers." Joseph looked up and smiled at her. The infectious quality of his smile was overpowering. She rolled on top of him. He groaned.

Nicole pulled up. "Did I hurt you?"

"Bring on the torture." Joseph wrapped her in his arms and she lay atop him with her head on his chest, listening to his heart. It beat slow and calm.

"How is it you're about to leave for the biggest two days of hockey in your life and your heart's beating like you're napping on a beach."

"Ahhhh, I like that place. Let's go to a sandy beach and just lie there." Joseph's eyes were closed. A long, thin smile crossed his face.

"Are you nervous?" she asked.

"No. I'm excited. But you have to smooth it out, like hands going across a cool bed sheet."

"Mmmmm, now there's a metaphor." She let her hands ride down his chest, down his hips, down his legs.

"Nicole, I've got a bus to catch."

"Yeah, yeah," she said, sliding up, kissing him.

"Please. I'm in a weakened condition."

"Too late," she said huskily. "No mercy."

Cory was a Thursday maniac. He always backed this particular day into the corner and took the most out of it. Especially when the weekend series was on the road. Friday's practice, he knew, would be nothing—just a light skate-around before the game. You'd skate in half-pads, learn the quirks of the other guys' sheet of ice—the way the puck came off the boards, whether the ice was fast or slow. Thursday was the last chance of the week to legitimately work on conditioning. Cory's regimen was nasty. He'd push himself and his teammates as far as he could. He'd skate like a madman in practice, hitting and forechecking and yelling at the guys to turn it up. More often than not, it boiled over to a point where Cory and somebody were pushing, ready to swing. Joseph would pull Cory away and tell him to chill. It's just practice.

And practice was just the beginning. Afterward, it was into heavy hooded sweats and onto the stationary bike. This was his time to go looking for what he was made of. He drove himself past his adrenaline-blissed centering place to the next stop, which wasn't pretty. He'd turn up the boom box as loud as it'd go, shut off the lights and ride himself darker and darker. Sweat dripping off his face, salt stinging his eyes, he'd push himself through doorway after doorway, to the dark core. Music banging on him, he'd go to the tamped-down anger, Cory's one abundant resource. He went wantonly.

Afterward, in the shower, light-headed, Cory slowly came back. His body began to adjust. The cold water of the shower revived him. Always, he started the shower cold, as his dad had taught him. Incrementally, he would warm it up. Incrementally, bad adrenaline was replaced by good. He made that trip every Thursday. He came to look forward to it.

"You're not just finishing?" Chevy said to Cory in the shower, shaking his head as he came into the locker room with his Badger-red duffel bag slung over his shoulder. Chevy had his road duds on. Shirt, slacks, sports jacket. Team policy. He reached into his jacket pocket and pulled out a beer. Cory stepped out of the shower. "You're going to burn yourself out, stud," Chevy said, smiling, taking a pull off his can. "Didn't your mom ever teach you about conserving energy? Using the off switch?"

"Plenty where that came from," Cory said, coolly, walking past Chevy.

"How do you see them playing us?" Chevy asked, trying to make conversation.

"What's the difference?" Cory toweled off.

Chevy got irked. "If something's up your ass, let's hear it. Your quiet superiority act is getting tired."

Cory looked up at Chevy. "Whatever."

"Why don't you learn to back off just a little bit, okay, superstar? You're exhausting. This game is supposed to be fun, remember?"

"Is it really necessary to drink *before* getting on the bus?" Cory asked, sarcastically. "Would it kill you to wait until you got on the bus to start popping 'em?"

Chevy dropped his bag off his shoulder and rifled his beer can across the room, exploding it off the tiled wall. "FUCK YOU, okay? You high and mighty little prick. You don't know shit. Since when did a sophomore tell the captain how to fucking act?"

"Start acting like a captain. You'll get no beef from me."

"What did you say?"

Cory had only his towel around his waist. Chevy took a step toward him, eyes igniting, arm drawing back, loading up a punch, a chain reaction of anger. He swung, his dress shoes slipping some on the wet tiled floor. Cory was too quick; the punch grazed him over the ear. Cory countered, stepping in as he threw, low, from his hips and his legs. His punch caught Chevy full in the stomach, and the air wheezed out of him.

Chevy crumpled, unable to speak but trying, balled up on the tile. All that came out were squeaks. Chevy was, of all things, smiling, as he writhed. Words eked out in fractured bits: "You." "Hockey." "Don't." "Dick." "Play." "Teammate." Then finally, laughing from the floor, his shoes sliding on the tile, fighting for air, Chevy said his piece. And the truth of it hit Cory harder than the punch he threw. "You can play," Chevy said, "but you don't know dick about being a teammate."

The WCHA championship would be decided in this weekend series. It was a standing-room only sellout; a border battle. Certainly, both teams would be supported in full, raucous force. Minnesota, on their home ice, was a point ahead in the standings, which made them the odds-on pick to win. But Wisconsin had blossomed in the role of the nothing-to-lose underdog. Their game couldn't have peaked at a better time. If they swept this two-game series, they would leave town with the title. A lot more than just pride was at stake, and the media was all over it.

With Cory and Joseph playing so well and being Minnesota natives, there was a groundswell of rare criticism about the U of M's hockey program. It had begun in the local media: why hadn't they been able to land two of the state's finest? Was Minnesota the premier hockey school it once was, or had it slipped? Usually U of

M hockey was above reproach—media darlings—but now they were fighting to hang on and win the title, and they had to beat two local ex–high school legends to get there. Some Minnesota fans found themselves suddenly whispering support for Cory and Joseph's Badgers.

Among the media, Hanna was down to cover the game for the Duluth Channel 6 news. She'd shown up for road trips before, staying with Chevy while his bunkmate would flop with some other player. But on this Thursday night when the bus rolled up to the Minneapolis hotel, it wasn't Chevy she was looking for. She hardly exchanged words with him as he walked by. Hanna and her cameraman wanted to talk to Cory. He was the story, the team's leading scorer, coming back to play in his backyard against a favored perennial national champion. Cory had always been comfortable, almost talkative, around Hanna. And she'd found him much more agreeable than his reputation. They got along for that mysterious reason people sometimes do; they seemed to naturally understand each other.

But more than that, tonight, she had an angle on a story that, if true, could be huge.

"Cory!" Hanna called into the wind. He came off the bus, head down, striding toward the hotel. She waved as he looked up. He gave her a squint, which was his best attempt to be accommodating; in truth, he was tired and didn't feel like talking. The Channel 6 news van idled in the background, staying warm. It was one of those early March nights where the wind came at you like winter was beginning rather than ending. Light snow snaked across the frozen parking lot. The freshmen got busy schlepping hockey duffels to the hotel lobby. Hanna's wavy auburn hair blew in the wind. She put her gloved hands on her ears to warm them. She freed one long enough for another quick wave.

Cory came over. "You should try a hat sometime," he said. "Works wonders."

"Company policy," she replied. "No on-camera women in hats. News director says it tanks the ratings. The cretin."

"I'm surprised he lets you wear coats." Cory managed a smile.

"Don't laugh," Hanna said, her dark brown eyes firing. "He's brought that up."

Cory looked at her hard with his gray-green eyes. "So, Hanna, what can I do for you at this hour?"

"Well," she said, trying to decide the best way to broach the subject, "how about you tell me why for tomorrow's series you'll be wearing Badger Red instead of Minnesota Maroon and Gold?"

"I play for the Badgers," Cory said simply.

"I'm aware of that," Hanna said. "But according to my source, it wasn't always supposed to end up that way. You did grow up just a few miles from the hallowed halls of the U of M."

"Thanks for the reminder."

"My camera guy's in the van. I'd be a hero in Duluth if I got an exclusive on your falling-out with Minnesota."

"Falling out?" Cory remained elusive.

"According to my source."

"How much do you know?"

"He says both you and Joseph should be skating for Minnesota, but Joseph didn't fit the 'profile,'" Hanna made invisible quote marks in the air. "And you weren't going anywhere without him."

"What source?"

"That's privileged." Hanna pushed her hair back, fighting the wind. "Let's just hypothetically say there might be an assistant coach who could talk all night if you can tolerate his company over beers. Like most guys, he'd give up his mother for someone to regale with his stories."

"Doesn't hurt if that someone look likes you do."

Hanna arched her eyebrow, surprised. "I'll take that as a compliment, which is no small victory coming from you." The wind brought a wonderful healthy color to Hanna's cheeks. She smiled at him. When she smiled, that's when the transformation was in full. It was the magic of Hanna Donnovan. Her smile took her from pretty to stunning. Her smile was full and white and just noticeably crooked. This was her magnetism. That smile had sealed her audition with the news station. That smile, Cory thought, would move her through the ranks in news as far as she cared to go. It was one of those rare million-dollar smiles that couldn't be painted on with make-up or outdone by a hip new haircut. It was natural and slightly imperfect, and that was the power of it. As long as there were cameras to capture her smile coming to life, she'd never go hungry.

"Why not get the story from Joseph?" Cory was testing to see just how much she really knew.

"I'm betting Joseph never heard any of this. Plus, you're the all-American boy. People love listening to you."

"Joseph's more American than I'll ever be. His people have been here longest."

Hanna took a step closer to Cory and looked up at him. Usually, he wasn't comfortable with this proximity, but with Hanna it seemed less intrusive. "You know that and I know that, but not everyone sees it that way."

Cory almost pushed her back with the ferocity of his eyes. "You're the picture-maker. Jesus, Hanna, you frame public view. It's your responsibility. I'll give you your story, but let it be about Joseph. My question for you is are you ready to take the lacquer off the hallowed halls of the University of Minnesota and expose them for the country club bigots they are?"

"So it *is* true?" Hanna said, shocked.

"Come on," Cory said, shaking his head. "They've got you fooled right along with the rest. Open your eyes, for Christ's sake."

Now Hanna flared up. "Just slow down and let me catch up here. You've had a few years' head start on this story. The U passed on Joseph back in high school because he's an Indian?"

"They wouldn't even send a lousy scout to watch him skate. They said he wasn't U of M material. When I got recruited, I begged them to look at Joseph, too. Just send a scout, I said. All I got back was rhetoric about taking care of myself. All the scholarships are filled, they said, except the one they held for me."

"Maybe it was true. I'm not saying it was, but maybe."

"Hanna. I heard them on the phone calls. Especially those first unguarded comments before they brought in the big artillery to spin it. The decision not to recruit Joseph had nothing to do with available scholarships. He wasn't as white as Minnesota snow. I told them to blow me. When Wisconsin called, Joseph and I were treated equally. That's your all-American story."

"Let's tape it," Hanna said.

"Will they run it?" Cory asked. "The University alumni influence runs broad and deep in this state."

"I didn't think of that."

Cory skipped ahead to processing what ramifications the story might have on Joseph. It could well be the catalyst he and the team needed to beat the favored U of M on their home ice. Hell, maybe Cory was an accessory to it all by remaining silent all these years. Plus the smugness of their program—their choirboy reputation—Cory wanted it recast in a more realistic light.

Cory looked at Hanna. "Drag your boy out of that cozy camera truck. Tell him you're about to break an exclusive that'll get a few highballs dropping on the den carpet."

On game night the next evening, even before both teams were fully dressed, word of "The Interview" was beginning to buzz through the locker rooms.

The first sign something was up came earlier, during the afternoon skate, when the Badgers coach was interrupted, left the ice—something he never did—and was gone for over 30 minutes. Hours later, in the pre-game chalk talk as the guys dressed, he broke away for a closed-door phone call. While the coach was on the phone, Cory walked over to Joseph. "Hey, man. Can I talk to you a minute?" he said in a low voice.

Joseph saw the tension on Cory's face. "Yeah. Sure."

Cory turned and walked toward the door. Joseph met him outside the locker room in the empty hallway.

"What's up, Ten Pounds?" Joseph asked, concerned.

"I might've fucked up." Cory squinted and rubbed his face.

"I doubt it," Joseph said, bothered to see his friend like this.

Cory dove in. He told Joseph about the recruiting story, how Hanna had taped it. Joseph listened very quietly, his eyes dark and hard with an uncharacteristic stillness. Cory finished by saying Hanna was going to try to get it on tonight's 6 and 10 p.m. news.

"I think the shit has hit the fan. That's why Coach has been pulled away today. I'm sorry, man. I should have talked to you first."

Joseph looked down, searching for what to say. He measured Cory with a long look and a frown. "Why now, Cory-boy? You sit on this for years. Why now, before the biggest game of our season?"

Cory looked Joseph in the eye and told him a half-truth. "Because the story asked to be told now. It surfaced, last night in the parking lot. Hanna had heard something, she asked me, I figured it had been stuffed in my shoeboxes long enough. So I gave it to her." Cory's eyes flashed in defense. "Hell, I'm tired of the lie. I'm not the all-American kid. You are."

"You're right," Joseph said. "You should have talked to me first." He took a wide berth around Cory and went back in the locker room

Across the hall in the U of M locker room, their coach addressed his team. He held a tape in his hand, waving it in the air. "Guys, I've got a copy of a tape here from our friends at Channel 4. They got it from a sister station in Duluth." He tapped the tape against the heel of his hand, his tone full of disdain. "Seems Mr. Playoff, Cory Bradford, has accused this team of some pretty unsavory conduct. He says we're Indian-haters for not recruiting Joseph Blackholm. Says we overlooked him because of his race. Now, everybody knows Cory is smart. A little too smart, if you ask me. But he's just trying to fire up his guys with lies 'cause he knows they haven't got a whore's chance in church against us. That boy's a damn liar. I personally tried to recruit both of them in high school. Tried like hell with full rides for the two. They turned me down flat. Wouldn't even see me. They said they were going with the Badgers and looking forward to coming in here and kicking our ass. Now they're desperate and they cook up this crock of shit. Hell, just ask Mike," he pointed to the assistant coach. "He was in recruiting back then. Didn't we, Mike? Didn't we make every effort to sign the both of them?"

Mike stood in the corner looking a little pale. "Fuckin' right," he said.

The coach continued. "So I say we go out there tonight and deliver a little message to Cory Bradford. We don't stand still while he spits in our program's face. Your mothers and fathers are going to be on their couches in their homes tonight and have to listen to this bullshit on every station." The coach again banged the videotape against his palm. "No one is going to embarrass this program. Not on our watch. We hung more national banners than any team in the WCHA. That boy needs to hear from us. Loud and clear. You hear me?"

The referee and linesmen took the ice, given the standard college welcome: boos rained down. Shortly after, both teams skated on, and the standing-room only crowd pounced. They loved their Gophers, and held back nothing. Air horns blasted. The band tore into the school's fight song. Screaming, whistling, feet stomped the floor in unison like a stampede. The despised rival Badgers were showered under curses and comments about their mothers' fidelity. The minority pro-Wisconsin contingent tried valiantly to be heard, but were drowned out. Cory's interview hadn't made the news yet, but the crowd didn't require any such motivation. Three stuffed badgers with nooses around their necks were hurled out on the ice. They bounced, spun, and skittered to a stop. The crowd noise rose an octave in appreciation. The officials scooped them up and tossed them in the penalty box. Tonight wasn't going to be pretty.

Gathered around the net, the Badgers were rocked speechless by the crowd. The legacy, the claustrophobia of the building, the deafening moment—the players could hardly spit. Chevy took charge. "Hands in!" The team closed in tighter, putting their gloves on top of each other's. Their helmets bumped as they leaned in. "Cory," Chevy barked, chewing on the corner of his mouthguard, "what's the fastest way to shut these assholes up?" By asking Cory, Chevy showed the team he was backing Cory despite their differences. It was galvanizing.

"Bury one," Cory said.

"Bury one," Chevy repeated, banging gloves with Cory, spitting.

"Bury one," Joseph repeated.

And the team chant around the net swelled. "Bury one. Bury one. Bury one." If they could score first, the Badgers knew they'd steal the momentum and rip the voice from this crowd.

Two minutes and twenty seconds into the first period, Cory buried one in high style. Upper-right corner. A gorgeous goal on an incredible effort. Despite two defensemen slashing and hooking him, he stopped, wheeled, and fired in a sequence so quick, the goalie didn't know what happened until the goal light flashed. The crowd went dumb. And slowly, surely, the Badgers took over the game.

At ten minutes, Cory struck again. Angry. Intelligent. Explosive. Cory brought every tool he had to bear on the game.

"He's making fools out of you!" the Minnesota coach screamed at his bench. "He's pissing on this program." He smacked Curtz, the team's muscle-head, on the side of the helmet. "Are you going to let that little fuck do that, on *our* ice? Do something, for chrissakes!"

The next time Cory was on the ice, the coach sent out his goon. Curtz tried to take Cory out clean, but he was too quick, sidestepping, causing Curtz to slam wildly into the boards. Curtz got hotter and crazier with each miss. He resolved to do whatever it took to take Cory out.

Up the ice Cory blurred, puck on his stick. Curtz came at him full speed. They were on a collision course, like two cars playing chicken. Cory picked him up in plenty of time, and knew the thug was skating out of control. One juke and Cory'd dust him. What Cory wasn't ready for was the cheap shot. Just as Cory was cutting past, Curtz shot out one of his massive legs. The impact point was Cory's knee. Curtz drove his leg forward and Cory's knee buckled. The snap of ligaments sounded like fresh carrots being broken.

Cory flew in the air, his leg flopping sickeningly. He landed flat, hard on his back. The air expelled from his lungs in a great deep heave. He lay motionless by the boards, trying to get air, wheezing, the cold of the ice freezing the sweat on his back. The crowd in the stands above stood. From over the top of the boards, it rained down on him. The whole damn section spat. The clear plex faceshield of his helmet took hit after hit. Spit echoes inside your helmet when it lands on your facemask from that distance.

As they stretchered Cory off the ice, Joseph came alongside. "I'm coming off."

"The hell," Cory grimaced. "You win this game. This is where you belong."

"It's just a game, Cory-man. I'm coming with."

"Fuck that. Think, Joseph. You're going to let that asshole get us both off the ice in one shot. Stay. That's what I want. That's what I'd do in your place. Do you hear? I wouldn't go." They looked hard into each other's eyes.

"But—"

Cory meant to put an end to the conversation. "You shouldn't have left last time. You should have stayed. I've have to live with that noble decision of yours. We won state because you took the ambulance ride. Everybody knows it. Don't be such a good guy this time, okay. I don't need it."

Joseph was stung. He shook his head, put his helmet back on, and skated to the bench. He felt himself getting angrier with every stride. Usually he contained it, but at the moment, he didn't care. Joseph looked around the ice to find Curtz.

As Cory was taken off the ice, the last thing he saw was the large black scoreboard passing above him. Minnesota: 0 Wisconsin: 2 Time: 8:30 Period: 1. His mind photographed the moment. Fuck. It was going to be the last time he'd see a scoreboard from the ice. He knew it.

Just as the ambulance was about to roll, there was a pounding on the door. The paramedics looked questioningly at each other, then at Cory. The pounding grew more insistent.

"Don't open those fucking doors," Cory told them.

The pounding got louder.

"Sorry, man," the EMT said to Cory. "We've got to check. Procedure."

"I can tell you who's out there. Please, just go."

The banging escalated. The EMT gave Cory a sympathetic shrug and reached to unlatch the door. Cory closed his eyes and grimaced with pain. "Fucking Joseph," he whispered aloud.

"Can I help you, ma'am?" the EMT asked.

"I'm coming with," the voice said, matter-of-factly. Cory recognized that voice. He opened his eyes. As the door shut, he saw the light cross Hanna's face.

Cory was wheeled to emergency surgery. Hanna walked quickly alongside the gurney. They were told they'd have to wait, likely no more than 15 minutes. The on-call surgeon was on his way. The doctor, ironically, was at the hockey game and would be scrubbed and ready shortly. Nurses and doctors hurried past in the brightly lit hallway.

"Don't you have a game to cover?" Cory asked.

"Please, don't. I feel terrible. I thought you might want somebody here." Hanna's eyes welled up. "That prick ran you because of the interview, didn't he? He was sent by the coach."

"I'd say your journalistic instincts are dead on in that regard."

Hanna reached for Cory's hand. Hers were cold. "I'm so sorry. God I'm sorry. If I hadn't been so damn pushy …"

Cory gave her a calm look, squeezed her hand and then took his away. "Hanna, I'm a big boy. I decided to go ahead with the interview. Maybe it was you who got used."

"I feel awful," she repeated.

Cory shifted on the gurney. "I know the feeling."

The nurses and doctors continued to stream by in the hallway. One nurse looked over and saw Hanna with Cory. She stopped, recognizing her.

"Hanna? Is that you?"

Hanna turned toward the nurse and tried to act pleasantly surprised. "Oh, hi. Jean, right?"

The nurse gave her a concerned smile. "Jean Anne, yes. You didn't faint again? Nothing's wrong, I hope?"

"No, no. I'm fine." They both looked down at Cory. The nurse asked, "What do we have here?"

Hanna squirmed. "This is my friend, Cory. He was hurt in the game tonight."

"Oh," the nurse said, confused. "But I thought you said his name was Mike."

Hanna's face flushed. Cory watched her carefully. "No. Mike's … Mike's someone else. He's on the team, too. But this is Cory. He's a mutual friend."

"Ohhhh," the nurse said, further confused. "Well, okay then. Good luck and take care of yourself." She smiled quickly, turned on her heel, and got out of there fast.

"What was that?" Cory asked. "You were here earlier today?"

Hanna looked at Cory. Hers was the look of someone not sure whether the next step should be forward or reverse. Cory didn't want to pry; it wasn't his nature.

"Why were you here, Hanna?" he heard himself asking nevertheless.

Hanna's eyes welled up. "Are you sure you're interested?" she asked. "This is territory you famously steer clear of."

Cory frowned, watching her. Tears building, running down her cheeks. "C'mon, Hanna." He considered taking her hand but didn't. "What is it?"

Hanna looked at him directly. "I'm going to be a mom. I got dehydrated today and fainted. Hit the back of my head pretty good so they looked me over quick."

Cory winced, but coaxed a smile. "A mom? You and Mike are having a child?"

Hanna wiped the tears away and her eyes fired. "No. I'm having a child. Mike *is* a child. You of all people should know that."

"So, you'll get married?" Cory asked.

Before she could answer, the surgeon arrived, dressed in scrubs. "Don't worry about a thing," he reassured Cory. Then, looking at them both, seeing the tears and concern, he added, "Hey, everything's going to be just fine."

Cory and Hanna watched each other in the hard fluorescent light of the hospital hallway. "If you say so, Doc," Cory said, still focused on Hanna.

PART TWO

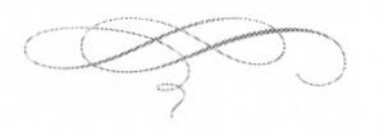

Summer 1981

CORY.

They ran in the dead still hours after moonrise. It was a blast-furnace August night under a fat full moon that threw shadows long and defined. They pushed down the middle of empty Highway 2. A pine palisade lined both sides of the road, cutting dark, serrated shapes out of star-tossed sky. Long constellations stretched across the heavens like soft strokes from some Godly paintbrush. Everywhere there were stars, layers behind layers, unsullied by light from unnatural sources.

Shirtless, sweat dripping on nylon running shorts long past soaked through, Pat, Joseph, and Cory ran shoulder to shoulder to shoulder. The only sounds: their breathing; their footfalls; the far-reaching hoot of an owl coming from the silvery timber.

Cory's right knee had made remarkable progress since the reconstructive surgery. First the doctors told him he'd likely walk with a cane the rest of his life. They then upgraded the prognosis to walking with a chronic limp. Then they said he might jog, lightly, a mile, but don't get your hopes up because an injury of this severity won't allow you to fully run. Finally, tired of being proven otherwise, they shut up and watched with grimacing admiration as Cory pulled himself up and over obstacle after obstacle. Always, he ended his therapy sessions in the pool. Back and forth, back and forth. Kicking and pulling until he had nothing left. The water would heal him. He knew that. He had always gone to the water.

Cory set goals in terms of weeks rather than the months doctors and therapists urged. He wore right through one physical therapist and demanded someone who could push him. In the end, it was Cory pushing Cory, as always. No one else was capable, or at least that's how he saw it. Finally the head of orthopedics had to come see for himself because frankly, he didn't believe the growing buzz of hallway talk. He'd seen Cory's MRI—just after the surgery—many doctors had; the injury had that kind of gruesome fascination about it. In his 25-year career, the department head had only seen one knee as severely injured and that belonged to a 60-year-old construction worker whose backhoe tipped, pinning his leg. The doctor personally came by Cory's room the day after surgery to tell him, "Son, you deserve to know this. I'm sorry. You'll never play competitive hockey again."

Cory simply asked for the details of the injury. Twice, Cory "interviewed" (Cory's word) the surgeon. He studied books on the knee. He asked questions of anyone who he guessed had even a sliver of information on the workings of the joint—including the night janitor he'd pass in the hall when he tried extra walking sessions to drive out the stiffness.

Less than six months later, he was not only running, but running sub-seven-minute miles. He needed to get back on the ice. Yes, hockey was college, but it was more than that now. He needed to show everyone he was truly a contributing part of the team that had won the national championship. If they could repeat, with Cory on the ice this time, then he could wear the championship ring they'd all been awarded. Cory didn't consider himself deserving at this point. Of course all the players told him otherwise at the post-tournament ceremonies. He had carried the team, he was their leading scorer, we just finished what you started, they said. But Cory didn't see it that way. Just as he never accepted the fact that he won the state high school championship from a hospital bed. It drove him. It ate him up.

"You're quiet," Father Pat said to Cory after the run. Cory was icing his knee.

"He's just gassed from running with the big dogs," Joseph teased. He had a water pitcher and was cranking on the hand pump just off the porch. The water flowed out and Joseph put his head under it. "Wheeeoooo! If this got any colder it'd come out cubes."

"How's the knee?" Father Pat asked, his tone a little too concerned for Cory's liking.

"Not good enough."

"You should lighten up, Attila," Joseph said, coming through the blackness, joining them on the porch. "It's August and you're already in better shape than most of the team."

"That's not the point," Cory said. Joseph filled glasses with the numbing cold water from the huge artesian aquifer that ran under the property.

"What is the point?" Father Pat asked, toweling off, finally beginning to dry. He took a glass of water. "Thanks."

"I don't think you'd understand, Father," Cory said. Then, softening some, "no disrespect."

"Try me," Pat said, in his best good-sport voice, trying to pull Cory out of a shell he'd withdrawn further and further into.

"I'm going to hit it early tonight," Cory said, getting up from the porch, unable to conceal the knee's stiffness. Joseph saw him wince in the dark.

"Maybe give yourself tomorrow off. It is Sunday. The Sabbath, a day of rest, right Father?" Joseph smiled at Cory.

"Forty-three days until the opener," Cory said, clearly communicating there was no time for days off. He looked at his watch, tilting it to the porch light. It read 12:07. "Make that forty-two. Good run, guys. Thanks." He headed in the screen door.

Joseph and Pat sat in the stillness of the porch, wrapped in the distant orchestra of crickets and peeping frogs, looking up at those magnificent stars. After another glass of water, Pat broke the silence. "He's not doing so well, is he?"

"No," Joseph said. "I guess he isn't."

"How long has he been like this? I mean Cory's never been chatty, but this is different."

Joseph put his head back on the wicker porch chair and exhaled a long deep breath. He rubbed his eyes. "Cory was on the bench with us for the championship game. The refs said no one could sit there who wasn't dressed for the game, so he put on his skates and pads and pulled on a jersey. I helped him to the bench; he glided on his good leg and let the other skate drag. Got a standing ovation. That applause hurt more than getting to the bench. He sat there for three periods even though his leg was supposed to be elevated, and when the final buzzer went and we won, everyone was out on the ice, piling on the goalie. I remember I looked back and saw Cory at the bench. Just standing there with his game jersey pulled on over his shirt. It was the happiest moment of my life until I saw that. Then some guys jumped me and pulled me down in the pile. By the time I was up again, Cory was gone. He won't take any credit for the championship, Father. Won't talk about it, won't wear the ring. Just says let's focus on getting it done this year."

Father Pat soaked the story in. He knew a little of what it felt like to be on a winning team, but to not have contributed to the victory. The false, hollow taste.

"He got the short end of that deal for sure."

Joseph nodded. "Now there's an understatement. The guy took us there, gets us ahead before he gets put out, and then doesn't get to feel what it's like to win it. How fair is that?" Joseph opened his eyes and looked at Pat through the darkness. "Where's the fairness in that?"

"There's a time for everything." Pat thought for a second. "Maybe it just wasn't Cory's. Who knows. Do you know what Monsignor Kief always said when I brought up the fairness of things?"

"What?"

"He says, 'Fair is a place your mom takes you in the summer to ride merry-go-rounds and eat corn dogs.'"

Joseph smiled and pondered the thought. "I could almost eat a corn dog right now. I'm starved."

"You're always hungry. And besides, I didn't think you ate junk."

"Nah. A couple-ten corn dogs won't kill you."

Pat smiled, resting his water glass on his forehead. They sat in the silent heat. The wind chime under the corner of the porch hung mute.

"Could use some breeze," Pat said. "Or an air conditioner."

Joseph sat quiet a spell. "When I was little, on dog days like this, my dad had an air conditioner he'd bring out when there was just a little breeze."

"I didn't figure your dad the air-conditioning type," Pat said.

"His air conditioner wasn't like most. Back before we built this porch, there was a smaller one off the side, screened in, about twelve by twelve. When there was a breeze, we'd all be in the porch after supper, and Dad would say, 'think we should turn on the air conditioner?' I'd play along and say, 'high or low?' He'd give it some serious consideration and say, 'judging tonight's breeze, I'd say high.' Then he'd bring the garden hose right in the porch door and spray down all the screens from the inside out. A film of water got trapped in the screens. The breeze blew through and the water would evaporate, cooling the porch. I kid you not. You could feel the difference. 'Too cold for you?' he'd ask. 'I can shut 'er off.' For about 15 minutes that breeze would blow cool. Then he'd spray the screens again."

"He didn't really, did he?" Pat asked. Just then a little breeze kicked up. The wind chimes bumped out a few perfect notes.

Joseph smiled. “Well, there’s your answer.”

They sat in the hush, hot quiet, thinking separate thoughts. On a clear summer night like this, when the stars and moon seemed to have been lowered closer to those who stayed out and cared to notice, the nearness to such wonders pulled questions from deep within. The stars tipped back their heads. Thoughts crystallized in the night sky. And they made their peace with them.

FATHER PAT.

For Pat, tonight was the night. He had some words that needed saying.

"Joseph, can you see if your mom's still up? She asked that I didn't leave without saying goodbye."

"Sure thing. Thanks for the run." He came over and gave Pat a clap on the back and took his hand for an extended handshake.

"Sleep well," Pat said.

"Maybe if I fill the tub with cold water," Joseph joked.

A few minutes later, HomeSky came out in cut-offs and an open-necked cotton blouse. The full moon shimmered off the perspiration on her collarbones. Pat felt a light-headed tingle as she came across the wide-plank porch carrying a mysterious trace of a smile. She sat close.

Quite out of character, he took her hands. With only the nerve to look there, at the moonlight on their hands, he spoke. "If I don't say this now, and quick, it won't get said." He studied her long fingers.

"Get on with it then," she nudged.

"Last week, I was offered a full-time job as the first-shift floor foreman. Salary. Full benefits. Pension."

HomeSky watched Pat, his head bent down. His long nose with the pronounced bend and bump where it was doubtless broken in some dustup from earlier days. His thinning, sandy hair. His white eyelashes practically luminous in the moonlight.

"I guess I'm not sure what you're telling me," HomeSky said.

Pat opened his hands, letting hers rest in his. His were working hands now, chapped and callused. Hers were much the same, yet with a feminine slenderness. "I used to chew my nails something awful," he started. That's as far as he got.

"If that's the depth of your flaws, I'd say you're better off than most." She gave his hands a light squeeze.

"What I mean is, look at my nails now. They're clipped. Things are finally getting right for me. When things were bad, my fingers told the story."

She looked at them. The nails were rounded and trimmed. She took his hands to her cheek.

"I still love you," Pat confessed. "I told you two years ago I did, and you said that wasn't possible." He looked into her eyes.

"I didn't believe it was."

"And now? What do you believe now?"

"I think yes. It's possible."

"Do you love me, HomeSky?"

"I can't answer that. I haven't allowed myself to love you. Am I capable of loving you? Yes. Ten times yes. But because I couldn't let myself be the reason you left the Church, those feelings were never given a chance. Now I'm beginning to understand it's arrogant to think I could ever be why you'd leave. Your reasons have much more complexity than one person or one place or one incident."

"Well, yes and no. My struggle is not as certain as one issue, but you are a big part of it. Maybe two years ago you could have been the sole reason. Today? I'd say you're more of a catalyst. I feel pulled away from church life. I want to remain in service. I've spoken to the tribal leaders about counseling, doing some secular outreach programs, maybe even going to night school to get a psychology degree. They told me I didn't need a piece of paper to continue to sit and talk and advise the community on affairs of the soul. That work, in their eyes, doesn't require certificates. Or a priest's collar, for that matter."

HomeSky nodded.

Father Pat shifted gears. "But I'm getting off course. I'm telling you this because you are the single most important reason I'm thinking of leaving. You're not the whole, as I'm sure you're relieved to hear. Either way, with you or without you, I think I'm leaving."

"When will you decide?"

"The plant needs an answer on the job soon. If I accept, and they can wait a month for me to switch over, I'll have eight years here at the church. I'd like to stay through my anniversary."

HomeSky looked at Pat in the bright moonlight. "Why did they even venture to ask you about the job? It's not every day someone offers a priest a full-time position."

"There are a few men I've gotten to know well there. I've confided in them about my struggle. It arose from there."

"Are you ready for this?" HomeSky asked, unsure of what answer she hoped for.

"Ready?" Pat smiled. "You can't prepare for a decision like this. You just make it. You make it, and then you live the life in front of you. Goethe wrote something that said if you get past hesitancy and commit fully, only then does providence move, too, and all sorts of things occur that never would have otherwise. You become more than your decision. God willing, more fulfilled. More to your true place. Unless I'm told in an immutable voice to stay, then yes, I'm ready."

"Those words must sound strange," HomeSky empathized.

"It's the first time I've spoken them aloud. They're ringing like a different language."

HomeSky and Pat looked at each other. They smiled, comfortable within the silence. HomeSky broke to a lighter note.

"First shift? You really must be turning some heads down there."

It took Pat a moment to catch up to the subject change.

"Oh, yeah. They've got a bit of a troublemaker running the floor. He's coming on when I clock out, so I just get whiffs of the whole thing. You may know him. Lu Ann's dad, Reg Cunningham? He's had the job forever. Always crossing swords with someone. They've had it. They're going to tell him step down or step out."

"I've never met him," HomeSky said. "I know Lu Ann doesn't even speak to him. His name is posted by the register. He tops the list of people she refuses to serve."

"That's the one. So the job is mine if I want it. Like I said, I'd arrange to do some other things on the Rez. I couldn't just extract myself from the people there. So that's where it sits."

"It's exciting. It's frightening. It's a lot to take in."

"Don't rush it. One thing we've got is time. It's taken me a long time to come to this place. Let it simmer."

Pat stood to leave. The night's heat kept his muscles from stiffening too badly. HomeSky thought, *he looks good on this porch in the moonlight. He looks right being here.*

"That's a funny expression," Pat said. "What are you thinking, if you don't mind the question?"

"Oh, but I do mind," HomeSky said, smiling softly. "A woman has some thoughts that are hers alone."

They smiled. Pat reached down and took her hand once more and gave it a tender squeeze. She looked at up him and whispered, "Now I really can't tell you what I'm thinking."

"Same here," Pat said. He gave her a priestly smile. "Good night then."

"Yes," she answered. "Indeed it is."

With a fan blowing on him, Pat stretched on the floor near his bed as he said his nightly prayers. He asked the same thing he asked for every night, although less desperately now that he felt closer to an answer: *Lord, please give me guidance, and the faith and strength to follow that guidance no matter which direction it turns me.* More and more he was thinking of his relationship with God in the context of son and father—small "f" father. Pat might not have turned out 100% as his father had hoped, but he turned out pretty well. He was at ease with the disparities between the ideal Pat and the real Pat. He finally had found a way to see his larger graces rather than the shortcomings in the margin.

He stretched his quadriceps and smiled at himself. A priest who prays while stretching and preaches in tennis shoes. What are you running from, son? He kidded himself, but he wasn't joking entirely.

HomeSky lay atop a bed sheet too hot to be under. She wore a light cotton shift, dug out of the bottom of a chest of drawers, where for years it had remained neatly folded under the layers of clothes. Typically, on a hot night like tonight, she would pull on one of RiverHeart's old t-shirts.

The moon's rays streaming through the window were intense enough to paint a rectangle on her bedroom wall. She looked into this squarish field of light and thought of the geometry of her life. RiverHeart as one corner. Joseph, the next. Pat and God the other two. Like corner pieces of a puzzle, they were fundamental in framing who she was. Each was irreplaceable to her whole. Why, then, did it feel as though she was replacing one with another? Was RiverHeart being replaced by Pat? Was she removing God by taking Pat, or accepting Pat, or whatever the right word was? She looked at the rectangle of silver light on the wall and decided this was not the case. They were her foundation. And embracing one did not eliminate the other. All of them together made her complete.

HomeSky rolled over and pulled a pillow to her side, hugging it tightly. And peace returned to her bedroom for the first time in many summers.

JOSEPH AND CORY.

Smiling, Joseph pulled out of sleep. A distant, rhythmic sound from his childhood floated up through the open bedroom window: CHOP! CHOP! CHOP! Outside, firewood was being split as the songbirds christened the morning. Pink light leaked beneath the drawn shade. Joseph sat up. For an instant, he was a boy of thirteen again and his father was putting up wood for the coming winter. He quickly regained his bearings, swung his bare feet onto the floor, and cracked his neck. Cory's sleeping bag was in the corner, rolled, with his pillow on top.

Downstairs, Joseph stepped silently out onto the porch, careful not to let the screen door bang shut. At the firewood bin next to the barn, his back to the house, Cory, shirtless, mechanically brought the heavy ax head down against the sun-hardened oak. He split and quartered it, kicking the pieces aside, stopping only to stack when the pile around his boots grew unmanageable.

Joseph sat on the porch and watched. Cory's back was muscle-roped, and V-ed down to a thin waist. His arms and shoulders were thick, quick, and very powerful. Joseph could only shake his head; was there nothing Cory didn't do well? Every stroke hit with explosive precision. For 10, 15, 20 minutes, Cory kept at it. Joseph could feel an intense disquiet radiate off his friend.

Then HomeSky, too, was there, on the porch. She stood. They both watched Cory's back. How it clenched and rippled with every vicious downstroke.

"I'm worried about him," she whispered, sitting down.

"How so?" Joseph kept watching his friend.

"He seems … so restless. Boxed in."

"That's what Father Pat said last night. Is it that obvious?"

"Look at him. He doesn't stop for a moment." HomeSky's worried eyes stayed on the young man. Cory shined with sweat. It jumped off him when ax met oak.

"He feels he's behind, Mom. And falling more so by the day. He said everything he's worked for is slipping away."

"But his recovery's been remarkable."

"Mom, his knee was ruined. That's the word one doctor used. They said he'd walk with a limp his whole life. Never skate again. He's out to prove them wrong. And he's got the heart to do it. He just doesn't have the knee. It's worse for him 'cause he's so smart. He understands too well the extent of the damage. He knows knees like a surgeon. He studied everything he could put his hands on. It's not a question of the guts to come back—his brain says it's not going to happen. It's eating him up."

"Did he tell you all this?"

Joseph smiled a sad smile. "C'mon, Mom. You know Cory."

She nodded, still watching.

Joseph continued. "It's all around him. It wouldn't be any more obvious for saying it. A few days ago, we were coming back from skating, stopped at Scalzo's gas station—you know, there by the corn fields?"

"Sure."

"I went in to pay for the gas, and came out and Cory was gone. The pump handle was still hanging out of the car, no Cory. I went behind the station where the fields start and there's this old oak just off the edge. Cory was under it. He was watching a kite caught in the branches. It was all wrapped up, but there was enough slack string to let the wind fly it a little, but then it would slap back into the branches. 'Damn shame,' he finally said, looking at the tattered kite. 'All that field and just one tree.'"

HomeSky put her arm around her boy. They watched Cory, swinging away.

Joseph and Cory ate breakfast in the dark before leaving for a week of voluntary practices held on the Madison campus. The coaches couldn't participate in summer workouts. According to NCAA rules, supervised practices couldn't begin until two weeks before the start of school. In fact, the sheet of ice wasn't even down in the arena yet. Nevertheless, the core of the team would meet, put on pads, and run the painted cement arena floor, playing ball hockey until they were drenched. They would scrimmage, work breakout drills, and start getting back into playing shape. But more than anything else, it was pure fun. It rekindled the intangible bond that a championship team always needs.

HomeSky found herself walking a fence line. Her mind was preoccupied as she moved quickly, rather than at the idle pace a hot summer morning normally requires. She was on the cusp of a decision there would be no easy return from. She wanted to call Pat, have him to the farm for dinner. With the boys gone and last night's talk still fresh, the outcome of such an invitation would likely advance beyond dinner conversation. Was she ready? Nervously, excitedly, she thought perhaps yes.

The high corn to her right was tasseling and in milk. The soybeans across the way were setting pods. As the hot wind combed through the broad soybean leaves, the field became a green sea.

HomeSky stood still. "So, should I ask him?" she inquired of the field. It swayed back and forth, ambiguous in reply. "I'll take that as a firm maybe," she said, smiling, moving on. She walked, her hand dragging against the corn shucks. HomeSky knew where she was heading, but got there without conscious thought.

At RiverHeart's grave, she sat. Sixty years ago, these quiet few acres were cleared of the encroaching trees and brush by River-Heart's father. Cleared and then burned, allowing the dormant native prairie grass to grow back uncontested. In the years that passed, every decade or so, these acres were again burned, each time bringing forth yet another dormant species of grass and wild-flower from the ancient prairie. Switchgrass, big bluestem, Indian grass, Canadian grass, heal-all. The lush, natural beauty, the diversity of this wild patch of restored prairie spoke to her. It would be as RiverHeart would want. It was time.

Father Pat's answering machine picked up just as he was coming through the screen door.

"Hi, it's me," he heard HomeSky's voice say, "wondering what you're doing for dinner. If you're not busy, I've got a nice venison steak that needs to be grilled before Joseph eats it. Call me."

Pat stood over the phone, unable to reach for it or walk away. Minutes passed before he sat down in the adjacent chair. He continued to look at the phone. As clearly as a person could feel himself at a road's dividing point, Pat was there. His stomach groaned with nervous energy.

"This is it," he said aloud. "You, most of all, understand my decision, Father. Of all the mysteries You have bequeathed, unconditional love is the greatest. I know as I move forward, I will not leave Your hand."

HomeSky was putting away the breakfast dishes when the phone rang. A phone rings differently in an empty house. Louder. And the rings seem to come farther apart. Careful not to be overanxious, she picked up on the third ring.

"Hello."

"Hi," Pat replied. "Dinner sounds great. What can I bring?"

"Just you."

"How about a salad? I picked some lettuce and tomatoes out of my garden. I have to use them up or they'll go bad."

"Perfect."

"What time?"

"Let's say six. I was thinking since we don't have the boys to feed, we could eat later."

"They got off okay, I trust," Pat said.

"Yes. They left before sunrise. They couldn't wait to get down to campus. Like two kids at Christmas. I'd almost forgotten how much they love the game."

"Good then. A late dinner sounds great. I'll see you around six, salad in tow."

"Great," she said, none too convincingly.

A drawn-out silence crackled on the line.

"HomeSky, are you as nervous as I am?" Pat asked.

"Oh," she said. "At least."

LICK.

Lick had been gone almost three years. In that time, the pack of dogs he ran with had become more like wolves. Once a dog gets a taste of running deer and living undomesticated, few ever look back. This pack was all muscle, tendons, rib cages, and matted fur. They subsisted like a family. If their kill was a deer, they'd share it. When they raided a chicken coop or brought down a calf, every animal got something, all the way down to the bone marrow.

They ran up in Canada, some fifty miles from the farm where Lick was whelped. Who's to say? What makes a dog start walking one night when the moon is full, to head for a home he hasn't seen in years? There really is no knowing.

As the venison hit the grill, it seared, sending up a hiss and a puff of smoke. Pat looked over at HomeSky on the porch swing. A few wisps of evening clouds had moved in, yet she looked to be in full sunshine. Her black hair was braided and pinned up so what little breeze there was could find her shoulders. Wearing a tank top and shorts, from this distance, she could have been mistaken for someone who was dating her son.

Pat had overdressed. He wore long pants and a shirt buttoned over a t-shirt. Standing next to a grill on a hot August night made him think, for the first time in a long time, about a cold beer. Maybe it wasn't the heat. Maybe it was nerves.

Joseph and Cory finished dinner at the college cafeteria. They had organized an afternoon red-against-white scrimmage on the arena floor, followed by flag football. That was more than enough workout for most of the guys. But for these two, seeing they were already in mid-season shape, it was just an endorphin appetizer. They planned to go out later and run under the full moon while the rest of the guys reacquainted themselves with the local bars.

At dinner, Pat and HomeSky revisited the topic of employment at the McKnight plant. The more they spoke of it, the more it took shape before them. They could visualize each other across this table every night. They talked faster; they apologized and laughed for interrupting. Excitement branched through them. Could Pat be fulfilled walking a plant floor? HomeSky wanted to know. Pat clarified that the job fulfillment would come in the form of a paycheck every two weeks. He would find *meaning* in other places, in other activities—in her. Talk like this made them light-headed. Much of the formality that had stiffened the early evening's conversation evaporated. When two people have been long apart, as the distance between them narrows, as emotions this long unattended are stirred, formality and caution don't stand a chance.

The boys grabbed a nap after dinner. Considering the long drive down and the afternoon workout, they'd already packed a lot into the day. In their dorm, they set an alarm for nine p.m. By ten, the moon would be high. A full-moon run was on deck. Just like they'd done so many times back at the farm, on a desolate stretch of highway lit by the heavens; it was confirmation that their friendship, their story, their determination was of a most unique kind.

After dessert, Pat and HomeSky took their iced teas and made for the porch. A slight breeze kicked up under the intense moon. The chimes bumped ever so gently. The front pasture was lit like a giant stage. Pat, pushing the screen door open, struck by the sight of the pasture rising out of the silver light, hesitated at the threshold. He saw something afar—a dog? a wolf?—making its way across the terrain. Then in that half-second before he could comment, he forgot everything; his hand taken gently by hers, guiding him backward, back in the house, a voice close to his neck, whispering "this way."

Lick had walked two days without taking food or water to arrive home under the full moon. He didn't approach the house, though the smell of food pulled strong. He angled across the front pasture and headed toward the ridge, slowly, head hanging low. Up above, on the ridge, was the high prairie grass. He had come home to lay in that grass. To die.

Cory and Joseph had run four miles out, and had just turned around to head back to the car. The highway rolled out bright under the moon. This was hilly country, this part of Wisconsin. The road bent sharply in front of them and then dipped downhill.

Even on a typical night, it would have been difficult to see the approaching headlights. But on this night, the kids driving the truck had the headlights off. It was something generations of boys from these parts did. Their fathers had done it when they were teens, as had their fathers before them. To drive this stretch of road under the bright full moon without headlights was part dare, part rite of passage, part of the innocence of growing up out away from the street-lit city. These weren't bad kids. These were unlucky kids. When their vehicle came flying out of the sharp turn, it was too late. All they saw were two shapes on the road. When they heard the thud, they thought they'd hit a deer.

Before they undressed, Pat and HomeSky sat on the bed. The moon provided ample light for them to look into each other's eyes, but his remained downcast. She asked if everything was okay. He said he was afraid he wasn't going to be very good at this. His chest had tightened and his heart beat so loudly inside him, he wondered, could she hear it, too? Please, she said. Don't worry. He looked up and saw his future waiting for him. He reached.

The dog circled slowly, five times. The tall blue stem began to fold and mat. Lick lay down. He closed his eyes to trace memories of ducks retrieved and scraps secretly brought to his muzzle under the table. His breathing slowed and slowed. Then his tail flicked one final time to the memory of crawling onto a warm lap as a puppy.

"JOSEPH!" Cory screamed, racing toward the ditch.

PART THREE

Autumn 1981

NOVEMBER.

As always, November was a son of a bitch. What was glorious and warm and colorful and autumnal, still fresh in your memory, vanishes in the hard turn of the wind. The breathtaking scenes torn down, withered, drifted under. Ice, snow, the relentless gray shoulders its way in. The occasional sun that cracks through has little heat to it. The body, fighting to adjust, finds little comfort in coat collars turned up, in leather gloves, in cold boots.

Pat parked the truck in the corner of the picked field, which lay under a dusting of dirty snow. The ground was plenty frozen to leave the truck there without possibility of it settling and getting stuck. He walked toward the slope of the ridge. The wind brought tears to his eyes that quickly crystallized.

The place on the ridge would be quiet, he knew. The lee side of the slash of trees, that halcyon place, where Joseph and his father lay side by side, where birds gathered in this weather, where deer bedded down after feeding. Pat, too, went to quiet himself there. He did most days. Now he sat on a deadfall for the final 15 minutes before the early dark. Dark came so quick and greedy this time of year.

In the blackness, Pat rose stiffly, left a feather and a dried flower petal at the graves, and carefully made his way back down the ridge to the truck with its yellowed dome light beaconing, thanks to the door he left ajar.

He drove out past the burned-out farmstead, his swing of headlights catching the pale beginnings of the newly framed house. He snapped off the static on the radio and wondered about HomeSky. Where might she be? How might she be? He rubbed his face and blew into his hands and considered cursing, but he was too tired for any of that. All he knew was he would rebuild what HomeSky had burned. It would be done by late spring when the warm winds returned home to fields ready to plant. Pat would bring forth something good that lay dormant under the ashes. What else could he do? It was the only thing that kept him from lying down and not getting up. He was bone-exhausted. Between working mornings at the plant, acquainting the new priest, Father Dan, with his parish, and counseling on the Rez, there was the farmhouse. The farmhouse would get built. Pat would see to it if it killed him. And if it did, damn it to hell, how much worse could that be?

THURSDAY.

By mid-November, the futility of it all finally pushed Cory's head back onto his pillow and pinned him. This was no small task. But his knee had already been drained three times in as many weeks and the Vicodin/Demerol combo he was ingesting like M&M's had ulcerated his stomach.

The five o'clock alarm went off. Time to swim. He snapped on the bedside lamp, pulled back the bed sheet, and grimaced. His knee had almost doubled in size overnight. He dry-swallowed one Vicodin and one Demerol tablet, twice the recommended dosage—and they're not to be mixed—but the truth could no longer be evaded. The blank prescription pad he used to forge refills had only two sheets left. Reality stood there laughing its fucking head off. So he lay back in bed. Something at the core of him gave way. *I quit. I'm a quitter. Add that to the list. No, put it first.*

Across the dorm room, Joseph's bed remained as it had for months: tautly made, with his zipped red hockey duffel bag on top.

Cory didn't know what to do with Joseph's belongings. Ever since HomeSky had disappeared, he kept them packed, ready, like she might appear out of the blue.

The drugs on an empty stomach fuzzed the edges of the ceiling as Cory stared up. He tried to keep the accident out of the room, but it was tenacious. Why hadn't it been him? If his knee hadn't slowed him down ever so slightly, would he have been out front instead of Joseph when the truck came around the curve? Nothing made sense. His intelligence, his ability to better the odds, his skill at anticipating what others couldn't—all worthless. It should have been me, he thought for the thousandth time.

Back when this year's hockey season began, to overcome the loss, Cory tried to be both himself and Joseph. No one player could do that. The coach told him he was trying to do too much. Take it slow, he cautioned. But before long, all the side-to-side and start-and-stop of the game, not to mention the endless physical aspect of college hockey, proved the doctors right: he would never play competitive hockey again. The knee couldn't sustain it.

Cory let the drugs shimmer through him. He liked these drugs not because they eliminated pain, but because they eliminated feeling. He turned off the bed light. He felt himself going blank, the acuity of the memories fading. His limbs got heavy, restraining him to the bed. He didn't give a shit. He just wanted to be left alone. He couldn't be Cory Bradford. Not anymore.

On the following Thursday afternoon, as the bus loaded up for an away game in Duluth, no one noticed that Cory stowed two duffel bags down below. He hobbled up the steps and took a seat up front by the driver.

For two months now, players weren't sure how to act around Cory. Avoid him? Razz him to bust him out of his funk? Frankly, he spooked them. Circles deepening under his eyes. Hardly looking up from the ground or saying a word. And it was no secret he was a walking medicine cabinet.

The coach dropped him to the third line, so he was seeing less and less ice time. The way he was playing, he deserved to be benched, but the coach kept him in uniform, half out of loyalty, half because he was afraid of what Cory might do otherwise. Cory just got quieter. Always sitting off in the corner of the locker room. He had gone weird, and it was worsening. After the last goal he scored, he just skated back to the bench and sat down. It was the damnedest thing. Even the home crowd grew quiet.

The snow had started. The bus merged onto the highway and swayed back and forth in the wind. In the back, music thumped and the cards were going like always. A few guys tried to look at homework, but the books didn't stay out for long. The further north the bus went, the heavier the snow fell. Just south of Lake Superior, it was near whiteout due to the lake effect.

Daylight quits early this time of year. The snow swirled out of the late afternoon blackness, lit squinting-white by the bus headlights. For hours, Cory had stared through the wipers, watching wet snow get pushed off the windshield. He watched for the sign: Highway 6 WEST. That road would take him over into Minnesota where he could hook up heading north.

The Highway 6 sign lit up momentarily in the headlights, and then was snuffed out by blackness. Had a person not been vigilant, he would have missed it. Cory stood and walked across the aisle to the driver.

"Pull over, Al."

"Yeah, right, Cory," the driver said, his eyes never leaving the treacherous road.

"Pull it over up here."

"Are you kidding me? What'n hell for?"

"Al. Right now."

The driver glanced at Cory. There was just enough light to see the intensity in Cory's eyes. He pulled over.

"Open 'er up." Cory gestured to the door.

"Damn, Cory," the driver said.

"Don't sweat it, Al." Cory gave him a faint smile.

The driver cranked open the door.

Coach Waldron looked up from his game notes and shouted at the driver. He came up to the front as Cory went out the door. Outside, Cory hauled two duffel bags out from the storage lockers.

"Cory," the coach hollered from the bus steps, "What the fuck? Get back in here." The wind muffled his voice.

Cory slung his and Joseph's hockey bags over opposite shoulders. All he was wearing was his travel sports coat and dress shoes. He slipped shouldering the bags but didn't go down; his knee shot him a reprimand.

Coach Waldron came down a step. "Cory, please now, boy. You're in the middle of bumfuck. You'll freeze." His voice was thick with asking.

Cory looked up at the coach—snow swirling around his head—his receding hairline blown farther back by the wind. Hell, he was a good enough man. He'd done right by Cory and Joseph in how he recruited them and treated them. Shit, the coach missed Joseph, too. Everyone was affected. He looked tired.

"You go get 'em this weekend, Coach. I'll see you back on campus in a few weeks. Your responsibility is to those 25 guys." Cory turned and started back toward the Highway 6 intersection. The snow, already five inches deep, slowly worked its way into his shoes. The coach stood on the middle step and watched the young man, with a red Wisconsin Badger duffel slung over each shoulder, limp down the side of the road. Darkness swallowed him up.

Back on the bus, everyone looked to the coach for some explanation. He saw fear in the faces of normally cocky players. "Cory said he has something he needs to do. He'll be back on campus in a few weeks." There was an extended guilty silence. "Fuck! That's all there is to it. Now let's get the hell out of here. Al!" he startled the driver, "that means you."

The driver yanked the door closed hard and inched the bus back on the highway. The coach sat in the front seat still warm from where Cory had been. In the next seat over, Cory's letter jacket was folded neatly. The coach let his head fall back on the headrest, exhaled heavily, and rubbed his eyes. "Mother of Christ," he said to anyone who cared to hear.

If you don't get run over hitchhiking in a snowstorm, the upside of the precarious conditions is that most cars are moving slow enough so their headlights afford drivers a good look at you. Cory's suit coat, tie flapping in the wind, and all-American looks definitely helped his cause. He had the duffels at his feet, one thumb stuck out, and the other hand in his pants pocket, rolling Joseph's stone between his fingers. Lost in thought, Cory didn't see the brake lights of the truck that pulled over up ahead. The driver rolled down the window and yelled against the wind. Cory finally snapped out of it and made his way over.

"Thought you were frozen solid there for a second," the good-natured driver laughed after Cory slung his bags in the truck bed and settled in the cab. Cold entered with him. The driver rubbed his large, chapped hands together.

"It's not so bad," was all Cory offered. Judging his tone, the driver didn't know if Cory was referring to the weather, or what put him in this spot in the first place. When asked, Cory said he was making his way home for Thanksgiving break and then diverted the conversation to cement, a topic near and dear to the driver's heart; Cory had noticed the words Rusty's Cement and Driveway custom-lettered on the truck door as he got in. Rusty spent the ride explaining how it was possible to pour cement, even in this weather, if your work is well covered and you mixed in the right polymers and epoxies to help it cure. Cory dropped just enough well-placed questions to keep the conversation about the driver.

As he pulled over to drop Cory at the next highway going north, he insisted Cory take his jacket and gloves. "I ain't pulling away 'til you do," the driver insisted. His eyes were dead set. "I can't be letting you out in this mess with only a church coat on. Take it now. Go on then." Cory thanked him and pulled on the old brown Carhartt coat frayed at the collar and cuffs from years of manual labor.

"Hate to take a man's coat," Cory tried one more time.

"Hell's bells. My wife'll send you a thank-you card at Christmas to be rid of it." He smiled and told Cory to take good care.

Cory headed north, leaning into the teeth of the blowing snow. The wind whistled across his ears, first stinging them, then taking away all feeling. He decided to walk for a bit up the road's shoulder. Highway 2, which ran due north from there, slowed down for one small town after another but never stopped until it made Baudette's one and only traffic light. After that, it cut a narrow ribbon through nothing but trees where finally, it dead-ended in Canada.

HOMESKY.

Her apartment in St. Paul was what they called an efficiency. HomeSky had never known the word in that context, but the ring of it suited her. Better yet, there wasn't much empty space to rattle around in. Empty spaces were no friend to HomeSky.

She had taken nothing with her except her purse, the clothes on her back, and a picture of Joseph from when he was a little boy in the summer sunshine. In the photo, he had his hand up to his eyebrows to shield the sun. His hair was a long, magnificent, straight black. He smiled big as he looked just off-camera. HomeSky imagined he was watching for his father.

HomeSky slept with the picture. She wanted only this memory. As much as she knew it wouldn't, she wanted time to reverse so she could smell nothing but the sunshine in her boy's hair. But what she smelled mostly was smoke. It was always there, on the wind, and nothing triggers memory like an aroma. Everywhere she went it came back to her, and she was there again, standing so close, watching the backbone of the farmhouse buckle as the fire glowed on her face. She backed away, as she often found herself backing away, from people at work, from people at the bus stop, in a crowded checkout line, when the smell found her. She backed away and went out and didn't look back. Just as she had that night.

HomeSky put the picture in her purse and left for work. Despite her care, its corners were wrinkled and turned up. She couldn't bring herself to tuck the picture in an envelope or close a book around it for safekeeping. She couldn't watch Joseph be covered like that. Not again.

She had found a restaurant on the bus line with an owner who didn't terminate her like the others had the first time she hurried out for fresh air. Her new boss just kindly requested she come back as quickly as possible. When HomeSky needed a minute, she'd catch his eye, grab her coat, and hurry outside until the moment passed. Other than that, HomeSky was a model employee. Exceedingly reliable. Very thorough. And friendly, but never to the point of intrusion like some wait staff are wont to be. Soon she became the quiet, adopted member of the family. A restaurant staff invariably becomes family. Instinctively, they all knew not to go too fast with her.

HomeSky had also taken up running. She felt closest to Joseph in the silence of a pounding heart. She had so much guilt to dispense with; thankfully for her, she found this one positive, life-saving outlet. She would stretch on the floor of her cold apartment, tie her key in her shoelaces, and run with abandon. Those who encountered her running might think: there goes a beautiful, strong, healthy woman. Nothing could have been further from HomeSky's reality. She was unforgivably ashamed of herself. She had no plan for moving forward. She had no secret hopes. She was saving for nothing. In fact, she often shorted herself when splitting tips. She worked. She ran. She ate a little now and then. She slept with Joseph's picture. By her reckoning, this was the life to which she was entitled.

When Pat crept into her thoughts, it showed physically. She would wince, as one might at the flashing onset of a migraine. She'd take her head in her hands. She tried to expel all thought of him. *I had a priest to my bed. I turned down the sheets. What kind of mother would expose her son to such wrath?*

She had taken a scissors to her long hair. She cut it straight in front but it was crooked along the collar in back. She brushed her teeth in the dark and washed her face without consulting the mirror. Occasionally she would catch her reflection in the window, turning from it like poison. She was beyond prayer. She felt no right to speak to God. Mostly, she waited. For the cancer or the bus or the rapist. God wasn't through with her yet. Of this she was certain.

HANNA.

How all of this transformed into such a tender mercy for her, Hanna hadn't a clue. But as an exhausted single parent, she had found real, inarguable happiness. Hanna's four-month-old boy, Pauly, centered her. She'd never known such a thing before. Yes, she had smarts. She had looks. She had personality. But she never had a flashpoint experience that put into tack-sharp focus that life wasn't about her. Not that she was a self-obsessed person—attention had always flowed her way. She had a magnetism about her.

Hanna hadn't heard from Chevy, Pauly's father, since before the birth, and she hadn't hoped to. She had made it abundantly clear that this was her child and the last thing either of them needed was another dependent in the form of a deadbeat hockey player clinging to his glory days. Chevy was just one of too many easy mistakes Hanna had made cruising through life. This mistake, though, finally held consequences. And she was glad for it. She was tired of exceptional luck. She'd been waiting for her streak to end. It was a relief, strangely, this demanding new life.

Hanna was back reporting and doing some weekend anchoring for the news station in Duluth. She had returned from maternity leave a month ago, and was making some progress. For example, leaving Pauly with the neighbor lady no longer made her cry. Not every drop-off, at least. All in all, Hanna was finding a new stride. She was happy.

Her acclaimed reporting from earlier that year—breaking Cory's story about the University of Minnesota's racially biased recruiting policy—had ratcheted up her credibility and celebrity as reporter. She was now more than just another news person with a cute smile and a shapely profile that played well on camera. She had doggedly stayed on the story beyond the initial interview, including two follow-up pieces from the hospital that all but insisted Cory's injury was a "hit" put out by the Minnesota coach in response to Cory's allegations. Her stories lived on the national stage for over a week—which is forever by that clock. Cory, finally, just wanted it all behind him. So he stopped returning her phone calls and wouldn't see her the last time she came down for his rehab sessions. All she wanted to do was talk. All he wanted was to get on with the knee.

In her few quiet moments, Hanna faced her guilt. She had gone digging for the story. Cory ended up hurt, she ended up promoted. The why of it, she wrestled with. Was it the sheer weight of the story demanding to be told? Or had Cory trusted her with the story as a friend? Or did she coax it out of him as she had so many others: with her brown eyes and her body language and her smile? What was she to do? The die was cast. Life had changed forever for them both. The only difference was now she had a child and, last she checked, Cory's scoring totals were abysmal.

And he had lost Joseph, too. She could only imagine how that was affecting Cory. Of course, Hanna was there for the funeral at the farm, along with the very small gathering. She drank coffee afterward and hugged HomeSky, who said Joseph always spoke of her affectionately. Hanna didn't know if it were true because HomeSky seemed so far away as they briefly talked. It was wrenching and unfairly hot for such a trying day. Hanna was into her third trimester and had a difficult time in the small, breezeless farmhouse. Cory hardly spoke to her. Cory hardly spoke, period. He went outside into the oppressive sun to walk the fence line.

But then came Pauly to lift her up. He was a miracle in flesh. His chubbiness was outdone only by his hair-trigger smile. Everything made him laugh. Say his name, get a laugh. Change his diaper, get a laugh. Drop his bottle and swear, get a laugh. He had his father's disposition, laid-back and easy-going—which was what attracted Hanna to Chevy in the first place—but affable nonchalance only gets you so far once you're out of diapers.

The three months Hanna spent at home with Pauly were the happiest she could remember. But she had to get back to work. There was no child support, and she'd have nothing of it even if there were. Plus she missed reporting, loved reporting. Her national news exposure opened a lot of new doors. Cities from L.A. to Philly were asking for her tape and resumé. Hanna politely declined, which made her that much more in demand. News directors personally picked up the phone to tell her she was committing career suicide working in podunk Duluth, playing for an audience of 20,000. So be it, she thought, as she said thanks but no thanks. She was back in front of the camera. She had an elderly Norwegian neighbor taking care of Pauly and loving him like family. And she was getting back into jeans she hadn't worn for months. The only bruise on the apple was the gouging ache she felt when her thoughts flipped to Cory. Which was random, but surprisingly often. She would see someone leaving a restaurant, or hear a voice or a song—something would trigger him—and she'd make a call. She'd get his machine, but no return calls. Then one day, the machine didn't pick up anymore, so Hanna stopped trying. She did, though, pay attention to the college hockey standings and game summaries. That was her contact. She'd look for his name under goals, assists.

Cory Bradford. Where are you? Her finger would go over the small print a second time, a third. *You've fallen off the earth.*

Hanna made her way to pick up Pauly after work. The snow had established a foothold on the afternoon and it showed no sign of relenting. The hilly streets were slow going as the dark of the late afternoon pushed people stomping into their warm entryways, pulling doors quickly shut, keeping them in for the night. Hanna wheeled her Buick Skylark toward the north side of town, trunk full of sandbags for traction against the endless slope of Duluth. On the radio, a melancholy guitar line played, reminding her of Cory. It had a sad, sweet, skilled quality. She saw his tumble of brown curls, the scar that divided his dark eyebrow, how he looked away while talking, a subdued smile on his lips as he commented wryly on some irony. Hanna promised herself she'd call after Pauly was fed and asleep. But even had she remembered, all she would have heard were empty rings. Cory hadn't been on campus for a week.

LU ANN'S DINER.

Pat had taken up a stool at the Formica counter. Taped on the back of the cash register was Lu Ann's latest hand-written sign making clear her position on things:

So far today I've done all right. I have not gossiped and I have not been grumpy, nasty, or selfish, and I am glad of it. But in a few minutes, Lord, I am going to get out of bed, and from then on, I am probably going to need some help.

Pat smiled and went back to what he was doing, which was nothing much. He'd forgotten how many cups of coffee he'd finished, but he was past the number where anything really tasted anymore. Good thing, too. The coffee had been sitting since morning. Cowboy coffee, Pat called it. Normally, coffee didn't last at Lu Ann's, but this was the slow time. The few days just before and after Thanksgiving always set everyone on a different schedule.

Busy preparing, shopping, cooking. Then came the recovery from big helpings of family, days off, and refrigerators full of leftovers. It put the town off its regular clock. A small town thrives on its eating routine. And in this regard, Lu Ann's was the center of the universe. The lull would last a few more days, but then Christmas trees would go up, the holiday yard lights would get strung, and out of the clear blue, thoughts of Lu Ann's potato pancakes, fresh bread pudding, and homemade popovers would strike without mercy. And Lu Ann's would be jumping again.

Two bachelor farmers sat in the window booth and Lu Ann worked them like a door-to-door salesman. She had some specials to move.

"Few people realize meatloaf is actually good for the skin," she claimed, showing them her cheek as if it were proof. "Brings out a glow. Especially this time of year with all the dryness. Puts a snap of sheen back in your hair as well. What do you say then? The special?" The farmers were docile as cattle. They nodded and went back to silently gazing out the window.

Sheriff Harris lumbered in through the door, stooping slightly so his brown fur hat would clear. He clapped his gloved hands together and declared, "Colder than a witch's left milker out there. Could fire a cannon down First street without touching a hair. The town's holed up like rabbits."

He got out of his coat and took a stool next to Pat. He slapped the cribbage board between them like a gauntlet and took a small fold of paper from his pocket. The year's tally: eighty-five for the Sheriff, seventy-four for Pat. They cut for deal and the Sheriff's two secured it.

Saturday night was cribbage night. First there'd be a few groceries, supplies, and whatnot for Pat to round up, then he'd get to Lu Ann's around six. His A.A. meeting didn't start until eight, so that left a couple of hours to eat and argue the nuances of cribbage with Sheriff Harris.

"How's the special?" the Sheriff asked, cutting to the chase.

"I don't know. I was waiting for you."

"Have you done any surveillance?"

"Sheriff. It's meatloaf. What would you have me do? Case the kitchen?"

"I noticed the Swenson boys each have a plate. Maybe you overheard something?"

"Deal the cards," Pat said, rapping his knuckle on the counter for luck.

The Sheriff went to his right shirt pocket for a Camel, thought better of it, and pulled a Vantage from the left. He took the rubber band off the cards. "You'd never pass for police work," he said, lighting up. Despite his disability, he was a wiz at shuffling cards.

A few hands into it, as the Sheriff expounded on the game's lost art of pegging, Pat interrupted.

"I need a favor."

"No. I won't spot you ten holes." The Sheriff grinned like a mongoose.

"Seriously," Pat added.

"Okay." The Sheriff cocked his head and squinted at Pat.

"I was wondering if you could find her. Just so I know she's all right. I wouldn't even make contact."

In a different time, the Sheriff would have strung him out. Which "her" was he referring to? he'd ask, just to watch him sweat the explanation. But that time was long past.

"I can do some nosing around. Five will get you twenty she's down in the Twin Cities. It's where locals go to disappear. Did she give you any inkling where she was heading?"

"Shit," Pat said, throwing down another lousy hand. "She didn't even give me an inkling she *was* going. We hardly exchanged two words at the funeral. She holds us accountable."

The Sheriff looked off and frowned. "I hope you put her straight on that."

Pat considered chewing a fingernail. "One thing I've learned from being around grief. It's not sensible."

Sheriff Harris nodded. "I'll vouch for that." He took a sip of black coffee. "When my Amanda passed, I had a spell. She sure was a neatnik," the Sheriff said, smiling some at the memory. "She cleaned constantly. Loved to vacuum, especially. Loved how it left the pile of the carpet straight and orderly. Well, as her brain tumor came on, she got more and more forgetful. It got so she'd vacuum some rooms two, three times over. Lost track of what was done and what was left. It brung her to tears. So mornings, before I left for work, I'd go around the house turning on lights in every room. Once she was finished vacuuming, leaving the room, she'd flip off the light. That way she'd always know. So, after she passed, damned if I didn't find myself going around the house putting all those lights on. Then I'd vacuum the house dark. Might be the middle of the night. I had neighbors ask me what I was doing at that hour with the house all lit up like a party. Hell, everyone has a spell. It's to be expected."

The Sheriff was still surprising Pat. Inside that off-putting exterior was a sensitive man. But he'd run you out of town at the mere mention of it.

"So, how you doing with all this?" he asked, noticing how Pat's clothes hung loose on him. "Looks like somebody's been chasing you up the skinny pole."

"Joseph's death nearly put me back drinking," Pat confessed. "Bought a bottle. Opened it. But I just imagined Joseph's sadness, me taking up with it like that again. Down the drain it went. My grieving, frankly, has been … work. Which can be a dangerous escape as well. But I'm going to get that farmhouse up and painted come spring. Something tells me it's the thing to do. If I just knew HomeSky was okay, I might find a little peace. Sleep's been touchy."

The Sheriff nodded. "I'll put the feelers out. For a guy up in Timbuktu, I can still turn over my share of rocks."

To say sleep was touchy was a sizable understatement. Tired as Pat was from his three-man workload, at night he rolled around in the possibility that HomeSky was right: maybe they, maybe *he* might be responsible for Joseph's death. His spiritual self told him that wasn't possible; the Father's hand wasn't directed by His children. But his emotional side couldn't be stilled, planting doubt upon guilt.

Most nights, after thrashing and flopping for an hour, Pat would take to the kitchen. At the table, he'd spoon a little ice cream into his decaf coffee. He'd try to disperse the pained thoughts, but he was haunted by HomeSky's downcast face. She'd hardly look at him after their night together. Once the shock of Joseph's death succumbed to the new reality, rather than reaching out, she withdrew further. She refused to speak to him. When Pat finally confronted her, she said she took a man of God by the hand and led him away from his calling. For her, their night and Joseph's death were inseparable. This was her punishment. Pat told her how impossible that was. God is not vengeful. Pat's relationship with God didn't *end* with his decision to leave the priesthood; it took a different form. But all this landed on deaf ears. She had decided it was so. That was all there was to say on it.

What kept Pat going was the farmhouse project. If he could bring something lasting out of the ashes of the homestead, something undeniably right, it could be like the meadow burnings that brought forth unforeseen beauty from what lay suppressed. This could be theirs from the floor joists up. Their home. Every memory sealed within its four walls would belong to them and no one else. It would be a new start.

Pat said his prayers, stretching on the floor along the side of his bed. He prayed HomeSky would find some peace. Be it with him or somewhere else, he begged. Let her find solace.

The Sheriff lined up his three beers next to a mug on the kitchen counter, rearranging their order as if one can might taste better if he drank it earlier in the sequence. He carried his glass into the living room and set the two unopened cans on the side table that held his latest puzzle. He was working on an upland bird print depicting half a dozen pheasants feeding on corn shucks under a dilapidated hay wagon. The Sheriff slid a few pieces around, but his heart wasn't in it. The fact that Cory hadn't called for two weeks worried him. Cory never missed a Thursday phone call. He'd talk about hockey and school, and the Sheriff would catch him up on the latest in the Baudette soap opera. But now, not a word.

For a man the Sheriff's size, finishing three beers was a task equivalent to a pickup truck hauling a hatbox. But his third, for relaxation, didn't do the trick. He paced. He looked out the windows. He washed and dried his mug. He cleaned his ashtray. He found three puzzle pieces of the rock pile on the field's edge.

As he got ready for bed, he pulled on the flannel pajamas Amanda had sewn for him. His size made buying off the shelf next to impossible. He took off his prosthesis and set it on the bed stand. His internal radar was picking up something. *Cory,* he asked the empty room, *what's wrong, boy?* The Sheriff thumped his pillow and decided that while he was inquiring into the whereabouts of HomeSky, he'd have someone look in on Cory, too. He knew a cop in Madison who could put him in touch with the head of campus police. That's what he'd do, he reassured himself. The bed quilt rose and fell to his breathing. He stared at the ceiling. He looked at the luminous clock face. He switched pillows. Then he pulled back the covers, went out to the front room in his robe, pulled a Vantage from the left pocket, and went back to cussing his puzzle.

CORY.

Cory wouldn't think to ask for help. It wasn't so much that the act would betray some internal code, it's just the thought never occurred to him. He had grown entirely self-reliant. Even now, as he sat on his Badger-red duffel bag in the howling cold of sunrise, wondering if he was losing his fucking mind, he didn't think to ask.

The gash where his hairline and forehead met could stand a stitch or two. The blood had caked dark and thick. Cory had no recollection of its getting there. When the pain pills dried up four days ago, he'd started on beer. He didn't care for the taste, but what the hell, it got him there.

He looked at the weathered sleeve of the brown canvas coat he'd been given hitching his way north. Just up from the cuff, it was carefully sewn with heavy thread. More than likely it had snagged on something unforgiving. That was a good man, he thought, remembering the driver's wide, honest face. A happy man.

A day back, or was it two? Cory had passed a highway sign reading, Baudette 40 miles. He'd stopped in towns along the way to eat something, asked if any of the establishments needed dishes washed or floors mopped or roofs cleared of snow. Then he'd find a bar, sometimes have a few beers, other times, not so few. He slept in garages left unlocked by people who had infinite faith in neighbors and providence. Hitchhiking, north he went.

For the first time in memory, Cory was without a schedule. He'd come off his iron track. No routine, no touch-points, no idea what day it was. He was ashamed. Deeply, completely, unforgivably. He had quit.

Behind him, the giant silver-black corrugated grain elevators ran endlessly, their blowers drying the harvest. He was on the edge of town. What town, Cory couldn't have cared less to know. He'd spent the night on the elevator's lee side, leaning his back up against a spot where a blower warmed the metal. He had made the road, but no farther. Sitting on his bag, Joseph's next to him, he waited for the morning's first cars heading north.

A pickup wheeled onto the gravel drive of the elevator yard. Cory and the driver locked eyes. The driver lifted his head in hello. Cory returned the gesture. The driver rolled past, thought better of it, and coaxed the old drive train into reverse.

He rolled down his window. "Mornin'," the driver said. He noticed the gash on Cory's forehead.

Cory looked at him blankly. "Good morning."

"Everything okay?" the driver asked out the window, trying not to sound overly concerned.

"Can't complain."

"You going up the road?"

Cory kicked one of the bags with his heel. "Baudette."

"I got a truck going there at nine. Why don't you come in the office for coffee 'til then."

"What time do you have?"

"Just past seven."

Cory thought about it. "Got any work you can keep me busy with until then? I'd rather earn the ride."

"That's not necessary."

"I thank you, then, for the offer." Cory looked away.

The driver saw the brown flaking of frostbit skin on the tips of Cory's ears. "Well, if you insist. No doubt I can keep you busy. There's always work."

Cory got up and shouldered his bags. "I'll follow you in."

Cory cleaned himself up in the bathroom. His unshaven, bedraggled image caught him off guard. He pulled a fresh pair of socks out of his duffel; his last clean pair. He soaped out the cut on his forehead. He scanned his face, looking at the tapestry of small hockey scars: above the bridge of his nose, trailing off the edge of his right eye, creasing his bottom lip, under his chin, through his left eyebrow where scar tissue prevented a thin seam of hair from growing back. All permanent reminders of the game that had thrown him aside. He tried, again, to recall the cause of the fresh gash in his forehead. Nothing.

He stared further into his bloodshot gray-green eyes, but saw only an unfamiliar dullness. The spark of clear certainty was washed out. After a lengthy pause, Cory spat at his image and made for the door. Thinking twice about the generosity of the grain elevator operator, he went back to the sink and rinsed the phlegm from the mirror.

Two hours later, Cory was sleeping fast and hard in the cab of a grain truck as it barreled north on Highway 2 toward Baudette. As luck had it, neither he nor the driver were much for small talk. Soon Cory was dreaming about the kite in the tree he and Joseph had seen last summer. Its string hopelessly looped, the wind picking it up and beating it into the branches. As they pulled into Baudette's town limits, the driver shook Cory. Cory jumped to alertness.

"Sorry," both said at the same time.

"You were really out of it there."

“Been a long couple days,” Cory said, glancing out the window, getting his bearings. Baudette had hardly changed. It always seemed old, but it never seemed to age.

The truck’s air brakes hissed as the driver set them. He pushed on his flashers, took out his log book, and nonchalantly asked, “Do you get to see your dad much, then?” He looked up into the silence for an answer and instantly realized he’d asked the wrong question. “Not that it’s any of my business,” the driver added quickly.

“Why mention my father?” Cory asked dryly, directly.

“Well, you talk in your sleep is all. You were asking for him.”

“Two pitchers of beer,” Cory said to the waitress at the Mutineer’s Jug. She had some tough miles on her.

“How many glasses?” She was thinking, it’s only 11:15 in the morning; he must be expecting company.

“One will do.”

She looked Cory over. Some of the miles in his face she surely recognized. She recalled herself at that age—the bad decisions—but swallowed the unsolicited advice. Live and let live was her philosophy.

Cory sat drinking beer like water. What he liked about drinking early was the lack of food allowed the alcohol to start in immediately on the right angles of reality. The waitress came by and asked if he minded her joining him for a cup of coffee. Cory politely said he’d rather she didn’t.

He’d come to like bars, which was quite a change in just a week. He liked them early, the quiet-empty, and he liked them late when they were crowded and he’d go unnoticed. It was damn nice to be a loser without feeling like you let anyone down.

Cory’s plan was to hitch out to the farmstead and visit Joseph’s grave. He hadn’t been there since the funeral and that was a lifetime ago. There were things that needed doing. He needed to put the small river stone in its rightful place, first of all, with Joseph. HomeSky had insisted Cory keep it, but the stone had become heavier than anything he'd ever carried. Cory took it from his pocket and rolled it on the table. Generations of wear gave it a surreal smoothness. There was a small vein of red running through its light gray coloring. He'd be glad to be rid of the thing.

He also planned to get out on the skating pond near the farmhouse, cut a hole, and sink the two duffels. Each was packed with skates, pads, helmet, and the home and away Badger jerseys. Among other items in Cory's bag were the shoebox of letters they'd exchanged, a scrapbook of clippings, and the Home Sweet Home needlepoint Cory had taken from the cabin on Lake of the Woods. The only keepsake he planned to save was the team poster from the national championship team. To him it was the truest memory of Joseph.

Cory unzipped his duffel and pulled out the cardboard tube that contained the poster. He unrolled the team photo out on the table and used the pitchers to hold it in place. He couldn't help but laugh. There was Joseph, and Cory, and a half-dozen other players smiling with the big fake teeth Joseph had passed out. The shit had hit the fan after the athletic director discovered the prank, but it was too late. The posters were printed and distributed. After the team won the championship, the sportswriter who covered the team did a piece about the legendary Teeth Poster. It became a collectors' item—like a stamp printed upside down or an incorrectly minted coin. This was the only possession Cory cared to hold on to.

Out on the highway, hitchhiking to the farm, Cory was somewhere between drunk and exhausted. Ten miles out, that was how far he needed to go. Cory remembered that Joseph used to skate that distance on the river to school. The few vehicles on the road were going into town, not out. Probably headed for early lunch—or dinner, as they called the noon meal in these parts. The recent snowfalls had pinched the highway smaller. Running parallel, the frozen Rainy River kept drawing his attention. With little prospect for a ride, he thought, what the hell. He'd skate it.

Sitting on his duffel, backed up against the bank of the river, Cory laced up his skates. They felt strangely unnatural. Cory had been off them for 10 straight days, the longest stretch he'd gone in a winter since he was five or six. The ice was blown clear in many areas, but snowed over in others. The day spread around him flat and white-gray. Nothing had shape nor shadow. Branches overhead veined the sky. In front of him, the river twisted and disappeared into the woods. The first few snowflakes of the day squeezed from the sky and landed noiselessly on Cory's hands, melting as he finished lacing his second skate. He stopped and looked at that left hand, where the tip of the index finger had been smashed with the rock. The nerves were never again right in that finger and the tip remained hooked. Every time he pulled hard on the laces of his skates, thousands of times over the years since, he'd always feel only the slightest tingle out of that fingertip.

With a duffel bag in each hand, Cory stepped onto the river ice. The sound of the blade striking ice, the feel, the glide of that first stride, was something akin to an aroma; it took him back to a place of origin. It was soothing in the way a mother's humming voice might be. Cory headed toward the forest where the river narrowed and ducked down under the canopy of trees, running quietly north toward the farmstead. He knew what to expect. The farmhouse had been burned and HomeSky had vanished. The Sheriff had also told him that Pat was going in earnest on a new building. He skated without further thought.

It was just after midday when Cory came walking over the rise in the drifted pasture and into full view of the three-quarters-framed farmhouse. He was instantly taken by the emptiness of the scene. The driveway was there. The outbuildings were there. But the skeleton of the house looked so forlorn against the sky—against the memory. A stack of lumber sat under a rustling tarp. There were no tracks in or out since last night's snow.

He went into the barn, and in one corner, where it had always been stored, found the ice chisel used for chipping holes to set the two-by-four posts of the plywood goal. The chisel was nothing more than a long, solid metal pole with a sharp chipping blade welded to the end. It was substantial to wield and had always made quick work of the ice.

Can I really do it? Bags over each shoulder, Cory made his way across the front pasture and saw the pond in the low dip of the land. He held for a moment, looking at the saucer of ice flanked on one side by cattails, opened to view by way of his approach. He pushed on.

Out on the center of the ice, as the snow came down heavy now, fat with moisture, Cory sat, then lay, eyes closed, feeling the flakes quickly melting on his face. He could hear the memories. The days here spent laughing. Pretending to be different NHL stars competing in the deciding game of the Stanley Cup, score tied, he and Joseph would come down this ice, teammates, snapping the puck back and forth, cutting in, one last pass, shooting, scoring the game-winner. Lick sliding around after them, barking, chasing the puck, playing keep-away. All here.

Cory's resolve returned. He had to jettison the uselessness of these memories. It was over, damn it all. The dream, the friendship—a child's fantasy. He stood, picked up the ice chisel, and with four powerful strokes gashed a fist-sized hole through the ice. For five minutes, he brought that blade down. Splinters of hard blue ice sprayed in all directions. Soon he had an opening large enough to drop the bags through.

As the water gushed and pooled on the surface, steam lifted on contact with the cold air. Cory tossed the chisel aside and looked at the black water. Falling snow mixed with the rising steam. Cory picked up one of the duffels. His 21 years, as well as Joseph's, were zipped inside. That's what he had to show for it. The joke was on him. Cory looked at his boot tracks leading onto the pond. The falling snow had begun to erase them. And at that moment, truly, it dawned on Cory what he was here to do.

"The hell," he said, dropping the duffel onto the snowy ice.

Then he stepped forward into the icy black water and was gone.

HOMESKY.

HomeSky wasn't the sick type. But she had felt something coming on ever since she got out of bed to her five o'clock alarm.

She knew she was needed for the restaurant's morning rush. Even more, she knew she had to hold on to *this* job. HomeSky dragged herself into the shower without glancing in the mirror.

Wrapped in towels, getting dressed, she couldn't warm up. She touched the old hot-water radiator just to be sure it was working. It wasn't the radiator. Try as she did to keep one foot coming down in front of the other, she repeatedly had to sit down on the edge of the bed. Chills raced down her back. She tried to eat some toast. Finally conceding, she called into work. The owner was gracious, told her not to worry, to get her rest. They'd be okay.

Not bothering to undress, she buried herself under the covers. She was still ice cold. She curled into a ball and let her eyes close, immediately dropping into a deep dream sleep.

Pat was standing in the uncut meadow. HomeSky observed from a vantage point somewhere hidden, high above. A boy came through the tall prairie grass toward Pat. He was a small boy, no more than four. The boy was radiant, almost incandescent.

Inseparable from his anguish, he reached out to Pat, crying, shaking from the sobs. The little boy put his hand to his mouth, overcome. Tears streaked down his flushed face.

HomeSky recognized this dream as the one she had years ago, the one she told Pat of when they first met. It was the dream Pat said called him to the priesthood.

The little boy dropped to his knees in the grass. Tears soaked his body. The grass closed over him.

Wake up! HomeSky urged herself. She knew who this boy was. Years ago, she didn't. Pat had been certain it was Joseph, but HomeSky knew her little boy and told him he was mistaken. *WAKE UP!* She tried again to pull herself out of the heavy mud of the fevered dream. *Go to him!* she called aloud. *He needs you.* She was so cold. The bed covers were leaden. She couldn't move.

Pat was having one of those days. He wanted to climb back in his pickup, go home, and start over. Two workers from the morning shift were out with what was known as the10-hour flu: hung-over. He covered for them. Meanwhile, he was trying to get one of the lines back up with machine parts that had been mothballed years ago. As if that weren't enough, the guy who Pat replaced, Reg Cunningham, was, even for him, especially foul. He was walking around itching for someone to pick on. Everyone was too busy so he found his usual easy mark: the plant janitor, a man with Down's Syndrome who went by the name Radio Voice.

Radio Voice was so nicknamed because he had an uncanny ability to memorize and mimic the deep announcer voices on the radio. Weather. News. Local auctions. High school football games; he did all the voices. It was his gift. His portable transistor radio and earpiece were constant companions. The only time the radio wasn't on was when Cunningham had removed the batteries as a joke. Radio Voice loved doing his impersonations for the guys at the plant and the townspeople. And delighted in the fact that everyone called him Radio Voice. Except for Cunningham. Cunningham called him Mongoloid.

At 11:45 the call came in. Pat remembered the time exactly because the shift was taking fifteen, although he was out on the fork truck because they were two semis behind. A girl from the front office came running out on the floor. Pat didn't like the look on her face.

"You've got a emergency phone call," she said, wide-eyed.

"What's it about?" Pat asked as they ran toward the office.

"I don't know. It's some lady. She said to tell you it's HomeSky."

The snow on the highway slowed him down some, but not much. By the time Pat's truck fishtailed into the drifted driveway at the farm, the footprints were almost covered. Pat found them, though, as they headed faintly out toward the front pasture. He jogged to the crown of the pasture and looked through the veil of heavy flurries, across the lowland to the pond. Cory was there, just as HomeSky had feared. Pat put his cupped hands to his mouth and took in a deep breath to shout. At that moment, Cory stepped forward and disappeared under the ice without a sound.

Three times Pat fell before he reached the hole. He went in.

PAT.

In the long hours afterward, Pat couldn't believe how cold Cory was. He asked the nurses to bring another blanket, but Cory just quaked and shivered. Pat buzzed for more blankets until the doctor finally came in and said it was the d.t.'s. Cory's withdrawal from pain pills was excruciating to watch. Pat had no idea it had gotten so bad. For that matter, no one did.

The phone rang in the hospital room. Quietly, Pat answered.

"Hello."

"Hi. It's me."

"HomeSky. Oh, thank God. I left the phone number everywhere I could think."

"You're talking so quiet. Is Cory okay? Are you with him?"

"He's here, he's fine. He's just across the room, sleeping. Exhausted. He's got pneumonia, but he'll be okay. The doctors say he's remarkably strong, of course. Listen, can I go to another phone and call you? Where are you? *How* are you?"

"I don't think so," she said. "I'm okay. I'm sorry ... I just needed to see about Cory."

Pat gripped the receiver harder, feeling her slip away again. "HomeSky, please, don't cut me out."

"Pat, I can't do this. I'm trying to sort things out. I really just needed to hear Cory was all right. I should go. I've done enough."

Pat whispered urgently, "HomeSky, you saved the boy's life. Can't you see? This was God working through a person He loves. You can't refuse—"

"Pat. No."

"Tell me you're okay, then. I've been lost in worry."

"I'm okay."

"Do you mean it? Will you call me? Or write? Something?"

"I can't promise anything."

"I need you, HomeSky. You know that, right?"

"Pat, I've brought this on—"

"No!" Pat raised his voice. Cory stirred. Pat dropped back to a whisper. "No. Don't do that. You must know better. Cory sleeping here is living proof of God's love for you. How else can you account for it?"

HomeSky was silent.

Cory sat up in bed. "Is that HomeSky?" he asked, the patchy beginnings of a beard on his face. "I'd like to talk to her."

"HomeSky," Pat said, "Cory wants to say hello." He listened to the silence, wondering if she was still there. "HomeSky?"

"Yes," she said softly. "Please put him on."

Pat stretched the cord over. Cory sat with pillows propped behind his back.

"Hello," he said into the receiver.

HomeSky's voice changed, got stronger, more assertive. "Hi. Pat tells me you're doing just fine."

"Yeah. Please, don't sweat it, really." He paused. "HomeSky, there's something I should have said back at the funeral. If anyone's to blame for Joseph's accident, it's me."

"No, Cory—"

"Please, let me finish." The emotion of Cory's months of grief was rising. His hand began to tremble. "You know how I felt about Joseph, right?" he whispered. "You and RiverHeart are the only ones who could have loved him more. But if it weren't for me going forward with that stupid interview, my injury wouldn't have happened and Joseph wouldn't have been hit."

"I don't … I don't see the connection." HomeSky's throat was almost too dry to speak.

"I broke the code and talked about the U's recruiting practices. Their coach marked me. Before the injury, I was always the faster runner. Rehabbing the knee slowed me down. It put Joseph out front where I should have been. That pickup got the wrong guy." Cory felt the tears filling behind his eyes. His voice cracked. "I'm so damn sorry …"

Pat moved to console Cory. As he leaned in, Cory held up one arm stiffly between them. Cory curled away, onto his side, his back to the room. He was embarrassed by himself. HomeSky asked, "Cory, are you there?" Cory began to talk again, softly, facing the wall. Pat tried not to eavesdrop, but couldn't help but pick up a few words: "Apologize … quit … pills … Why? … I can't … Yes … sure."

"Cory?" Pat said as Cory handed over the phone to hang up. He looked at him earnestly, trying to break through. He knew Cory always kept his distance, but it hurt him to not be able to make at least some fraction of contact.

"I apologize for all of this," Cory said, looking down at his hands on the crisp hospital sheets. "Hell, I've ah … I've been struggling for a while now. You know what I'm saying. I don't want to be anyone's pain in the ass."

Cory finally looked up at Pat. He looked thin, Cory thought. Bone-tired.

Pat respected the distance between them—as badly as he wanted to go across the room and hug him tightly. He simply leaned in from his chair and spoke. "Cory, I love you. You're an amazing person. An inspiration to me and everyone who's known you. As for Joseph, you did so much for him. He talked of you with such affection and awe. Did you know that? I wouldn't know where to begin telling you how he felt about you. You could never be anyone's pain in the ass. You've made such a point of being nobody's pain in the ass, I think it's actually harming you."

Cory shook his head. "I didn't mean for what happened to happen. I know how it must look, but I went out there to get rid of those stupid fucking hockey bags. I just wanted to be done with it." Cory exhaled. "I don't know."

Pat tried to slow the conversation down. He could see Cory withdrawing again. "Do you remember when we met?" Pat asked. "We sat on that dock at Lake of the Woods and we looked at each other in disbelief at all that was happening? And me trying to pull some sense of it out of there. Me, a royal screw-up." Pat looked at Cory, who, to Pat's surprise, was watching him closely. "Cory, I've made a pile of mistakes, but I know one thing. It takes a long time to make sense of the life we've been given. The past eight years you've been handed, I wouldn't wish on anyone. Mine have been no picnic either. And yet, when I walk around the rectory—a rectory, don't forget, that my recklessness burned to the ground—and stand in the church courtyard watching the pigeons flying over the bell tower, I feel lucky. You and Joseph and HomeSky are my life. And you, my dear boy, are so far, so many, many millions of miles from being the pain in the ass you speak of, you should never think it again."

"Pat," Cory pointed out matter-of-factly, "you pulled me out of a frozen pond."

"Cory," Pat said, "I've been pulled out of worse."

The men looked at each other. Cory broke first. He shook his head and smiled faintly.

"What a pair," Cory said.

Pat nodded. "God broke the mold. So," he said, filling the silence, "what did HomeSky say, if you don't mind my asking?"

"I can't really go into it."

"You know, it's very hard being excluded from this."

"I know."

"Did she give you a phone number, or where she's living?"

"Her phone number. I said I might need to talk to her."

"So what will you do next?"

"Who knows? I'm a 21-year-old with a knee a 70-year-old would take a pass on. Hockey was my ride. Ride's over. I've got thirty bucks to my name."

"You could get an academic scholarship to any college in the country. There's more to you than hockey."

"No. That's where you don't get it. Hockey changes me. It's the only thing that's ever, I don't know, released me, I guess."

"Things change, Cory. You're looking at living proof."

"Don't get your hopes up."

"Why don't you stick around here for a while? Take a few deep breaths. There's a pull-out couch at the rectory. Father Dan has been exceptionally gracious in letting me stay until I get the farmhouse done. He'd be happy to have you, I'm sure. And I could use a hand out at the farm. I'm hoping to paint it by spring. Doesn't matter how late spring comes up here, my chances are slim right now. I bet I could get you on at the factory, too. Loading pallets, driving a fork truck, getting on a ladder to change light bulbs, nothing too fancy. But I've found the work a welcome distraction. What do you say?"

"I need to get back to you on that," Cory hedged.

Pat's eyes sparkled with a bit of optimism. "Okay. Think it over, but don't overthink it, as a great man once said."

Cory thought. "Joseph?"

"The one and only." Pat smiled. He paused. "Do you want to talk about what happened?"

"No," Cory said automatically.

"But it's okay to ask for help—to ask me—you know that, right?"

"Sure." Cory answered quickly.

"Please, Cory, I really want you to think about that. You're darn lousy at asking."

"This is an unusual pep talk."

The men looked at each other. Pat decided he'd pushed enough for the time being.

"One thing I can't figure," Cory added, taking Pat by surprise. "What do you make of HomeSky knowing I'd be at the farm?"

"It was divine intervention, sure as you're sitting here. God's not ready for you just yet."

"Maybe He doesn't want me. Keeps sending me back."

"What do you mean?"

"Forget it."

"Come on. Tell me."

"I don't know. The accident with my dad, the collapsed lung in the state tournament, now this. I keep getting sent back." Cory forced a laugh.

"That's not the way God works," Pat said with conviction. "You've only begun to make His mark on this world. Your work here isn't finished."

"Do you feel you've let Him down? You know, by leaving the priesthood?" Cory watched Pat's face carefully to see if he'd pried too deep.

Pat turned to Cory. "No. I'm an ex-priest, not an ex-Christian. God is only let down when we squander His gifts. Our obligation is to use them to leave the world a little better, and to have a great time doing so. I admit, I do need to work harder on the great time part of things." Pat risked, "You should come to church with me and talk to God about this stuff. About what's happening to you."

"I don't think so."

"Why not?"

Cory just shook his head. "I couldn't lift my eyes in church."

"Cory—" Pat began, but was quickly cut off.

"Let's give it a rest for now." Cory looked ready for sleep as he let his head sink into the pillow.

"Sure enough. But I want you to think about staying, just for a few months. Okay?"

"I can't make any promises," Cory said, closing his heavy eyelids. He kept this final thought to himself: *I'm done making promises.*

CORY.

The months slid into the dead of winter. Routine became like the deepening ruts in the ice-covered street: harder to escape once momentum deposited you there. It was a noiseless time. Bundled people moving briskly in straight lines, slightly stooped, unwilling to lift their faces into the wind to say hello. Pant legs stiff as stove pipe with a cold that goes right to the bone. Temperatures plunging to 20 below zero without factoring for the wind. Parked cars life-lined to long orange extension cords so block heaters might keep the oil from going to pudding. Parishioners wearing snowmobile suits to Sunday worship and keeping them zipped until the second reading. For days on end, all you saw of neighbors was the white string of smoke leaving their chimneys.

If anything, Cory was doing worse now. Yes, he'd taken the job at the plant and had accepted Pat and Father Dan's offer to stay with them. He was helping out here and there at the farm, but often as not, he'd disappear for nights in a row to the Mutineer's Jug. He'd take the back booth, put his back to the bar, and polish off a couple of pitchers just watching the wall. Sheriff Harris would join him occasionally for his three beers and twice as many cigarettes; he'd drive Cory home. Or Pat would come looking for him, have a coke, and they'd leave. But Cory withdrew. He retreated behind a beard. He let his hair go. He put on weight. You'd hardly recognize him. Which was the goal.

At the plant, besides Pat, the only co-worker Cory had more than two words with was Radio Voice. The oversized innocence of this mentally retarded janitor drew Cory to him. His ready smile and quick, small steps broke Cory down, made him care to be human. As for everyone else on the shift, fuck 'em. The others whispered. Cory figures he's too good for us. He's been in the newspapers, on the TV, so he thinks he's above us. They left him alone. All except for Reg Cunningham, Lu Ann's dad, who relished the fact that a phenom had gotten his wings clipped and sunk to his level. To the stink, to the din, to the hopeless repetition of the plant. He tried to pull Cory into his little clique of production line malcontents, but Cory simply got up and left whenever Cunningham pulled up a chair. Cunningham could take a hint. He started addressing Cory as College Boy, and had it out for him. And, of course, Pat was the enemy; Pat had replaced Cunningham as foreman. Anything he could do to undermine Pat and sabotage productivity, he did.

What especially gnawed at Cunningham, though, worse than Cory's indifference, was how Cory spent time with Radio Voice. "Would ya look at College Boy and Mongoloid," Cunningham would say, elbowing his cronies, thumbing across the break room as Radio Voice slurped his coffee next to Cory reading the paper. That Cory found Radio Voice to be more interesting company than Cunningham was unforgivable.

One word described the kind of work they did in the pulping plant: monotonous. Cunningham and his boys got through the doldrums by endlessly tormenting Radio Voice. They'd take the batteries from his transistor radio. Clog the toilets before defecating so Radio Voice would have to clean up the overflow. They'd put his mop bucket out to freeze overnight and laugh the next morning when Radio Voice, confused, struggled to free the mop. They'd hide his overshoes, sew a sleeve shut on his coat, unplug the vending machine before he'd use it, and endless other juvenile pranks to entertain themselves. Cory minded his own business. He didn't say anything. But he was always there, plugging in candy machines, helping with messes, putting new nine-volt batteries in Radio Voice's transistor, setting things right. But on Radio Voice's birthday, they went too far. And Cory made it his business.

"Hey muff divers," Cunningham said to his boys. "C'mere. I've got the plan of all plans for Mongoloid's birthday." They crowded together in the break room, laughing, but became suspiciously well-behaved the moment Radio Voice and Cory walked in.

"Hey, Mongoloid," Cunningham said to Radio Voice.

Radio Voice ignored him, like Cory had taught him.

"Hey!" Cunningham repeated sharply, "I'm talking to you."

"That's not my name," Radio Voice said, looking at the floor tiles.

"I hear it's your birthday. Is it true?"

Radio Voice's face transformed. He looked up, his almond-shaped eyes widened and sparkled, his head nodding fast over and over. "Yes, Mr. Cunningham. It sure is. Today. Now."

"The guys and I chipped in and got you a present. We'll give it to you at lunch, when we have an hour. Maybe we'll have a cake."

"With candles?" Radio Voice asked.

"Why not," Cunningham laughed. "Right boys?" His table joined the laughter.

Cory looked the men over. He didn't like it.

Radio Voice spent the next two hours watching the clock. Lunch couldn't come fast enough. He'd hardly start a job before he came shuffling back out to the floor, his wide face turned up to the clock, seeing how much time had passed since he last looked.

Cory would turn him around and give him a gentle push back toward his work. "Knock it off, now," Cory said firmly. "I'll come get you when it's time. Go on now before we both have to work through lunch to make up the time we're losing."

"No lunch?" Radio Voice said, mouth opening in panic.

"No. Don't worry. Just get to work now. There'll be lunch."

At lunch, Cunningham and his pals were standing around the large break room lunch table. A few were smoking, and the others just grinned, looking down at the wrapped present in the middle of the table. Next to it was a Hostess cupcake from the vending machine. Cunningham stuck a candle in it while he shoved the second cupcake from the package in his mouth.

"Birthday boy," he said, spraying chocolate crumbs. "Get your butt up here and see what me and the boys got ya."

Radio Voice, all 250-plus pounds of him, nearly knocked two workers over getting to the table. He froze when he saw the wrapped present. You'd think he'd never seen a gift before.

"Thank you," he said, slow and heartfelt.

"Light the fuckin' candle," Cunningham barked at one of the smokers.

Cory slipped through the circle of workers. On the table sat a smallish wrapped box. The paper was festive. "Go ahead, blow out your candle," Cory instructed, breaking the spell the package had put on Radio Voice.

He blew out the candle, which promptly re-lit. A prank candle. Radio Voice thought it was funny. He laughed along with the crowd, and tried again.

"Sure is a tough candle, Mr. Cunningham."

"You ain't blowing hard enough," he told him, hardly able to contain himself.

Cory stepped in and pinched the candle out with his fingers. He looked Cunningham in the eyes. "See what you got there, Radio Voice." Cory nodded toward the present, still eyeing Cunningham.

The paper was off in record time. Inside the cardboard box was a white enameled coffee cup with a flying eagle on it. Radio Voice loved it instantly.

"Look at that bird, Cory," he said in amazement.

"It's an eagle."

"Wow. Thank you. An eagle."

Cunningham spoke up. "Go ahead. Try it out. Me and the boys know how much you like your coffee. Now you can leave your own cup up in the cabinet just like the guys."

It was true. Radio Voice did love coffee. He could drink four or five Styrofoam cups in a sitting. Hot as it was, it didn't seem to bother him. The real coffee drinkers on the shift each kept a mug in the break room over the coffeepot. There was a Minnesota Vikings mug, another that said *I need a cigarette*, a mug with breasts on it, a mug that said *OLD FART*, another that read *Duck Hunters Blow Their Wad,* and a plain white one with a piece of duct tape marking it.

Radio Voice carried his mug in two hands carefully over to the pot. The boys watched him with far too much interest for Cory's liking. *What the hell are they up to?*

Pouring a full cup, Radio Voice beamed, making sure the eagle faced him as he drank. "I like to look at the bird," he said. Every sip seemed to bring more chortles and grunts out of the guys. They tried to hold back, but as Radio Voice made his way through that cup of coffee, they were splitting at the seams. When Radio Voice finished, he lifted his mug, smacked his lips in pleasure and said "Ahhh." That did it. The boys lost it, howling with laughter. Cunningham was doubled over, pounding the table. "D'ya see that?" he exclaimed, tears in his eyes. "Ahhh," he mimicked Radio Voice, his hand up to his mouth, pinky extended. "There's nothing like a little piss with your coffee, I've always said." The boys hooted. The smile froze on Radio Voice's face, his brow wrinkled, confused.

"What did you say?" Cory said to Cunningham.

"I rinsed out the cup for him," Cunningham said, as he pantomimed unzipping his fly and urinating. Radio Voice remained across the room, holding his empty mug.

"What does he mean, Cory?" Radio Voice asked.

Cory felt the blood rising in his neck. "You pissed in his cup?" he asked, throat dry.

"Well, no. Not *just* me," Cunningham said, laughing, looking at his boys.

Radio Voice let go of the mug. The last sound Cory heard was it shattering on the tile floor. Cory didn't hear, for instance, the crash of the break room window as he launched Cunningham through it, landing him flat on his back in shards of glass out on the cement plant floor. He didn't hear the sound of his fists breaking Cunningham's nose, his left cheekbone, his right front tooth. He didn't hear the begging whine of Cunningham's voice. All he heard was a low rumbling in his ears as he sent Cunningham into and over the iron assembly line conveyor, and then into a stack of pallets, and then into a fork truck, and then into a steel bay door. He didn't hear Pat yelling to let go, to please let go. He didn't hear the sickening crack of a two-by-four as Pat brought the board down across the back of his skull, knocking him unconscious. And most of all, he didn't hear Radio Voice sobbing above him. Because if he had, God as his witness, he would have come to and done it all over again.

Cory awoke in jail. His cell door was swung open. The deep drone of Sheriff Harris' voice came from around the corner. It was a forceful monologue. Likely he was on the phone. Then it all came streaking back to Cory. He lay there, staring at the ceiling, running it through over and over. *Well, if I killed the bastard, the door wouldn't be unlocked.*

"Hey Sleeping Beauty," the Sheriff said, suddenly at the door. "How long you been with the living?"

Cory sat up on the thin mattress, leaning his back against the cool wall. It wasn't easy getting upright. His head felt like it was filled with wet cement. He had a lump the size of a halved cantaloupe. It itched where it was shaved and stitched.

"Did the asshole live?" Cory asked.

"Lucky for you he's tougher to put down than a swamp moose," the Sheriff said. Cory just nodded and closed his eyes.

"You've been out almost 24 hours. I had to come by a few times and put a mirror by your mouth like they do at the old folks' home to make sure you were breathing."

"You should have used a pillow on me."

"You'll notice there ain't no pillow in the cell. I took your belt too."

Cory opened his bloodshot eyes. He felt like hell but he looked something worse. Ragged beard, a shaved patch of hair gone from the back of his head, right hand swollen to the size of a small ham. "So now what?"

The Sheriff exhaled and pulled up a chair outside the door. "Are you done? Have you cleared this shit from your system? There can't be more of this. You nearly took a life, for chrissakes."

"I'm done with it."

"You well better be because Cunningham's got a winter in a bed to look forward to and pile of hospital bills the plant's insurance guys won't much care for."

Cory rubbed his discolored right hand.

"I've been on the phone through the night and here's how we're going to sell it: Cunningham was up working a stuck pallet when he fell off the fork truck and the load came down on him. We installed a clean piece of glass in the break room so hopefully they won't notice a thing in that regard. The claims guy is due up at the plant tomorrow. All the workers have agreed to the story. They shut up, they don't lose their jobs for what they did to Radio Voice. Same goes for Cunningham. And the company won't leave him high and dry with bills. You, you're out of work. As far as anyone is concerned, you've never been an employee at McKnight. You've been erased."

"Cunningham agreed to this?"

"Let's just say I presented it in a way he couldn't refuse. I told him the beating was long overdue and reminded him of a little incident some years back when he and his pack put a whipping on a young teacher who got involved with his Lu Ann. Plus there's some issues about him poaching a few bucks I've chose to ignore, not to mention the nights after closing time I've had to follow him home because his truck can't seem to stay on the right side of the painted line. I told him it was in his best interest to keep one friend in town."

Cory looked at the wall. "Why go to the trouble? I know how you feel about twisting the law. Why not just let what I've got coming come?"

The Sheriff's eyes flashed. "You've gotten your fair share, and then some." He lit up a Camel. "This has been coming to Cunningham long before you got in between. You just had the nuts to serve it up to him." The Sheriff drew hard on his cigarette. "Justice and the law, I've come to see, don't always paddle in the same direction. As for you, it's time to snap out of this. Got me? You're a hell of a good kid, but you're out there on the thin edge. Shit, you got talent enough for three lifetimes. Don't blow it feeling sorry for yourself. You've had some shitty breaks, no arguing. But enough's enough. Maybe that board the ex-padre put down on your head will get you thinking straight again."

"Oh. So that's who got me," Cory said with a trace of a smile. He rubbed his eyes. "I appreciate what you've done. I don't know where to start, so I'll just leave it at that if that's okay."

"I'm not the one to talk to." The Sheriff ground the cigarette butt under his size 15 steel-toed boot. "Pat called for the umpteenth time. He'll be stopping over on his lunch hour. You've got him worried sleepless."

Cory nodded. "Thanks again. Am I free to go?"

"No charges are being pressed. Just keep a low profile for a day or two 'til this thing blows over. And let me know where you're going in case I have to reach you."

Cory said he would. "What about my belt?" he added as the big Sheriff lumbered away. "You ready to trust me with that?"

"Check the bathroom. On top of a clean shirt of mine. Won't much fit, but I put yours through the washer and it still looked like someone gut a deer in it. Guess I should have bought some spray stuff for that."

"Thanks," Cory said. He went to the bathroom. As he put on the large shirt and tucked a generous portion of it under his belt, it came clear to him that he didn't need a lecture from the Sheriff or Pat at the moment. What he needed was a beer. And had he not stopped long enough to take a leak and wash his face, he would have gotten out of there clean and ended up at the Mutineer's Jug. But once again, the timing of events dictated otherwise. As Cory pulled on his canvas coat and pushed through the front door of the courthouse, he sent Pat tumbling down the steps on the other side.

THE CHURCH.

Pat went shoelaces over ears down the steps. Cory hustled down after him.

"Shit. Sorry about that." He gave him a hand.

Pat checked the working condition of his limbs. "Are you breaking out?"

"No. Sheriff said I was free to go."

"Then slow down a second, okay?" Pat winced, brushing himself off. "Where you in such a hurry to get to?"

"I don't know. Just needed some fresh air."

"Got plenty of that. No need rushing after it." Pat slapped Cory on the shoulder. "Okay. I've got an hour for lunch and a bag of Lu Ann's burgers in the truck. You're coming with me."

"Where we going?" Cory asked, his feet firmly planted.

"It's a surprise. C'mon."

"I've never been much on surprises," Cory said.

Pat winked. "It's high time you learned."

They ate as the pickup rolled over the plowed blacktop of Highway 2. Cory was famished, as Pat had anticipated. Of the five cheeseburgers in the bag, Pat had one and a half. There wasn't much room for talk between bites. Outside, it was another in a string of flat gray days. The winding road was salt-bleached a wispy gray. The oversized snow tires hummed loudly. Pat could feel Cory's tension.

"How's Radio Voice?" Cory asked.

"He's fine. Mad at me for hitting you. He says he won't be my friend anymore."

"I'll talk to him."

"Sorry about that knock I put on you," Pat said.

Cory felt his stitches. "Good thing you did," Cory held up the burger, "or I'd be eating jail food instead."

"You didn't look like you were going to let up, Cory."

"No. I guess not."

"You've got to get this out of you. You've got to find some peace."

"Yep," Cory said, trying to avoid the discussion.

"Seriously. The answer isn't in the back booth of the Mutineer's Jug. Take it from an ex-drunk."

"Shit. It's not about beer; I don't even like the stuff. It's just a door that gets me out of the room."

"How so?"

Cory chewed the inside of his mouth, clenching his jaw. "I just want to be left alone. Okay? Why is that so much to ask? Out, away, alone. That's it."

"Bullshit, Cory. Alone is no answer."

Cory looked at the cracked dash of the pickup. He looked at the rosary hanging from the rear-view mirror. "I don't claim to have any answers."

"Well I do," Pat said crisply. "I know the answer because I've been through the door you so fondly speak of. That door's a mirage. I know it and you know it. This probably sounds like fortune cookie philosophy, but you need to redefine yourself. The old Cory's gone. Time to accept that, give the new Cory a shot. There'll be some crappy days, believe me, but you learn to like the new guy. You have to look him in the mirror and offer him some encouragement. Let me ask you, how do you feel about Cory Bradford?"

"Is this a multiple-choice question?"

"Answer me, Cory."

The tires hummed. "Ashamed."

"Why?"

"I quit."

"No, really, why?"

"I just told you."

"No you didn't. No more bullshit. Why?"

"I don't know what you're getting at."

"Don't lie to me. Why are you ashamed? Say it. Get it out." Pat was pushing hard now.

Cory let out a mock laugh. "Save the therapist stuff, okay."

Pat persisted. "Why are you ashamed, Cory Bradford? C'mon. Say it."

Cory looked out the window, swallowed hard.

"What are you hiding? Say it. It's your dad."

"That's enough!" Cory swiveled around and glared at Pat. "Enough now."

Pat kept going. "It's not Joseph, is it?"

Tears built behind Cory's eyes. He fought them. "Leave him the fuck out of it."

"It's not Joseph and it's not the knee and it's not quitting the team and it's not Reg Cunningham. What is it? Say it and be through with it."

Tears rolled down the sides of Cory's face. "God damn it, shut up!"

"I think your dad—"

"NO!" Cory's eyes flashed on Pat. "No more. That's the end."

"Oh no. We're just getting started. What are you going to do, beat me up like Cunningham? Free yourself from this thing. It's been lodged in there too long."

Cory slumped forward and buried his face in his hands. Quiet tears squeezed through, dropping onto his coat. Pat looked at Cory's crooked left index finger.

Pat's tone softened. He exhaled deeply. "You can't blame yourself for what happened to your dad, or what didn't happen to you. It's time to stop with that now. It's long past time."

Cory took his hands away. His face was blotched and wet. His nose was running; he dragged his coat sleeve across. "What do you know? You weren't there."

"Look at me," Pat said. "See this eye?" Pat faced him, pointing to his right eye. "Look at it."

Cory looked at the white eyelashes. He recalled being startled by the sight when they first met.

"That's my reminder. I told you the story. The young man from my parish—my friend—how he and his fiancée asphyxiated themselves and their unborn child in my garage because I went to their parents about their pregnancy. This is what I got for that betrayal. I used to ask God, why do this to me? Why leave me this reminder, this *mark*, to greet me every day in the mirror? I walked around with that question for years. Then one day, looking at my reflection, the answer smiled upon me. You know why He did it?"

Cory shook his head.

"Because God was sad, too. He wanted me to know that. Every day, He felt my sadness, too. I wasn't alone with it."

"Maybe so. But I walked away untouched," Cory said. "Not a single lousy scratch. Explain to me why I had to do this." Cory held his crooked finger up to the gray light coming in through the windshield.

"Oh, Cory," Pat shook his head sadly. "That was the least of your injuries that day. It's time you understood how badly you were hurt."

Cory clenched his fists and spoke to his feet. "What do you do when you're not happy despite the achievements? How do you face yourself when people say you're great but you know better?" He looked up at Pat. "What do you do when you've got this thing that won't take its knee off your back and let you up?"

"You ask for help," Pat said quietly.

"I don't know how," Cory said, shaking his head. "I see that as giving up."

"It's not about *I*, Cory, that's the irony. Didn't Joseph teach you that?"

"Sure. Look where it got him."

"In heaven," Pat insisted. "We all should end up so lucky."

"What, spend an eternity in the palm of His hand? What a joke. All I've known is the back of His hand. No thanks. I'll stay on the ground where He dropped me."

"Is that what you really believe? C'mon Cory, you're smarter than that. Who gave you those legs to stand back up on? The fortitude to get back up? The spirit to get back up? The life to get back up? God is here. He's holding the sense of it all, waiting for you to make the first move."

"What move?"

"You have to be open to the *why.* What could the meaning be? But you're a locked door. You're Me, Myself, and I—"

Cory jolted. "What?"

"Me, Myself and I. That's you. That's your Holy Trinity."

"Weird you'd say that." Cory's countenance changed, slackening. "When I was rowing Dad on Lake of the Woods, every time I'd dig the oars in, I'd say 'me' on one stroke, 'myself' on the next, 'I' the next. It was my cadence. When I'm out running and I'm gassed, I say those words on the footfalls. It's been my advantage."

"Maybe," Pat countered gently. "Maybe it's your weakness."

Cory grew serious. He squinted slightly, as he always did when he was processing. "I've got to think that through."

"Fair enough," Pat said, in a brighter tone. "Now I want to show you something pretty amazing." They turned off the highway onto the long, winding driveway of the Rez church. The truck rolled down the middle of the plowed road, fenced on either side by large green pines. Snow flocked the branches. The small church sat nestled up ahead.

"This, you're going to like," Pat smiled as he pulled in.

"It may shock you," Cory said, "but I have seen a church before."

Pat looked at Cory. "It's not actually the church we're here to see."

They stopped in the center of the empty parking lot and looked at the 100-year-old pipestone church with its hand-set stones jutting out in wondrous asymmetry. Above, a century-old stand of Norways towered shoulder to shoulder. "Let's go," Pat said, opening his door. They slid out. Pat dropped down the tailgate, and gave it a slap. "Have a seat." Pat zigzagged the parking lot, kicking through the frozen gravel, apparently looking for something. He freed three stones of a satisfactory size and loosened up his throwing arm, windmilling it. Cory sat on the tailgate and watched as the snow-capped, dark green crowns of the Norways swayed, their needles saying hush, hush. Looking back at Cory, Pat gave him a nod.

The first stone he threw was errant and ricocheted off the roof of the church spire. The second hit high off the pipestone just to the right. Pat's third rock was dead on, going cleanly into the bell tower, striking the lone copper bell, releasing a deep, resonant peal that vibrated the quiet air. Four nesting pigeons came flushing out, wheeling into the sky. Quickly they came into formation, in unison, each sensing the other, turning as one. They circled high over the church, dipped down around the pines, came swooping over the parking lot, rose as one over the roof, over the treetops. They made pass after pass, these cruising gray shapes, vectoring so precisely, in harmony. Pat and Cory's heads craned back, squinting, watching. Without a sound, connected by a shared force, the birds set their wings and lit back into the tower. Pat walked over to the truck.

"I like to come here. It does my heart good, them flying together. They move independently, but not alone. Like community. For me, it's the perfect embodiment of the church. A simple reminder. For somebody else, it's just four pigeons." Pat shrugged his shoulders.

"This is a nice place," Cory said, still looking high above the church roofline, into the trees. "Peaceful."

"I miss it at times, not being here every day anymore, blessed by this quiet. But I make a point not to let more than a few days get between us. Plus, it keeps my throwing arm in shape."

Cory looked away. "What's it like, changing your life? Becoming someone else?"

Pat blew into his gloveless hands. "I don't think of what's happened as me becoming someone else. I think of it as becoming something new. That said, it's hard." He smiled at Cory. "At first, especially. We've got a lot of our identity wrapped up in this person we've built, both internally and in what we show the world. When that image changes, and becomes less … what's the word? … impressive, I guess, we feel lessened. I've gone from being a priest to being a plant foreman. People used to cross the street just to say hello. Acquaintances would invite me to Sunday supper, call ahead and ask if I preferred squash to sweet potatoes. They'd see my clerical collar and wait for me to go first through a door. Kids would shake my hand while their parents smiled. I liked that attention; I have to admit. Now I'm a guy who needs a new pair of boots and a haircut. Nobody looks twice. But I'm happier, and that's what a person needs to look for. God prefers a happy foreman to a disillusioned priest any Sunday." Pat smiled. "Every father only wants happiness for his children. It's that simple. So this decision, or destiny, for me, this change, God has been in on it, too. I didn't move alone. I had to look hard at my life and face the question marks. You live many lives in this one, that's what Joseph's father said. It's all about moving toward your true place. And God only knows what and where that'll be. These transitions and possibilities that you never saw coming to greet you—or flatten you—it's all for a reason. But, to answer your question, to change your life is … alive. Change is the very definition of alive."

"I have to change," Cory said, looking up at the bell tower. "I know that."

"You are changing, Cory. Just understand, you don't have to go it alone."

"Okay. Thanks for showing me your pigeons." Cory paused, and then in his inimitable way, hopped off the tailgate and got back on task. "We need to be getting you back to work. One of us has to bring home a paycheck."

A few nights later, on the well-worn fold-out couch after a long day of putting up rafters at the farmhouse, Cory sat, near asleep, with the TV on. The ten o'clock Duluth news spun in with its flashy graphics and overly dramatic intro music. Duluth was northern Minnesota's largest city, so it was the default news station for towns like Baudette. Cory was paying little attention until the co-anchor said her good evenings and smoothly segued into the night's top story. Her voice snapped his focus to the TV.

"Hanna," Cory said quietly, sitting up.

Sure enough, Hanna was doing the lead. A small plane had engine failure but landed safely in a dairy field just outside of the Duluth city limits. They cut to an interview. The young pilot had amazing composure. He talked about the experience like it was no more dangerous than hard-boiling an egg. He said he didn't rile easy. He said if you wanted to encounter hair-raising, you should get in a car with his mother behind the wheel.

The newscast returned to Hanna. Cory didn't hear much of what she said, he just watched her. First and foremost was that smile of hers. She lit up the screen; she always had. Even back when Hanna was doing little more than reporting on cats getting rescued from trees and handling the on-ice college hockey interviews, people always asked what it was like to be near her. Cory just shrugged. No big deal, he said. Which it hadn't been. But now he saw what the others had.

And another thing surprised Cory. He was sorry when the newscast signed off and the cameras pulled back and the set lights faded. "Don't be an idiot," he chided himself. But he sat there nonetheless, feeling sad. Through the bank of commercials and through Johnny Carson's monologue, he sat there.

Finally he rose and clicked off the TV. "Maybe," he said to himself.

HANNA.

"Hectic!" Hanna blurted to a passing co-worker who asked her how things were going. "But thanks for asking," she added over her shoulder. She sped down the corridor of the news station. She had 15 minutes before the 6:00 news countdown. And she had a pimple you could mountain climb. Make-up, that's what got left behind when she grabbed her diaper bag rather than her purse while rushing out of the house. Absent other alternatives, she was going to resort to a trick of the trade: liquid paper from the copy room blended with a dab of lipstick.

Hanna had spent her day playing with Pauly, then dropped him off with the neighbor, rushed to work, prepped, and was about to co-anchor the Six, or the rehearsal, as they called it, because many of the 10:00 stories were just polished versions of the earlier broadcast. She would finish the Six, pick up Pauly, eat, give him a knockout feeding at 7:45, drop him off, sleeping, back at the neighbor's, return to the station, prep for the Ten, do the Ten, go back and get Pauly, one more feeding, put him down, and then collapse into bed, reading only three-quarters of a page of a book before being out.

But they had their precious mornings to dally around after breakfast, to play and dance and nap later together on the couch under a blanket she received for opening Pauly's savings account up the street. She loved those early hours when the eastern sun came in hard through the windows, deflecting off snowdrifts that blew ever closer to sill-height.

Hanna lived only 15 minutes from the news station, so she didn't waste much time in a car. Her neighbor's daycare rate was $1.50 an hour, $2.00 weekend nights. These were but a few of the daily reminders that she'd made the right decision to stick with small-market journalism.

She and Pauly rented half a duplex; Pauly helping out where he could with pennies from his piggy bank. The house was a peeling yellow one-story with laundry in the basement that seemed to be constantly running loads of miniature clothes so perfect they could make Hanna cry folding them. There were two bedrooms in back, hers and Pauly's nursery, a small kitchen, and a living room in front with an old couch and armchair set she'd snapped up at a garage sale.

Weekly, a call would come in after Sunday morning worship, always beginning with the same question: "Are you ready to come home yet?" "No, Dad," she'd say. "I am home, and you and Mom are welcome to visit anytime. Say, how's work?" was the question that would, without fail, get her dad off the trail for 10 minutes or so, complaining about one thing after another at the car dealership he owned. Hanna's mom would jump on the other line and correct her husband at every opportunity until finally, exasperated, he'd just hang up and head downstairs to the workshop to spend hours with things that didn't talk.

Hanna loved her parents dearly, but they drove her nuts. She promised Pauly it would be different with them. They'd always be best friends, she told him, but she was smart enough to know that was easier said than done.

Hanna changed Pauly, put him in his footie pajamas, gave him his knockout feeding, dropped him off, and made it back to the station for the Ten. As tired as she was when she got there, the adrenaline of co-anchoring revived her. She loved the pressure, the high, the pre-broadcast chaos, tapes running back and forth between editors and producers, and especially the post-show buzz just after the newscast signed off and everyone was jazzed about pulling together yet another nightly miracle.

After the team pushed back from the news desk and got unwired, they met in the studio with the entire night crew to banter back and forth about which bar they'd descend upon. Franky's had the best popcorn. Twin Anchors had cuter waitresses. Hanna said her good nights.

"C'mon, *Mom*," one producer taunted. "For Christ, it's Saturday night."

"Not at my house," she shot back. "Great job tonight."

"You're the best!" they said, pointing at her dramatically.

She turned and pointed at them. "No. You're the best!"

And then in unison, "Oh, you're right!" They laughed. It was their usual shtick.

"Get your beauty sleep," the news director cracked.

"You're one to talk," she jabbed, much to the delight of her peers. Hanna was his pet, and the only one allowed to return fire.

Outside, as she braced against the parking lot wind, hat pulled down, scarf wrapped around her face, she saw someone standing beside her car. The wind teared her vision, but no doubt, she recognized the silhouette, the stance.

"Cory," she said, approaching. "What a nice surprise."

Cory smiled faintly. He liked the sound of her voice. Not even the wind could dampen her spirit. "I figured this was yours." He kicked at the bumper. It had a red and white Go Badgers Hockey!

sticker on it. "That's got to be like putting a bullseye on your car in a town like this."

Hanna pulled her scarf down around her neck. Cory was struck by her smile. "I like the Bulldogs fine, but I *bleed* Badger red."

They stood in the loud silence of the parking lot wind.

Hanna spoke first. "I hardly recognized you with the Jeremiah Johnson beard."

Cory let it glance off. "Seems we have a thing about surprising each other in frozen parking lots."

Hanna flashed to the night of the interview, when she and her cameraman had waited almost two hours for Cory and the team bus to arrive at the hotel. "God, Cory. I'm sorry about all that."

"Hey, I'm joking." Cory looked her in the eyes for the first time. "Just a stupid joke."

"Cory Bradford telling a joke," she kidded.

"I'm turning over a new leaf," he said, posturing a smile.

"So," she started, "how are you?" She took a step in and touched his coat sleeve.

"You can say what you're thinking, Hanna. What am I doing freezing my ass in your parking lot at," Cory checked his watch, "at five to eleven?"

"Okay …" was all she could muster.

"I left the team. I'm living in Baudette, of all places. I saw you on the news." Cory stumbled. He didn't know where to go next. "You left some messages that I never got back to you on. I apologize about that. I just wanted to say, it wasn't your fault. The interview, the knee, all that bullshit. I don't know what I'm doing here blathering like an idiot. Guess my better judgment is frozen solid."

Hannah looked at Cory's tattered canvas coat, the old Red Sox cap he borrowed from Pat. "You must be freezing. Come on. Let's go to my house. I have to pick up Pauly—you have to meet my little man," Hanna's eyes sparkled with such love. "He's incredible. It's just a few minutes from here. Come on, warm up. I want to know what you've been up to."

Cory shook his head. "Maybe we should find a better time. I'll call …"

Hanna came closer. "No you won't." She looked up at Cory and grabbed both of his arms as if to shake him. "Come and tell me how you've been, Cory Bradford. Come and meet my son."

Cory half smiled and looked away. "I'll follow the bumper sticker."

While Hanna fed Pauly in the nursery, Cory was up and down more times than he could count. His hot chocolate had gone cold, just two sips short of full. Once, he actually had his coat and hat on, one hand on the doorknob, but stayed. The ball cap remained on, though. One look in the hallway mirror with it off, the shaved path of stitches, it startled even him.

Hanna came out from the back bedroom. "Come here a sec. I have something to show you."

Cory walked behind her, tentatively. Hanna took his hand and they approached the room with the door ajar. Lullaby music crept into the hallway. Hanna smiled back at Cory as they entered Pauly's room. A small night lamp on a dresser cast a light across the crib. There, on his back, one tiny hand balled on the blue blanket, the other reaching above his head, his face turned toward them, his breathing whistling just audibly through his perfect broad little nose, his face as serene as a saint, Pauly slept. Hanna, still smiling, looked up from Pauly to whisper something, but she was struck quiet by what she saw. Cory's eyes were moist. Captivated, he watched the boy's stars-and-moon blanket rise and fall so infinitesimally beneath his breathing. Cory could have stood there an hour. Hanna touched his forearm. "Amazing, huh?" she whispered.

Out in the front room, Hanna opened a beer. She exhaled, beat, and flopped down next to Cory on the couch. "It's the only one I got," she said taking a long swig. "We'll split it."

"No thanks," Cory said, a little distant, still thinking about the sleeping child.

"Oh, that's right. You don't drink," Hanna said, thinking of the old days.

Cory laughed roughly. "Oh, Christ, Hanna," he said, rubbing his face.

"What?" she asked quickly. "I don't mean anything's wrong with that."

Cory took his hands away from his face and looked at her. Studied her. Smiled at her.

"What?" she said, self-consciously. "You're looking at me funny."

"Why is it, Hanna," Cory said with uncharacteristic frankness, "that I say something and you go somewhere else, and you say something, and I don't know what you mean? It's always been like that with us—like we're in different rooms."

Hanna smiled, cheeks reddening. "I don't know. You've always been something of a mystery to me."

"Hanna, I don't even know how to talk to you."

Hanna put her beer on the coffee table and folded her legs under herself and looked at Cory. "Okay," she said, plunging in. "I'm nervous around you because you're intimidating. You've always kept everyone away, except you'd talk to me for some reason, and I didn't know if it was some game you were playing because you and Chevy were always competing and I didn't want to be the prize—I know that sounds egotistical and I'm already regretting bringing this up—but you're a hard person to get comfortable around because, I'm sorry, you have unbelievably high standards and I'm blabbering now so I'll shut up and stick my other foot in my mouth because I'm sure it will fit, too."

Cory looked at her. Then down at the sofa cushion. "Okay," he said, taking a deep breath. "Here we go. First, I do drink. Or did drink. I'd actually like to drink that beer sitting there, but that wouldn't be a good idea because I'd end up in the back of a bar somewhere." He looked up at her. She frowned in confusion. "It started with me taking pills for my knee. I'd toss down an extra one here and there because hell, I was feeling sorry for myself. Pretty soon I was hooked. When the pills and the lies ran out, I started on beer. That's about the time I quit the team. When it comes to beer, I'm pretty much a pitcher guy. It cuts down on the time I have to talk to waitresses. I got drunk for a week or so straight and ended up going to Joseph's farm. I had this bright idea about getting rid of some stuff, hockey crap and whatnot, so I chopped a hole in the pond where we always skated, but I went in instead and pretty much wouldn't be here if Pat, you remember Pat, he's the priest from Joseph's funeral, but he's no longer a priest—which is another story—I wouldn't be here if Pat hadn't pulled me out. So, how's that for incredibly high standards?" Cory looked at Hanna. She was wide-eyed, but trying her best not to look stunned. "I can stop now," Cory said, "or I could get to the part where things gets weird and out of hand." He looked at Hanna and smiled. "That's a joke. Second of the night."

Hanna forced a return smile. "All right," she said, tentatively. "But what was Pat doing out at the farm?"

"You are an ace reporter," Cory said. "So, keep going?"

"Keep going."

"Pat was there because he got a call from HomeSky. The two of them hadn't talked since Joseph's funeral. Out of the blue, she calls, pulls Pat off the factory floor, tells him to haul ass out to the farm. As it turns out, she dreamed I needed help. I guess it was me as a kid or something."

Hanna looked at Cory like, you're kidding, right?

Cory shrugged. "Don't ask me. All I know is I woke up in the hospital. Part of me thinks all this is some dream and I'm going to wake up. But, you know, here we are so I doubt that."

Hanna shivered. "I got goose bumps." She rubbed her arms. "So you stayed up there after that and then you saw me on the news?"

Cory grimaced slightly. "Well there's more. There's an assault and some limited jail time and some pigeons at a church, but that's really not why I came to see you."

Hanna looked at him. She bit her thumbnail. "All right …"

"There's something I thought I might tell you. Shit, this is weird for me." Cory stopped, looked off.

"Don't go away on me now, Cory," Hanna said.

"You sure?" He looked square at her.

"I'm sure."

He nodded. "You know about how my dad died."

"Yeah," Hanna said. "You and Joseph couldn't put on skates without some reporter retelling the story."

"Well this part, nobody's been told. Not even Joseph. This is where it starts. The real beginning." He looked at her. She nodded for him to continue. "I'd grab another pillow there. The going gets a little rough."

DAY ONE: OCTOBER 15, 1973.

A sandy-haired boy no taller than his dad's shoulder led the way down the twisting, worn, tree-rooted trail that opened to the docks and to the lake. The wind snatched his cap. He set down his fishing gear and took up chase. He laughed and stomped and finally brought his boot down, pinning the cartwheeling hat. He pulled it on and grinned at his father.

His dad walked past. "Pull that damn thing down now before you lose it for good."

Stepping onto the weathered dock, they made their way to the boat. Waves licked the planks under their boots, pounding the frosted beach. For as far as the eye could stretch there were icy fall rollers. The water spraying off their white crests was cold enough to sting flesh like battery acid. The wind sucked the breath from the boy. Boats lifted, creaked, straining the ropes that moored them to the wooden dock. Rim ice had formed along the quiet cuts in the shoreline. Out on the horizon, Lake of the Woods was empty.

"Leave some room. The walleyes will be jumping into the boat today," the boy shouted to his dad as they put their gear and lunches into the boat. The father kept his head down, busy, attentive to the equipment. He was mentally rechecking his list. They wore heavy coats and wool overalls. It was a day for sitting next to the cast iron wood-burner and playing euchre, but the father would hear none of it. They had paid for three days' fishing. Weather be damned, he'd accept not a minute less.

"You take her," the father shouted into the wind. "Take the stern." The boy's face grew instantly anxious. He was thirteen, remarkably capable, but he was scared. Handling an outboard motor in these waves was a true arm wrestle, even for an adult. Keeping the speed up and the bow cutting straight into the oncoming waves was imperative. Meet a wave at an angle, you'll get sideways, and be flipped like a bottle cap.

"I don't want to, Dad. Not today. Okay?" The boy's face scrunched up.

"Only one way to learn," the father said, settling heavily into the bow. "Untie us and get us going."

The boy remained on the dock. His stomach knotted. He looked out at the cold tangerine sun just over the eastern horizon; there wasn't a degree of heat to be found in it yet. The father looked hard at his boy. The boy simply shook his head no. His nose was running.

The father's brow creased. "What in hell, now. Take it, I said. There are walleyes to be had."

"You," the boy pleaded. "Please. Okay?"

"I don't want to say it again. Get your backside in the boat and drive. You can do it."

The boy's shoulders began to shake. Tears rose, rolled from the corners of his eyes. They burned on his icy cheeks. The lake roiled all about him.

"Ho-ly shit," his father said, shaking his head. Standing now in the bow, a wave came in under the boat and he lost balance and fell against the boat's aluminum gunwale, barking his shin. "God damn it!" he hollered into the wind. "Get in the front of the boat. Look at you." He shook his head in disappointment. "Jesus, what a baby."

The boy pleaded. "I'm not. I just don't want to drive. I'll fish." The boy's cheeks were streaked with tears.

"Look at you," the father repeated, now standing on the dock. "I thought we left the girls at home. Get in the front." He pushed the boy forward.

"I'll untie—" the boy started.

"NO!"

The boy looked at him, pleadingly.

"Not another word!" his father ordered. "You're a damn disappointment. That's all I have to say to you."

The boy sat rigid in the bow, facing forward, straight into the wind and the waves. His father pushed off. Typically, in the bow, a person would sit with his back to the elements as a boat runs up a lake, but the boy cinched his hood tight and faced forward. He didn't want his dad to see him crying. The motor was cold and wouldn't start. Each impatient, hard rip of the starter cord was like a lash across the boy's back. One. Two. Three. Four. Five. Six. He prayed the boat would start. Then the motor coughed to life.

The boy's father cranked the throttle. The boat banged eastward, into the October waves, straight into the cold sun.

EPILOGUE

MAY.

Cory took off his coat and hung it over a low branch. The spring winds had finally turned favorable. The morning sun shined with purpose. Finally, the moment they had worked so hard for had arrived.

The farmhouse was done and the raw exterior stood ready for paint. For five weeks now, he and Pat had bunked on the floor in sleeping bags. They'd worked every spare minute the spring light afforded. On a morning like this, when you could stand back and watch the sunrise touch your accomplishments, everything in that beautiful split second made sense.

Cory walked to the barn to get the old wooden extension ladder. You wouldn't notice the limp had it not been pointed out to you. The river stone braided into the hank of hair behind his ear gently tapped with each step. It was confirming, that touch. He was excited about the day.

Cory's face was lean now, clean-shaven, his hair trimmed but longer than he used to wear it. The winter weight around his waist was long past gone. His muscles had hardened, become denser, dropping his weight to below what he played at. Cory had gone from looking like a hockey player to looking like a drug dealer to looking like a rancher. The pounds he once needed to survive on the rink were just a nuisance to carry on open land. His pants hung on him.

He got the long extension ladder, the cans of primer, white paint, pans, and assorted brushes. They'd begin on the east-facing side of the house where the sun would be working with them. Cory couldn't have asked for a better day to paint, but he did ask, and that was something in itself.

His watch read just past nine. Cory squinted up at the ridge. Pat was coming down now. They'd agreed to get started by nine. He didn't want to give it away, but almost had when Pat asked what it was about nine that made a difference. Cory said he just wanted to get at it. By nine the sun would have the dew off the wood.

The frost had gone out of the front field, giving the dirt the illusion of growing blacker and more fertile by the day. Pat skirted the field too soft to walk, taking the fence line in. Soon the dirt would be turned and fertilized and the corn would go in and the beans too. Cory would stay for that; how much longer, he couldn't say, but he wanted to see the seed into the ground, so if HomeSky should come home, those neat running rows of green shoots would be lined up to greet her. And there'd be the white-painted farmhouse, too, and the wrap-around porch, the flower boxes, and the kitchen windows that opened to the breeze coming off the front pasture. He wanted to leave that for her. They'd talked only once since the phone conversation in the hospital. HomeSky called to make sure he was getting on all right. She wouldn't say about herself, or her plans. She didn't know. She said it'd be lying to be too optimistic.

As Cory held the ladder away from the building, Pat pushed the extension up until it locked into place. They set the ladder's feet and stood back to look at the parallel rungs waiting to carry up that first brushstroke.

"You go ahead," Pat said.

"No, I don't think so. How about you go up for one, then me for one?"

They pried open a can and stirred it creamy. Pat dipped a brush. Cory dipped a brush. First one, then the other, they climbed. Back on the ground, they stepped back, looking at the two paint strokes glistening on the boards.

Behind them, a car turned up the gravel drive and crunched up the gradual slope, coming to a stop alongside them. It was Hanna with Pauly, asleep, buckled in the car seat. A stepladder jutted out of the tied-down trunk. Then, behind her, the Sheriff's cruiser pulled in with an aluminum ladder hanging out the back, properly flagged with a red cloth. Pat looked at Cory. Cory gave him a touch of a smile. Lu Ann pulled in, her son driving the old station wagon with their ladder out the back window. Next came Father Dan from the Rez with Radio Voice waving. Peterson then, along with his two teenage boys shouldered into the cab, two ladders tied down in the box. Bonaducci from the grocery store pulled onto the grass, as did Johnson and his eldest boy from Johnson and Sons Moving. The Mogas had to park over by the barn, same for old man Fredrickson. The yard filled. It was 9:30. Right on time, as people from these parts are known to be.

"What have you gone and done?" Pat asked, smiling at Cory.

"You never know what might occur to you just watching pigeons fly," he replied.

The farmhouse stood there, two swipes of paint on it, as the community gathered around, looking up, admiring the structure, ladders going up on all sides. Hands were shook, comments exchanged about the weather, about how much the children had shot up.

Pat put his hand on Cory's shoulder. Cory nodded, and went off to help Hanna with Pauly. He took the child, held him high, framed against the bold blue sky, making him squeal.

Pat stood back and took it all in. The sun was warm on his shoulders. Friendly faces filled the yard. A breeze blew in off the front pasture, lifting his shirt collar. He turned his face to the sun, absorbing everything he could. He closed his eyes to the yellow light and listened. The voices. The songbirds busy making nests. Laughter.

"HomeSky," he whispered to the morning wind. "Come home."

READERS' COMMENTS

Readers value what other readers have to say about a book—as do I. While *Fall to Grace* is still fresh in your mind, please go to **fivefriendsbooks.com** and share your thoughts on this novel in the Readers' Comments section.

Thanks.

ACKNOWLEDGEMENTS

Let me begin by acknowledging my friends. Having a story to tell is the direct result of friendships. I could not have told this story alone. Kelly, thanks for the patience and sacrifice. The next one will be shorter. Mom, you'll skin me alive if I don't mention you, and reasonably so. You're the reader in the family who passed down the gene. Thanks. A number of you plowed mightily through early drafts of this book; know that your edits and pep talks were instrumental. Thanks to my editor, Leif Fedje, for your Germanic Norwegian persistence, and the team at Mori Studio for a job well done. Lastly, for all the favors I cashed in on this book, thanks. If you have a couch to move, I'm your guy.